Dani Wade astonished her local librarian as a child when she carried home te[n] books every week—and actually read them all. Now she writes her own characters, who clamour for attention in the midst of the chaos that is her life. Residing in the southern United States with her husband, two kids, two dogs and one grumpy cat, she stays busy until she can closet herself away with her characters once more.

Robyn Grady was first contracted by Mills & Boon in 2006. Her books feature regularly on bestseller lists and at award ceremonies, including the National Readers' Choice Awards, the Booksellers' Best Awards, CataRomance Reviewers' Choice Awards and Australia's prestigious Romantic Book of the Year.

Robyn lives on Australia's gorgeous Sunshine Coast, where she met and married her real-life hero. When she's not tapping out her next story, she enjoys the challenges of raising three very different daughters, going to the theatre, reading on the beach and dreaming about bumping into Stephen King during a month-long Mediterranean cruise.

Robyn knows that writing romance is the best job on the planet and she loves to hear from her readers! You can keep up with news on her latest releases at www.robyngrady.com

ENTANGLED WITH THE HEIRESS

DANI WADE

THE CASE FOR TEMPTATION

ROBYN GRADY

MILLS & BOON

First Published in Great Britain 2020
by Mills & Boon, an imprint of HarperCollinsPublishers,
1 London Bridge Street, London, SE1 9GF

Entangled with the Heiress © 2020 Katherine Worsham
The Case for Temptation © 2020 Robyn Grady

ISBN: 978-0-263-27912-2

0120

MIX
Paper from
responsible sources
FSC® C007454

This book is produced from independently certified FSC™ paper to ensure responsible forest management.

For more information visit: www.harpercollins.co.uk/green

Printed and bound in Spain
by CPI, Barcelona

ENTANGLED WITH THE HEIRESS

DANI WADE

This book is dedicated to my daughter, Nicole, who is finding her purpose and passions in life just like Trinity. I'm proud of the woman you have become, but you'll always be my little curly-headed "baby girl." Go forth and conquer!

One

Trinity Hyatt walked down the museum hallway, keeping her steps light on the tile floor as if she were a child trying to sneak past her parents. As if the sound of the gala from the west wing wouldn't cover her brief getaway.

She just needed a moment, a moment away from the speculative gazes and prying questions. A moment to breathe…

But then she thought back to the headline she'd seen when she turned on her computer this morning.

Suspicious Marriage Threatens Local Jobs

That damn blogger… Her mother had drilled into her growing up that using profanity was only for the uneducated, but Trinity had found its occasional use more than satisfying as an adult. Since the mental slip was the only form of anger Trinity allowed herself, she hoped her mother forgave her this time.

Didn't the anonymous columnist understand how much words hurt? Not to mention how the photograph that accompanied the story made Trinity relive the moment standing beside Michael's grave as half the country watched and ultimately judged her. Why couldn't her online tormentor see the grief on her face? Why couldn't this person tell her tears were genuine?

Trinity locked away the memories of the painful whispering and curious stares during tonight's charity gala, brought on by today's post. Instead she tried to focus on her momentary solitude in one of her favorite places in New Orleans.

So many memories from the familiar hallways of the ASTRA Museum flitted through her overtaxed mind, bringing a welcome peace. She remembered holding her mother's hand as they walked in the blessed quiet, without worry over someone yelling at them or telling them to leave because they didn't fit in because they were too poor. The museum had been open without cost every Saturday. They'd often made the trip across town on the bus to spend a few hours away from her screaming father, looking at the paintings and sculptures, appreciating the beauty that drew them even though they knew nothing about art.

Later, Michael had wandered these halls with her, filling her mind with stories of the artists and the sometimes harrowing journeys the pieces went through before coming to be displayed in the Southern United States.

They were both gone now, to Trinity's never-ending grief. But she tucked it down inside and locked it away, because Michael had left her with a very important job to do. And she would. She would step back out into the charity event with her head high and represent her best friend and everything he'd worked so hard to build.

But for just a moment, she needed peace and calm to surround her.

A twinge of guilt stole through her as she reflected on her husband…though it was still hard to think of him as such. Ten years her senior, Michael Hyatt had been her friend and mentor of sorts for a long time. Then they'd barely been married a week. She had trouble accepting that he was gone, though the explosive crash of his private helicopter had taken him from her just a little over six weeks ago.

The ache he'd left behind weighed on her day and night.

Coming to a standstill in front of a hundred-year-old painting of a peasant woman holding her infant son, Trinity stared at the muted colors. Her vision blurred, the familiar details disappearing as her brain simply drifted. Even the ache this particular portrait always evoked inside her remained subdued. Children were another part of her life to be mourned, and she didn't want to handle that tonight.

When her eyes felt too full, she let her lids close, ignoring the solitary tear that flowed down her cheek.

"She looks happy… At peace, wouldn't you say? Despite what must be hard life circumstances."

Startled to hear an echo of her own past thoughts on this particular painting, Trinity turned. She hadn't heard anyone approach. But the man now standing beside her took her very breath away.

His dark hair had a touch of premature silver at each temple. The color echoed the cool gray of his irises, which had subtle green striations. His bearing was distinguished enough that he fit into the elegant surroundings of the museum, but he didn't have the soft edges that a lifetime of high living gave many men in this world. Head and shoulders taller than her own average height, he left Trinity feeling dwarfed. He filled out his tux just enough to hint at muscle without too much bulk.

His gaze dropped to her cheek, leaving Trinity uncomfortably aware of the cool air over her moist skin. As casually as she could manage, she wiped the tear away. He didn't mention what he'd seen.

The very look of him mesmerized her even more than the paintings. An embarrassingly long moment drew out before she could force herself to breathe in a long drink of air, then she offered a small nod. "Yes, I've always thought so."

For the briefest instant, a surprised expression crossed his features. She noticed a faint lifting of one dark brow, so quick she wondered if it had even happened.

Trinity stiffened. The question of whether or not he was a reporter hadn't occurred to her, but having seen that same expression on the faces of the people who hounded her day in and day out, she couldn't help but wonder. Had he followed her here on purpose?

Having swallowed the story that she'd been raised in a rural, strictly religious household, most press hounds didn't expect her to speak with a cultured accent or intelligent words. After all, she had to be a money-hungry hick to have come from obscurity to inherit the entire Hyatt fortune. It was the very image that Michael's family had painted of her.

That idea sold more stories, more of the candid pictures they hunted her down for. They didn't want to look for the truth, the *deeper* truth of who she was, of what she'd survived.

But the man's expression disappeared so quickly that Trinity wondered if she was just being paranoid because of her current situation. Now his cool gaze trailed down her sapphire gown, one of the few Michael had personally picked out for her. For once, Trinity wasn't left feeling vulnerable and exposed. Instead a small wave of unexpected heat flowed over her.

"Needed a little breather from the party?" he asked quietly.

Though it was probably a banal piece of small talk, Trinity was shaken at how much it echoed her own thoughts. She tried to brush it off. "These things do tend to get a little stuffy at times."

"I agree. In many ways."

Goodness, that grin reached all the way to the core of her. Something Trinity had never experienced before…and wasn't really comfortable experiencing now.

To her relief, his gaze moved past her to the elaborate cream-and-gold walls of the rotunda, pausing at each of the twelve specially chosen pieces displayed permanently within this space. "This isn't just peaceful. It's unique. Gorgeous," he said, his voice deepening in a way that sent a tingle down her spine.

What was wrong with her tonight?

"You've never been here before?" she asked to fill the silence.

Part of her was resentful that this man, and the sensations he seemed to be calling to the surface, had interrupted her time in this special space. The other part of her couldn't quell the fascination that kept popping up in unexpected, uninvited ways.

I'm a widow, dang it. A recent one.

Unaware of her inner turmoil, the man answered, "No. This is my first time. My first time in New Orleans, actually." He held out a hand. "I'm Rhett Butler. Nice to meet you."

Trinity felt her mouth drop open in a most unladylike way. "Seriously?"

"No," he said, flashing another hundred-watt smile, "actually my name is Rhett Brannon. But when in the South…"

Stinker. "That's good. I was beginning to think your

parents had a strange sense of humor." Not that his dark good looks and riveting charisma wouldn't allow him to double for Rhett Butler.

Something deep inside warned her not to make nice. The outstretched hand reminded her of a snake she knew was dangerous. It caused a combination of fascination and fear in her suspicious brain. She couldn't risk one misstep in the game Michael had begged her to play.

She stretched her hand out and politely shook. "Thank you. I'm Trinity, Trinity—Hyatt."

Her hesitation was automatic. Even after almost two months, she had a hard time grasping that her last name had changed, that there was now a paramount need to present herself as Michael's wife. He had counted on her. The charity counted on her. She had to do the right thing.

"Trinity, huh?" Rhett said, not showing any recognition of who she was. Was he simply a good actor? Or did he really not know? "That's an interesting name, too."

Definitely. "My mother was highly religious." She let a small smile stretch her lips. "I've always wondered if it was a reminder to me. To never forget the Father, Son and Holy Ghost."

"And have you?"

She was startled enough to answer honestly. "Some days are easier than others."

The rueful grin that stretched his lips fascinated her more than it should have. "I can agree with that," he said.

A small silence fell, bringing with it that uncomfortable sense of awareness of his masculinity and presence. It only eased a little as he motioned for them to stroll farther around the rotunda.

At least she didn't have to look directly into those mesmerizing eyes. But the silence didn't sit well with her. "So what brings you to NOLA?" she asked.

"Business. Some people I'll be working with brought me along tonight."

"Generous of them."

His grunt could have been a confirmation, but she suspected she heard a bit of skepticism behind the sound.

"Are you here with your husband?"

Surprise shot through her, until her quick glance found his gaze resting on the band encircling her ring finger, the tiny cluster of emeralds and diamonds twinkling in the lights from above. "No," she murmured. "I'm a widow."

It still felt weird saying it out loud. It still felt strange to realize she and Michael had been married. For her, it had essentially been a business proposition—with infinite benefits considering the fortune she stood to inherit. And a favor to the man who had been her best friend, even if it had turned out to be the hardest job she'd ever faced.

And she faced it alone, now that Michael was gone.

Rhett cocked his head to the side, an obvious question in his expression.

"My…husband, Michael Hyatt, passed away recently in an accident."

Rhett's nod was slow and sage. "Yes, I believe I heard about that. Helicopter accident, wasn't it? Very sad."

Of course, he would have heard of it. Michael had not just been a lifelong friend and the owner of the charity Trinity had run for him, he'd also been a wildly successful, multimillion-dollar businessman. The question was, what else had he heard?

As if he sensed her subtle withdrawal, Rhett paused to meet her gaze head on. There was nowhere for her to hide. "Please accept my sincere condolences for your loss."

Startled, she felt pinned by both his look and his words. His wasn't one of the trite *I'm sorry*s that preceded the endless questions she wished she never had to answer again.

"Thank you," she said simply.

"You're welcome." A smaller version of his grin appeared, but dang if it wasn't just as charming.

For a moment, Trinity found herself drifting, wishing she wasn't Michael's widow, wasn't the most talked-about person in New Orleans at the moment, and was simply a woman who could respond to that smile without a worry in the world.

But she wasn't. Time ticked inside her head, counting off the seconds until someone realized she was missing from the elite crowd.

"I really should be getting back," she said. Someone had surely noticed she was gone by now. Especially Michael's aunt and uncle. They didn't miss a move that she made.

And neither did the press.

Defeat weighed down on her as she remembered reading today's post and photos on the *NOLA Secrets & Scandals* blog. She'd never have noticed it on her own. Jenny, her secretary, had pointed it out. The hints about a money-hungry widow threatening the livelihoods of countless families gave her an idea of what information the author had hunted down, but not an idea of when the full story would hit... As if Trinity didn't have enough to stress her out.

Didn't anyone understand that she shared the questions—and fears—about how her husband's death and the lawsuit filed against his estate by his aunt and uncle would affect the business's 50,000-person global workforce?

She assured herself time and again that she was carrying out Michael's wishes. But she had to wonder what he'd been thinking to put a global empire and the fate of that many people under the direction of a charity program director like herself. Still, despite her many misgivings, she never let her worries surface in public. There were too many people eager to use them against her.

Though the question haunted her night after night, she was determined to do her very best by all of them...including Michael.

But those worries were nothing compared to the butterflies in her stomach and unfamiliar heat in her core caused by the man walking by her side. "Yes, I definitely need to get back."

"But we're just getting to know—"

Trinity sped up, snagging her shoe in her dress in her clumsy attempt to get away. She tripped and flung out her hand to catch herself.

Without warning, she found herself engulfed in musky male scent and heat. Her body froze, but her instincts knew exactly what they wanted. She breathed deep, sucking in the hint of cologne and the savory scent of him, imprinting his essence on her lungs.

Immediately guilt snaked through her. She pushed against his arms, needing to be free. But he didn't release her until she was once again steady on her feet.

"Please don't," she gasped, recognizing her response to him with rising fear. Attraction by itself, let alone to a man she knew nothing about, was the last thing she needed in her life.

Unfazed by her protests, Rhett simply arched a brow as he pulled back. "I assumed from our talk that you didn't care for a crowd."

Puzzled, she said, "Yes?"

"Well, if your hand had hit right there—" his gaze turned to the wall where she would have landed, right on the frame of one of the beloved portraits in the rotunda "—then you would have set off the alarm and brought a whole load of people running."

And caused an epic scene being found in the arms of another man six weeks after her husband's death. Her cheeks

burned as she imagined it. She quickly covered them with her palms. What a nightmare.

"Thank you," she choked out, unable to look up into Rhett's gray-green gaze.

But he was having none of that. He tucked firm fingers under her chin and lifted her face, displacing her own hands covering her embarrassment. Then he removed his arm from her, creating a small, intimate space between them.

Then she felt his thumb rub against the fullness of her bottom lip. A jolt of electricity shot through her. His eyelids lowered, and he gave her a slumberous, searching look that sent aftershocks down her spine.

"My pleasure," he said quietly. Then he was gone.

"So I see you've met our little gold digger."

Something about Richard Hyatt's voice always hit Rhett like nails on a chalkboard. Suppressing a wince took effort. He turned to find the heavyset man standing behind him, years of self-indulgence stamped on his pale, bloated face. His wife stood beside him, looking like his polar opposite. From the first moment Rhett had met with them, the couple had reminded him of the Jack Sprat nursery rhyme. Patricia Hyatt was pencil thin and her expression remained hard no matter the topic of conversation.

Somehow Rhett couldn't imagine the pale, vulnerable woman he'd met in the rotunda marrying into a family that included these people, but appearances could be deceiving…as Rhett knew better than most. He'd been on the receiving end of dishonest treachery more times than he could count, personally and professionally, but it was his ability to look beneath the surface of a pretty face and find the hidden ugliness that made him a master at his job.

Well, he preferred to consider it a true calling.

Trinity appeared genuinely innocent, from her wide, doe-brown eyes to the emotions that had flitted through her expression when she'd thought she was alone. There was a purity to her beauty that drew him in, urged him to let his guard down and believe that she'd been a true bride to Richard's deceased nephew, not a grifter. There was also something about her that woke sensations that weren't usually a part of his investigations.

But crying in public when there was any chance she might get caught? That had his Spidey senses tingling.

Was she simply a great actress? Had she taken advantage of Michael Hyatt and caught an unexpected win when he died so suddenly? Had she wormed her way into his bed, then into his will? From what he'd been told, that seductive innocence was a lie…and it was Rhett's responsibility to prove it.

Still, something about the whole scenario didn't quite fit. Rhett's instincts were usually spot-on from the moment he met someone. But with Trinity, the signal seemed to be intermittent. Not that he would be voicing that suspicion to his new client.

"Do you think it's wise to be speaking with me tonight?" he asked before indulging in a miniscule sip from his whiskey glass. Normally, he didn't drink on a job, but he did need to look the part in tonight's crowd. And blending in, playing the part, was something at which Rhett was extremely skilled. He glanced around, noting that Trinity hadn't returned to mingle in the crowd yet. But if she did, he wanted this meeting to look as casual as possible.

"Just a brief chat," Richard said, his gaze shifting back and forth over the surrounding crowd in a way that was blatantly suspicious. He extended a meaty hand. "You know how to make it look like a first meeting, don't you?"

Rhett smothered a sigh before shaking the other man's

hand. Working with amateurs who thought they knew everything was such a pain in the ass.

"Of course," he said, his tone smooth and his voice pitched low. "It's nice to meet you, Mr. Hyatt. I had the pleasure of meeting Trinity Hyatt moments ago."

Richard smirked, as if pleased Rhett had taken his direction, but Patricia snapped, "Don't call her that. I will never acknowledge that woman's so-called marriage to my nephew. Ever."

She might not, but that didn't mean the law wouldn't. Rhett didn't bother making the distinction. That was their lawyer's job.

"Regardless, our meeting was quite satisfactory. I don't foresee any problems with proceeding."

Satisfied smiles appeared on Richard's and Patricia's faces. As much as the Hyatts' obvious greed for their deceased nephew's estate left a bad taste in Rhett's mouth, he couldn't deny their suspicions had basis in reality. Trinity Romero had become Trinity Hyatt a mere week before her new husband had died in a helicopter crash, taking her from a lowly administrator at one of her husband's charities to a very wealthy widow. A claim her new family was already protesting in court. She did have a handwritten copy of his new will, but her lawyer insisted the official copy had been with her husband in the helicopter he'd died in on his way to his lawyer's office.

Convenient.

"I knew you were the man for the job," Richard was saying. "Our lawyer knew exactly who to turn to. A man like you will make her putty in your hands in a week—"

"Maybe less," his wife murmured, eyeing Rhett in a most unladylike way over the rim of her wineglass.

Richard ignored her. "You'll get the truth from her, then

we will have evidence for our court case. Anything to put this whole debacle behind us."

"Remember, I cannot guarantee that time frame, Mr. Hyatt."

Richard's ham-handed slap on the back left Rhett uncomfortable but he knew better than to show it. Clients were never happy if you gave any hint of not trusting them.

The pat was accompanied by a hearty, "I have full faith in you, my man. And it seems like others are starting to get on board."

Rhett knew what Richard was referring to, as anyone in his position should, but still asked, "Meaning?"

"Apparently New Orleans' resident gossip blogger, one of those anonymous channels that dishes all the dirt, has started digging into Trinity's secrets. That should help our cause," he said with an overly loud guffaw. "Our lawyer will send you a link before the meeting tomorrow."

Again, Rhett didn't let on that he knew about the gossip column. He was nothing if not thorough. No single thing was left to chance. Rhett had seen the alert just as soon as the post had gone live. *NOLA Secrets & Scandals* was exceedingly popular in the city and gaining ground across the South. In less than three months, the Instagram page connected with the blog had gained over 100,000 followers. It had caught on not just with gossipmongers, but within the upper classes, who relished knowing and spreading the secret tidbits the blogger exposed.

Rhett shifted a little in his jacket, for once wishing he'd sent his partner, Chris, instead of taking this job himself. But Chris had his hands full with a case involving a gigolo trying to swindle an elderly woman out of her fortune; Chris's job was to seduce the old lady right out from under him so her children would ultimately receive their rightful inheritance.

On the surface, what their company did sounded down and dirty, but it really wasn't. They might whisper a few sweet words or hold someone a little closer than publicly proper, but there was a line that was never crossed. A line that Rhett had never wanted to cross. After all, he'd had enough betrayal in his life without deliberately putting himself into a situation that could only have a bad ending.

They were coming down to the wire on that case, but Rhett couldn't wait for Chris to wrap it up. Oh, Rhett could certainly do this job. Trinity's beauty eased any hardship caused by her gauche in-laws. Just the thought of the hunt, the subtle maneuvers required to ferret out the information he needed to undermine any claim she had on the Hyatt estate set his blood pumping.

He just had to ignore the other things about Trinity that made his heart pound.

As his new clients eased off with a casual wave and a not-so-subtle wink, Rhett indulged in the barest sip of his whiskey. He casually zeroed in on the very spot where Trinity was standing. He'd known the moment she'd reentered the museum's grand ballroom. His brain had registered every glance she'd thrown his way, no matter how much she'd tried to hide it. So he let the distaste he'd felt for his clients' motives show momentarily on his face. He wanted her to see that he'd met her in-laws and didn't care for them that much.

He could almost feel her curiosity and concern across the space between them.

Now he let himself make eye contact, then he lifted his glass in her direction, catching her wide-eyed surprise as he acknowledged a connection neither of them had put into words. Regardless of what her in-laws might say, what society might whisper or what his own conscience might condemn, getting to know each other was going to be a very sure pleasure.

Two

Trinity tried not to be alarmed by the number of people seated around the table at the emergency board meeting of Hyatt Heights, Inc. *It looked like a world peace negotiation instead of a business meeting.*

There were the lawyers: stone-faced as they set up their laptops. There were the businessmen: some familiar and friendly faces, some not so much. Then there were Richard and his wife, Patricia, whose faces had never been friendly in all the years she'd known them.

They'd never pretended to love Michael, though he was their only nephew. Instead they'd spent all their time complaining to him about Hyatt Heights losing money and the waste of running *Maison de Jardin*. The home for abused women and children had become Michael's life passion after his parents had been killed in a car accident in his midtwenties.

That was when Michael's unlikely friendship with Trin-

ity had started. They'd both been dealing with the repercussions of losing their families, though in different ways. Trinity as a victim of violence who found shelter with her mother at *Maison de Jardin*. Michael as the rescuer who took them in and gave them hope and a future. It had led to a lifetime connection that had shaped her entire world.

Trinity forced her thoughts back to the present, rather than let herself get lost in the bittersweet memories of her best friend. Despite the comfort they gave her, she somehow knew she needed all her focus on the here and now. People didn't just call an emergency board meeting for any old reason, right?

Those darn posts... They had to have something to do with it.

"Doing okay, Trinity?" Bill LeBlanc asked from her right side.

She gave him a small smile, grateful to have the one other person who had known her husband as well as she had by her side through all of this. An old-fashioned Southern lawyer in his ever-present vest and bowtie, Bill looked right at home amid the arched windows and wainscoting of the boardroom at Hyatt House, the private mansion from which Michael Hyatt had run his business and charitable foundation. Bill's only regret was that, as Michael's lawyer, he hadn't been able to finalize the will before Michael's death. But he was doing all that he could to help Trinity honor his client and friend's wishes.

"I feel completely unprepared," she said low, not wanting anyone else in the room to overhear. There were a few people here who would jump on any weakness like sharks scenting blood in the water.

What she needed was a strategy. Being perceived as a strong leader by the board of Hyatt Heights was essential. If she inherited Michael's position, she would be CEO of

the corporation, and a majority shareholder, but still needed the board on her side to put through the initiatives and decisions that could be supported by the other shareholders.

An injunction had created a temporary board director to serve in Michael's place during the court case, while Trinity still handled Michael's other businesses and whatever tasks the temporary board director asked of her. So she and Richard were "auditioning" while the case was ongoing. If she didn't prove her worth, Trinity could still lose the CEO position, though the shares would remain hers through inheritance.

Which would make carrying out Michael's wishes even harder. The two board meetings she'd attended since her husband's death had included talking points and presentations and charts that Bill had briefed her on before they'd arrived.

Not today. There'd been no preparation, no warnings. Trinity knew on an intellectual level that she needed to focus on getting through this without hinting how much she was out of her depth. She was a smart woman, but her crash course in billion-dollar businesses over the last two months had been steep.

Plus, her sleep last night had been repeatedly interrupted by the image of bright gray-green eyes that left her restless and needy in a way she'd never felt before. A way she was definitely not comfortable with.

"It will be fine," Bill assured her as the meeting was called to order.

Richard Hyatt sat with his wife and lawyer at an angle across from Trinity and Bill, which should have been enough to put her out of their line of sight. Still she shifted in discomfort as she noticed the couple's gazes trained in her direction. What trouble were they stirring up now?

She had to wonder what influence Richard had used with

the temporary board director to get everyone to show up for this. He acted as if winning the case for Michael's inheritance was a done deal and he'd already been elevated to CEO, instead of still being only a member of the board.

"This meeting at my request to the chair was called with some urgency to address issues brought to my awareness this morning," Richard said, taking to his feet as if to assert his superiority over the others around the table. "How many of you have seen this?"

He clicked a button on the remote in his hand, which caused a portion of the back wall to slide down. The large screen behind it was already on, displaying a photo of Trinity. She could easily read the headline on the screen.

Suspicious Widow Fights for Control of Hyatt Estate

Trinity couldn't hold in a gasp, though she would have given anything not to react after Richard smirked in her direction.

But he didn't stop there. "I told the board you'd be bad for business, but they wouldn't listen."

His words were lost in the cacophony of voices as board members asserted their opinions. They clicked on the keyboards before them on the table's highly polished surface. He'd gotten his point across, and that was all that mattered.

Trinity pressed her shaking fingers together. The headline and blog post were only the beginning of the ugliness. There were also photos. The series of pictures included one of her at the funeral, one from the charity event the night before looking particularly standoffish, and a picture of her marriage certificate. She tuned out the noise around her as she read the short captions and comments.

They included vague claims about how unfit Trinity was, simply because she'd never been part of New Orleans's

upper crust and ran a charity for a living. There were specific details about her short marriage to Michael and a link to documentation about the court case filed by Richard and Patricia, all under the hashtag #NOLASecrets. A few Black Widow comments thrown in didn't sit well with her either.

"Where is this from?" Bill's sharp voice jolted her from her absorption. She'd assumed he knew about the rumors making the social media rounds.

"That new gossip blogger who's all the rage at the moment," Patricia said. "Everyone who is anyone is following her blog and other social media." Her eye roll was almost comical.

Another board member interrupted, his voice sounding panicky. "It's only a matter of time before this hits other news sites. *NOLA Secrets & Scandals* is really making waves."

"It already has," Richard said, his voice calm. There was an ominous glint of satisfaction in his gaze as he trained it once again on Trinity. "Our stock has already begun to drop."

There was a flurry of rustling as phones were pulled from pockets and briefcases. Those with laptops began furiously clicking. The murmurs grew louder as the board members confirmed for themselves what Richard had said.

Bill scoffed, looking up from his own phone. "We have no idea whether this was caused by that hatchet piece. The stock is barely down from yesterday."

"Mark my words, it's going to fall, and fall fast," Richard assured him. "I mean, look at this post." He clicked on a link in the sidebar. The headline read, "Suspicious Marriage Threatens Local Jobs." Then the next line, "And it's all her fault."

Trinity allowed herself to blink slowly once, twice, before saying, "I thought you said it was the blogger's fault."

"There wouldn't even be a post if it wasn't for you. Obviously, *they* agree it's your fault, too."

"You don't even know who wrote this," Trinity argued, though she knew it was futile.

"The public doesn't care, little girl. Shareholders just read the news and start dumping their stock. Prices go down. People lose jobs."

Bill interrupted with, "This isn't news. It's rumors. Once the truth comes out in court—"

"When?" Richard demanded. "In a year? Two years? How much damage will be done in that amount of time?"

Trinity's heart picked up speed.

That's when Richard and Patricia's lawyer saw an opening. "Let's not forget that if the stock drops, you might all be booted off the board."

Larry Pelegrine, one of the men who had been kind enough to answer Trinity's questions over the last six weeks, spoke up. "Now, we can't allow this to get out of hand. Not because of how it might affect any one of us individually," he said with gentlemanly emphasis, without directly pointing out the crass slant of the lawyer's words, "but because of the thousands of people who work for the Hyatt companies. They have families to support. Families that need groceries and health insurance and—"

"We get it," Patricia said, her voice turning snide. "We need to help people…and ourselves."

How in the world could the other board members not see just how focused Richard and Patricia Hyatt were on bettering themselves, without caring about the effect of their actions on others? Or that their selfishness was the exact opposite of Michael's vision for his companies and charitable foundation?

Larry leaned forward. "Look, as much as I hate to say it, the reality is that if the company's valuation goes down,

people *will* lose their jobs. And that valuation is partially
reliant on how the outside world views the company, regardless of the truth."

The rest of the board members nodded and muttered to
each other. Bill cast a sympathetic glance in Trinity's direction. She pressed her palms against her thighs beneath
the protection of the table's edge. She and Bill and even
Larry had worked hard to promote her abilities and skills to
the rest of the board for the last six weeks. After all, she'd
single-handedly run *Maison de Jardin* for Michael since
she was twenty-three. It wasn't a small operation, by any
stretch of the imagination, though it was miniscule compared to the entire Hyatt Heights operation.

She could feel the understanding and support they'd
been working so hard to cultivate slowly sinking out from
underneath her like sand beneath a wave on the beach.
Once the court case was settled, the winner would own
the largest portion of the company and would most likely
be the CEO, giving them the most sway with the board.
She needed them to believe in her, so she could use her
power for the things Michael would have wanted. Richard had his own seat, but no true power if he didn't inherit
Michael's estate.

One voice rose above the rest. "We have to do something."

Trinity was bombarded with questions and comments
from all sides. She slowly drew in a breath, trying to think
amid the chaos.

"I think this will help everyone see what I mean," Richard said.

This time he clicked to display a file. At first when Trinity looked at the handout, the figures and columns jum-
bled before her eyes; then, she started to sort through the
data. She could see Bill doing the same out of her periph-

eral vision. The negative projections on how their work-force and revenue would be impacted by the bad press hit Trinity hard.

No matter how much she told herself that this wasn't her fault, that what had simply started as a favor to her best friend had gotten completely out of control with his unex-pected death, it didn't make her feel any less responsible for what could happen to innocent people along the way.

Patricia drove the nail in harder. "That's an estimated five thousand people with families in New Orleans alone who will end up unemployed."

A city in desperate need of jobs. Trinity knew that.

"You don't know that," Bill asserted, a little of his spirit reappearing.

The woman didn't seem to care about a little thing like facts…or decorum. She leaned forward, hands planted squarely on the table, and looked Trinity directly in the eye. "That means they're gonna need all the charity they can get. You know, the same kind your clients receive over at *Maison*," she said, a snide twist to her voice. "That's something your brain can actually grasp, right?"

Trinity felt herself withdraw from the unexpected attack, but forced herself to hold completely still. It was the only coping mechanism she had. If she held still, no one could see her, no one could take a swipe at her. Or in this case, gather any more evidence to use against her.

She forced her voice to stay steady as she said, "The last thing I want is for families to lose their income."

"They will as long as you hang this board up with your court case."

Trinity raised a brow in disbelief. "I'm not the one who initiated the case."

"That's not how the press sees it." Richard nodded to-ward the screen .

Larry stood up, his height and girth commanding attention. "Let's focus here. We need to do something about this before it gets to be a huge problem. The issue here is the need to sway public opinion in such a way that it will reassure our investors and raise stock prices." He sighed. "I believe I've got an idea."

His glance in her direction was almost apologetic. "Even before this bad press, I looked into a business consultant to help you. Now I realize hiring him might reassure our investors that our corporation is not simply being run by someone completely inexperienced."

Bill grunted, but Trinity laid a hand on his arm. Let everyone think she was inexperienced. She was, to a certain extent, though years spent talking aspects of his business through with Michael had taught her some very valuable things. Not that she'd expected to ever have to use that knowledge. But now that he was gone, she was more than grateful.

"That sounds like an interesting proposition," she said instead of rejecting the proposal outright.

"He's here, actually. He was in town and I asked if he would meet with you," Larry said.

That took her back a little bit, but at least it expedited things.

"Here?" Richard asked, his voice booming in the room. "Let's bring him in."

Trinity winced. How lovely—another businessman to "fix" the problem of her inexperience. Even if she won the case against the people trying to take her inheritance away, consultants like this would be telling her what to do.

The room went oddly quiet as Larry stepped out into the hallway. Trinity felt a sick kind of anticipation build inside her. Logic said if this consultant could help, it would be a

good thing for a lot of people. Fear said he could end up being just one more person to criticize her after analyzing her every move.

The door opened and Larry stepped back inside with another man following close behind.

Trinity took one look into the gray-green eyes she'd never expected to see again and wished the floor would open up and swallow her whole.

Rhett saw the surprise in Trinity's eyes as he walked into the room but didn't experience the usual thrill he felt as the game started in earnest.

Angry tones and placating words swirled around the periphery of his awareness. Still Rhett couldn't tear his gaze from the wide-eyed woman seated halfway up the table. Her slender elegance seemed out of place amid the stout men in power suits who filled the room. Today her wealth of dark hair was pulled back from the fine cheekbones, making Rhett wish to see it loose and tumbling in waves around her shoulders as it had last night at the museum.

Today her expression was more guarded. He sensed the hard barrier she'd placed between herself and those she surely saw as adversaries, giving her the calm, blank stare of a sphinx. Where had she learned to do that? Or did it come naturally to her? Was it always her reaction to the men surrounding her?

Or had he truly caught her in an unguarded moment the night before, a time when she'd been alone with her thoughts and unprepared to defend herself against her enemies?

Rhett wasn't sure, but the question came from somewhere deep inside of him. It wasn't just curiosity about information that would help him do his job. No, this was

a bone-deep desire to solve the mystery in front of him. Would he be satisfied with exposing her as a liar? Or would finding evidence of her less-than-stellar character leave him with a bad taste in his mouth for once?

Because Rhett wasn't just good at what he did. He was exceptional. He had yet to complete a case without finding something to prove his client's suspicions valid. This one would end the same...even if the chase was much more interesting.

As Larry introduced Rhett to the board, Trinity blinked, slowly, almost deliberately, then turned her gaze toward the man seated beside her. Her lawyer, Rhett remembered now from his files. Something about her breaking eye contact with him finally jump-started his adrenaline.

"I don't see how this will help," Bill complained. "Why would his presence sway public opinion at all? It just looks like a PR move, which will hardly be reassuring."

"He has a proven track record of inspiring confidence in investors," Larry countered. Rhett had met the man earlier this morning, when Richard and Patricia had filled Larry in on Rhett's secret assignment. "We tell the media and our shareholders that we're addressing the concerns of our employees and making sure the business is in the best possible hands."

Protests rose around the room once more; the group sounded more like unruly schoolchildren than business professionals. Only Trinity sat quietly in the midst of the chaos.

It didn't take long for Rhett to reach his limit. He gave the black tabletop before him a firm smack. Once the room quieted and he had the full attention of those around him, he asked in a firm tone, "Do you want to make the best of this situation or lose everything you helped Michael Hyatt work so hard to build?"

The room went utterly still as Rhett deliberately moved his gaze from one man to the next. Even the background hum of the air conditioner seemed to subside. Then his attention fell on Trinity.

Her gaze was trained solely on him; she ignored everyone else. Something about her attention shook his control for a moment.

Startled at her reaction, he deliberately pulled his mental barriers back in place, then moved effortlessly into the spiel he had prepared to convince the board of his usefulness to their present dilemma. His cover story as a business consultant rolled smoothly off his tongue.

A brief discussion ensued, one Trinity continued to follow with that sphinxlike expression on her face. He knew she was soaking it all in, but she showed very little reaction to his pitch. Until the end.

When he was done speaking, she stood up. It wasn't an attempt to intimidate, as he'd seen the other men do earlier in the meeting through the small spy camera Richard was carrying for him. No. Instead, tranquility radiated from her, garnering the attention of those around her.

Rhett didn't understand what that magnetism was, but he was determined to find out.

All eyes were riveted on her as she said in a solid voice that held no hint of hesitation, "Welcome, Mr. Brannon. We appreciate your willingness to take on our unusual situation."

He heard a quickly stifled hiss from Patricia, but Rhett didn't look her way. He found himself too fascinated with this new, unexpected side of Trinity, this authority that seemed to come naturally to her. The woman he'd met last night had been hesitant. Shy, even. In this moment, she was commanding.

For the first time, he wondered why the Hyatts saw Trinity as more of a nuisance who stood in their way rather than a true threat. They should be much more concerned. Because his instincts said he was now facing someone who might prove to be a more than competent adversary when crossed.

"Gentlemen," she said, her tone brooking no argument, "there's been enough discussion for today. I believe hiring Mr. Brannon as a consultant is an acceptable solution all around."

She glanced toward the interim board director, who nodded. "This meeting is adjourned. You all know your way out," he said.

As one, everyone stood and headed toward the door. Not a single person lingered. Rhett could see why. Trinity had closed the discussion with a force of personality that hadn't been in evidence earlier.

His spy camera hadn't caught her saying very much in the meeting, but that didn't mean she hadn't made an impact. It was almost as if she'd sat in the room, blending in like an old-fashioned wallflower, while she soaked in every word being said. But when she'd made her decision, it was time for everyone else to get the hell out of Dodge, so to speak.

Impressive.

Whispering among themselves, the crowd, led by Richard and his wife, filed out the door held open by a butler. Rhett would have gotten lost in the sprawling mansion if not for the butler leading the way.

It possessed an opulent, dark beauty in the curved arches of every window, the elaborately carved entryways and myriad displays of art and books in every nook and cranny. Quintessentially Southern, it reflected the rich, spicy atmo-

sphere of the city with splashes of bright color and nods to the rich, turbulent history of the land.

Gorgeous, but stifling. Did Trinity find the elegance oppressive? Her focus on her responsibilities, while admirable on the surface, could simply be part of the act. Dutiful widow and all. Would she welcome him into her confidence to help her with the duties she'd inherited, even as he gathered the evidence to take her down? Though it was just an assignment, his heartbeat gained speed at the thought of working so closely with her.

No, he needed to proceed with caution. He needed to get close to her, yes. But only to do his job. He needed the real motive...not the real woman.

Still, enticing Trinity to have a little fun could serve his purpose well.

Trinity exchanged a few quiet words with her lawyer when Bill paused beside her, but she didn't move as he headed on through the door. Rhett didn't miss the hard look Bill threw his way. That man would have a background check completed before the end of today. Too bad he would only find what Rhett wanted him to know.

Somehow, without the words being spoken, Rhett knew Trinity expected him to remain behind. Sheer curiosity held him still. He was psyched to see what other surprises she had in store for him.

As his gaze returned to her, he caught the briefest of moments when her whole body seemed weighed down. Her shoulders drooped. Her head hung forward a few inches. Her expression was lined with despair. It was only there for a moment, as if the demands of speaking earlier had drained every last inch of her energy.

Then the moment disappeared, and she was once more closed off to his prying eyes.

As soon as the last board member cleared the room,

Trinity nodded to the butler and he firmly closed the carved wooden doors. Not missing a beat, she turned to Rhett and fixed him with her gaze.

"Tell me exactly what game it is you think you're playing, Mr. Brannon."

Three

Watching Rhett's gray eyes widen with shock was even better than the special scenes in the movies that were her big indulgence now that she was an adult. Her mother had believed films were sinful, but Trinity had no such hang-ups. There was nothing better than losing herself in scene after colorful scene…except maybe throwing Rhett off guard by stepping outside of the carefully constructed box he'd obviously placed her in.

She had a feeling he wasn't often at a loss for words. Today his presence was even more commanding than last night. He'd stepped into a room full of powerful business-men without any hesitation. He'd taken up the reins of the meeting as if he'd been born to lead and established his abilities with just a few simple words.

This was a version of the man she'd met last night. Still gorgeous in that glossy-magazine way, but without the flir-tatiousness and single-minded intensity of the night before.

Today he'd been performing for the entire room. Last night he'd been focused only on her.

Or so it had seemed.

What was he really up to? She needed answers.

"You knew who I was last night." The words weren't a question, because they both knew the truth. She waited for the excuses to start rolling in.

"Trinity."

His deep voice held the same intimate tone that it had the night before, except now they were in a boardroom, instead of what had seemed like a very private meeting of their own. Still she had to suppress a shiver as her skin prickled.

This time it was her turn to be taken off guard. His dark good looks, the pull of his powerful personality sucked her under. What was the point in asking questions? It would be easier to sit and stare for a while, let his sexy energy distract her from the truth that had to be lurking behind that charming smile. It would be such a relief to drop the suspicions and defenses the situation seemed to require.

"You're right," he said, the ready confession surprising her. "I did recognize you—after you told me your name."

That made sense. The story of Michael's death and her inheritance had certainly been in the news lately. "It still didn't occur to you to introduce yourself? Your real self?"

One thing Trinity had learned in life was that you never got anywhere if you kept backing down...and she wasn't moving forward with this plan until she had some answers.

"Well, yes," he conceded.

His gaze dipped, making her suddenly aware of her arms crossed over her front and how defensive she must seem. She forced herself to relax, but that seemed to warrant another quick look from him, one that lingered just long enough to cause gooseflesh to break out over her forearms.

"But?" she prompted. *Eyes up, bucko.*

"But I wasn't sure whether this plan had been shared with *you* yet. Besides, I didn't know the job was definite until this morning. I just flew in last night. It was simply... a tentative offer."

His logic was perfectly reasonable. He'd been right to wonder. After all, she hadn't been told why he was here... or that he was here at all. Something she couldn't fault him for, as much as she'd like to.

So why did her suspicions linger?

It didn't help that a slight smile graced his lips, almost as if he were amused by all the questions. Defensiveness rose inside her, a desire to build a protective wall around herself, so he couldn't see or touch or know any part of her that might tell him just a little too much about the real Trinity Hyatt.

This was *business only.*

She forced herself to focus on that. "Why would you come here just to consult in a situation like this?"

He shrugged. "It's what I do. Teaching people to run their businesses properly, or more efficiently, or simply to evaluate and suggest new processes. People who inherit businesses like you have are sometimes more in need of those services than most."

"Isn't that kind of like 'those who can't do, teach'?"

That sounded rude when she said it out loud, but maybe she wanted to push him away. Just a little.

"Not when you're as good at it as I am."

He said the words with a perfectly straight face. So why did she feel like he was insinuating something that had nothing to do with business?

Determined to distract him, not to mention herself, she asked, "Do you usually conduct business by lying to people? The people you're supposed to be helping?"

He straightened, though his facial expression didn't change. "I wasn't lying. I just didn't reveal everything right when we met because nothing had been decided upon."

Warning bells went off in Trinity's head at his dangerous logic. They got even louder as he leaned over, resting his hands against the edge of the boardroom table, a wide smile appearing on his lips.

Why did her heart speed up, just like it had earlier? They were only talking. She knew Bill, Richard and the butler, Frederick, were just outside. Frederick wouldn't leave her unguarded with a stranger. There wasn't any danger here. But the response had to be fear…right?

Then Rhett spoke. "Besides, I definitely didn't want to kill the mood with something as boring as business."

"If I had known—" Trinity sputtered.

"You never would have spoken to me about art or beauty or feelings last night," he finished for her. "All of it would have been off the table." He leaned a little closer. "While I appreciate what you're saying, I simply wasn't ready to break the mood."

Implying he'd felt all or more of the attraction she had as they'd stood alone in the rotunda. But she had been willing to walk away because discussing those things with him made her feel much more than she should. Regardless of the fact that her husband had only been dead six weeks, and the fact that getting involved with anyone would give the press one more reason to flay her alive, Trinity was fully aware that she wasn't experienced enough to handle a man like Rhett.

He had the sophistication of a man who knew exactly what he wanted and exactly how to get it. She was completely naive by comparison—she knew that. Could she work with the businessman to stabilize the situation at the

company and still give the fascinating charismatic version of Rhett a wide berth?

She glanced down at his hands resting on the tabletop and frowned. She had to establish the rules as strictly as she could. It was up to her to set the tone, stake the boundaries.

"Just how much is this consulting job going to cost me?" She had no doubt that this would come out of her portion of the inheritance.

He frowned, as if he disapproved of her attempt to bring the focus back to business. But he didn't back down. Instead, he gestured toward the scattered papers still littering the slick black surface of the conference table. "Does it really matter?"

As much as she hated to admit it, he was right. She wasn't in a place where she could bargain…not when the livelihoods of over 5,000 people were at stake.

When they left the boardroom, Rhett could feel Richard approaching them. Even if he hadn't been looking, Rhett would have known by the way Trinity straightened. The way she gathered herself gave her almost another inch in height. Was she readying herself in defense…or to go on the offensive?

Relief spread through him as Bill arrived, too, so Trinity wasn't alone with Richard. Her feelings weren't something he should care about—as a matter of fact, the more uncomfortable she was, the more likely she was to make a mistake. Which was to his advantage.

So why was he worrying about her so much?

His phone vibrated. Rhett glanced at the display before excusing himself.

"Rhett here," he said, connecting the call after walking a few feet away.

It was his standard greeting for his business partner, a

signal to Chris that Rhett had to be careful about his words because someone might overhear him.

Once he was at a safe distance, he turned back around and met Trinity's gaze. She didn't immediately look away.

Chris's voice distracted him. "What's this I hear about you wanting me to take over your job? Has some woman got you whupped already?"

"In twenty-four hours?" His partner was way off base, though Rhett had the uncomfortable feeling this job wasn't going to follow his usual patterns.

"Well, it could happen," Chris said.

"In what universe?" The ribbing had the familiar comfort of a worn pair of jeans, calming Rhett's concerns.

"Stefan was really worried. He said you sounded funny on the phone," Chris said. "I figured lust must have hit hard and quick."

"I'm impervious." At least, he hoped so.

"That's what they all say."

Picking up the cue, Rhett and Chris said in unison, "But for us it's the truth."

"Seriously, Rhett," Chris said, his tone finally turning serious, "what's the problem?"

Rhett was silent for a moment, unsure how much to get into. In addition to the trio standing nearby, several board members still lingered across the anteroom near the impressive arched window. "Nothing I can't handle. Last night was weird but I'm over it."

"That was quick."

Oh, the odd premonitions he'd had about Trinity were still there, but Rhett refused to cave into his feelings. "I've got it under control."

"You sure?" Chris asked.

"Yeah. I have no doubt I'm gonna find something here. It's just a matter of digging deep enough." It always was.

"Just be careful you don't enjoy it too much."

Though the warning came with the territory, Rhett felt it on a much deeper level than usual. "I know better than to get involved."

"Hey, we all need a reminder sometimes. We were made to be cynical. Sometimes we just listen to our man parts more than our common sense."

Rhett knew better than to protest. That would just make him sound defensive.

Apparently, silence made him sound guilty, too, because Chris kept up his lecture.

"If it was just one time, life would be different. You and I both would be different," Chris said. "But we were exposed to the truth too many times. Never forget your dad and Veronica...or Mickey and Tracy...or even Lily and—"

"Uncle Joe," they said together. They'd had this discussion many times before. Both of them had families littered with betrayal. Every couple Chris mentioned was an example. It had been a training ground for the work Rhett now did.

"Dude," Chris went on. "Anastasia taught you well."

The mention of his former fiancée was just another reminder for Rhett to harden his resolve. He was fully aware of how dangerous lust could be to a man. Especially when he was staring at the incredible silhouette of Trinity from behind. Her height might be an inch or two below average, but her curves were fully present and accounted for...

And he was accounting for each and every one. He needed to take Chris's words to heart and get his head in the game. "Roger that," he said before signing off.

Now Rhett could move on to the next stage in his plan to insinuate himself into Trinity's life.

He approached the little group just in time to hear Rich-

ard say, "At least you're being sensible. It won't do any of us any good if you ruin everything before we take over."

"If you take over," Bill countered with a stern glance.

Richard smirked. "It's only a matter of time."

Trinity held still, not reacting to the men's conversation, though her gaze remained on Richard's face long enough for the man to actually fidget in his designer leather shoes. *Impressive.*

"A little snag," Rhett said, raising his phone to indicate the call.

"Anything we can do to help?" Bill asked with a lawyer's version of a polite smile.

Rhett hoped so. "Can you recommend a place to stay? My secretary said the hotel wasn't able to extend my reservation because of a convention or something."

Bill frowned in concentration, but Richard didn't think for a moment. "You don't need a hotel."

To Rhett's fascination, Trinity showed her first touch of annoyance by pressing her full lips firmly together. Was she holding back a protest for what she could see coming? How would she feel if she knew he and Richard had arranged this ahead of time?

Doesn't matter, numbskull.

"You can stay right here," Richard replied gleefully. "Hyatt House has plenty of guest rooms. Right, Trinity?"

When Trinity replied, she spoke with a little too much control. "Of course. There's plenty of space here."

"And it will save you a few dollars, too," Richard added.

"I'm a little more concerned with how others might view Mr. Brannon living here with me, since I'm so recent a widow—"

"Please, call me Rhett."

"You don't have a reputation to protect, anyway." Rich-

ard just had to step in one more time. Did the man have no tact?

Once again Trinity's face went completely still at Richard Hyatt's insult.

"Richard," Bill rumbled in warning.

But Rhett ignored his secret employer and focused entirely on Trinity. He clasped her fragile hand in his and raised it to his lips in an old-fashioned gesture. This gave him the opportunity to watch her guarded expression crack just enough, her eyes widening as his lips met her skin. He allowed only the briefest of touches before he pulled back and said, "Don't you worry. I understand my job here, and my expertise is completely at your disposal."

Confusion mingled with caution in her expression. Not letting his satisfaction show as she puzzled over the double meaning of his words, he went on, "You have my word that my behavior will be completely professional. The gossips would find me completely boring."

For once, Rhett wasn't sure that was a promise he could keep.

Four

Why did walking down the hall, Rhett at her back, make Trinity so uncomfortable?

Not in the sense of being scared. It was more of an awareness that he was watching her, moving with her, that sifted through her skin into her very consciousness. It was craziness. She didn't know this man at all. Keeping her distance was the best option, especially considering she'd be working with him starting today.

She couldn't get away.

She knew for a fact that there was only one room ready at a moment's notice inside Hyatt House, and it was directly across the hall from her bedroom.

So much for keeping her distance.

Rhett's voice interrupted her obsessive thoughts. "I appreciate you letting me stay here on such short notice," he said.

So polite. Why was he being this nice to her? He had to be working with the enemy. That thought stopped her in her tracks, and she whirled around to face him.

"Did Richard know why you were here before I did?" she demanded.

She caught an expression of surprise he probably didn't want her to see, considering how quickly it disappeared.

"I saw you speaking with him at the event last night."

Rhett was quiet for a moment longer than she expected, which made her want to squirm. But she refused to let herself. Now that she'd started on this road, there was no reason to back down.

Finally, he said, "I was introduced to him last night, but Larry was the one who initially contacted me. Look, I know this situation is highly unusual. You want to learn more about the businesses. Let me help you do that…and be seen doing it. For everyone's sake."

His words made sense. Still, she had to stay on guard. He was too convenient, too accommodating, too—attractive.

"How much can you teach me? And can you do it in enough time to make a difference with the press?"

He inclined his head, as if approving of her questions. "Right now, I'm at your disposal. Let's just evaluate where you are, what you'll need, and go from there. I have to know more about you."

"Why?"

"I need to know how you learn, what you need to learn, what will put you on the fast track to success."

"That sounds…" Trinity suddenly realized she was rubbing at her temple and forced her hand down to her side. What it sounded like was way too much one-on-one time with this man.

"Good, right? Trust me. This process will lead to good things."

That she wasn't so sure of. She only made it a few more feet down the hallway before gesturing to an open door. "This will be your room."

Rhett stepped to the door and glanced around before turning back.

But that gave her a few seconds to observe the way his suit jacket fit his wide shoulders. The slight curl of the black hair brushing his collar. The confident stance that said he was in control, even in these unfamiliar circumstances. She hated to admit her toes curled a little.

It had to be the weariness from all these weeks of constant turmoil, stress and being under observation. She was plumb worn-out, as her mother would say. That was all.

As he turned back to her, she adopted the most pleasant version of her hostess smile she could manage under the weight of the exhaustion slowly descending over her. "Your luggage will be brought up when it arrives. Luncheon will be on the back patio in an hour."

A tempting half smile appeared on his sculpted lips. "You don't have to feed me, too."

She spoke before thinking. "My mama would have a fit if I didn't feed a guest." Hearing her country twang peek through brought her up short. "Besides, it'll save me money, right?"

Wow. This exhaustion was weakening the very facade that had gotten her through the last six weeks. *Try again.* "I apologize. That was inappropriate of me."

"No. I understand where it came from."

Though she resisted it, she could feel both her body and spirit soften as he gifted her with a look of understanding. "Still, I apologize. My only excuse is I'm very tired. I would normally never make a guest feel unwelcome. Please join me for lunch."

"I imagine this has been a very stressful time for you." His hushed tone urged her to confide in him, and for just a moment, Trinity wanted to. She knew she couldn't, she

most definitely shouldn't, but it was more tempting than she would admit to anyone.

Why was he saying all the right things? Trinity needed to get away from the whirling suspicions clouding her brain before her tightly held control cracked wide open.

"Let us know if you need anything to get settled in," she said as she slowly backed away.

"Thank you, Trinity."

The way he said her name had her scrambling across the hall to her own room and into the en suite bathroom. She had to get away. His gaze had been searching, seeing way more than made her comfortable.

With shaking hands, she opened the taps and let cool water run over her wrists. Closing her eyes, she refused to look into the mirror before her. What did Rhett see when he looked at her? A gold digger? A helpless widow about to ruin her dead husband's legacy? Someone pretending to be more capable than she was?

Then the more dangerous question: What did she want him to see?

That one she refused to wrap her head around.

Maybe it would be best to lie down for a little while before she had to face him again. Getting some rest might tamp down the mood swings and give her a more solid perspective. Normally Trinity was the one logical, proactive person in the room. She just needed a few minutes to process everything that had happened in the last twenty-four hours.

She reached above her head to remove the pins from her hair, breathing a sigh of relief as the weight fell from her scalp. Then she unbuttoned her suit jacket. As she walked back into the bedroom, she shook the heavy length out and pulled the hem of her camisole from the waistband of her skirt.

"Trinity, I—"

To her dismay, Rhett stood at the open door. His brows were raised high as he took in her disheveled appearance. Even though she was fully clothed, something about his look made her feel closer to naked than she'd ever been in a man's presence.

"What are you doing in here?" she demanded, pulling the two sides of her jacket closed in an attempt to feel more secure.

His gaze followed the gesture, then traveled up to her loose hair. He cleared his throat before saying, "I had a question and saw you come in here. The door was open."

He seemed reluctant to pull his gaze from her hair, but finally did look around the room. She knew what he would see. Michael had let her decorate it to her taste, so the room had the feel of an old-fashioned library, with an antique bed that matched the bookshelves lining half the room. There was a writing desk and feminine purple bedding and curtains. The room had made her incredibly happy when Michael had designed it for her.

Now she felt like her very self was being exposed from every corner...something she did not want Rhett to see. But he was too quick for her.

Finally, his gray-green gaze made its way back to her, the intensity bringing a burn of guilt to her cheeks. Though she wasn't quite sure what she had to feel guilty about... until he asked, "Is this your bedroom?"

With those words, she knew he'd guessed part of her secret. She could only pray he didn't guess it all.

There were so many questions Rhett had wanted to ask Trinity. So many things he wanted to know about her. Some of them involved business—which he would get to in good time. Many of them did not. He knew he had no true rea-

son to dive deep into her personal life except insofar as it helped him build his clients' case. But that didn't stop the burn of curiosity low in his gut.

He kept their conversation as innocuous as possible during their quiet lunch together, not wanting to set her further on edge. Her stiff body language and wary glances when she first came to the table warned him that their time in her bedroom still upset her, even hours later. She hadn't wanted him to see her private space.

Or was that just an act for his benefit?

She very politely thanked the young lady who served their meal and very properly laid her silver and napkin in place for it to be easily removed. Genteel actions, but they felt learned. Had her husband taught her all the right moves? Had she learned them so she could earn her place when the time was right?

Why didn't Rhett want to believe that?

"We can work in my office," she said, her gesture for him to follow her quiet and elegant.

The questions continued as he followed her to the wing of the massive mansion that housed the business operations. Would Trinity have taken over her husband's office? She didn't appear to have shared the master bedroom with him.

The room she was sleeping in was too lived in, too much like *her* for her to have moved in a mere six weeks ago. No. It wasn't the room of a widow trying to get away from the memory of her dead husband. It was a room designed for her. That intrigued him most of all.

The Hyatts would find it intriguing, too, he was sure. Which meant Rhett had to figure out exactly what it meant.

He wouldn't be sharing anything just yet. When the time was right, he'd ask the questions nagging him, and hope he knew what to do with the answers.

Trinity led him through one of the elaborately carved

oak doors into a room with high ceilings supported by numerous bookshelves. There was a heavy, polished desk with a clean desktop containing multiple computer screens, now dark.

Trinity kept walking through a side door where she paused beside the desk of a smiling woman with an air of quiet competence.

"Anything I need to see, Jenny?" Trinity asked.

The secretary frowned. "Well…"

"Besides that," Trinity said, wiggling her phone to indicate she'd already seen the posts.

"Sorry, Mrs. Hyatt," Jenny said.

Rhett watched the interaction with interest. The Hyatts would have everyone believe that Trinity was nothing but a gold digger. But the staff in the house seemed to be devoted to her, or at least friendly. Did they just know her better? Or had they been fooled?

"Jenny, this is Rhett Brannon. He's going to be helping me out with the businesses for the foreseeable future."

Rhett smiled as Jenny nodded an acknowledgment in his direction.

"Please have an office space set up for him across the hall."

"That's not necessary," he protested.

Trinity turned her sage gaze his way. "I want you to be comfortable here. That includes having your own space."

Was she buttering him up? Or was this genuine Louisiana hospitality?

Rhett smiled his thanks despite his questions and followed Trinity into the room beyond.

This office was a smaller, more feminine version of the one they'd left behind. It was also more old-school. Whereas Michael had appeared to be the epitome of a modern businessman who did the entirety of his work on his computer,

the same could not be said of this office's occupant. Though Trinity had a monitor and keyboard, there were no other indications of expensive technology. Instead, the wall facing her desk appeared to have been taken over by an army of whiteboards. Each one seemed dedicated to aspects of Michael's businesses that she seemed to be tracking.

Personnel. Income. Expenditures. Contracts. Stock market numbers for the last week.

"Wow," he said, not realizing at first that he'd spoken aloud.

He turned back to where she stood behind the small but gorgeous teakwood desk just in time to catch a glimpse of a becoming flush staining her cheeks before she looked down. A few framed photographs of her with Michael taken over the years caught his eye.

"There's a chair by the table over there if you want to make yourself comfortable," she said softly, as if she couldn't force the words out any louder.

Glancing around, he spotted the chair and crossed the room to retrieve it. "Not a lot of visitors?" he asked, attempting to lighten the atmosphere.

"No. Just Michael and Jenny."

The table across the long, narrow room was littered with piles of papers and binders. It was pushed against a window looking into the lush gardens of Hyatt House, overflowing with blooms and foliage in the damp July heat. Before turning away, Rhett noted some spreadsheets and graphs with neat, tiny handwriting in the margins. She'd been keeping track of an abundance of details. To do the right thing? Or to find her own ways of taking over?

Or both?

Again, Rhett's unease returned as he set the chair across from her desk and sat down. Usually he had his target pinned and figured out within hours of their meeting. Defi-

nitely within a day. His doubts and questions about Trinity were unusual. He certainly didn't enjoy the constant second-guessing. He needed answers. ASAP.

You know why she's trying to throw you off track, his inner cynic said. But the rest of him, the part admittedly attracted to her, reminded him to keep an open mind. He liked to think he could do that—it wasn't his fault the people he was brought in to condemn usually proved his inner cynic right.

The inner struggle drove him to his feet once more, and he crossed to the wall of whiteboards. "What made you decide to use this method?" he asked. He told himself that being able to see the data out in the open like this was good for his investigation.

"Michael and I came up with it. I've always been a visually oriented person, and writing things down helps them stick. Typing information into a computer doesn't do the same thing for me, hence the whiteboards. Michael, on the other hand, was more at home with spreadsheets and data-mining programs."

That made sense. "So he knew you pretty well?"

"As you could tell by the photographs, we've known each other a long time."

Long enough for you to learn his weaknesses?

"He taught me a lot through the years, about business, art and people. Though very few people want to acknowledge those years we worked together."

"What did you do before you married?" he asked, though he knew the answer already.

"Same thing I do now," Trinity said with the smallest of enchanting smiles. That pinpoint of happiness drew Rhett into her words. "I managed Michael's charity, *Maison de Jardin*. It's a shelter for abused women and children."

"Sounds fulfilling."

"It is." Her smile grew even softer. "And heartbreaking. And satisfying. Michael wholeheartedly believed in the charity and wanted to ensure it continued— despite his aunt and uncle's wishes."

Rhett let that pass, for now.

"Michael and I spent a lot of time together. Not just at the charity." The very fact that she didn't elaborate made Rhett all the more curious. "He tended to process issues and problems out loud. When we were together, he would talk through the ins and outs of business strategies just as much as he spoke about art and movies and travel."

"Sounds boring for you."

"Nothing with Michael was ever boring." The sad shadow that crossed her expression brought an odd tightness to Rhett's chest. "He wasn't just my husband, he was my best friend."

But was he her bedmate once they were married? Rhett wanted to know—even though it wasn't his place to ask.

Or was it? Was she lying about her husband's intentions in marrying her? Or her intentions? After all, other than sex, why would Michael have married a woman much younger than him, so much below his own station in life? Or was Rhett simply blowing the evidence of the unshared bedroom out of proportion? He knew more than anyone how odd the rich and famous could be. And people slept in different rooms for a myriad of reasons…it didn't necessarily mean they hadn't been intimate.

But how would that knowledge affect the court case? If he could get her to confide the true emotional depth of her relationship with her husband… After all, wasn't that what he was here for?

But first, he had to get her to trust him.

As he focused in on her expression once more, Rhett noticed she seemed to be struggling with something just as

much as he was—though he hoped his expression wasn't nearly as revealing as hers.

"Look—" she paused to swallow hard "—I know other people must have mentioned that I grew up at *Maison de Jardin*. That is true. I did."

At least she wasn't hiding her roots from him. This part of the story intrigued him more than he wanted it to.

"My mother and I moved there when I was ten after... Well, it doesn't matter. But Michael was very good to us. We came there just before his parents died. He was very lost and spent a lot of time helping at *Maison de Jardin* during that very dark period of his life."

"So it meant a lot to him?"

"It did. More than a lot of people know." She grimaced, seemingly struggling to say something. "I don't want to appear judgmental or—"

"Trinity." He waited until she met his gaze head-on before continuing. "Whatever it is, just tell me."

He really wanted to know. He needed to know. And holding her gaze with his own deepened that need in a way he didn't want to examine.

"Michael's aunt and uncle—there's something you don't understand. Something no one on the board seems to understand. This court case, it has nothing to do with the businesses."

Wait a minute... "How so?"

"Oh, in the long run, the income from the businesses might help them. But that's not why they want the inheritance."

Her gaze went to the wall over his shoulder next to the door to the other offices. Rhett turned to find a gorgeous portrait of a house. No, house was an understatement. It was three stories of astonishing Queen Anne brick architecture. It had three chimneys. A turret on the third floor.

Arched bay windows on the lower level and a balcony over the front door. It was enormous and in incredible repair despite what must be significant age.

Some houses were portrayed as scary. Some majestic. Some transcendent. Despite the obvious grandeur of the building in the painting, Rhett felt a sense of welcoming, of the promise of protection within its walls. The small nameplate at the bottom confirmed that this was *Maison de Jardin*.

"You see, whoever gains control of Michael's inheritance doesn't just gain his place on the board of Hyatt Heights. They gain full control over the charity."

"There's no board for the charity?" Rhett asked, tiny alarm bells sounding in his brain.

Trinity slowly shook her head. "There are no checks and balances, which means they would be able to do with *Maison de Jardin* whatever they want." Her gaze returned to the painting. "There would be no one to stop them."

"From doing what?" Rhett's voice came out hushed, though they were alone in the room.

"What they've wanted all along...sell *Maison de Jardin* to the highest bidder."

Five

Trinity paused outside the door to the breakfast room and took a few deep breaths. The faint clink of silverware told her Rhett was already inside. She'd tossed and turned, knowing that he slept just across the hall. The anticipation she felt at seeing him again confirmed she needed to keep him at arm's length.

She'd never been one to be charmed by a handsome face, but she was beginning to wonder about herself. Then again, the understanding and shock he'd exhibited when she'd talked about her in-laws yesterday might have something to do with her curiosity, too.

Sympathetic people had been few and far between in her lifetime, much less since marrying Michael. Since his death, she'd restricted her comments about the Hyatts to private discussions with her lawyer, so she wasn't sure what had prompted her revelation the day before. Some days she simply felt so alone in the task Michael had left for her. Ap-

parently she hadn't been able to resist unburdening herself when Rhett seemed to lend a sympathetic ear.

Still, the last thing she needed was to get too attached. Her life was already complicated enough, and she had too many obligations that other people might not understand.

So suck it up, buttercup! Time to go back to standing on her own two feet.

With that little pep talk, she forced herself through the doorway and gave Rhett a cautious smile. "Good morning," she said.

She let herself absorb the atmosphere of one of her favorite places in the house. A double set of French doors, open to the coolness of the morning, allowed in dappled sunshine and the scent of flowers from the luscious gardens outside. She could even hear the buzzing of a bee as it worked the blossoms of the bougainvillea that framed the doorway.

With a quick but deep breath, she turned to the buffet along the opposite wall. Normally the cook who had been with Michael since he'd been a teenager would have prepared a simple breakfast just for Trinity. But the presence of a guest called for a more elaborate, traditionally Southern spread of biscuits, grits, gravy, bacon, sausage and omelets that left the buffet overflowing. It was a little overboard for just two people but the cook missed preparing meals for visitors, who had been frequent when Michael had been alive.

"Have a chance to look over those cash flow concepts last night?" Rhett asked.

The focus on business helped her relax slightly. "Yes. And I've started working on a strategy guide for you and Bill to vet…" She couldn't stop the frown that pulled down her brows. "Although I still feel we should do more to help the employees themselves, rather than focusing solely on creating profits."

"You can—by ensuring them a stable and profitable business that guarantees jobs and income."

His matter-of-fact tone was understandable but frustrating. "But the business would be nothing without its employees. Shouldn't we reassure them we're concerned about their welfare?" That would take more than words. She knew. She'd been there.

"I understand your concern, but it's idealistic," he said as he lowered his plate onto the small table next to a window overlooking the patio. The mounds of omelet, bacon and biscuits barely made a dent in the offerings, but Rhett looked happy. "Right now, we need to ensure the business is the strongest it can be."

"Actually, a focus on employees was something Michael felt very strongly about." Her appetite shriveled as she thought about betraying his legacy. Still, she spooned a small portion of scrambled eggs and a biscuit onto her plate. "Employee benefits and policies was something he and his uncle continually disagreed on."

"He sounds like a good guy."

Why had Rhett's voice suddenly hardened? Trinity glanced over but his expression was neutral. "You don't believe me?" she asked. "Michael knew how to be tough when he needed to be."

"And now is one of those times," he said, Rhett's voice softening as he watched her. "I'm not saying take advantage or short the employees in any way. I'm just saying the focus has to be on the bigger picture. For now. The kindhearted rarely survive long in big business. With these companies on shaky ground, you need to remember that. Be tough."

He was right. This was something she could not fail at, so taking Rhett's advice was essential. There was too much at stake. "I guess my own experience is with an organization like *Maison de Jardin* that's less focused on profit

and more focused on people. I know that, but it's still hard to get away from."

When he didn't respond, she glanced over at him to find him watching her with a little more intensity than before. He chewed slowly, looking deep in thought. She felt the urge to squirm but calmed herself by pouring a cup of her favorite chicory coffee and taking a sip.

From behind her, he said, "I understand that. You've done a good job there, I'm sure. The skills are transferable, but the focus is just different."

His words nagged at her as she crossed to her seat and set her plate on the table. She couldn't stop herself from asking, "Are you always tough?" She bit her lip as she sat down, but couldn't hold the next question inside. "Is it always about the bottom line for you?"

If she hadn't been watching him, she would have missed his reaction. Because it wasn't the words he spoke, or rather, didn't speak. It was his face.

It was as if his expression cracked, whether from surprise or irritation or something else, she wasn't sure. But almost immediately she recognized that she was seeing Rhett's true self, one he rarely—if ever—let anyone see. His gray eyes went wide. She saw a mixture of shock and pain there that both saddened and intrigued her. She leaned forward before he was able to lock himself down tight.

She opened her mouth to ask more, propelled by some internal need for answers, but her phone rang. They both started at the sound. It took her a moment to pull her gaze away from his face to focus on the noise. Bill's name scrolled across the screen.

She connected the call but had to clear her throat before any words would come out. "Yes?"

She only caught a few rushed words, but her brain refused to comprehend them. "I'm sorry. What?"

"There's been another post. You might want to take a look." He paused a moment before going on, "I'm sorry, Trinity."

She barely acknowledged his words as she hung up. She was too busy trying to access the site on her phone. Dread settled hard in her stomach. Why was this person tormenting her like this?

Sure enough, the new post was all about her. This blogger didn't play around. There were already dozens of comments. But it was the picture that held Trinity captivated, cutting off her breath for long moments.

The post consisted of two photos side by side. The one on the left was a picture of a picture. Someone had obviously gotten their hands on the old photograph—one she knew was framed here in the house. Her at fifteen, all awkward smile and hand-me-down clothes. A twenty-five-year-old Michael stood by her side, dapper in his dress shirt and tie. They stood outside *Maison de Jardin*, comfortable in their friendship, even at that age.

The second picture featured her now, dressed to the nines in the sapphire gown she'd worn to the museum event because Michael had picked it out for her. Then and now. Poor and rich. Awkward and soberly mourning, though no one else would believe it. Certainly no one who had commented had taken that view.

And then the hateful caption:

Planning ahead? Guess she got what she worked all those years for.

Trinity's throat closed up.

She could remember the very moment the first photograph had been taken. The happiness she'd felt having her best friend by her side. Having his acceptance of her as

something like a sister, despite the differences of age and wealth between them.

To have it used against her in this comparison post was vaguely ironic in a way she couldn't fully grasp through the hurt of the accusation. She forced herself to take a shallow breath.

Of course, people thought that. They had to. But the only ones to ever say it out loud were Patricia and Richard. To see it on the screen for anyone to see...

Suddenly she felt a warm hand at the nape of her neck, right over the tense knot developing there. The tightness melted immediately.

She wanted to dive into that warmth, to hide in a cocoon where no one could find her. Just as her eyes drifted closed, she remembered.

This was Rhett. He couldn't be trusted. After what she'd just seen, such personal ammunition that could have been taken from this very house, she was beginning to think no one could.

So she forced the starch back into her spine and subtly pulled away. For long moments, he lingered by her side, his close presence both calling to her and inciting fear. Finally, unable to stand it any longer, she looked up to see him staring at the screen of her phone.

Part of her shriveled up inside to have him see it, to expose him to the rumors about her, even though someone had probably told him before now.

"Started gold digging at a young age, huh?"

Rhett could sense the stiffening of Trinity's muscles, her defenses rising against the accusing eyes of the world.

Usually he would never have been that crude but he had a growing need to get some real insight into Trinity's intentions. Good or bad, he simply needed to know.

Though he'd only meant to be flippant, Trinity's face spasmed in pain, leaving him with an uncomfortable feeling. One that wasn't familiar. It took a few seconds before he realized he was contrite.

"Where do they get this stuff?" he scoffed, surprising himself as he attempted to take the pressure off.

That shouldn't be his mode of operation. He should be pressing harder, not consoling her, but he couldn't seem to help himself.

"People only see what they're looking for," he continued.

He'd said the words time and again to his partner. It was his way of explaining why people could fool others over and over and get away with it. The truth was in the eye of the beholder.

He couldn't stop his gentle squeeze of her neck, but then he made himself let go and step away.

But the urge to touch her again wouldn't subside. The feel of her warm, silken skin lingered against his palm. Instead he focused on what he'd just said. Were his comforting words only an attempt to get into her good graces? Or was her vulnerability getting to him?

Finally, she turned those oh-so-soulful eyes away from him. Only then could he focus once more on the pictures still displayed on her phone.

In the first photograph, Trinity looked so innocent that it almost hurt. So young. So eager. So ripe for the picking. Her expression seemed to hold an awareness that Michael's friendship wasn't normal for someone in her situation. Had Michael taken the opportunity to make her more than a friend at some point before their marriage? Surely, he had in all those years that they'd known each other.

Then why had he suddenly married her when he did?

In the photo, Michael exuded confidence and knowledge of his place in the world. And a comfortable sense of

belonging at Trinity's side that Rhett was suddenly jealous of, even though they weren't touching. Why had someone ten years Trinity's senior felt the need to befriend one of the children in his care?

That's when Rhett spotted something that made him double back. He leaned in, unsure if it was a trick of the light. The photo was grainy, obviously a picture of a picture. But was that an angry, raised scar snaking along Trinity's hairline?

Slowly he reached out to rub the tip of his finger over her cheek in the picture. "What's this?" he asked.

The jolt of her body told him he'd gone too far, but he wouldn't back down. And he didn't pull away from her. He couldn't tell if he was staying so close to put on the pressure or to savor the feel of her. When he didn't move, she finally spoke.

"People have made up my story to suit themselves my entire life," she said, skirting his direct question. Her voice was shaky at first, but grew steadier with each word. "Guess it's more interesting than the boring truth."

"I doubt anything about you is boring," he countered. It was meant to charm her but he realized it was true.

The scar fascinated him. It was red and raised but still partially hidden by her hair in the picture. A quick glance showed no evidence of scarring at her now-smooth temple. Had the injury been less severe than it appeared in the photo?

As if she knew he was looking, Trinity turned to gaze out the bay window of the breakfast nook.

"You didn't answer my question."

Trinity was instantly on her feet, her chair skittering back a few inches on the polished wood floor. "It was an accident," she said, her voice clipped.

Her movements were tight as she crossed the room,

stalking over the tile floor until she could press her palms down against the smooth wood of the buffet. Instinct told him she wasn't surveying the food for a second helping. She wanted away from him, but she hadn't left the room.

Why?

He couldn't stop himself. As if his body had a mind of its own, he followed her, stepping closer than he knew she would be comfortable with. Watching her. Needing that reaction on some gut level.

"What kind of accident?"

The sudden anger that vibrated off her surprised him... and intrigued him even more.

"Why should I tell you anything?" she finally barked. "So you can use it against me like everyone else?"

He wanted to refute her words, be angry that she would assume such a thing. But the truth was, his assignment was to do exactly that.

"Why would you assume I want to hurt you?" he asked instead, his voice low and quiet.

Her face suddenly scrunched up in confusion. "I don't know, I just—" She shook her head as if to clear her thoughts away. "You wouldn't understand."

"Try me."

There was no denying his need to touch her. He took another step closer, reaching his hand around until he could cup her chin. Turning her face to his woke the urge to kiss her, but he held himself back. Barely. Her answer was more important to him.

"Tell me, Trinity."

"Why should I?"

She backed away, giving him a better view of her face and the protective curve of her arms around her waist. Still he kept his connection with her, skin to skin.

"Because I need to know." The words came out of no-

where and were the most honest thing he'd ever told a target. Nerves exploded in his gut for the first time in a long time. A target. He didn't want to think about her that way... ever.

She shook her head slightly. "I don't think you'd understand. Most people don't." She swallowed, drawing his gaze down to the smooth column of her throat. How vulnerable. How tempting. "Very few people understand what it's like to live under such hostile scrutiny. Everywhere I turn, someone is waiting to twist the truth to suit their own devices. I've lived in this fishbowl for weeks. Have you?" Her voice hardened. "Can you even begin to understand what it's like to not be able to trust anyone anymore?"

Rhett felt his eyelids fall to half-mast. His gaze dropped from her soulful brown eyes to the pale skin he stroked with his thumb. Despite his resistance, his mind took him back to another time. The defining moments that taught him the very lesson that had changed his path forever. Hardened him. Broken him.

"Oh, yes, I understand," he murmured.

Though the back of his mind was screaming at him to shut up, he couldn't keep the words inside. On some level, he owed them to her for his many deceptions. "I know all about being scrutinized and used. Women aren't the only ones vulnerable to that treatment."

"What happened?" she asked, her soft voice barely registering over the memories flooding his brain.

He felt his mouth twist, knowing he was revealing the true amount of cynicism in his heart. It was an emotion he normally kept deeply buried beneath a charming facade. "I trusted the wrong person. I thought I was in love, only to find out she simply wanted me for my money."

Six

Trinity's anger melted immediately, leaving behind an uncomfortable mixture of awareness and sympathy for the man standing so close to her. The heat from his body drew her. Made her want to sway closer until he gathered her into his strong arms and protected her from the prying eyes of the world.

But no. She'd learned early to stand on her own two feet. Protection was a fairy tale even Michael hadn't been able to provide.

Rhett's expression betrayed his surprise and regret over what he'd said. Given her own reluctance to share, she couldn't blame him. It must be even harder for men to reveal that they'd been blindsided like that.

"I'm sorry, Rhett," her sympathy compelled her to say. Maybe he was something of a kindred spirit.

He stepped away from her. "I'm not."

That was definitely surprising. "Why?"

"It taught me a lot." Though the words were confident,

steady, Rhett's smile was strained. "It put me on the path I'm on today. There's no sense regretting it."

But are you happy that it happened? She couldn't speak the words, even though they resounded in her head. As hard as it had been since his death, she would never have given up her friendship with Michael for anything. Could never regret accepting his marriage request...even though it had led to some of the most deeply unhappy times of her life. She hadn't known the scrutiny and backlash she would face.

Or how much of her life would be exposed. She'd learned from a young age to keep to herself. Then growing up in a group home, where everyone seemed to be in everyone else's business, she'd become very private. So much so, she'd rather keep hidden or just not talk. Being thrust into the public eye was more devastating than she was willing to let on.

As if he'd read her mind, Rhett said, "Enough of my sordid history. So what happened? Fell off your bike? Got hit in a sport?"

Trinity wished it had been any number of mundane childhood accidents. Ones easily explained away. But she hadn't spoken of the incident since it happened. Luckily the scar had long ago moved up under her thick hairline, covering the source of so many questions she'd had to brush off in her early teens.

She'd never even spoken of it with Michael. Though he hadn't had to ask the details. He'd learned them from her devastated mother while Trinity had been hospitalized after the brutal beating her father had given her.

"Car accident?"

Rhett's expression had grown more somber, showing a concern she hadn't expected.

"Tell me it was a car accident and not—"

"We didn't own a car."

He blanched, and his reaction struck a chord in her. Which prompted her to tell the story she hadn't told a soul in her life.

"We met Michael at Children's Hospital. Mama and me." She swallowed, wrapping her arms around her stomach. "He had walked over after visiting his father, who was in an adjacent hospital after a car accident that proved fatal, and found my mother crying in the emergency room lobby. Alone."

She tried to cover the rest of the story as straightforwardly as possible. "My father had slammed me against the fireplace, cutting my face open from temple to ear. Mama didn't know what to do. Even though he'd been abusive before, we stayed because there was no place to go. But this was the worst he'd ever hurt me."

Trinity swallowed hard. Why, after all these years, did this memory make her throat tighten? It wasn't like she cared about her father. He'd been cut from her life that very night.

Michael had made that possible.

"She took me to the hospital. We had no money, nothing from home. Just the clothes on our back. We knew we wouldn't be able to return without serious repercussions. Michael—he took care of everything."

He'd paid her hospital bill in cash. Had overlooked their lack of possessions and money and driven them to *Maison de Jardin* as soon as Trinity was released. Sent a couple of huge guys to their house to get their clothes. It was the first big step he'd taken to help another person *in person*, as opposed to just writing a check, and it had made as big an impact on him as it had on Trinity. Especially since his dad had been dying in a nearby hospital bed.

"How old were you?" Rhett asked, his quiet voice breaking her out of her reverie.

"I was ten," she said. "Michael was twenty."

He'd taken a special interest in her from that moment on. Never romantic. Despite the differences in their upbringings and social status, they'd eventually become inseparable. He'd helped her get her degree, and she'd formally gone to work for him while she was at university. Informally, she and her mother had been helping run the charity for years.

The wound that started it all was hidden now, just like her story had been. She felt a twinge of regret. Would Rhett think less of her for it? Lord knew there were many through the years who had looked down on her for living on charity most of her life. Her mother, too. But they'd never stopped giving back—both to *Maison de Jardin* and to the other women and children who had passed through the home over the years. Michael had relied on them, and they'd repaid him with everything they had.

Even to the point of marriage...

Trinity lifted her chin. Regardless of Rhett's reaction, she knew she'd made the right choices in her life. "*Maison* is a godsend to women like my mother and me. It must continue. Those lives are worth way more than the cost of some land."

Silence reigned in the cozy room for long minutes, leaving Trinity acutely aware that the two of them were alone with each other. The air felt thick with revelation. She wasn't sure where to look or what to say next.

At long last she dragged her gaze from the gardens outside to look into Rhett's eyes. Where she'd expected to find judgment, she instead saw an intensity that penetrated any barriers she might put up between them. She'd already felt raw. Now she was bare.

"You're very right, Trinity," he finally said.

No words of trite sympathy. Just a simple acknowledg-

ment. Her body relaxed. She drew in a deep breath. "Would you like to see it?"

He was more than likely working for the enemy. The best she knew to do was to lure him over to her side. To help him see the good in *Maison de Jardin* and the women and children there.

But part of her request was personal. For the first time, she needed to share a part of her life that very few had seen.

He tilted his head to the side and silently regarded her. What was she doing? Was the risk worth it?

She wasn't even sure if she was relieved when he said, "I believe I would."

"You're going soft, man."

Rhett scoffed at his partner's words later that night while ignoring the twinge of guilt they kicked up. "I just think this is important."

"Whether your clients are telling the truth or not isn't important."

"Since when?" Had they really come to that point?

Chris was silent for a minute. "Maybe that's the wrong way to put it. Yes, we want to do the right thing. But when was the last time a client was wrong?"

Never. Rhett didn't want to admit it, because it would undermine his position, but he knew where Chris was coming from. "I just think there's more at stake here than a simple inheritance."

On the surface, the charity seemed like nothing compared to the overall worth of Michael's estate. Why would the Hyatts dismantle it? Was Trinity right? Were they looking for fast cash?

Besides, the charity Michael had started seemed to do a lot of good. He remembered Trinity's story. Were the Hyatts actually heartless enough to do away with all that? "What

if these people are looking to get their hands on the building and land just to sell it quick?"

"Then that's their prerogative. But if you're worried about it, don't you need more evidence than just the word of the woman you're there to investigate?"

True. Rhett rubbed his hand over his face. Was he losing his edge? He tried to tell himself this was about protecting a home for abused women and children—the very one he would visit tomorrow. So why did he keep seeing soft brown eyes that begged him to look deeper?

"Just look into it from your end," he barked.

"All right. Though I think it's crazy."

Shaking his head, Rhett quickly concluded his call with Chris but couldn't stop the pacing. He needed to find out more about both *Maison de Jardin* and Michael's aunt and uncle. Questioning Trinity was an option, but could he trust the answers he would be given? He wanted to, but having Chris dig deeper was a better way to go. And he needed to stay objective, no matter what.

He paused inside the door to his bedroom, knowing what he had to do. It wasn't like he hadn't searched for information in a house before in the dead of night.

This was no different.

Hell, it should be a lot easier, since Trinity and he were alone in this portion of the house…right next to the wing that held the offices.

Having made his decision, he wasted no time, utilizing stealth and speed as he made his way to the lower floor. He might find nothing. They might keep the office suite locked. He might encounter someone along the way. Cleaning staff. The butler. He'd just have to see.

He passed the door to the little office they'd given him, using only the flashlight on his phone to show him the way.

The door to the other offices was almost directly across the hall. The knob turned easily beneath his palm.

She is too trusting.

He wasn't as lucky inside. Without turning on the lights, he tried the tall filing cabinets along one wall of Michael's office. They were all locked. The computer was password protected. The cabinet on the hutch above the desk was also locked. He glanced toward the secretary's office. Maybe he should check there?

His heartbeat remained steady. Hands sure. But his mind raced, running through the options that might be open to him.

What he hoped to find, he wasn't sure. But he needed more facts than what he had. Facts, not conjectures. Or at the very least, clues as to what Michael Hyatt had been thinking. Who else would know his family and all their secrets?

He stood, uncertain for a moment. *Think...think...*

As if by divine guidance, the light from his phone caught the edge of something under the desk he hadn't noticed before. Bending down, he realized the desk had a hanging drawer. Even as he reached for it, Rhett knew it wouldn't be locked. Something just told him this one had been overlooked.

Sure enough, the drawer slid soundlessly open.

There was a small crush of tabs to peruse. Rhett quickly realized why this drawer was probably open. It held all of Michael's personal files—Trinity and her secretary were probably accessing them a lot dealing with the legalities of Michael's death. Health insurance. A surprisingly large medical file. Household bills. Original documents. All things Rhett found himself uncomfortably curious about.

And there it was, all the way in the back.

Background Investigations

A quick glance at the top page looked like a financial accounting…and not a good one. Richard's name appeared a time or two. Definitely a file Rhett needed to take a look at. The next one back looked just as intriguing. *Maison de Jardin.*

The folder was slim, which probably meant it held something innocuous like deeds and insurance documents. Not much more. Still, it wouldn't hurt for him to borrow them both for a few hours.

Carefully he made sure the drawer was firmly shut, then crossed toward the door. He was only halfway there when the light from the hallway blinked on, creating a bright line beneath the door.

Someone was coming.

His heart rate picked up. He rushed back to the desk and dropped the folders beneath it. No time to put them away. He hurried back toward the door, so that he grabbed the handle at the same time as the person outside. But he kept plowing forward, his alibi forming in his mind already.

Then he made contact with soft curves in all the right places.

Instantly his body went on high alert…but not because of fear or nerves. Holding this woman evoked pure adrenaline. Something he'd never experienced before. He couldn't fight it. Didn't want to. He could only enjoy the rush.

"Trinity," he groaned.

Her muscles were taut, as though she were preparing to pull away from whomever she'd run into. Blinded by the light from the hallway, Rhett had only touch to rely upon. He felt her relax, her body melt into his. He leaned into the sensation, supporting her weight as his mouth came down on hers.

Her lips were pliant, almost as if she were expecting this. And he couldn't wait any longer. He pressed into her from lips to knees, desperate to imprint her body with his. Her curves felt so right. She was no longer the elegant representation of a lady by day, but instead the full impression of a true woman by night. A woman who needed him, if the way she clutched his biceps meant anything.

He lost himself in the exploration of her lips, tracing the seam with the tip of his tongue until she opened for him. She was sweet without sugar and left him aching for more. Her taste, her response seemed to have been made solely for him. She moaned low in her throat, sending a thrill down his spine.

He knew kissing her was wrong. But right now, it felt oh so right. Nothing would make him walk away…not even a pesky thing like logic.

Once more her fingers dug into his upper arms, her body pressing closer. He let his hand slide down the curve of her spine to lock her against him. The throb of his body made him moan. He was forced to pull away to gasp for air.

"Trinity," he muttered, his voice turned guttural in his need. "I want you so badly."

In an instant her body froze. All that precious molten movement shuttered to a stop. Hands that had clutched at him now pushed him away, demanding release. He could do nothing but obey.

"I'm sorry," she gasped, backing away one step, then another. "I'm sorry. I just can't do this."

Then she spun on her heel and disappeared into the light.

Seven

The next morning, Trinity paused at the top of the stairs as her stomach cramped. She panted through the sensation. There wasn't much else she could do.

After all, meeting Rhett this morning wasn't optional. It was an obligation. A necessity.

She'd wanted to show him *Maison de Jardin*, especially after their discussion yesterday. If she could get someone of his stature to see the value of the charity, she might have an ally, and she could sorely use one. But after last night, they needed to have a very uncomfortable conversation.

Only after her humiliating flight back to her room last night had the questions come. She'd been so startled by his presence, and then his kiss, that she hadn't properly questioned why he'd been in Michael's office to begin with. How could that not have been her highest priority?

The urge to laugh and cry at the same time almost overwhelmed her. If only he knew. She'd been so far out of

her league last night…but no one would believe her if she told them. Just the memory of Rhett's kiss was enough to evoke shivers.

That was the last thing she needed to be thinking about right now. She forced herself down the steps one at a time, a deliberate pace even though this was the last place she wanted to be and Rhett was the last person she wanted to face.

Her brain refused to rehearse the questions she needed to ask. Instead her attention was caught by Rhett's appearance through the side doorway. He came to a stop at the bottom of the stairs.

Trinity tightened her grip on the banister. It wouldn't do to fall just because this man threw her off.

His expression was somber this morning, just as she imagined hers was. She tried to lighten the mood with a slight smile, though she probably failed. Mornings after weren't something she knew how to deal with. And he wasn't giving her any visual clues on how to proceed.

Luckily her driver, Roberto, came through the front door just as she reached the bottom of the stairs. A blessing of a distraction.

"Everything is packed and ready, ma'am," he said in his slightly accented voice.

Trinity calmed…for the moment, at least.

"Thank you, Roberto." She cast a quick glance toward Rhett. "Shall we?"

She didn't even wait long enough to catch his nod. Instead she strode across the foyer with a confidence she was far from feeling. She heard his footsteps behind her.

Of course, she was simply walking into a trap of her own making. Roberto held the door for them to enter the back of the Bentley, and then she was confined for the next thirty minutes with the very man she'd been kissing last night.

Why did her brain keep reminding her of that? How exciting it had felt to have his arms around her. How the sexy scent of him had filled her senses. How her body had leaped to life at his touch.

Stop it!

Rhett didn't have the same reservations about bringing up what happened as she did.

"Trinity, I'm sorry about—"

"Why were you in Michael's office last night?"

It was the only way she could come up with to cut him off at the pass.

"I apologize, Trinity. I should have explained myself last night, but then we…"

He just couldn't keep from mentioning it, could he? Her face burned and she turned to look out the window.

"I didn't turn on the lights when I went downstairs last night because I didn't want to disturb anyone. In the light from my flashlight, I took a wrong turn. The door wasn't locked, so—"

"I'll have to talk to Jenny about that."

She sounded super prim. Wow, she really was turning into an old maid. Still, they had to be more careful. Even though she knew everything in the offices was secured, that didn't mean they needed to leave the door unlocked with a guest in the house. Jenny had been the last one out the night before.

"I had just realized my mistake and was heading back out when I…ran into you."

Suddenly she felt his hand rest lightly on her arm. As much as she wished she could continue to avoid his gaze, that touch compelled her to turn around to face him. Still, she couldn't drag her eyes up to meet his, but instead stared intently at the smooth gray fabric of his polo.

"I am very sorry about last night," he said. "Everything about it was unexpected, but—"

Out of the corner of her eye, she caught sight of his hand going up to run through the silvery strands that stood out against dark hair. She couldn't help but let her gaze follow. Why did he have to be so handsome? Why did he have to seem intelligent and helpful? Why did he have to be affiliated with *them*?

Her heart pounded as she remembered the feel of his lips moving over hers. So powerful. So commanding. She'd wanted nothing more than to surrender.

But she didn't trust herself to make good judgments right now. Michael was the only man she'd ever trusted. And when it came to romance—if that was even something Rhett was interested in—she was the last person who would know what to ask.

No, it was safer right now to focus on the chaos already in her life, rather than inviting more.

"But what we shared last night—"

"Please don't."

Thankfully, her harsh whisper silenced any words that might be far too tempting for her.

"Even if I wasn't a widow of only six short weeks—" she swallowed hard, forcing herself not to reveal the truth that would make his judgment even more harsh "—I simply can't get involved right now. It's just too much."

She waited for him to offer an excuse or argue. Instead he watched her in enigmatic silence for a few moments before he said, "I understand."

He didn't seem to be judging, but she couldn't help but notice that he backed down quickly. And didn't that make her a hypocrite? She didn't want any romantic complications in her life, but her ego would have appreciated him arguing a little harder for them.

She turned back toward the window, hoping to hide her confusion. What the heck was wrong with her?

Thankfully they were turning onto the *Maison de Jardin* estate. It wasn't huge in terms of land. Over the years, all estates in the Garden District had shrunk as the city encroached on them. But the house...that was another story.

As soon as the car stopped in the front drive, Trinity was out the door; she didn't wait for Roberto to come around and open it for her. She paused in the drive, taking a moment to breathe in the smell of hyacinth and roses. Her gaze roamed over the outside of the mansion. Every time she returned here, that stone facade greeted her, welcoming her home. And yet she always saw it with fresh eyes, no matter how many years she'd lived here.

"How long has the house been here?" Rhett asked from the other side of the Bentley.

"It was built in the 1870s, I believe," Trinity said. "James Hyatt brought big shipping to New Orleans with luxury liners he operated all over the world. He wanted nothing more than to have a large family, but every generation seems to have only birthed one son."

"This is breathtaking," Rhett said, his gaze roaming over the ornamental brick and the landscaped grounds.

"The inside is even more fascinating," Trinity assured him. "When James built the house for his first bride, he spared no expense. The idea was to create a legacy that endured. The fact that she never had children was the deepest sorrow of her life, according to her journals."

She turned to smile at him. "I can only hope the purpose Michael and his parents put the house to has made her happy."

He didn't scoff or brush off her sentimentality. "I'm sure it has."

"His second wife was able to give birth to a son, the only child of that generation."

As she stepped around the car toward the front door, Rhett's hand closed around her arm right above the elbow. She glanced back at him in surprise, unable to suppress the jolt of awareness that came from the contact. If she'd hoped that her reaction to his touch the night before had been a product of the night and her own isolation, she'd been fooling herself.

He must have felt it, too, because he immediately let go, pulling back and spreading his fingers in a gesture that said *I come in peace*. His tongue swept out over his lips. Did his mouth go as dry as hers? Was his brief glance down to her lips a hint that he wanted to kiss her as much as she wanted him to?

Even though she'd told him no.

"Trinity," he finally said, "I just want you to know... I see your point."

She tilted her head to the side. "What point?" Her heart pounded; she was anxious to hear his next words.

He gestured to the house and sculpted grounds. "About the house. I don't know what the whole story is, but I can see that this property would be very valuable to someone who wanted to off-load it."

His gaze was assessing, seeing the worth of what was in front of him like a true businessman. But she found herself hoping he could see even more than just dollars and land values. Would he see the worth of the people who called *Maison de Jardin* home?

If he could, she just might have an ally after all.

Rhett may have been impressed with the outer trappings of *Maison de Jardin*, but the inside was awe-inspiring. The fact that the Hyatts could have bought any house in Louisi-

ana to make the base of their safe house for battered women and children, but chose to place it on the original family estate, spoke to the quality of people they were.

People who didn't do anything halfway.

"Rhett Brannon, this is Madison. She's my replacement as director here at *Maison de Jardin*."

Madison had flaming auburn hair, pale skin and freckles. She appeared strong despite her less-than-average height and was dressed practically in jeans and a T-shirt.

Rhett glanced over at Trinity as she and the other woman shared soft smiles. Did Trinity's hold a hint of sadness? Had she truly found her calling, like her mother, in running *Maison de Jardin*? Or had she seen it as an opportunity to better herself?

Despite the Hyatts' poisonous description of Trinity, he was leaning toward the latter explanation. Her motives seemed pure. It left him a little stunned that he was ready to admit this to himself about a target for the first time in his entire career.

Then he realized the women were watching him expectantly. He must have missed something. "I'm sorry?"

"Would you like a tour?" Trinity asked.

"Oh, of course."

Rhett noticed a few women watching from the doorway of another room down the hall, and how they retreated as Madison led them that way. They entered an impressive two-story library, but Rhett had a hard time focusing on the incredible book collection. The three women were now watching him warily from near the fireplace, their expressions ranging from subtle defiance to wide-eyed fear. He almost closed his eyes as he realized the source, but reminded himself they didn't get the luxury of turning away from what had happened to them.

Instead he nodded with as much respect as he knew how

to show with a silent gesture, and kept his distance so that he didn't spark any sense of threat.

Still, their expressions lingered in his mind as Trinity and Madison led him through halls and rooms filled with warmth. Dark shiny woods were everywhere. Fireplaces for the rare winterish night in the bayou. Intriguing nooks and crannies that he could just imagine young women like Trinity using to curl up with a good book. And there were enough creaks and groans to elicit a friendly ghost story or two.

"This is the floor Michael's parents had made into suites," Madison explained as they came to the third-floor landing. "It houses women with small children so they can all stay together, as opposed to the single women and teenagers in the individual rooms on the second floor."

Suddenly a door opened and a tiny figure in black ran down the hall to slam into Trinity's legs. Rhett automatically reached out to steady her, but she braced herself pretty well. She barely swayed as the munchkin called out her name. But it was the soft smile easing her expression that enchanted him.

She knelt down next to what Rhett realized was a toddler in a costume, just as a woman came out of the same door. "Barrett," she called. "Come back here."

The little boy twisted around with a serious expression on his light brown face. "Not Barrett, Mama," he said, making his annoyance plain despite the half mask he wore. "I'm Batman."

Rhett pressed his lips together to keep his laughter inside, noticing that Trinity and Madison did the same.

Batman's mama was not as amused. "No, you're Barrett. And you could hurt Miss Trinity doing that."

"It's okay," Trinity said. She smiled down at the young man. "Did you want to show me your costume?"

"I'm Batman."

"I see. And a very handsome Batman you are."

"I'm a superhero."

"Do superheroes like cookies?" Madison asked, garnering the toddler's full attention. "Because I believe Roberto just unloaded some cookies that Miss Marie might not have put away yet."

Barrett rushed for the stairs, his mother in full sprint behind him. "This kid!" she exclaimed as she rushed past.

Madison and Trinity giggled. "Poor Sofia has had her hands full from day one with that one," Trinity explained.

"I can tell."

"I do need to check that Sofia got herself registered for her radiology tech classes," Trinity said. "Madison, why don't you show Rhett the big surprise downstairs?"

Rhett watched her go, then followed Madison down the opposite hallway. He felt oddly cold without Trinity's running commentary on *Maison de Jardin*. Madison did her best to keep up the history lessons until they came to a set of ornately framed glass doors. "This is the solarium," Madison said as she let him through.

Rhett's eyes grew wide as he took in what was essentially a two-story greenhouse. Fans circulated the warm air.

"Mrs. Hyatt, Michael Hyatt's grandmother, had it added on to the original house and planted during their first decade of marriage. She did love her gardens."

"If the gardens at Hyatt House hadn't convinced me, this certainly would have."

"She also wanted an 'outdoor area' that the children could enjoy, regardless of the weather. It maintains a steady temperature, and thanks to careful choice of materials, we haven't lost a single pane of glass despite numerous hurricanes in the intervening years."

Incredible. The brick-and-glass structure was home to

numerous Japanese maple trees, climbing roses in shades of pink, cream and red, and some kind of pink flowering tree Rhett wasn't familiar with.

He managed to drag his attention away from the fascinating scenery back to the woman with him. Reminding himself that he needed all the information he could get for his job, he asked, "How long have you worked here?"

She looked not quite as old as Trinity, maybe mid to late twenties, with the same haunted shadows in her eyes and determination in her attitude.

"I started helping out a couple of years back." She nodded toward a thick patch of trees and bushes. "My family estate is over there. But I only went on salary last year after my father died. I learned the ropes from Trinity and her mother. As a lifelong caregiver, I felt I had a lot to offer. And Trinity really needed help after her mother passed away."

"How did she pass?"

"A heart attack. Very sudden and sad. We all lost something precious that day." She glanced around the solarium. "I just hope we don't lose everything now...without Mr. Hyatt to protect us."

"Do *you* think a sale is a possibility?" After seeing the place, Rhett could certainly see how anyone would view *Maison de Jardin* as a cash cow.

She involuntarily scoffed, then quickly put her hand over her mouth to conceal it. "Well," she said after clearing her throat, "the last six years I've been here, the current Hyatts have never set foot in *Maison de Jardin*." She shrugged, shaking her head. "I hate to see it end, but thanks to Trinity, we at least have a contingency plan."

That wasn't something Trinity had mentioned to him. "What do you mean?"

Madison didn't seem put off by the question. "I'm not

surprised she hasn't said anything. Trinity tends to keep to herself, especially when it's something that might make her look good."

With a glance over her shoulder to make sure her boss wasn't around, she said, "As soon as Mr. Hyatt passed, we had a meeting. She promoted me and said she was essentially stepping down as director. But what that really meant was that she still does just as much work, only she doesn't get paid for it."

"What do you mean?"

"The salary she would have been paid is now used to buy clothes and stockpile food for the families currently living here. She's setting up educational trusts for the women and children we help, even some who have moved out." Madison squeezed her eyes shut, then blinked away the moisture that had filled them. "If the Hyatts win their lawsuit, she wants everyone set before any sale happens."

Rhett stared over the young woman's head at the black iron scrollwork around the door. His blood pounded in his temples. The evidence was right in front of him. Who did he want to believe?

"That's incredible," he said, speaking more to himself than Madison.

Her smile was big and broad this time. "No, that's Trinity."

Eight

"Madison says you're still paying for some of the women's education even though they've moved on from the house."

Trinity glanced up from the salad she'd been picking at, realizing that she hadn't been tracking the conversation. Going to *Maison de Jardin* was just as upsetting these days as it was inspiring, with all the worry about the future and the burden of keeping everyone safe placed squarely on her shoulders. It was all exhausting. Far too much for her to enjoy lunch at her favorite French Quarter café, located in one of the historic hotels. But feeding Rhett seemed like the proper thing to do.

"I'm sorry. I guess I didn't get the chance to finish talking to you about what we try to do. But yes, some of them get scholarships to continue their education even after their time with us. It just depends on their needs and our ability to meet them."

"How do you know you aren't being taken advantage of?"

She paused to stare at him, her fork halfway to her lips, but he didn't back down. "You know it happens with a lot of charities," he said.

She did. "Yes, and I'm not trying to say it hasn't happened to us. But I'm not naive, nor that trusting. Michael did have some safeguards in place. For instance, all payments go directly to the school and GPA criteria must be met, whether it's a trade school or four-year degree. Stuff like that." She chewed the bite of salad, then wiped her mouth. "Look, I'm not saying the charity is perfect. But it does so much good. I'd hate for it to end because of greed."

The thought of that beautiful building being handed over to two people who couldn't care less about it lingered in her mind like a bad penny. Trinity had always known *Maison de Jardin* was worth a lot of money, given the fact that it was in a prime location on the outskirts of New Orleans' Garden District. But it had been her home, and continued to be the home of so many women and children who desperately needed it.

"You don't think they would offer to simply move the charity somewhere else?"

"Oh, I'm sure they would, because that would make them look like they're doing the right thing." She threw down her napkin with more force than necessary. "How long would that last once the cameras were turned off? Besides, would they offer the same level of help we do now?" She shook her head. "Even if they didn't mine the coffers immediately, I'm convinced Patricia and Richard would slowly steal away every educational fund, clothes fund and food fund until there was nothing left...then probably blame the missing money on mismanagement."

He took a healthy swallow of his Sazerac with cognac, a drink this hotel was famous for. Then he stared down into the elegantly cut crystal glass for a moment before he

said, "Well, you're definitely convinced that nothing good will come of this court case. Otherwise you wouldn't have given up your salary like you did."

Startled, Trinity simply stared at him for a moment. Then the truth dawned on her. "I guess Madison told you?"

His expression said *you got me*, but he didn't look the least bit repentant to have been discussing something so personal behind her back. "She did. I'm sure she told me a lot of things you would rather keep under wraps." He leaned forward, meeting her gaze with an intensity that made her uncomfortable. "This isn't a safe course of action, you know."

"I will not let those women be left out in the cold." Trinity tightened her grip on her fork, only realizing she was doing it when the cool handle bit into her fingers. "Besides, I'm not giving up yet. All this worry might be for nothing. I'll be well taken care of once the courts decide in my favor."

But she wasn't fool enough to think winning against the Hyatts would be easy. They were more than willing to play dirty. To be honest, she had to wonder if that blogger was working for them. Still, she believed she wasn't fighting a losing battle.

She had to believe in Michael's plan.

"We've built a family," she insisted, even knowing she sounded more emotional than a businessman probably cared to hear. "These women continue to reach out to each other, celebrate every move-out day together, notify us of job openings and childcare options. They donate food and clothes their kids have grown out of."

She paused as the waitress came to deliver the check, struggling to get her emotions under control. More than anything, she hated to appear weak. As a kid, it had almost gotten her killed. Now, her strength could mean the

difference between *Maison de Jardin* remaining a home or becoming a commodity. "I refuse to give up on that."

Even if it meant giving up on her part of it. All her life, she'd only wanted to serve the women in need she saw around her. Just like she and her mother had so desperately needed someone when Michael found them at the hospital. But if having *Maison de Jardin* survive meant she had to move on to the role of director of Hyatt Heights, Inc., then that was what she would do.

Rhett remained quiet as they left the restaurant and slowly walked down the sidewalk. This little café was one of her favorites, tucked away on the side of a hotel in the French Quarter where she could walk around and enjoy the historic buildings, black iron railings and flickering street lamps. Here she could simply think as she strolled. They continued along the street for a while, as she texted Roberto where to meet them. She breathed in the cooler air flowing between the buildings. New Orleans summer heat was rarely kind or forgiving.

"I think what you're doing is incredibly risky," Rhett said. His serious tone disappointed her. Sometimes it was exhausting when people didn't understand you.

She paused, surprised by the rebuke even though she knew many would share his opinion. What she was doing *was* risky. But these women were worth it.

Despite his words, his hands were gentle as he turned her to face him, lifting her chin to get her to look up at him. "If you lose your inheritance, what would happen to *you*? That salary could be all you have to fall back on."

She opened her mouth to defend herself, though she wasn't sure she had the words. He laid a finger over her lips. "But I also think what you're doing is very, very brave."

"I've been without before," she whispered around the tightness in her throat.

"Which just means you know more than others what you're sacrificing." His gray gaze bored into hers, making her want to shift, make any movement that would relieve the tension building inside her. No man had ever looked at her like he did right this moment, with a mixture of admiration and heat that caught her off guard.

She couldn't pull away when he wrapped his palms around her jaw, cupping her face as if it were utterly fragile and utterly precious. Then his mouth covered hers in a firm kiss.

What started out as admiration quickly transformed into something deeper, something mutual. A restrained version of the night before.

Something Trinity wasn't sure she could resist for long.

Rhett ignored the buzz of his phone in his pocket as he greeted members of Hyatt Heights's board and upper management from the companies the next day. This Saturday crawfish boil at one of the executives' mansions seemed to be the Southern version of putting him on display, replacing the press conference he'd refused to attend.

In true New Orleans fashion, he could hear live jazz playing through the open French doors on the far side of the great hall. The spicy scent of the food being served under the large tents on the back lawn also drifted in, reminding Rhett of his empty stomach. Crawfish boil wasn't his favorite dish, but hopefully he'd get a big bowl of gumbo at some point. He'd become addicted to that and po'boys since he'd come to NOLA.

Hyatt Heights would have hired the best chef in the city. They spared no expense, especially when they were trying to convince their employees that everything was perfectly fine.

Somehow, he had a feeling this crowd was gonna have him too busy shaking hands to truly enjoy the chef's work.

Bill had told him he and Larry wanted a casual environment for him to win over the board members and executives. Any conversations with the upper management would hopefully filter down to employees and set people at ease—or as much at ease as they could be, knowing the ownership of the corporation might be in dispute for a while. They also hoped that these reassurances filtered out to the public from today's event.

After touching base with a couple groups of attendees, Rhett stepped off to the side to check his phone. The entire time he swept his gaze over the room, looking for Trinity. They'd been separated quickly after they'd come in. The longer they were apart, the more Rhett felt anxiety creeping over him.

Then he saw his waiting text message. You were right. Hyatts deep in debt. Details sent via secure email.

Good to know. Chris had done what Rhett asked, even if he had disagreed with what he perceived as Rhett's motive behind it. Frankly, Rhett's train of thought was beginning to worry him a bit, too. For the first time since he'd started in this profession, the very person he'd come to investigate might just be the innocent in the situation.

Though his brain fought the idea, his body seemed to be fully on board, which was troublesome in and of itself.

When he looked up from his phone, he saw the Hyatts bearing down on him. A deep breath helped him brace for what he knew he had to do.

"Let's find a place to talk," Richard said as soon as he was within speaking distance.

"Are you sure?" Rhett asked with a polite smile for anyone who cared to look their way.

Richard didn't need to answer. His wife was busy an-

swering for him. "Since we're the ones in charge, I don't think it's your place to ask questions."

Rhett simply stared her down. She might think she was in charge, but he had a few tricks up his sleeve she might not be aware of. His quick glance for Trinity came up empty once more.

Richard led them to a nearby office and closed the door after they all filed inside.

"Since you don't seem willing to give us a report otherwise, I think you should do it in person," Patricia said, her tone indicating this was her due.

Amateurs. "You and Larry were told you probably wouldn't get an update because of the sensitive and up close nature of this investigation. Doing it this way, in person, actually increases the risk of exposure."

Patricia threw her husband a look. "I don't think we're getting our money's worth."

He wasn't about to let this opportunity pass. "Since you aren't paying my salary, I think you are."

Both looked surprised.

"Didn't think I would realize that, huh?" Rhett was ready to play hardball. "Other than my initial fee, Hyatt Heights is paying my salary as a *business consultant*. Isn't that convenient?"

"You signed a binding contract," Richard insisted.

"That I did," Rhett conceded. "But that contract was separate from the one I signed for consulting. I've waived portions of your fee out of generosity. Would you care to pay your portion?"

Both sputtered at the implications.

"Now, I am continuing my investigations, I assure you. Because I want Michael's inheritance to go to the rightful person."

"Well, that person is not the woman who married him

for his money just a week before he died. Hell, she probably had a hand in killing him."

Rhett didn't bother to comment on that. The investigators of the helicopter crash had easily ruled it an accident. The experienced pilot had flown for Michael for years and lost his own life—it had nothing to do with foul play.

"I will figure out if she married him for his money," he said, "but I do have a few questions for the two of you."

Did he come right out with it? Or take a subtler approach? Patricia and Richard didn't seem the subtle type.

"Why would you question us?" Patricia had the ruffled chicken feathers posture down to an art.

"Because it's important for me to understand what is happening on all sides of the situation." Especially during his unexplained crisis of conscience. "I visited *Maison de Jardin* yesterday. It's a very beautiful, very *valuable* property."

He didn't miss the quick glance the couple exchanged.

Richard was prepared for this subject. "I see you've heard the rumors about how easy it would be to sell the place."

"Of course, it would be," Patricia concurred. "But that's never been our intention."

Rhett wasn't buying it. No one could look at that place and not wonder what it was worth. "You never encouraged Michael to sell the estate and move the charity to a smaller property?"

"Many times," Patricia said with a wave of her hand. "But that was before. It has nothing to do with us fighting for our rightful place as Michael's heirs."

"Besides, the businesses are worth far more than *Maison de Jardin* would ever be," Richard assured him...a little too glibly.

"But the businesses wouldn't be as easy to liquidate if you needed money."

"That's not an issue," Patricia snapped.

"According to the IRS it is."

She gasped. "We are *not* under investigation here."

That's what she would want him to think. He didn't miss the fact that she didn't dispute what he was saying. "I have to ask *all* the questions. As I've said many times in my career, if you haven't done anything wrong, you have nothing to hide."

"Don't compare us with Trinity and her like," Patricia hissed. "We aren't criminals."

Yet.

Richard had a cooler head. "He's right, darlin'. And we have absolutely nothing to hide." He nodded at Rhett. "Yes, our finances have been strained lately, and it's no secret that Michael had many buyers approach him with offers for *Maison de Jardin* through the years. His parents, too." Richard took a few steps closer, meeting Rhett's gaze head-on. "But we simply want what is best for the companies. That's the important part right now."

Patricia's phone dinged while the men stared each other down. Rhett ignored her until she held her phone out to her husband with a smirk. "Well, if you wanted to create even more negative press for her, you're doing pretty well," she said.

Richard's surprised expression didn't bode well. "Yes, sir," he said. "You are certainly good at your job."

Then he turned the screen around so Rhett could see the posted picture of him kissing Trinity.

Nine

The first giggle didn't quite register. It was just background noise that Trinity easily dismissed.

Then she heard another giggle. Then another, accompanied by a rising swell of murmurings that set her teeth on edge. She was used to this, ever since she'd first gone out in public after Michael's death. But this might be the worst she'd experienced. It was like a dream she'd had as a teenager about walking through the school halls in her pj's with everyone she knew laughing at her when she passed by.

It might have nothing to do with you.

But a quick glance around showed furtive looks being thrown her way. It was definitely about her. What horrible thing had that blogger posted now?

Before she could dig her phone out of her pocketbook, Bill appeared at her side. "Trinity, how could you do this?"

Uh-oh. "Do what?"

One flash of his phone and heat burned across her

cheeks. She didn't even have to see the comments. She could imagine what they were. There she was, in full color, getting hot and heavy with Rhett on a public sidewalk. At least, that's what the picture made it look like. Only the two of them knew the kiss had been brief, and in her mind innocent. While it had been wonderful, it hadn't been an action *inspired* by lust or arousal.

Though it had ultimately sparked both, at least for her.

But she'd felt like it had started as Rhett's way of showing admiration. Something she hadn't had in a long time. No one else knew the context, the conversation that had preceded that small moment in time.

Bill took her arm, leading her back through the house toward the front rooms. They were halfway there when Larry joined them. He shook his phone at them, though the screen was black. "Bill, this is not the impression I was trying to make."

Trinity wished a hole would open up and swallow her. Never having had much of a love life, she wasn't used to it being talked about by anyone, much less by strangers. She'd avoided the spotlight her entire life, only to find herself living in it permanently since Michael's death.

She wasn't sure how much of this she could take. To her dismay, she was finding that her loyalty to him might actually have its limits.

The men continued flanking her on each side, making her feel like she was being escorted out in shame. Her stomach roiled, the smell of spicy food setting off a wave of nausea as her emotions washed over her. How could this be happening? How could Michael have left her to this?

She ducked her head, hoping to hide the tears that welled up. Picking up her pace, she rushed on, just hoping for a bit of privacy before she broke down.

But after a moment, someone stepped into her path. Be-

fore she could even look up, she knew it was Rhett. It was his smell. She felt his touch on her arm. She immediately wanted to collapse into his arms and let the world disappear. Which made her straighten her spine and squeeze her eyes shut.

Then she heard Larry from her side. "Isn't our situation enough of a soap opera at the moment? What were you two thinking?"

Would the embarrassments never end?

"Excuse me?" The hard tone of Rhett's voice was a warning Larry ignored.

"The purpose of tonight is to allay our stockholders' fears, soothe our employees' worries." Larry shook his phone. "This doesn't exactly say 'focused on keeping our business stable.'"

"Let's not talk about this in the open," Bill said, leading Trinity into a little alcove near the front door.

She wanted nothing more than to just bolt out the door and be done with today.

Larry trailed behind them. "You've embarrassed us, Trinity," he scolded.

Rhett pivoted to face him. "Do not talk to her like that. It's uncalled for."

They all stood frozen for a moment. Trinity could barely breathe for the emotions squeezing her chest. Until now, only two people had ever stood up for her during her lifetime. One was her mother. She'd done it quietly, with actions rather than her words. Michael had done it through support, but never direct confrontation.

But here was Rhett defending her out in the open.

"Look," he went on, "the kiss was a simple thank-you. Not the seduction that picture makes it look like."

He glanced back toward the crowds in the open space of the living area. Here and there, someone looked their

way but no one had made a move to pursue them. "Even if it had been, we're adults. What happened yesterday should have been between the two of us. Not between us and the whole world."

"Not when her husband just died and we are fighting for his inheritance," Larry hissed.

The two men stared each other down as they jockeyed for dominance.

Bill's voice was much softer. "It does look bad."

"Public opinion doesn't sway a judge," Rhett insisted.

The slow shake of Bill's head made Trinity's stomach sink. "This is the South. It depends on the judge."

Rhett squeezed the bridge of his nose between his thumb and forefinger, blowing out a deep breath. "Right now," he finally said, "we just need to get Trinity out of here."

Larry straightened with an almost audible snap. "That defeats the purpose of this little shindig."

Trinity let her gaze find Rhett's. She could feel her mask falling into place. The same one she'd used to tell her daddy she didn't care how much he yelled and hit her. The same one she donned in the boardroom when Richard and Patricia flung insults at her. The mask that hid the real feelings that people only used against her.

"It's okay," she said. Even though she knew it would be hours before she could seek the safety and solitude of her suite at Hyatt House.

Rhett searched her face with his gray-green eyes, making her wonder if he could see beyond the mask to the humiliation and pain beneath. She hoped not.

He nodded enigmatically. Then he stepped across their little circle to wrap his arm around her shoulders. "If that's the case, we will go all in," he announced.

He led her away from the little group, but he didn't let go

as they paused at the top of the steps leading into the living area. If anything, he pulled her a little closer.

She glanced up at him, unsure what he was planning. His proximity sent shivers down her spine despite the twenty pairs of eyes turned in their direction. "What should I do?" she asked, desperate for even an ounce of the calm demeanor he seemed to have adopted like a well-worn sweater.

He smiled down at her, a look so intimate it took her breath away. The feel of his arm holding her close was the most secure she'd felt in her entire life.

"Hold your head high, Trinity." Then he led her into the crowd.

A week later, Rhett strode down the hall of Hyatt House, irritation feeding his quick stride. This was the third morning in a row that Trinity had missed breakfast and he was having no more of it. She was coming to breakfast if he had to carry her there.

He knew where she would be. The library or the office. He'd found her in both places for the last few days, crouched over books he'd recommended or drawing up notes and plans for the businesses. While he admired her dedication—he'd rarely seen a CEO more dedicated than she was—he had to admit he was worried.

First, she was avoiding him. After all the attention from the *NOLA Secrets & Scandals* blog post, he *shouldn't* blame her. But he did. Her avoidance left him aching to see her, talk to her and, if he was honest, touch her again.

Second, she was working herself into an illness.

He walked through Michael's empty office into Trinity's. There she was, behind her desk. Only she wasn't really sitting. Instead she was propping herself up by her arms and shoulders on the cluttered desktop. Her face was buried in

a book, but she wasn't reading. Her hair fanned over her face, hiding her closed eyes from view.

Rhett paused for a moment, almost in awe of the softening he felt in his chest. No matter how much his brain said it was dangerous, he couldn't fight it. He admired her determination, her loyalty and her grace under pressure. The way she pushed herself to learn and grow for the good of people she would probably never meet.

It was so unlike how he'd first heard her described: as a charity director who had conned a billionaire into marrying her.

He slowly advanced across the room, uncertainty slowing his steps. What should he do? Part of him wanted to carry her to bed. His intentions weren't entirely pure, but he had a feeling the only way she'd stay there would be if he wrapped her up in his arms and held her still until sleep became irresistible. He could just imagine her soft warmth molding against him as she surrendered to the rest her body needed so badly.

But then all his pure intentions would probably go up in smoke.

Should he wake her? Find a way to make her more comfortable where she was? She'd wake up with a terrible backache once her nap was over. It was hardly restful.

For the first time in his career—hell, since the moment he'd realized his fiancée was preparing to take him for all he was worth—he put aside his suspicions and let himself feel.

He felt the weight of responsibility and a touch of guilt that he had given her what was essentially busy work to satisfy a bunch of men who couldn't believe in her. He felt admiration for her hard work and dedication. He felt an anxious need to touch her in a way she'd never forget.

What was that about? It was certainly something he'd

never felt before. Something he dared not put into words…
even in his own mind. But that didn't mean he wouldn't
act on it.

Steeling himself against what could only be a weakness, he strode across the quiet space. With a firm touch,
he rubbed her back until she stirred in the chair. It took a
few moments before her eyes opened. Even then, she looked
up with a hazy cloud over her gaze that warned him she
wasn't fully awake.

Was she always like this? Would he need to kiss her
awake in the mornings, slowly bringing her to consciousness in a sweetly sensual way? Or was she normally an
eager riser, with this haziness only brought on by too many
late nights and too much studying?

He knelt beside her chair. "Good morning, Sleeping
Beauty. It's time for breakfast."

She looked cute with her unguarded frown and wayward
hair cascading in all directions.

What the hell was he thinking?

He firmed his tone. "You will come eat. We'll discuss
what needs to happen next after you have some food in
you."

She stood, self-consciously tugging at her rumpled
clothes and smoothing down her hair. Her balance still
seemed a little unsteady as they made their way back down
the hall.

"How late were you up last night?" he asked, his tone
hushed to match the quiet atmosphere of the house before
the bustle of the day.

She mumbled a little, probably expecting to get away
with not really answering, but he paused and looked down
at her. He wouldn't have asked the question if he didn't
want the answer.

Her gaze skittered away from his before settling some-

where on the floor ahead of them. "Three…maybe four. I'm not sure."

Yes, this definitely had to stop.

When they got to the dining room, she simply dropped into the chair at the table and stared out the window onto the rain-soaked patio. Only one of the French doors was open this morning, letting in the sweet, cool breeze. He filled her plate with eggs, fruit and the biscuit with strawberry jam and butter she had every morning. To his relief, she dug right in without complaint. He waited until she had a good portion in her before he started.

"You're taking on too much," he said, not bothering to beat around the bush.

Her confused look wrinkled her adorable brow. "I have to prove I'm competent."

And he'd been a party to making her feel that way, something he could now admit he regretted. "At the expense of your health? Your ability to think and reason? All of that diminishes with lack of sleep, exercise and food. Then where will you be? Where will the residents of *Maison de Jardin* be?"

He let a touch of irritation creep into his voice. "On top of that, you've been giving up your salary. I'm all for helping others, but your sense of self-preservation seems to have gone right out the window. You're too sensible for that."

For the first time, Rhett got to see anger flush those gorgeous cheeks. She narrowed her eyes but couldn't hide her tears. "I don't understand what you want from me," she said through clenched teeth.

"For you to cut yourself a break."

Her irritation was replaced by a look of surprise. He had to wonder if anyone had ever bothered taking care of her, instead of her always being the responsible one. Had Michael ever pampered her? Loved on her?

"Look, you're working very hard. But if you burn out, you can't help anyone, can you?"

Her shoulders slumped, which made him feel like a bully. But this was important, dammit!

"You need rest and a day off."

She looked skeptical.

"An entire day," he insisted.

"I don't know."

How could he tempt her? "If you could do anything fun, what would it be?"

She didn't even hesitate. "I'd go to the movies."

He hadn't expected that. He'd rarely seen her watch television—she was always so focused on books and paperwork. "I'm not sure if being in public is a good idea, but we'll make it work." Maybe he could rent out a theater for the day?

A small grin, her first for the day, tugged at her bow-shaped lips. "Actually, follow me. I have a surprise for you."

Ten

Trinity headed into the theater room, energy in her step for the first time since Rhett had woken her up at her desk. She heard his quick intake of breath and smiled. It was the same reaction she had to this room every time she walked through the door.

"Michael had this built for me," she said, her voice hushed as if not to disturb the memories that lingered here.

She'd spent so many nights here beside her best friend, watching the latest action releases, laughing over old comedies and peeking through her fingers at the villain on the big screen. But in truth, she didn't want the reminder of her dead husband to cast shadows on this moment.

Michael had gone all in on an old-fashioned theater look: velvet curtains, iron lantern fixtures, and a full-wall screen. But the seating was modern. In the center of the room was a comfortable-looking oversize power lounger big enough for two. Pairs of oversize leather recliners were lined up around it from the screen to the back wall. Trinity strolled

over to it and pushed a single button. With a whir of machinery, the top half dropped all the way back so the viewer could actually lie down if she wanted.

"This is incredible," Rhett said.

Trinity couldn't help but smile. "Michael had two rooms combined to make this theater about five years ago. He claimed it was perfect for entertaining, but we both knew he did this for me. I love watching movies. It's my favorite way to unwind. But he didn't like going to an actual theater because of crowds and travel time and such, so this was the compromise."

Rhett cocked his head to the side to study her. "I never would have pegged you for a movie buff."

"All it took was one good movie and I was hooked," she said, smiling at the memory. "As I mentioned before, my mother was very religious. Extremely conservative. She believed that movies were sinful. So was television unless it was the news. I wasn't allowed to watch anything. Not even cartoons."

"That must have been weird when all of your friends were talking about the latest TV show."

She shrugged. "Honestly, I spent a lot of time reading, so it didn't bother me much until I became a teenager. The whole 'being different' thing made me even more of an outsider than our low income did." She couldn't suppress a sheepish grin. "But once I got older, I would sneak away to the dollar theater and spend the day watching movie after movie. It was wonderfully decadent."

Rhett moved closer, close enough she imagined she felt the heat radiating off his body. Part of her had a hard time believing they were having this conversation. Was he really interested? Or just humoring her?

"Anyway, now I don't have to leave the house to watch

movies." Trinity gestured around the room. "I can indulge whenever I want."

"When was the last time you did?"

Everything inside her went still. She forced the words out through her tight throat. "Michael and I had movie night a couple of days before he died."

Without noticing him move, Trinity realized Rhett was almost touching her. "This looks like the perfect place to spend a rainy day," he said, his voice soothing, coaxing her to relax.

"I have so much I need to do today," she objected, feeling the familiar guilt over taking a day off.

"And it will still be there tomorrow."

"My mother always said that was a lazy person's excuse." And she'd been fond of saying so.

"That explains this strange complex you have." Rhett placed his hand on her back. The concentrated heat she remembered upon waking this morning returned, loosening her muscles, pulling her into the plan. "But I think this is the perfect place to spend a day relaxing, renewing your energy. Don't you?"

She looked around the shadowy room, imagining the joy of spending an entire day indulging her favorite pastime. "With buttery popcorn?"

"I think Frederick might be able to scare us up some. Maybe lunch, too."

"Us? Will you join me?" She swallowed, afraid to look at Rhett. If she saw rejection in those gray eyes in her fragile state, it just might cause a breakdown.

He was silent for so long, her fear multiplied. She had to force herself to meet his gaze, braced for what she might see. Even in the shadows, she could make out the crinkle of laugh lines around his eyes as he smiled.

"I wouldn't miss it," he said.

Why was her heart speeding as if she'd run a race?

"Now," he went on, "go upstairs, change into some lounging clothes and bring whatever you need to be comfortable for the day back here. I'll look over the movie selection."

"If you're joining me, you need to change, too." She dared to let her gaze stray over the button-down shirt and dress pants he sported.

His grin only grew bigger. "You're on."

Trinity took a few extra minutes for a quick shower to wash off the last of the grunge from sleeping in her clothes. Then she put on her softest lounge pants and T-shirt and returned to the theater room carrying her pillow and blanket. She tried not to think about a day spent watching movies with a man who made her heart race and her palms perspire. If he enjoyed this as much as she did, she might be completely hooked.

More than anything, she forcefully pushed away the guilt of letting her work slide for the day. As Rhett had said, it would still be there tomorrow. And nothing urgent was pending at the moment, so this wouldn't do any harm.

The thought of taking a mental break made her want to whimper in relief. Her head felt overstuffed from studying, and she was exhausted from trying to create profitable, secure scenarios for Hyatt Heights's future. She needed rest. She knew that... She'd just been afraid to take the time off.

Trinity dumped her pillow-blanket combo, then moved over to where Rhett was perusing the list of movie choices. She felt a little more comfortable at the sight of the lounge pants and plain white T-shirt he'd put on. She peered past his arm to see what part of the list he'd made it to, recognizing it right away.

"What about a superhero marathon?"

He glanced back at her in surprise. "Are you just saying that because I'm a guy?"

"Why would you think that?"

"It's just not the kind of movies I would have expected you to like."

"Why?" She slapped her hands on her hips in mock indignation. "Because I'm a girl?"

"*Touché.*"

"What kind of movies do you think I actually like?" She was almost afraid to find out.

"You know, romances or tearjerkers."

"So cliché." Trinity shrugged. "I got into superheroes at *Maison de Jardin*. We as residents didn't need a ton of extra emotion, and romances were excluded on sheer principle, since most of the women there were in the first throws of broken relationships. What we needed most were calls to action. There's nothing more inspiring in that department than superhero movies."

"You're a girl after my own heart."

She wondered if she really could be.

"Uh-uh. Phone off."

The side-eye she cast him was just adorable.

"I'm serious," Rhett said. "The last thing you need is a text message making more demands on you or a phone call with bad news. We've had enough nasty surprises over the last couple of weeks."

And that was an understatement. But he'd pushed her enough for today. He simply watched in silence while she contemplated the empty screen of her phone. Hopefully the promise of a drama-free day would convince her to just turn it off.

Sure enough, she eased her thumb to the off button and held it down.

"Good girl."

She gave him a piercing glance. "Now you," she demanded.

Turnabout was fair play.

Rhett didn't usually turn off his phone for anyone. Yes, he might have a slight addiction, but he needed his gadgets to stay on top of his game. But under Trinity's mock-stern gaze, he, too, shut down his link to the outside world.

As he watched her create a little nest on her side of the lounger by raising the headrest to a decent angle and draping a soft fluffy blanket over the cushion, he wondered what came next. Would he be expected to keep his hands to himself with this sexy woman right beside him? *Boring.* But how was he supposed to know how far to take this?

Excitement and a touch of unease tightened his gut.

His uncertainty almost got the better of him as he stood beside the lounger not moving even after she settled in and pushed the button to start the first movie. But when she glanced up at him, it broke through his inertia. He sat down beside her. Close but not touching. Not nearly close enough.

They were about thirty minutes in before she passed the tub of buttery popcorn to him and asked, "So what do you think?"

"Definitely the most unique date I've had." His entire body tightened as he realized what he'd just said.

He was almost afraid to look over and see her reaction. She'd gone so still, he thought at first she might be angry. A quick glance proved she was watching him instead of the screen, but her expression was guarded in the flickering lights.

"Is it a date?" she finally asked.

He wished he had a prepared statement ready. "Would that be a problem?"

She reached for another handful of popcorn and chewed thoughtfully before answering. He couldn't tell if it was a delay tactic. "We *are* working together."

Two could stall. He munched on his popcorn for a minute or two, enjoying the salty, buttery goodness.

Finally he said, "On the other hand, we've already spread the idea that we're an item around to most of the people who know you. Even some people who don't." He indulged in another handful of popcorn as he reflected on the crawfish boil Saturday, when he'd put his arm around her and they went out to face the hostile, curious crowd together. Signaling that there was something going on between them.

Was he meant to be a white knight instead of a sneaky spy?

"I say we go with it." This time he wasn't playing around. Something deep inside was driving this. It was time he owned up to it. "I want to see where this leads."

"I thought you were just being nice at the party, getting me out of an awkward jam."

He'd thought so, too, at first. He took a deep breath as he waded into deeper waters. "I wasn't sure at the time why I did that. Normally I would never take that step, especially publicly. I drew a hard line in the sand a long time ago. I don't sleep with clients… I certainly don't get involved."

"Because of your fiancée?"

Rhett's gut contracted as if she'd hit him square in the stomach. He'd left himself unguarded, and she got in.

"I'm sorry," she quickly followed up. "I didn't mean to pry—"

"No." In for a penny… "You've had your private life made very public. I'm just not used to talking about mine."

"Was she involved in your business?"

"Not that I was aware of." He hadn't meant that to sound quite so bitter. In all honesty, he wasn't harboring a lot of resentment. He had in the beginning, but he'd channeled all of that negative energy into building his current business.

"I don't understand," Trinity said, distracting him from his thoughts.

He cleared his throat, trying to formulate the most straightforward answer. "I found out that what she really wanted me for was my bank account. I was her chance to live the high life without having to do any of the work." He stared at the flickering screen without really seeing it. "It's a lousy feeling—one I wouldn't wish on anyone."

"No one wants to be used," Trinity said, her voice almost lost in a loud explosion from the movie. "Or accused of being a user. That's what I don't understand—do Richard and Patricia really think Michael wasn't smart enough to defend himself against something like that?"

"I wasn't."

She was silent for a moment before she asked, "Did you know her long?"

He shook his head. "Less than a year."

"Michael and I had been friends for over fifteen."

Rhett needed to start trusting that Michael had known what he was doing.

Her gentle tone contrasted sharply with the loud sounds from the screen as she went on, "I'm sorry you went through that. Once that faith in others is broken—I know from experience that getting it back is hard. Especially with no one to lean on."

Rhett liked to think he didn't need anyone for that, but didn't everyone? "Men are a little different than women in that regard, I think," he said, ignoring the gruffness that crept into his voice.

"I'm sure they like to think so."

He glanced over at her but her smile was soft, encouraging rather than judgmental. "How would you know?" he teased. "Didn't you grow up in a house full of women?"

"Human nature is what it is."

He'd always thought so. Now he wasn't so sure.

Eleven

She was so warm.

It had been years since Trinity had felt this kind of snuggly, secure warmth that made her want to burrow in and hide from the light of day. Or rather, the light from the movie screen.

Consciousness slowly returned as she became aware of the source of both the light and sound. The flashes against her closed eyelids made her want to turn away from the intrusion, toward the source of the heat at her side. Toward the smell of citrus and musk.

She forced her eyelids up.

Under other circumstances, opening her eyes to the sight of a man lying beside her would have been shocking. It was disconcerting…since it had never happened to her before. But something about knowing this man was Rhett Brannon settled her mind then and there. This might be new. Just a little bit scary… Okay, a lot. But she didn't want to be anywhere else but beside him.

He wasn't pushing her away, so maybe he felt the same.

She could tell from the soundtrack that they'd reached about the middle of the third movie. She wasn't sure when she'd fallen asleep, but obviously she'd taken liberties and made Rhett serve as a pillow. Did he mind?

A squeal of tires on the big screen sent a shock through her. Involuntarily her fingers curled into his chest as if to give herself an anchor. She watched in fascination as his hand drifted up to cover hers.

If possible, she relaxed even more.

"Sleep well?"

The vibration of his chest beneath her palm as he spoke prompted her to rub small circles in his cotton T-shirt. She swallowed down her shyness and tilted her head back until she could see his face. "Yes," she admitted. "Um, thanks for providing a replacement pillow?"

He grinned, his teeth flashing white in the dim shadows. "No problem. I stole yours anyway."

He reached out and pushed her hair back away from her face. It must have come loose while she slept. Her heart sped up as his fingers tugged on the silky strands, then even more as he rolled to his side, easing her back against the cushions.

The headrest of the lounger was still elevated so they were level with each other but she still felt dwarfed by him. Not physically, but because of his intensity.

His hooded gaze stole her breath. She couldn't look away.

"Trinity?" he said, his voice a soft question that surprised her.

He was asking for permission to continue and she found herself considering whether she should give it. Some women might not bother thinking about it. She imagined

them throwing themselves at this willing man lying next to her with abandon. But Trinity had never been that carefree.

Rhett had proven he cared about her. It wasn't about a quick roll in the hay. He'd supported her through some difficult situations. Today alone said that he cared about her as a person, rather than just a convenient body. Was that enough?

Instead of passively offering her permission, Trinity reached up to rub her thumb along the strong edge of his jaw. Rough stubble scratched her fingertips. What would that scruff feel like against more tender skin? Against her belly or her thighs?

His eyes slowly closed, but otherwise he didn't move as her hand wandered down to the side of his neck. She indulged her curiosity, running her fingers through his hair, testing the textures. The dark hair against the nape of his neck was softer; the gray coming in at his temples tended more toward coarseness. She trailed her touch to his full lips, then down over his chin.

She let her palm fall to his shirt once more, detecting the faint texture of chest hair through the fabric. As she approached his belly button, his stomach tightened, the muscles rippling beneath her touch. She wanted so badly to close her eyes and focus on the feel of him, but she couldn't drag her gaze away from the expression on his face.

It wasn't pain or ecstasy but almost a surprised fascination. She didn't know how else to describe it. He practically soaked in her touch.

She shifted so she could use both hands. She pressed her palms into his muscles, testing the resistance. The feel of him leaning into her touch sent a thrill through her. She followed the corded muscle of his chest out to his shoulders and grasped them with an intensity that conveyed exactly what she wanted from him.

He followed her lead, leaning forward to kiss her forehead. Then he brushed his lips over her brows, her cheekbones, exploring her just as she had explored him.

Finally, his lips brushed hers, the tang of salt giving way to sweet surrender. She pulled him closer, her grip tightening. The ache of need spread through her body.

He didn't hurry. He took his time exploring her mouth. The dance of lips and tongue set off tingles that spread in waves over her skin.

She couldn't hold back the moan from deep in her throat. Everything he did felt so good. Better than she'd ever imagined.

He moved even lower, letting his body slide against hers, producing delicious friction. She felt the heat of his mouth against her throat. Her hips rose against him without her permission. So intoxicating.

Mewling sounds escaped her as he licked along her neck, then suckled gently right below her ear. She gasped, clutching him to her. She wanted, no, needed, him closer. She tilted her head back, giving him an all-access pass.

Only then did she realize that a light was intruding on the darkness. Opening her eyes, she realized the movie was over and the wall sconces had automatically turned on. They weren't super bright, but it felt like it.

She tried closing her eyes again. Tried focusing in on Rhett—the feel of him, the heat of him. Instead her mind started to race. What if someone came in? What if she did something stupid? What if something went wrong?

And was she ready to expose her most intimate secret to him? The thought rolled over and over in her brain, leaving her whimpering.

This had to stop. She had to stop. Panic sped up her heartbeat, left her gasping.

Some of it must have gotten through to Rhett because

he pulled back just enough to look down at her. "Everything okay?" he asked.

She wanted it to be… More than anything. But her brain simply wouldn't shut off. She licked her lips. What should she do?

"Trinity?" he said, once again stroking her hair back from her face.

She didn't want to say it out loud, but her body chose for her. "No, I'm not okay."

Even as she tried to rein in her panic, Trinity felt it slipping through her grasp. Control was a thing of beauty in her world. The one thing that allowed her to steer in the face of wave after wave that threatened to capsize her boat. Right now, as her heart raced out of control and she struggled to breathe, control seemed forever out of her grasp.

She pulled away, pressing her palms into the soft cushions as she forced breath in and out of her lungs. She tried stretching to relieve the tightness from her back and neck, anchoring herself to keep from losing her balance. But it wasn't the physical symptoms that were the most daunting—it was the constant racing of her thoughts.

Why wouldn't they stop?

"Trinity," Rhett said from the opposite side of the lounger. His voice wavered as her brain cried out for more oxygen, making it a struggle to understand his words. "What's the matter?"

But she couldn't tell him. Nothing would allow her to voice the fears his touch evoked. It was a can of worms she simply wasn't ready to open. After all, she'd spent the last eight weeks pretending to be the epitome of Michael's true love. She knew she'd been his closest friend. She'd told others time and again that she'd been his best friend. But that wasn't what they wanted to hear. She was either his one true love…or a gold digger.

To tell anyone that she was still a virgin after becoming a widow would shatter the illusion of why she and Michael had married…because no one wanted to hear the truth.

Knowing that she wouldn't be able to hide that knowledge from Rhett if she slept with him wasn't something she was ready to deal with. The last thing she wanted was to rehash her relationship with her husband right after having sex with someone else.

She clenched her fists into the cool silkiness of the cushions, forcing herself to focus on the tangible connection as she continued drawing air in and out. In and out. In and out.

"I'm sorry," she finally gasped. Which felt juvenile and lame. What woman has a panic attack because a sexy man wants to touch her?

What was wrong with her?

"I'm sorry," she said again, her voice steadier this time. "I just started thinking…and I couldn't stop."

He stood nearby, dwarfing her with his height. "That doesn't sound like the result I was looking for."

The amused tone in his voice at least cut the tension a notch. "Yeah," she gasped. "Not helpful."

"Do you need anything?"

"This is gonna sound nuts." And probably was, but she couldn't talk about her biggest concern. Not openly. So she moved on to the next one. "But I started to think about some person, some photographer, suddenly jumping out of the shadows and taking pictures of me. Of us. Isn't that crazy?"

"I hope that doesn't happen. That's the last thing I want people to watch me doing." He laughed.

"Hey, what about me?" she asked with fake indignation. It was easier than focusing on her panic attack, and she was grateful to him for leading them in a less intense direction.

He shrugged. "I'm pretty sure you'll be beautiful regardless of what you're doing."

"Flatterer."

As self-conscious as that made her feel, at least they weren't dwelling on her other issues…

But Rhett wasn't about to be kept at arm's length for long. He reached out and wrapped his arms around her shoulders. His warmth at her side made her feel supported, but it wasn't sexual in any way. She hooked her hands over his forearm draped across her front, anchoring herself.

"You probably think I'm being overly dramatic," she finally said.

He rested his forehead briefly against hers before straightening again. "Look, everything has happened very quickly," he acknowledged. "I understand that. You've barely had time to mourn your husband."

Trinity felt a jolt burst through her. Her husband. Difficult to remember. Hard to forget.

"And now all of this other stuff with the businesses and charity and the press." He squeezed her against him for a moment. "I think being touchy and emotional is a normal response."

"That's making allowances," she said, hearing echoes of her mother's stern voice in her words.

Rhett shook his head in denial. "No. Most days you're regal, moving through it all with a poise I can only envy. But everyone is human. Even you."

She lifted her chin so she could stare at him.

"What?" he asked.

"Michael used to say that," she answered, reluctant to bring him up but needing to be honest. *Just try your best. Everybody makes mistakes.* "He didn't accept deliberate slacking, but he also remembered that the people around him had limits."

"Sounds like a smart man."

At first, she thought Rhett was retreating as his grip

loosened but then he eased one of his large hands around her to rub her back. He gave her comfort. Something she'd had very little of in her life…and none since she'd lost Michael. Would Rhett understand what that meant for her?

"He was my best friend," she said, hating that she sounded lost, forlorn. She couldn't help but wonder what Rhett would say if he found out that Michael hadn't been more than that.

Rhett's touch at the base of her neck distracted her from her worries. "Don't worry about this, Trinity," he said.

She barely suppressed a huff of laughter. Rhett added his own chuckle.

"I know. Easier said than done." He tipped her chin up to look into her eyes. "But there's no obligation here. No plan going forward. Take your time to think it through, and decide what you really want. Okay?"

Trinity nodded, but deep inside, she feared this was a choice she wasn't ready to make.

Twelve

Trinity smiled as Roberto helped Madison into the back of the limo the following evening. The redhead looked flushed but beautiful in her silky lavender gown. Not a look Madison was used to sporting. At *Maison de Jardin*, they normally favored yoga pants or jeans, but this was something the younger woman needed to get used to if she was going to represent the charity at fund-raising events.

"Ready?" Rhett asked with a smile. He was sitting next to Trinity on the plush leather back seat.

Madison raised a skeptical brow. "No."

Trinity couldn't hold back a small chuckle. She knew the other woman well.

Madison smiled a little. "I'm not a huge fan of crowds," she conceded. "Spending most of your life in a sickroom will do that." She rushed on, as if she wanted to change the subject. "But I'm really grateful that you offered me an invite. And this dress!" She fingered the material, testing the smooth texture. "It's so gorgeous, Trinity. Thank you."

Trinity smiled over the nervous chatter, remembering her own first society fund-raiser. She'd been a bit younger than Madison, and definitely more soft-spoken, but she understood the nerves that came with the job. Having Michael at her side had only helped a little. "It's okay. Just relax. And remember, I'll be right there with you." She glanced over at Rhett. "Have I mentioned this is Madison's first event?"

"I never would have guessed it." He winked at the younger woman. "You look gorgeous, Madison."

Definitely a flatterer.

"Don't worry," he went on. "You'll soon realize it's always just the same boring people talking about the same boring things—"

Trinity cut him off. "You're making it worse. She's starting to turn green."

They all laughed, which helped Madison's color return to normal. The lush foliage, wrought iron gates and decorative stone and brick of the Garden District floated by as Roberto drove them at a leisurely pace to their destination.

"So you live in the Garden District but don't go to the upper-crust parties?" Rhett teased, making Trinity want to elbow him in the side. She knew he was trying to provide a distraction, but worried Madison wouldn't want to discuss her history with a stranger.

"My family used to be pretty well-known," Madison conceded with only a slight hesitation. "But after my mom died, my father withdrew from almost all social contact. Then he got sick, so…"

"I'm sorry to hear that," Rhett said.

She shrugged and said, "It doesn't bother me. I'd rather be useful than pretty, as my father used to say." She paused to nibble on her lip for a moment. "What if I don't know what to say? I mean, it's not like these people will be in-

terested in how I can feed twenty people every day or co-
ordinate their laundry."

The women shared a smile as Trinity remembered her
own challenges juggling the two sides of the job. The prac-
ticalities of running a charity for women and children were
worlds away from anything the glamorous people who supported it had to deal with.

"A lot of it is listening," Rhett offered. "Everyone wants
to be heard, right? Listen and pay attention. Offer your
unique perspective on whatever the subject matter is."

Trinity knew that advice to be sound. "If I've learned
anything in the last few months, it's that you don't need
to be formally educated to have an opinion. A lot of people at these events have advanced degrees but no practi-
cal experience. Just bring that to the table and know you
have an insider's view of what charities like ours need on
a day-to-day basis."

Surprising Trinity with a quick kiss, Rhett winked at
Madison. "But it helps to have someone beautiful and intelligent at your side."

Trinity glanced down, her heart picking up speed at the
sight of Rhett's hand clasped around her own. He'd decided
to fully embrace whatever this was between them and didn't
seem worried about providing more fodder for the press.

She'd prefer not to appear on a certain blogger's website
again, but wondered what else could possibly be done to
her at this point. She'd been called a gold digger, a hooker,
a woman willing to use her body to get what she wanted
from a young age. Couldn't get much worse than that.

She hoped, since this was a ticketed, private event at
a private home, she didn't have any worries on that front
tonight.

As if he could read her mind, Rhett squeezed her hand,

drawing her attention up to his gaze. He lowered his voice so only she could hear. "Worried?"

"Should I be?" Why she wanted to appear brave to him, she wasn't sure. He'd seen the worst of her fears, anxieties and exhaustion. Who was she kidding?

"No." His gray gaze was steady on her. "I say go all in. Give 'em what they want to see."

She worried at her lower lip, probably ruining her carefully applied lipstick. His attempts to take care of her went straight to her heart. "It's easier to fade into the background."

"They aren't going to let you, are they?"

She shook her head, acknowledging the truth. Richard and Patricia wouldn't stop with their accusations. They'd take every piece of evidence they could find and twist it to support their own version of events. They wanted to make her out to be a grasping harpy who stole their inheritance from them, and threatened the livelihood of thousands of families, when in truth they would simply drain Hyatt Heights of every last ounce of profit they could, all while pretending to be innocent.

It would support their version of the story if she were seen as moving on from her husband in an unseemly amount of time. Never truly mourning him, though she'd mourned him for months before he'd actually died. That was their twisted truth.

But she looked at Rhett and knew of the truth. Someone so supportive and understanding couldn't be a threat to her. She could trust him to help her find her way, and a way for the company, without being swayed by media coverage. As she glanced back down at their intertwined hands, she realized that's what she wanted. It was exactly what she needed in this moment.

But was she brave enough to take what he was offering?

* * *

Rhett should have had a moment of downtime while Madison and Trinity made a trip to the ladies' room, but one gesture from Richard over near a back hallway changed all that.

Rhett's thoughts churned as he crossed the crowded room. More than anything, he knew he couldn't give the Hyatts what they wanted. Trinity just wasn't that kind of woman—the sneaky, conniving woman they wanted her to be. And he couldn't portray her that way for any amount of money.

The boisterous music from the live band clashed with Rhett's inner worries.

The fact that he was taking a target's side like this for the first time in his career still left him a little off-kilter. But this wasn't just about his attraction to her. Even if he wasn't with Trinity in the long run, he would stand by her side to the end of her ordeal.

He just hadn't figured out how he would do that yet.

After all, he had signed a contract with the Hyatts. His salary wasn't paid by them, now that he was being paid as a consultant for Hyatt Heights, but he could only imagine what it would do to Trinity to realize he'd been hired to spy on her, not "consult" with her on Hyatt Heights's businesses. And that was a conundrum he hadn't figured out how to fix…yet.

Rhett followed the Hyatts and Larry into a small anteroom that blocked some of the noise from the main hall. No sooner had the trio surrounded him than Richard pounced. "We want more information. Why haven't you found anything yet?"

Because there's nothing to find. "I don't have anything of interest to report."

Patricia took two steps and was in his face, anger pinch-

ing her already narrow features. "Then you aren't trying hard enough. Everything can be twisted to tell a story, if you just look at it from the right angle."

Larry cleared his throat. "Now, wait a minute…"

"We're running out of time," Patricia said over him, not bothering to keep her voice lowered. "I want evidence now, not when you're done having your way with her."

Rhett's control slipped a notch, pushing him to straighten up and brace himself. "Do *not* speak about her that way."

"We can still use it to our advantage," Patricia said, her expression turning sly. She reached out and gripped one of his biceps with her red-tipped fingers. "Just give 'em some more pictures. A new boyfriend eight weeks after the tragic death of her husband always looks bad." She shared a glance with her husband. "That should shine a light on her true motives, right?"

"What?" Larry exclaimed.

"Shut up." Patricia was determined to run the show. Her nails dug a little deeper. "We want evidence. I don't care what kind it is."

Larry's expression grew panicked. "I do."

Richard carefully pried his wife's talons away from Rhett's arm. "I think we can all work together here. Especially considering the new member of our team."

Rhett narrowed his gaze on the man's face. "What are you talking about?"

"We put out some feelers on that gossip blogger…" Rhett's glare didn't seem to faze Richard. In fact, the man seemed to relish the tension growing in the small room. "And made arrangements for him to be here tonight."

"So it's a man?" Rhett asked.

Patricia wasn't fussy about details. "Don't know. Don't care. As long as you give him or her some good photos tonight, it will keep the controversy going."

"Since you enjoyed the last kiss so much, surely you wouldn't mind providing another," Richard said with a smirk.

While kissing Trinity was never a hardship, the last thing he wanted was to put her on display. "I don't think—"

"You don't need to think," Patricia interrupted. "Simply do as you're told."

Rhett straightened, unable to stop himself from looming over the thin woman. "You don't seem to understand my job here. I'm an investigator, not some flunky here to *make up* evidence for you."

This time Patricia let her pointed red nail creep down his chest, forcing Rhett to subdue a shudder. "I'm sure Trinity would be interested to learn this about you. Don't you think?"

Richard chimed in, "Or we can find someone more accommodating to do it for us."

Rhett wasn't ready for that. He needed more time to figure out how to get them out of this mess with the least amount of damage to Trinity.

"So you want what? Me to pose for a photo with her so they can shame her again?"

Larry edged toward the wall, a frown marring his normal good ol' boy expression.

Patricia smiled, seeming to sense imminent victory. "Just prove what the world—and the board—already suspect. She's just in it for the money and doesn't care what happens to Hyatt Heights or the family name. You're at least good for that much...or should we find something else on Trinity for the blogger to expose?"

The look the couple shared said they already had something devious in mind. Rhett worried he couldn't keep the disgust from his expression much longer. Better to keep his mouth shut, for now.

"Just think about it. I'm sure you'll make the right decision," Patricia said before she sipped her pink martini and walked away.

Richard gave him a stern look before following her out into the bustling party.

Larry patted at his sweaty forehead with a handkerchief, looking on the verge of tears. "I didn't mean for this to happen."

"What? Finding yourself in league with the villains?"

"I didn't mean for Trinity to get hurt. I just wanted to scare her into doing the right thing."

Rhett wanted to explode, but forced himself to keep calm. How could Michael have left Trinity surrounded by these people? "How is scaring her the right thing? Or turning the companies over to those people? Is that what you think is right for Michael's legacy?"

Larry pressed the handkerchief over his mouth, letting his head drop forward. Emotions turned his cheeks ruddy. "What should I do?"

It seemed obvious to Rhett but he spelled it out anyway. "Get started swaying the board in her favor...and find me that blogger."

Rhett returned to the party to find Trinity standing next to a high-top table by the dance floor. He followed her gaze to see Madison watching the dancers, a tall man at her side. "Do we know him?" he asked as he placed his hand at the small of Trinity's back.

"Actually, no," she said, studying the couple. "I haven't seen him on the charity circuit before." She turned to Rhett and was silent for a moment. Her smile slowly faded. "Are you okay?"

"Yes." Rhett struggled to clear his throat. The last thing he wanted was to put Trinity on display, but he didn't trust Patricia not to do something harmful if he didn't comply.

He wished he didn't have to do this. "You look beautiful," he said, regret tightening his throat once more.

"Thank you. You aren't too bad to look at yourself."

"Then let's not waste this moment. How about a dance?" That should provide plenty of interesting pictures.

Trinity eyed the antics on the dance floor with a skeptical look. "I don't know. I've only really slow danced."

"This is New Orleans," he coaxed. "It's time to learn how to party."

Without giving her breathing room, he pulled her out onto the dance floor. He had learned that giving Trinity too much time to think left her paralyzed. Sometimes you had to jump-start the action to get her to, well, act.

She shouldn't have worried about her dancing. They shared lots of laughter, lots of teasing, and some very sexual tension. Finally, the band slowed enough that he could pull her close, and bury his fingers in the curls now falling at the nape of her neck.

It wasn't until he glanced sideways and caught sight of Patricia and Richard watching from the wings that he remembered exactly why he was on the dance floor. According to their smug expressions, it was time to start worrying.

Thirteen

"I just think it would be an interesting way to include donors in the everyday running of the charity," Trinity concluded as she set her plate on the breakfast table the next morning.

Heavy clouds loomed outside, warning of an incoming thunderstorm. It still felt like early morning, even though they'd skipped their customary breakfast in favor of an early lunch. Rhett had been grateful for the extra time to sleep. They'd gotten in late after dropping a very chatty Madison off at her home. After the sleepless hours Rhett had spent trying to brainstorm a way out of this whole mess, he was grateful they were getting a late start on their day.

Feeling sluggish, he simply wanted to stretch out on one of the chaises beneath the bougainvillea vine and soak in some warmth. The weather had other ideas. Also, Trinity was firing on way more cylinders than he was this morning.

"Don't you think?" she asked.

He grunted as he lifted his first cup of hot, black chicory coffee to his lips.

She shot him a half grin. "Rough night?"

"You have no idea."

He thought she whispered, "Oh, I probably do," but he couldn't be sure.

He'd wrestled half the night with his decision to put Trinity on display at the party last night. Even though she hadn't felt it, he had known what he was doing. His body was tense with anticipation for the call letting them know a new post was up. It would come today.

At least these photos were something he could control, rather than something the Hyatts cooked up on a whim to damage Trinity's reputation further.

Their phones buzzed almost simultaneously. Rhett didn't bother to look at his. His focus was on Trinity.

He watched as she checked her notifications and turned pale. The guilt washed over him, forcing him to squeeze his eyes shut for a second, maybe two. Then he heard the clatter of her phone on the table and her footsteps as she ran back into the house.

By the time he opened his eyes, she was gone.

He wanted to run after her, but knew he needed to see what had been posted. Her reaction had been unusually strong.

Reaching across the table, he picked up her phone. The screen lit up as he turned it to face him. Rhett blinked for a moment, his brain not quite comprehending the image. The video still showed the face of a man he didn't recognize. It wasn't until he scrolled down to the headline that it all made sense.

Widow's Father Confirms She is After Money

Nice. Guess he wouldn't be winning any father-of-the-year awards, now would he? But the man never had before, so why start now?

At least Rhett knew what Patricia had been scheming.

He walked with heavy steps up the stairs to Trinity's room. Somehow he knew she would be there, surrounded by her books and artwork. He almost expected her to be curled up in the bed. Instead, he found her braced, her back turned as she stared out the panoramic windows.

Even from this angle, he could tell she had her arms locked around her stomach. Was she crying? Was she raging? Whatever she was doing, it was too quiet for Rhett's comfort.

"Trinity, are you okay?" he asked, wincing even as he said the words. Of course, she wasn't okay. That was a stupid question to ask. But where else could he possibly start?

"I'm fine," she said, her tone biting and cold.

"It's all right to be upset."

"Oh, I'm not upset." The tremor in her deadly quiet voice set off alarm bells. As she turned to face him, he saw no evidence of tears.

"I'm not upset," she repeated. "I'm furious. How dare he? How dare they?" She stomped across the open space, then turned and headed back again.

Rhett felt like he'd sold his soul for nothing, even though he knew this wasn't about him. He had no clue how to make this right. At all. But he had to find a way. He wanted to hold her, comfort her in a way he'd never thought he was capable of, but the emotions bouncing off of her kept him at bay.

So he let her pace it out, hoping his continued presence, his willingness to listen was enough.

"You know what makes me angry?" she asked, her voice loud enough to ring in his ears. But he refused to wince as she went on. "I'm not angry for myself, but for my mother."

She paced back to the window, laying her palm against the glass as if to feel the water running down the other side. "You see, I know whatever he says, he's lying. He always has. I'm old enough to remember." She released a soul-deep sigh. "I remember his lies, to us and to himself."

She shook her head. "My mother never contradicted him, never argued. Maybe she put up with his abuse longer than she should have, but she tried to keep peace in our house." Her hand dropped to her side. "Until she knew she couldn't anymore." She turned to face him. "It's a losing battle when you're up against someone stronger than you."

She absently rubbed her fingertips over the scar above her right ear. "She made the choice to leave, but the lies didn't stop until someone more powerful stepped in. Only Michael was able to truly gut him from our lives. My father just wanted control. He would have plagued us forever without Michael's help."

She pointed a shaky finger toward her phone in Rhett's hand and he reflexively squeezed it. "Whatever he said about us, it's a lie. But my mother isn't here to defend herself, is she?" The way she hugged herself made his chest ache. "Would she want me to? In the midst of all the other chaos in my life, do I really want to engage with…this? Counter whatever he might have said about us? Or ignore it all?"

She slumped forward. "It's all so exhausting."

Rhett bent forward until he could meet her gaze with his own, his chest aching at the emotion in her brown eyes, and asked, "Does he even deserve a response?"

She shook her head adamantly. "No, he doesn't."

"Then we'll let Bill deal with it," he assured her. "Whatever he said."

He approached her with cautious steps, for once unsure exactly how to comfort her. "You aren't alone in this," he said. "It may feel like it sometimes, but you aren't alone."

The twinge of unease as the words left his mouth was muted. Over the past few days, he'd become more comfortable being there for her. He wasn't sure how it had happened. If it was simply the sheer peace of her presence, the purity of her drive to do the best for everyone involved, or the draw of her sophisticated beauty…but the change was definite.

To his surprise, he welcomed it.

He didn't know what the next action to take was or how to fix any of this. But the peace was there. The conviction that she didn't deserve any of what the Hyatts were doing to her.

The belief that Michael had made the right choice.

Then Trinity took a deep breath, looked down at her phone still in his possession, and asked, "Will you watch it with me?"

If Trinity had ever thought she'd see her father again, it had never occurred to her it would be in a rainy room in Michael's house, in full color on the screen of her phone with Rhett's arm securely around her.

She took a deep breath against the sense of unreality as the video began to play.

Her father's face was more bloated than she remembered. Probably from years of drinking the beer he'd always liked so much. At least he appeared tidy and clean-shaven. But she could still recognize the essence of his character in the features. What he truly was.

A bully.

"I was never nothin' but good to 'em." To Trinity, the slight whine in his voice set her on edge. "Until they fell in with that Hyatt dude. I wasn't wanted for nothin' after that."

The interviewer's voice was disguised, sounding mechanical as he or she asked questions from off-screen. "Where did they meet Michael Hyatt?"

"Don't rightly remember," her father replied with a shrug. "They was always disappearing, not telling me where they'd go."

Trinity could feel herself tightening up, barely able to contain the rebuttals running through her head. Her inner defenses were hardening. She forced herself to remain silent, as if to prove something to a man who wasn't even in the room.

Her father continued, "Guess all that money and a fancy house was too much to turn away from."

The interviewer asked, "So your wife wanted money?"

"Doesn't every woman?"

Rhett coughed, then cleared his throat. He hugged her a little closer.

Her father continued, "Nothin' I did was ever good enough for 'em. They was always whining and crying. Enough to put me in a rage."

Guess the audience wouldn't realize quite how accurate his words were.

"I'm pretty sure if that girl of mine was in the right place, she'd take full advantage of getting in that guy's pants—"

"Oh, turn it off," she snapped.

Rhett paused the video and stared for a long moment at the frozen screen. "How awful," he muttered.

Trinity turned her head to look up at him, watching his throat muscles work as he swallowed.

He pulled back a little so he could look down at her. The slight frown between his brows touched her. Very few people would care about her feelings in this matter. Life had taught her that much.

"How are you?" he asked.

A sad sort of chuckle escaped, surprising her. "Actually, it's a relief."

"Why?" he asked, the frown digging a little deeper.

"Because that man is obviously full of himself. My memories were right."

Rhett nodded slowly. "But not everyone will see that. Even if they do…"

"That's not my problem."

Trinity struggled to put her sudden apathy into words. It wasn't really that she didn't care. Some part of her did. But the overwhelming feeling at the moment was a kind of numbness seeping over her, giving her a respite from the constant upset caused by other people's actions.

She'd been *reacting* since she'd first learned of Michael's death, and faced public outrage over the inheritance. Even before that, going back to when Michael had asked her to marry him and told her the reason for his request. It was as if her own emotions were being played by an orchestra of other players, but she never got to voice her own personal song. The numbness was a relief on several levels, even though she sensed it was a protective move to shut down the roller coaster she couldn't seem to get off.

"These past weeks have taught me the hard way that I can't control what everyone thinks," she said. "The reality doesn't make me happy—I've spent my life trying to help others—but it's foolish to sit around and stew about it."

Still, the struggle wore her down. Why, for a few minutes, could she not be happy? She wanted to actually live rather than simply struggle to breathe. To figure out the fix to everything around her.

She glanced down, her gaze catching on the sight of Rhett's hand on his thigh. So strong. So masculine. She remembered the feel of it on her body, and wished for once that she hadn't chickened out the other night.

Maybe there wouldn't be any repercussions. At her age, maybe he wouldn't even be able to tell that she'd never been with anyone else. After all, who would suspect it?

She inched her fingers over to his, then let them glide over his skin in a tiny stroke that felt awfully big.

Lightning flashed outside the windows, followed moments later by thunder loud enough to shake the house. The storm was raging. Wind beat against the house with the full ferocity of nature. It mirrored Trinity's emotions.

She swallowed the lump of fear in her throat and wrapped trembling fingers around Rhett's palm. She could sense his gaze on her, but couldn't force herself to look up.

She wanted this for herself, this one thing. And she would have it.

"Trinity?"

A questioning, searching tone, but not a rejection. She took a moment to gather what little courage she could find, then forced herself to look up and meet his gaze with an open one of her own.

She could see when the realization hit him. Of their own accord, her fingers stroked over his hand again. She allowed herself to test the textures of his skin. To ground herself in the moment and let the last weeks of turmoil completely slip away.

The last time he'd touched her, he'd been hesitant, almost as if he were asking for permission. This time, he already had it. With firm confidence, his hand slid up from her shoulder into the fall of her hair. The feel of him cupping the back of her head made her want to melt into his warmth. Her neck, shoulders and back relaxed in automatic response.

Her eyelids slid down. In the darkness, she could focus on the touch, smell and feel of him. The rain against the windows and roof created a cocoon where it was only the two of them. The rest of the world washed away beneath the deluge.

He twisted his upper body toward her. He began massaging her scalp with both hands. Breathy moans escaped her

parted lips, but she couldn't stop them. Refused to smother them. They blended with the ping of raindrops.

Then his lips covered hers.

Giving herself over to her desires, Trinity refused to hold anything back. She reached out, grasping the front of his shirt with her fists. Her head spun with the overwhelming sensations. Being able to just feel, instead of constantly thinking, left her desperate for more.

No one had ever done this for her...except Rhett.

Then suddenly he was gone. Trinity opened her eyes to find him standing beside the bed, his gaze darkened with an intensity that made her shiver. His body shadowing her made her feel small but not afraid. Rhett had never used his strength against her; he never would. But now he crowded forward. She crawled back. Their gazes remained locked.

As she reached the middle of the bed, he grabbed her foot with both hands. She watched as his skillful fingers found each buckle, loosened each strap and slid each foot free. Since when had removing sandals been so sexy?

Then, one at a time, he enveloped each arch in his big hands and began to work magic. Squeezing, rubbing, pressing... Trinity let herself fall back onto the comforter, no longer able to hold herself upright as her body rejoiced. The focus wasn't just on her feet; every inch of her seemed to revel in his expertise.

Then he guided her feet until they rested flat against the top of the bed. Her legs were spread wide beneath her flowing skirt, knees bent. She knew it wouldn't be any barrier at all. He loosened his tie, pulling it off over his head. Then he unbuttoned the first button on his dress shirt. Then the next. Then the next.

Finally he paused, fingers poised to finish the job, and asked, "Are you ready?"

Fourteen

Rhett blew out a heavy breath, attempting to steady his fingers. The shaking was unexpected. Of the intense emotions buffeting him right now, nervousness wasn't one of them.

He refused to think about what that might mean.

Instead, he focused on stripping down to his boxers quickly so he could turn his attention where it mattered. To Trinity.

Her reactions seemed just as intense as his. Gratifying, for sure. But more important, they fed his own response in a way he'd never experienced before. It was a mutual exchange of energy that pushed them both higher. He wanted to experience every part of Trinity with a thirst that went beyond mere physical desire...and he wanted the same for her.

Rhett slipped his hands beneath her skirt to cup the backs of her knees. Her skin was soft, silky smooth. He swallowed hard on a moan. Palms flat, he traced her sup-

ple muscles up to her hips, feeling as if he'd been granted something very special, something only between the two of them. When his fingertips found the edge of her panties, he paused, letting another breath out. Her hips lifted slightly, granting permission. He could hear her panting, see the desire in her eyes even as the thunderstorm darkened the room further.

Hooking the fabric in his thumbs, Rhett pulled her panties down. He watched their slow progress beneath her skirt, down her legs, his body throbbing its approval. Somehow knowing she was naked yet still clothed blew the top off what seemed so simple. So sexy.

Her naked toes dug into the duvet. He wanted to touch them again, kiss them. But urgency pushed him higher.

Just as he had done with his own shirt, he unbuttoned hers one button at a time. Her pale skin peeked out between the parting fabric. Ribs and stomach trembled with her rapid breathing. He peeled back the layers, groaning at the sight of her breasts encased in pale pink lace. Trinity was a lady down to her skin. But her watchful gaze told him he held the key to turning this proper lady into the woman she ached to be.

He buried his face in the smooth skin of her stomach, taking in her sweet smell accented with a hint of need. She pressed against her heels, raising her body to meet him. He traced her contours with his lips, then nestled his face between her breasts. He let his body ease down onto her, testing her tolerance for his weight. There were no protests, only clutching hands and tilting hips.

She felt incredible beneath him. Her tiny gasps told of her aching need, ratcheting his own higher and higher. Her fingers dug into his back, urging him to give her more.

He tried to hold out, tried to make himself wait so he could indulge in this experience as long as possible. He

popped open the front clasp of her bra, then swept one cup aside to free the trembling mound beneath. Her skin was so pale he was almost afraid of leaving marks. But he couldn't stop himself from touching her. He followed her lead, learning what made her gasp, what made her moan and what made her beg.

Only when he couldn't ignore the urgent pull of his own body did he finally slip his hand beneath the flimsy barrier of her skirt once more. Lying on his side next to her, he could watch her face as he found her most precious of spots. Knowing he might not be able to control himself later, he forced himself to lock down his desires and focus on hers. With exquisite expertise and a dawning wonder, he teased her body.

Her expressions of surprise and excitement fascinated him. He could have gotten drunk off the headiness of pleasuring her. Her cries echoed the thunder. When he could hold himself back no longer, he pressed his fingers urgently against her. The firm lift of her hips and her silent scream only fed his own pleasure as he slid his fingers firmly inside of her.

He didn't expect the resistance, the tightness, the way her pleasure turned to a gasp of pain. He immediately froze.

She didn't move, so he tried again. This time, she let out a cry of discomfort.

"Trinity?"

He wasn't prepared for her to squeeze her thighs together, to force him out. She shook her head. "I didn't realize…" she moaned. "I've never…"

Virgin. The word echoed through his brain. That couldn't be right. There was no way—

Virgin. Rhett pulled back, from her, from the bed… How was this possible? He'd done his due diligence. He'd asked the common questions about her marriage. He'd watched

her, spied on her, seen how they'd lived. Nothing too un-usual for the rich types he'd spent his life watching. Noth-ing to indicate…this.

Virgin. She hadn't been intimate with Michael as his wife. Their marriage hadn't been normal…real. Did that mean the Hyatts were right, in a way? Had she somehow duped Michael into an arrangement that gave her access to his fortune…but no intimacy in return? What had she been to Michael, if they hadn't fully consummated the marriage?

Memories of being duped into what would have been a similar relationship flooded his mind. The hurt. The be-trayal. Had Michael known before he married Trinity? Had she tricked him into marriage, then reneged on the deal later?

Rhett suddenly realized that he was now standing be-side the bed, staring down at Trinity. His heart raced. No desire remained, only a growing wave of betrayal. The re-alization that Trinity hadn't told him the real truth. How had he let this happen to him *again*?

With that thought echoing in his brain, he met Trinity's look with his own and said, "How could you keep this from me? Let me think that…" He ran a harsh hand through his hair. "Let me think your marriage was real. That your re-lationship with Michael was real."

He ignored the frantic shake of her head, the way she sat up and wrapped her shirt tightly over her nakedness. Instead he let that sense of betrayal build, connecting with the remnants from that confrontation with his fiancée so long ago. He'd told himself he would never be vulnerable to a woman again. Yet here he was.

Now another woman had drawn him in with her sweet-ness and charm, feeding him the bits and pieces she wanted him to see to gain his help and favor with the Hyatt Heights board. He thought back to his ex-fiancée, how she'd been

gaming him for his fortune. He'd narrowly escaped her scheming but it had left a permanent scar.

Rhett had spent the rest of his adult life making sure other people didn't get scammed like he had. Like his father had. Now look at him.

The first woman to make him question the convictions built by years in this job had proven that she wasn't what she seemed. She wasn't a devoted, grieving widow in the true sense. She could very well be someone who'd scammed Michael out of his fortune.

It was the first time Rhett had ever turned his back on those instincts. He'd believed Trinity wasn't capable of deceiving him, wouldn't even want to. And yet, here they were.

A flash of heat swept over his skin—a mixture of anger and embarrassment. He wanted answers, but couldn't even formulate the questions. He paced back and forth, needing an outlet for the emotions ricocheting inside of him. Finally, he halted next to the window, pivoting to stare at the woman still sitting on the bed.

Her expression had smoothed to a blank mask, just as he'd seen it do in times past. But this time, he wondered what she was hiding beneath the smooth façade. Trinity just sat like a blank doll in the middle of the bed.

Silent.

Deep inside, the urgent need to know the truth she'd been hiding from him spread. He didn't care how dark or ugly her secrets were. He needed to know the scope of the deception that had broken every last instinct he'd relied on to guide him for years. He had believed in her and she'd let him down.

"Tell me the truth. The real truth," Rhett demanded from across the room, running a rough hand through that silver-streaked hair.

Trinity had felt a slight relief as he'd moved away from her. Common sense told her she had nothing to fear from him. At least, physically. But then again, she'd never seen him under this amount of pressure, expressing this much emotion. And life had made her cautious.

Her vocal chords remained frozen. She should have accepted the inevitable and kept Rhett firmly at arm's length. But she hadn't. She'd been greedy, wanting something for herself.

And ended up in this nightmare.

There was no going back. But how could she explain the truth she'd been living? Rhett saw her marriage as a lie. Michael had seen it as security. For Trinity...it had been the only way to say thank you to the man who had saved her life.

"I should have trusted my instincts," Rhett said as he paced across the room. "People said you were a gold digger. How could I have just brushed that aside? Your marriage *was* a lie. I want to know just how much of one."

In an instant, the deep freeze inside Trinity melted. Gathering a cloak of stoicism around her, she eased herself to the edge of the bed and rearranged her skirt over her legs. To the best of her ability, she blocked out Rhett's critical presence across the room. With steady effort she put her bra back on, then buttoned up her shirt.

Only when she'd finished did she realize he'd stopped speaking, stopped pacing.

She turned her gaze in his direction, thankful for the shadowy room and the sense of protection it gave her. She doubted she could have handled this conversation in a spotlight of sunshine.

"What do you want to know?" she asked.

Her voice wasn't as steady as she would have liked, but

at least she wasn't going to break down crying. Showing weakness never led to anything good.

His voice was low, but gravelly with emotions. "Why are you a virgin?"

"Because I've never had sex, of course."

She couldn't interpret what his grunt meant. That she was telling him something obvious? Couldn't they just skip to the part where this conversation was over and they both knew where they stood? That would be great. Yeah…

"You were married to Michael."

She nodded, not trusting her voice. The next question was a given.

"So why are you a virgin?"

"Because Michael wasn't able to consummate our marriage."

Rhett's deep intake of breath told her he was going to demand more answers, so she plunged forward, hoping not to have to break her final promise to Michael. "Even if he'd been able to, Michael would not have wanted to have sex with me. I told you, and everyone else who would listen… Michael was my best friend. We were friends since I was a kid. But he was not romantically interested in me."

"Then why on earth would he marry you?"

Trinity buried the sting of those words deep down inside.

"Michael wanted to protect his estate from his aunt and uncle. He knew their interests in his assets stemmed from their desire to sell them off. The only way to keep that from happening was to have another heir."

"It's not the only way…he could have simply willed it to you."

"Which he was doing. But Michael wasn't taking any chances. He knew they would challenge whatever he put in place. The more ties he could create, the better chance his choice would be honored in court."

"So he planned to what? Use you as a surrogate?" His incredulous tone wreaked havoc on her nerves. "Have children but not sex?"

This time she couldn't hold back a wince. It was never nice to know that someone thought you were good enough to be used, but not worthy of the true experience of love.

"I never said that."

Not that Michael had meant it that way. But Trinity had known that by doing as he asked, she was giving up on her own dream of a family in her own way. Not that prospects had been beating down the door of *Maison de Jardin* to date her. Yet another reason why she was having this conversation…

She tried to distract him instead. "We didn't share a room. You knew that."

"Lots of couples do that. But they still have sex. Especially on their honeymoon. You were married a week, for Christ's sake. Hell, you'd known each other a whole lot longer. Why wouldn't he—"

The urgency in his voice told her his frustration was growing. How long could she hold the questions at bay? Was it a betrayal of her dead husband if she told the truth? The whole truth?

His next question was delivered with very tight control. "*Why* did you marry him?"

Trinity pressed her feet together, wishing she had shoes on. Then she pressed her knees together, and her thighs. The precise movements distracted her from her acute distress. "Because he asked me to."

"This wasn't a simple marriage, a *normal* marriage."

"No," she finally conceded. "Michael had very specific demands for our marriage. It was my job to fulfill them, whether he was here or not."

"*Job.* So this *was* a business arrangement? I should have known."

More of a legacy.

She tilted her head back to meet his gaze. That direct confrontation was hard for her, but she knew better than to avert her gaze. That would just make her look even more guilty.

"So he paid you?" he persisted.

She could feel her mind pulling away, shrinking away from the implications of his words.

But Rhett wasn't backing down. "Did he pay you to pretend to be his wife?"

"Not in the way you think," she answered, hating how small her voice sounded next to his.

Only then did she notice the coolness streaking down her cheeks. Tears. Trinity wasn't sure when they'd started, only that they were gathering along the curve of her jaw and falling to her shirt below. She refused to reach up and brush them away. That would only highlight their existence.

"Enlighten me," Rhett said. "I refuse to be fooled again. Not in this lifetime. Not by you."

Just like that, her heart cracked. Weariness seeped out to spread through her body and flood her system. It was all she could do to keep herself upright. She'd spent her life supporting others. It was her purpose, her calling. First her mother, the women at the shelter, Michael.

For one glorious moment, she'd thought she'd found someone who could be there *for her*, *with her*, in Rhett. Now she knew that wasn't going to happen. Not the way she wanted.

After this, he'd never feel the same way about her again.

So why continue to fight the inevitable? Weariness weighed her down. Maybe if she told him the truth, he'd leave her to grieve in peace.

"Michael needed a wife very quickly."

"And he chose you?"

"He knew he could trust me."

Rhett shook his head, denying the truth. "Why would a man in his position trust you? Why would he let himself get into a situation where he had to?"

"There are things in life even the rich can't control." Still her loyalty refused to give in, to unlock the words held inside for so long.

"Such as?"

It took some effort to force the forbidden words past the tightness in her throat. "Michael was very sick."

Rhett froze. "How sick?"

Trinity squeezed her eyes closed, then broke her promise to her best friend. "Stage four pancreatic cancer."

Fifteen

Rhett heard the words but felt them more like a blow. The knowledge that Michael had been that sick, facing his own mortality, could support either interpretation of Trinity's motives...depending on which side he wanted to take.

"There were no remains left to test," he said.

Trinity shook her head. At least the tears seemed to have stopped for the moment. He hadn't liked how the sight of them softened him.

"No," she said. "Dying in the helicopter crash meant no true evidence of his illness except protected medical records. No way to prove he was dying already. No way to judge the severity of his illness. And no way for the Hyatts to claim he wasn't in his right mind when he chose to marry me to protect his charity. Unless the judge could get the medical records released...if he even knew to ask."

"Was he?"

Trinity glanced up at him, her expression resigned. "Was he what?"

She knew what he meant, but she was going to force him to state the obvious, huh? "Was he in his right mind?"

"Right until the last minute. I was on the phone with him just minutes after the helicopter took off. Though luckily not when they went down. According to the investigation, the accident was a mechanical malfunction...not deliberate tampering."

Despite his roiling emotions, Rhett was glad Trinity hadn't been on the line to hear it as it happened. It was something he wouldn't wish on his worst enemy.

"Michael knew exactly what Richard and Patricia would do with his estate once they had their hands on it. His doctor had only given him a month, at best. He wanted everything in place before he announced our marriage."

Her shaky breath brought on a mixture of guilt and skepticism Rhett still couldn't quite suppress.

"I promised Michael I would protect his secrets and protect his vision for the future of the charity. He knew the board would help me run the companies, though he'd hoped to make his own announcement about me taking his place...closer to time."

"So why open up about this at all?" Rhett didn't like the hoarseness of his voice, the hint that he might be buying a tale he couldn't corroborate with the man himself. His demands would not have made her tell him this sacred of a truth if she'd been determined to keep the secret from him.

For just a brief moment, a grief so visceral flashed through her stoic expression that Rhett actually took a step back. But that didn't protect him from her words.

"You're the only person who has seen every part of me. What's the point of holding back anymore?"

In that moment, Rhett knew that words would never have convinced him. Neither would papers or files or sig-

natures. That one flash of emotion proved to him that Trinity was on the level.

And that he was a total asshole.

Simply because experience—the very thing that had warned him not to trust her—had taught him that emotions that intense could not be faked. There was always a hint of insincerity. Something Rhett was a master at sniffing out. But with Trinity, there had been nothing to hold that grief back...and to know that he had caused at least part of it meant he was lower than low.

Rhett usually trusted his instincts. The fact that he'd been warring with them the whole time he'd been with Trinity had worn him down. But this time, he would listen without hesitation.

He crossed the last few steps to her side, noting for the first time how he'd pressured her. Oh, on some level, he'd surely known that, but only now did he acknowledge it.

So when he reached her, he knelt down, forcing himself to look up at her instead.

"Trinity, I only have one more question," he said.

She tilted her chin back to meet his look, mask once more in place, even though every line in her body spoke of a weariness he knew had to go bone deep. "Yes?" she asked.

"Will you forgive me?"

She shook her head as if to clear it. "I don't understand."

Rhett felt awkward and juvenile and humbled. He'd made assumptions based on his past and hers that he shouldn't have. Why should he expect her to understand? He wasn't sure how he'd make it right but he refused to let himself skate through this.

"I told you, once before, that I'd been betrayed. By a woman."

She nodded, the blank mask she'd adopted softening

with curiosity. Seeing that genuine emotion told him he was on the right track.

"Well." His throat tightened as he grew more reluctant to give up his secrets. But it was only fair, as much as he had refused to discuss this in the past. Only two other people knew: his partner and his father. But after what he'd said to her, she deserved an explanation rather than living with the belief that this was all her fault.

"My ex-fiancée... I found out quite by accident that she'd decided to marry me not for love."

Trinity remembered his earlier words about his ex-fiancée and her quest for riches. "Oh, Rhett. I'm sorry."

He shrugged, though his feelings on the matter were far from casual. That one incident had changed the course of his entire life. "I'm sure there are any number of men who would have been happy with that arrangement if they'd have known about it up front. I was not comfortable, nor happy. She had targeted me and come into the relationship knowing that's all she wanted, but spent months convincing me her feelings were much, much deeper. So I broke our engagement in quite a cold fashion."

"What happened to her?"

"She went on to marry a man within our social circle... twenty years her senior."

Trinity gave off an air of growing awareness, as she seemed to grasp the similarities between the situations. "I see."

"He was a retired military man. Quite well-off. Once she became pregnant, I simply couldn't handle even chance meetings. I embraced my—work—and was grateful to be away on travel more often than not."

He'd wished that their encounters hadn't bothered him, that he'd felt nothing at all. Instead every time he'd seen her, the barbs had sunk deeper. Which in turn fueled his

passion for his work. Though he'd never accused anyone of going after money without proof, he had to wonder now if he'd missed something along the way.

He certainly had with Trinity. Or rather, he'd lost his own ability to sniff out the truth.

"It's not an excuse. Rather, an explanation." Hopefully one that would help her feel better when the time came for her to know the whole truth.

In this moment, he realized he wasn't going to be able to hide who he really was from Trinity. She deserved better. And for this to move forward—whether just toward healing or an actual relationship—he would have to be honest. Only he didn't know how to do that yet.

He glanced back at her, only to find her gaze brushing hastily over his chest. Because it was bare? Did that part of him, any part of him, still attract her?

Heat pooled low in his belly, urging him to return to the sweetness of their first encounter.

Her first encounter.

His heartbeat sped up. He shouldn't. But he wanted to. Then her gaze lifted to his and he saw the spark there also. She still wanted him. But was he doing the right thing? Or the selfish thing? Could he walk away and let Trinity feel rejected by yet another person in her life who should care for her?

For the first time in this whole situation, Rhett led with instincts alone. "I lied. I actually have one more question."

"What's that?" Trinity asked, caution drawing out the two words. He didn't blame her. But he could show her another way.

"Will you let me stay with you?"

Trinity called herself every kind of fool for even entertaining the idea. But her body remembered. Her body

wanted. She'd never thought she'd be the type of person who could give her body without letting her heart be fully involved, but for just once in her life, she considered risking the heartache to have this one moment with him. Could she wall off her heart for a little while so she could have this memory of him?

A moment she might never have again.

She tried to let reason prevail, just as she had her entire life. "I'm not really sure that's a good idea," she said, though she didn't even sound convincing to herself. It *wasn't* a good idea. Things between them were already messy and complicated. He was probably doing this out of guilt.

"I know, and that's my fault," he said, confirming her thoughts. "I want to make it up to you."

Her body went cold at his words. She didn't want someone who felt like he *had* to be with her. But he had wanted her earlier. She might be innocent, but she wasn't naive. Rhett had wanted her.

Could he want her again?

Out of the corner of her eye, she looked him over once more. His button-down shirt hung open, leaving his sculpted chest and abs in partial view. Her mouth watered. Remembering the feel of him against her didn't help keep her on the straight and narrow.

Half-dressed and his hair askew from running his fingers through it, Rhett was the sexiest man alive. In this moment, there was only one thing that would keep her from indulging.

She forced her chin up once more, took a deep breath and plunged ahead. "I don't want this to be about me." She swallowed hard, forcing the words out despite her churning emotions. "I would want it to be about us."

It took a minute for her meaning to hit him, but she could see a visible change when it did. His body relaxed

for a moment, then every inch of him tightened. Those gorgeous gray eyes and wide smile lit up the darkened room. He looked like she'd given him a gift.

The last thing she wanted was for this to be about making up for his judgments. That wasn't how she wanted to remember it. Because she knew without a doubt that soon a memory would be all she had.

Suddenly the air in the room changed, as if it had been electrified. Rhett reached out a hand to her. She wasn't sure what he had in mind. A moment of panic contracted her lungs. But she couldn't stop herself from reaching out, from taking what she truly wanted.

Tears burned against her eyes as he helped her to stand facing him. She would do this and keep those emotions tucked deep inside. There was no way for her to eradicate them. She'd always been emotional. But she'd had a lifetime to perfect how to hide them. She only hoped that skill served her well today.

Rhett rubbed the back of his knuckles right beneath her jawbone, then tucked his hand down along her neck. The feel of him against her sensitive skin made her shiver. His fingers slowly worked her top buttons open.

Her reaction this time was just as aroused as before, only mixed with anxiety over what was to come. She mourned the loss of that pure excitement, but willed away the sadness with each brush of his knuckles against her skin.

Once all of the buttons were undone, he slipped the shirt back and off her shoulders, leaving her in her skirt and bra. She expected him to go straight for that front clasp. Instead he traced her shoulders with his palms, then trailed them down her arms to her hands, igniting all of the nerves along the way.

After a moment, he lifted her hands to the opening of his shirt.

Startled, she glanced up. He watched her through a hooded gaze that sent her temperature soaring upward, but he gave no verbal directions. She grasped each lapel and squeezed tight. Could she do this?

The citrusy smell of him mixed with the smell of fresh-fallen rain from outside. The scent filled her head. She tightened her grip. There was no way she could give up on this, even though there was no future in it for her. There couldn't be.

But she blocked that out and focused only on the moment. On slipping her hands beneath the panels of his shirt. On the smooth texture of his skin stretched across taut muscles, except where a sprinkling of hair broke the heated expanse. Trinity let her eyes close, concentrating on the feel of him beneath her palms. She brushed her fingers along the edge of his waistband, then down the front of the cotton boxers.

How she had the courage to cup the hardness of him, she wasn't sure. His groan echoed in the air. It was a music her entire body was attuned to. She wasn't sure if she would melt or tense when he touched her, but she was very sure the heaviness growing low in her belly was all for him.

When he put his hands on her, all hesitation ended.

A trail of fire traveled over her skin, led by the touch of his hands, then his arms, his chest, then there wasn't a single part of them that didn't touch. Bare skin pressed against bare skin was more intoxicating than she'd ever imagined it could be. And when he laid her down on the bed, his muscled body covering hers, she thought she'd found heaven.

There was barely a hint of pain this time, just an unfamiliarity as his body stretched hers. She lifted her hips, eager to be wholly a part of their coming together. Not passive or accepting. She couldn't keep her hands still. Instead,

they pulled him closer, tracing the muscles of his arms and back as he worked over her body.

The feel of him moving with her, her minute responses to his every movement, left her breathless. He buried his mouth against her throat. Every nerve ending in her body went electric. She heard herself cry out. Her nails dug into his back.

As his own cries filled her senses, she knew she'd just created the memory of a lifetime.

Sixteen

"Son, only you could find yourself in this situation. I've always told you this line of work would come back to bite you."

It was so easy to picture his father on the other end of the phone, with his head full of silver hair, seated in his favorite armchair before the fire in Seattle dispensing those words. Rhett would have grinned at the fond indulgence in his father's voice, if he wasn't in some serious need.

"I chose this line of work, as you call it, because I wanted to help people."

"You mean help expose people? People like your ex-fiancée, and your stepmother, and—"

"Dad," Rhett interrupted in a warning tone.

"It's a legitimate question. You don't need to work. So why would you do this day in and day out? Why would you do something that just keeps you mired in suspicion and lies?"

Because I'm good at it. Or rather…he had been.

"Well, this would definitely be the moment you've been predicting for years," Rhett conceded, but he wasn't ready to give in completely. "But I would like to point out that I've never been wrong before."

"There's always a first."

"This is a pretty unique first," Rhett said, his brain distracted with thoughts of the woman he'd left working in the office at Hyatt House and the unusual challenge he'd found in her.

"I'd say," his father agreed. The story had just come tumbling out as soon as Rhett had found a safe space, and a safe ear, to talk.

"I just…" He hated to admit this, but he didn't see that he had any choice. He couldn't see where to go from here. His usual strategic plans had failed him. "I know Trinity is hardworking and doing her best to take care of both the charity and the employees of the companies. I've seen it in her dedicated study and brainstorming and conscientious work. I have no doubt I could win her case in an instant if I testified to everything I've seen. But—"

"But?"

"You and I both know that her being a virgin would be a damaging piece of information in a court case over her dead husband's inheritance." *Tell me I'm making the right choice. Was he looking the other way because he wanted to be right? Because he wanted Trinity to be innocent?* "At the very least, once the public got ahold of that information, it could be used to sway the board against her."

"It could."

He let the silence play out for a minute, not wanting to ask the question outright. But he finally gave in and said, "Am I missing something?"

"You've seen evidence of her true character with your

own eyes?" his father asked, no-nonsense and able to zero in on the essence of the problem just as Rhett had known he would.

"I have."

Rhett thought back over the past few weeks, trying to look beyond the looming memory of last night. He knew he was being swayed by the intensity of becoming Trinity's lover...her first lover. "I believe her to be a good person. A person who's trying to do what's right by the charity and the businesses." Unlike the Hyatts.

"Then trust those instincts."

"But—" Hell, he couldn't actually love her... Could he?

"Trust them. I'm learning to."

What? "Dad, what have you done?" Slight panic sliced through him as he wondered what his father had gotten into while he'd been halfway across the country.

"I've found Candy."

"Really, Dad? A woman named Candy?" He shouldn't be biased against a name, but considering his father's choices in the past...

"Yes, sir. And my instincts are leading me true."

He'd be the judge of that. Taking care of his father had always been his job. "I'll decide that when I get home. Do not sign anything."

"No, you won't. And I don't need to. She has her own money."

That's what they all wanted them to think. "Dad—" There was no one else to step in. He had to protect his dad's heart from being crushed yet again.

"Rhett, it's time for you to let go."

There was no force in his father's voice. No harsh directive. Only a calm acceptance that Rhett couldn't quite grasp.

"What are you talking about?"

"Son, despite our family's history of unfortunate encounters, there is still happiness to be had in this world. I'm ready to have it, rather than holding it at arm's length because I'm afraid."

"I'm not afraid."

"I beg to differ. Otherwise, why would you be calling me for an opinion? You're a strong, decisive young man. You don't need me to tell you what to do. Your instincts will lead you."

They hadn't been helping so far. Rhett felt like this whole case had been one challenge to his instincts after another.

"Now, as for this young lady of yours... She'll be tried in the court of public opinion, regardless of what the judicial system says."

He'd known his father would get it right off. "Exactly." And Rhett did not want to watch her go through that. But how did he warn her without coming clean about himself?

He would do whatever he could to prevent the Hyatts from getting the information he now knew. But what about the rest? "I don't know how to protect her."

"You can't."

"But knowing what she'll face alone..."

"You can't stop the reality from coming to her." His father sighed. "We both know that. When she chose to help her friend, like you said, she chose what she would face. You can only stand beside her. Guide her. Uplift her. But you can't protect her."

But he wanted to. For the first time in his life, he wanted to protect someone from the consequences of her actions, rather than expose them. Thinking about the soft, sensual woman he'd held last night being vulnerable to Richard and Patricia Hyatt as he'd come to know them turned on a fierceness Rhett didn't know how to handle. And know-

ing that he'd been part of the plot to destroy her made him
feel ashamed.

"I don't want her to find out about me."

"You know it will never stay a secret."

"I do know that." The question was, would he lose her
over it? He deserved to, but that didn't keep him from wanting to fight to keep her.

Trinity frowned at Rhett as he sat at the small table
across the room from her desk. He wasn't working. Instead
he stared out the window at the sunshine that had finally
decided to make an appearance.

She didn't care that he was slacking off. It was the infer-
nal tapping of the pen he held against the papers in his other
hand. *Tap. Tap. Tap.* Whatever he was thinking so hard
about had him oblivious to the noise that Trinity couldn't
ignore.

"Are you okay?" she finally asked, her voice a little
louder than she intended in the quiet office.

With a start, Rhett glanced her way. "Yes. Why?"

She dropped her gaze to the pen, which he'd stopped
tapping. "Just wondering."

He didn't acknowledge her look, but she knew he got
her point because he gripped the pen in his fist. Still he
didn't say a word. So as much as she didn't care for confrontation…

"Plus, you've been acting weird all day." She cleared
her throat, not sure where she got the courage to say the
rest. Why did adult relationships come with so many difficult conversations? "You know, if you regret yesterday,
it's okay. I won't hold you to any implied commitment."

His raised brows indicated a surprise almost as big as
hers for having said anything in the first place. Then a smile

spread across his sculpted lips, offering a hint of relief to her growing angst. "No, Trinity. It's nothing like that."

"But it is something, right?"

Busted. She almost laughed at the consternation in his face and the way his body tightened up. If there was one thing she was good at in her life, it was reading people. Rhett wasn't hiding the signs very well.

Before she could tease him, the door to her office swung inward.

Of all the people she'd expected, Patricia and Richard were not the ones. She tensed.

Jenny rushed in after them. "I'm sorry."

"Leave us," Patricia demanded.

If she hadn't been so nervous, Trinity would have laughed at the way Jenny held ramrod straight, refusing to leave until she received the nod from Trinity. Some people still understood loyalty, and Trinity was grateful for the few people in her life that hadn't turned their backs on her since Michael had passed.

"What can we do for you, Patricia?" she asked as the door closed with a quiet snick.

"Rhett, so nice of you to join us," the other woman said instead of answering.

Rhett stood, bracing himself as he faced the Hyatts. "I didn't realize I'd been given a choice." The Hyatts exchanged a glance that he ignored. "As Trinity asked, what can we do for you?"

Richard chimed in this time. "Oh, it isn't about what you can do for us. We have an offer you won't want to refuse."

Patricia glanced Trinity's way with a smirk. "Especially you, my dear."

"What?" Trinity did not like where this was going. The very vibe of the room had changed, darkening despite the sunshine streaming through the slats of the blinds.

Add the fact that Patricia and Richard never visited Hyatt House outside of business meetings, and this felt wrong on every level.

An ambush. Trinity's stomach tightened, bracing herself against the wave of malevolence in Patricia's look.

"We are here with a very sweet offer for you, my dear," she said, her smarmy tone contrasting her steely look.

"Then talk to her lawyer," Rhett broke in.

Richard raised a brow, confusing Trinity as he said, "Careful now."

Rhett clenched his teeth, his face freezing even as his gaze was shooting daggers into the other man. The level of emotion between the two men seemed out of proportion, though Trinity appreciated Rhett's defense.

She frowned, further unsettled. "Look, if this is about the court case, Rhett is right. You need to speak to Bill."

"I don't think it will go to court. *Now.*"

"Why?" Trinity braced herself for yet another blow. After all, that's what the Hyatts were good at, right? But she could hope... "Are you withdrawing your suit?"

"No, but you will withdraw your objections and willingly turn the estate over to us."

Trinity huffed out her surprise, glancing around at the other people in the room. "Um, no. I won't."

Patricia stalked closer. "Of course, you will. Unless you want us to reveal everything we know about you to the court."

"And what would that be? I have nothing to hide. And someone has already made my past an open book on social media, so—"

"Oh, I'm sure the judge will be very interested to learn that you were a virgin when your husband died. Non-consummation might have some influence over how he decides the case."

Trinity felt her body go ice-cold down to her fingertips. Even her brain froze, keeping her from uttering a single protest. Then a sickening wave of heat washed over her. She swayed before steadying herself. If there was one thing she would control in this meeting, it was whether or not she would go down.

Rhett stepped into the outer edges of her vision. "Non-consummation does not change whether or not she can receive his inheritance. The judge won't be influenced by that."

"But public opinion might," Richard said. "I'm sure the board would love to be led by a woman accused of enticing a lifelong friend into marrying him, then not even gifting him with her body before stealing his money."

"Stop it," Trinity barked, struggling for air but unable to hold the words back. "That has never been true."

"The public doesn't care." Patricia smirked before she went on. "And I'm sure a certain Instagrammer will be happy to spread the news for us…as well as how we found out that juicy little tidbit."

In that moment, Trinity realized her first mistake was that she hadn't denied their claim immediately. Second, in her shock, she hadn't even thought about how they'd found out about it. There were only two people who knew. Her…and…

She turned her gaze to Rhett, who stood still as a statue without a single denial on his lips.

"Please tell me you did not do this," she pleaded, ashamed that the words had to pass her lips.

"I did not," he said, not averting his gaze from the snakes in their midst.

"Oh, he pretty much did, though he didn't include it in his weekly report."

Trinity blinked. "I don't understand."

"Oh, you will," Patricia said, her tone indicating just how much she relished delivering the blows to her enemy.

Richard jumped to fill in the details. "Your boyfriend here has been working for us the whole time."

"As a business consultant? Larry brought him in."

"No." Patricia's smile was wide and satisfied. "As a spy."

Trinity's throat went dry. She licked her lips, wondering where all the moisture in the room had gone.

"He was brought in to tell us everything we needed to know about you to break your claim on Michael's estate. And he has."

Rhett stalked forward. "I don't know how you got that information, but it was not from me. And I told you just now that is not a legally binding reason for her not to inherit."

Patricia didn't seem to care. "You will withdraw your claim and sign everything over to us, free and clear. Otherwise, we will discuss your sexual history, or lack of it, in court, for it to become public record."

She glanced at Rhett. "If you're lucky, we will keep silent about your part in this. Not make your little career public news."

"You signed a nondisclosure agreement," Rhett said, squashing Trinity's last bit of hope that this was all a nightmarish mistake.

Patricia turned to leave before throwing her final words over her shoulder. "You have seventy-two hours to comply."

Seventeen

For the first time in a long time, Rhett had no words. Maybe for the first time in his lifetime.

As he watched Trinity stare into her room from the hallway later that day, he knew they had to talk this out. But she looked so forlorn as she watched an army of staff pack her belongings, he knew he couldn't put it off for long.

He still didn't understand why she wanted to move out. The first thing she had done upon leaving the office downstairs—without a word—had been to instruct Jenny to have her stuff packed and a moving van called.

With an excess of caution, he stepped up beside her and asked, "Why are you doing this? It's crazy."

Trinity was silent for so long that he wondered if she would answer at all. Finally she said, "You know, I've long known that there were advantages to having money. But when you have none, it's hard to imagine them in detail. The possibilities don't occur to you, because they would

never be an option under normal circumstances. That's why people consider the behavior of celebrities eccentric. Only now I realize, if I want to move in a matter of hours, as opposed to days or weeks, I can."

She tilted her head just enough for him to get a glimpse of her profile. Of her strained smile.

"And no one can stop me," she said.

"You don't have to do this. Don't give in to them, Trinity." Of all the things happening right now, he did not want Trinity to lose this incredible space Michael had created for her.

For a moment, her tone went from flat to hard. "Do you really think I'd ever want to sleep in that bed again? Ever?"

And that was all on him.

He didn't know who had overheard him talking, but someone had to have passed that information along to the Hyatts. Now that he thought about it, maybe getting her out of this house was for the best. The last thing she needed was someone spying on her...someone *else* spying on her. *Damn.*

"I promise you I did not tell them—"

She cut him off. "I do not care to speak about that."

Should he honor her wishes? Should he push this?

"Will you go to *Maison de Jardin*?" He wasn't even sure why he asked. After all, it wasn't like she had another family home to return to.

"Yes. For now."

A safe house. Exactly what she needed right now. He wished he could be with her, but he would need time to figure all of this out.

"You're welcome to stay here as long as your contract with the Hyatts permits," she said. "But I'm not paying a dime past yesterday for your consulting services to Hyatt Heights."

"I understand—"

"I doubt you do. But I'm being more than generous. My only stipulation is that you stay the hell away from me."

Rhett searched hard for something to say, feeling her slip away with every word. "Trinity, I didn't know you when I took this job."

"Is that really your job?" She cocked her head but still refused to look him in the eye. The sphinxlike profile that had intrigued him from the beginning was set off nicely by the warm wood doorframe behind her. He took in the high cheekbones. Thick eyelashes. Delicate nose. Her fragile beauty made his shame even worse.

"You've made a career out of discrediting people?"

He wasn't surprised by the sheer disbelief in her tone. She'd thought she'd known him. Now she faced the reality of his lies. He'd never worried about the people he left behind before this. Of course, many of them didn't know he'd exposed their dishonesty. He didn't stick around for that part.

The reality of his chosen career wasn't pleasant or comfortable. Watching Trinity have to suffer for it made it feel like someone was tearing tiny little wounds into his heart every few minutes.

"I simply gather information about people and pass it along to the clients who need to know it." Even he could tell he was grasping for an explanation. He'd never been ashamed of what he'd done until this morning. But looking at it through her eyes...

"You spy on people," she clarified for him. "I thought you were helping me, teaching me." The words choked off for a moment.

Loving me. He'd refused to acknowledge it, but now he could see what had been happening all along. Rhett had risked his heart—something he'd vowed not to do for the

last ten years. Now here he was, trying to figure out a way to fix the situation that he'd complicated with his own lies.

Still, he was grateful to see at least a glimpse of emotion. The last thing he wanted for Trinity was for her to be permanently locked behind the blank mask caused by her wounds. She should not have to live like that.

"I'm sorry," he said, then had to clear his throat as the emotions constricted it. "I've been trying to find a way to get you out of this for a while." And he still would, somehow.

"Why bother?"

Reaching out, he used his knuckle to guide her chin in his direction. He waited until her brown eyes met his before he said, "I expose people who deserve it. People who are trying to steal from others. It didn't take me long to realize that you weren't one of those people."

Her eyes widened slightly, exposing the whites, before she turned away once again. His fingers went cold immediately. Her voice was once again distant as she said, "It doesn't matter now. Once they realize I'm not giving in, the Hyatts will make sure no one believes anything I say anyway."

No. No. No. "It doesn't have to be that way. We can ask Bill to make it inadmissible in court." Anything to keep her from being further exposed to the judgment and condemnation she'd already experienced.

"In court or on the internet…what difference does it make?"

The hopelessness in her tone seeped under his skin. "Then don't do it. Walk away."

"Why? So y'all can win?"

"No." He dragged one of his hands through his hair, wishing he could pull it out by the roots. "Because fight-

ing for this in court is not worth your reputation, your sanity, Trinity."

She shook her head slowly, sadly. "Have you ever owed someone your life, Rhett?"

He swallowed hard. "No."

"Then you wouldn't know if it's worth it or not." She started to walk away from him down the hall. "Right now, I simply want to be back in the only home I've ever really known. For as long as I'm allowed to be there."

Rhett returned to his own room, unable to handle the sight of her walking away from him. He deserved it. He knew that. But he wasn't ready to give up yet. Pulling out his cell phone, he dialed Larry's number.

"Tell me you have something for me. Now."

"I can't believe I'm one of those women who is fussing over what to wear," Madison said, then let out an exasperated sigh. "Living in a sickroom means dressing for comfort and flexibility. Not in frills and ruffles."

Trinity gave her a half-hearted smile. "I don't really think you're the ruffles type."

"Definitely not." Madison shuddered. After accepting a date with the man she'd met at the fund-raiser, her nervous preparations had begun. "But I figure a man like him will be expecting more than jeans and a T-shirt."

"You never know. Everyone has their own preferences."

And their own secrets. That had never hit home for Trinity more than it had over the last three days. With her deadline for the Hyatts fast approaching, her thoughts were consumed with worry and need.

Any minute now, her secrets would be spilled to the world. She just wasn't sure which direction they would come from. When she wasn't talking herself out of a panic attack over it, she was wondering what had happened to

Rhett. She shouldn't care, shouldn't want to know. Yet she found herself obsessing over whether he'd gone back home—wherever that was. And whether he'd given the Hyatts more details about their encounter. Whether he cared about the humiliation she was about to face.

She shouldn't spare him a single thought. So why was he all she could think about?

Madison got up as the kettle on the stove started to sing. The house was relatively quiet at this time of the day, with the children in school or day care, and most of the women at work or in classes. Madison had come by to check on Trinity and immediately set about making tea when she saw how listless she was. Trinity wasn't used to having so little to do. Her days had always been full to the brim with charity stuff, then after Michael's death, it had been the business. Being at loose ends was not boding well for her sanity.

Madison's chatter about her upcoming date was a welcome distraction.

"I don't even know what we're doing. It's a surprise," Madison said as she set up the tea and poured. "Do you think we'll have anything in common?" She cupped her hands around her teacup as if to warm them. "I'm used to spending time alone, a lot. I hope he doesn't find that weird."

"You'll be fine," Trinity assured her. Her brain raced with warnings she wanted to pass on to the younger woman, but she kept her mouth shut because she knew they were a product of her current situation.

"I'm sorry," Madison said.

Trinity looked up from stirring her tea. "Why?"

"I'm prattling on about some guy. That's probably the last thing you're interested in right now." She offered a small smile. "I just don't really know what to say to make any of the things you've experienced better."

"Don't be sorry. It actually helps take my mind off things."

Any minute, the other shoe would drop. She'd instructed Bill that she would continue to deny the Hyatts' control of Michael's estate. She had no doubt now that they would drive it into the ground, starting with *Maison de Jardin*. Regardless of whatever paperwork had been signed between the other parties, Trinity was not bound by any nondisclosure agreements. She would do whatever she had to in order to defend the estate from Michael's greedy relatives.

After all, people's livelihoods and protection were more important than a little humiliation on her part. But so far, news had been quiet.

Too quiet.

"I just can't believe Rhett was working with those people." Madison shook her head. Trinity had shared some of the bare bones of the situation once she'd moved back to *Maison de Jardin*. "He seemed genuinely interested in the charity while he was here. Surprised by everything we did to help these women get back on their feet. I thought he was a good guy."

"Me, too," Trinity said softly. "Guess we can be taken in by just about anyone, huh?"

"Scary."

"I see women come through here all the time. Their husbands or boyfriends are charmers at the start. Until they become controlling, petty, angry. Then they change." Because it was all about them, never about the women they loved.

"Did Rhett change?"

"Yes, but I thought it was for the better. Now I know it was just another lie."

Madison squirmed in her chair, reminding Trinity that she was speaking to someone on the verge of a new relationship. She shouldn't be ruining it for her. Despite every-

thing, Trinity wanted to believe love was possible…just for other people. Not for her.

She'd never risk her heart…or her body…again.

"It will be okay, Madison."

The younger woman smiled, but Trinity couldn't miss the knowledge in her eyes. Madison might not have been abused, like many of the women in this house, but her life had never been an easy one. That was for sure. She deserved some hope.

"You go and have a good time, Madison. Everything here will work itself out. I promise."

As if to challenge her words, her cell phone started to ring. Trinity hesitated when she saw Bill's name. It took a moment of gathering what tatters of grace she had left before she could answer.

"Yes?"

"Have you seen the new blog post?"

"No, Bill," she snapped. "It's not like I have alerts set up or something." She'd finally turned them off. She was tired of knowing about it the instant bad news made its way out into the world.

"You might want to take a look at this one. I'll call you in a little while."

Trinity rolled her eyes as she ended the call. She'd thought women were melodramatic. They had nothing on silver-haired Southern lawyers. She stared at her phone for long moments, unable to force herself to open the internet browser. Her mother had taught her to face life head-on. Trinity was fast losing that lesson these days.

Maybe she could hide in her cave for another five or six hours?

The doorbell rang, providing a welcome distraction. As she and Madison headed for the front foyer, the weight of her phone in her hand reminded her of everything she was

avoiding. Had they gone to the gossip blogger with stories of her virginity? How she'd duped Michael out of his inheritance? Why was no one willing to believe that she'd done all of this to help a friend?

She needed to stop hiding and at least arm herself with the knowledge of what she would be facing over the next few weeks. Pausing on the edge of the foyer, Trinity forced herself to unlock her phone.

Just as she clicked on the app, Madison opened the front door. Trinity couldn't look up from her search. Now that she'd determined what needed to be done, she had to do it immediately. She didn't hear the steps approaching her. Instead, when the blog opened on her phone, she scrolled down to the first picture and was shocked to see Rhett Brannon.

Then his voice intruded, "Hello, Trinity."

Looking up, she found herself staring into those gray eyes in person.

Eighteen

Rhett followed Trinity into the sitting room attached to her bedroom at *Maison de Jardin* and slid the door closed behind him. He wasn't taking any chances on anyone overhearing them. What he had to say was too important, too personal.

When she reached the slim side table near the window, literally as far from him as she could get, she stopped and turned to face him. "If you've come to talk to me about the blogger, save your breath. I see you've done some kind of interview…just like my father."

He wouldn't admit to anyone how much it hurt to be lumped into the same category as her abuser. "Have you watched it?"

"Not yet."

Well, he had been impatient to see her again. Maybe he should have waited another hour or two, but he hadn't been able to stay away. Her closed expression and short answers weren't giving him much hope.

"Do you plan to?"

"Why? What will I hear? A first person account of how I threw myself at you to lose my virginity? That would make for really sensational gossip, wouldn't it?"

A spark of frustration lit inside him. "I would never do that to you."

"I don't know you at all," she argued. "How would I know what you're capable of?"

How could he prove he was trustworthy? He'd done the only thing he'd known to do. Now he needed her to watch it.

"I've always been me, Trinity. Yes, I hid things about myself, especially in the beginning. But I strive to give as much of the truth as possible."

"So you don't slip up?"

He couldn't really refute it. That's exactly why he'd done it in the past. "Given the nature of my job, what do you want me to say to that?"

"I honestly don't know."

He did. She was angry and lashing out, and she had every reason to. He should be soft and accepting but that wasn't Rhett. If there was a playbook for winning back the woman you loved after being a complete horse's ass, he hadn't read it. But he wasn't about to let her shut him out with anger.

"I'm not going to apologize for doing my job, but I am sorry for how it ended up hurting you." He took a deep breath. "Now let's move on to something more productive."

Oh, she didn't like that. Her body tensed and she wrapped her arms around her stomach. "Okay, then answer some questions for me," she demanded. "How in the world do you make a living doing this?"

Wow...from shaky ground to even shakier. "Since I don't need the money, it's not really a true living."

"You do this for *fun*?"

From her tone, her anger was growing. "No. I do it to keep people like me from being taken advantage of. From being lied to and stolen from."

That softened her just a little. At least, her voice. "Your fiancée?"

"It happened to me. It happened to my father. People lie and steal all the time."

She thought about that a moment. "So you run a sort of undercover security company."

"Not anymore."

She shook her head. "What?"

"First, no one is gonna hire me once they watch that." He gestured to her phone. Her eyes widened as the implications started to take hold. "And second, I don't think I have the stomach for it anymore." He couldn't take his eyes off of her, even though she refused to look at him directly. "A sweet Southern woman taught me a better way."

She shook her head, squeezing her eyes closed. "I can't. I can't do this, Rhett."

"Yes. You can." He stepped closer. "I know you've been hurt. I know *I* hurt you. But I'm trying to fix this, to make it right."

"By spilling even more of my secrets?" The fear and sadness in her eyes made his stomach churn. "Did you tell them about Michael? About how sick he was? That was a confidence I gave you. I promised him I wouldn't tell—"

"I didn't." Rhett grabbed her shoulders and gently shook her. "I promise I did not tell them anything you wouldn't want me to." He wanted nothing more than to end the panic and pain on her face. "Watch it," he said. "Now." He needed her to see.

Rhett cringed as his voice on the recording filled the room, but he refused to move away from Trinity. He would be here with her through this, even if she didn't want him,

until he knew she was safe. Safe from the Hyatts and safe from him.

Even though he couldn't see the screen, Rhett recognized the tinny distortion of the interviewer's disguised voice asking, "Can you introduce yourself, please?"

"I'm Rhett Brannon, currently contracted as a business consultant for Hyatt Heights, Inc."

"So you were requested to help Trinity Hyatt learn to run the businesses she stands to inherit from her late husband, is that correct?"

"Through Hyatt Heights, yes."

"Are you employed by anyone else?" the interviewer asked.

"I'm not at liberty to say."

"Are you contractually obligated to deny answering that question?"

Rhett hesitated before he answered. "Yes. I've signed a nondisclosure agreement with another entity who required me to work closely with Trinity Hyatt. Something she was unaware of at the time."

"Since we are very concerned here about whether this woman is qualified to carry on Michael Hyatt's enterprises, can you tell us whether you believe she duped her dead husband into giving her his businesses?"

Rhett remembered how this part of the interview had made his blood pressure rise, though he couldn't hear any anger in his response. It had probably shown on his face, though.

"I've interacted extensively with Trinity Hyatt, with her lawyer and the staff at Hyatt House who knew Michael Hyatt after years of working with him. There was no duplicity on her part. She and Michael were very close friends for many years, and I believe that's the reason he asked her to marry him."

He paused a moment before going on. "People get married for many different reasons. We assume, in this day and age, that it's either for love or for money. But that's not always the case. I believe Michael saw in Trinity someone who could complement him in business, in social situations and in companionship. That was his choice to make. Unfortunately, he passed away before he could make the world understand why he made that choice."

Rhett went on to talk about his experience with Trinity in business matters. He'd kept it as general as possible, to avoid any legal trouble for himself or Trinity. He and Bill had briefed the blogger on what he could say, which hadn't stopped the person from asking him, "If Trinity Hyatt is such a good person, why do you think so many bad things have come out about her?"

Rhett remembered the punch of sadness that had accompanied his answer. Trinity had never deserved the things dished out to her since Michael's death.

"Two things. First, money talks. Greedy people will say whatever they want to get people on their side. Especially if saying those things profits them in some way. We can't change that, only counterbalance it as best we can. In the end, people will believe what they want. Second, drama sells. There's a reason why controversy is what you end up posting about on your blog and social media channels. Because more people will click on it, read it. We don't need more drama in our lives."

He took a deep breath before he went on. "We need love. Trinity taught me that."

Rhett tensed, recognizing the moment the interviewer went off script.

"I've heard a rumor that Michael and Trinity Hyatt's marriage wasn't consummated. Can you confirm that for us?"

Trinity abruptly paused the recording. "I can't. I just can't hear this," she said.

He laid his hand over hers, aching as he felt the slight tremor beneath his palm. "Trust me, Trinity," he said. "Trust me to do right by you."

She didn't, he knew that. He deserved it. But she didn't deserve to live without faith. Doing this interview had been just as much about giving that back to her as setting the record straight. "Please."

It took a few seconds. But like the strong woman he knew, she finally pushed the button so she could listen.

On the video, Rhett said, "I've heard that rumor, too, and it makes me sad."

"How so?" the interviewer asked.

"Michael Hyatt was a trusted member of this community, held in high esteem by his fellow members of society, the members of his board and by his employees. Why can we not trust his judgment? He chose Trinity. For whatever reason, he chose her. Why do we not believe he knew exactly what he was doing when he made that choice?"

"People get duped all the time," the interviewer insisted.

"Not by people they've known for over fifteen years," Rhett said, his own experiences with Trinity bolstering his confidence. "He knew Trinity since she was a child. He knew what he was doing. Trust that."

Trinity gave a small squeak, but he didn't turn to look at her, afraid of what he would see.

"Do you think the Hyatts will win?" the interviewer asked.

Rhett thought for a moment before he responded, "They'll continue to fight. And because they are willing to fight dirty, they might even win. I've offered to testify as much as I can on her behalf. But all Trinity can do is her

best. For Michael's sake, for the trust he put in her, I know she will give it her all."

Rhett listened as the video wound down, hoping his words were enough to make Trinity see how he believed in her. He may not have been able to win the case for her, but he hoped he'd been able to make the path an easier one.

Trinity couldn't stop the shaking deep down in her core. The fact that Rhett had protected her privacy meant the most to her, but he'd also defended her...and defended Michael.

"Why are you doing this?" she asked, barely able to force her voice above a whisper.

"I want to make things right," he said, but the way he fidgeted while they watched the video, his tense stance and clenched fists, indicated it wasn't as simple as that.

"Why?" she pushed.

Something was missing. She needed to know more.

Whatever was missing was big. Trinity could tell as Rhett pivoted on his heel and stalked to the far side of the room. His hands dug into his hair, making it stick up at odd angles. Oh, yeah, this was big.

Was she ready?

Finally, he blurted out, "There's something I left out."

Was she ready? Did she really want to know? Trinity swallowed hard, then asked, "What?"

To her surprise, Rhett connected his gaze to hers. There was nowhere for her to hide from the emotion in those gray eyes. "That I love you," he said with a quiet intensity that shook her foundation.

She could only blink. "Why?"

He gave a huff of laughter. "Trinity, so often you sell yourself short. You're intelligent, intense, hardworking, compassionate." He strode back over to her, as if he couldn't

stand to be that far away from her. It felt good…though she didn't want to admit it. "And you're beautiful in every way. Even if I lose you through my own sheer stupidity, I will never, ever be able to forget you."

Each word hit her heart like a knock on a door, begging her to open and let him in. Did she dare risk it? What if— no. No more questions. She would have to step out in faith, like her mother had always told her.

"Why didn't you tell them that on the video?" she asked.

"Because not everything should be public."

Good answer.

"I can't stop what the Hyatts may put out there about you. And I'm horrified about the part I played in giving them that information."

"How did it happen?" Trinity needed to hear him say it for herself.

"Someone spying on the spy." His mouth twisted in a sarcastic smile. "I believe someone overheard me having a conversation over the phone about conscience with my father…when I thought I was alone."

"With your father, huh? About me?"

Rhett nodded. "For the record, he's never approved of my career choice, despite some episodes in his life inspiring it. Our family isn't the luckiest in love."

Rhett hesitantly reached for her hand as if to underscore his words. He brushed his fingertips along the back first, then slid them around to completely envelop her hand. Ever so slowly, she curled her fingers up around his. Accepting, but still cautious. His smile said he understood.

Okay, she wasn't going to even think about him telling his father she was a virgin. It was too embarrassing, even though she could now understand the issues it raised for him.

"Well, I found myself in a unique situation," Rhett said,

"and he was eager to make me admit I wasn't always right about these things."

"Smart man." Trinity smiled at the idea of his father trying to keep Rhett humble.

"We've had some ugly times, he and I. He's never agreed with how I've handled it."

"Betrayal by someone you love is never easy," she murmured. "I'm sorry you both had to go through that."

"I'm not. I wouldn't be here if we hadn't. If I hadn't."

"I know the feeling."

"I wish you didn't," he said, taking her face between his palms. "I've done so many things wrong since I've met you, but I want the chance to make it right.

"Which reminds me," he said, "I've investigated a few things through my connections, and my suggestion to you is to get rid of Maggie. She's head of the daytime housekeeping crew, by the way, and has contacted Patricia Hyatt on her cell phone several times."

Trinity remembered the slight woman, though she'd rarely had much to do with her. Had that been on purpose?

She couldn't stop herself from reaching up and cupping his cheek. She didn't want to talk about them anymore, to give more headspace to the people who had set out to harm her. "What about the things you've done right?"

"They're hard to remember when I see the pain on your face."

"Let's try," she said, wishing she could erase the regret from his expression. "You believed in me, encouraged me, protected me in a room full of gossips eager for blood."

"They were quite rabid."

"So I think, all in all—" she paused to swallow "—you might be a keeper."

"Are you sure? An unemployed thirtysomething with a

father to take care of and a sad track record with relationships. I think *I'm* the risk now."

"Are you sure about giving up your company for me?"

Rhett pulled her close, speaking against her hair. "My father told me it was time to let go. I've decided he was right."

"I learned something from my father, too."

He squeezed her a little closer, the comfort of having his body against hers something she couldn't believe she was actually experiencing.

"What's that?" he asked.

"I learned that some people's actions can make you angry or sad or amused or irritated. But there is only one reason that someone's actions truly hurt."

"Why, Trinity?" he whispered against her.

She knew he regretted what he'd done. It was there in his touch, in his tone. As much as she hated to hurt him, she needed him to understand this.

"It only hurts if you love them."

That had him drawing back, looking deep into her eyes with that incredible gray gaze. "Thank you, Trinity. Nothing could ever mean more to me than knowing you love me."

"I do." The words truly were a vow, though they weren't standing in a church to say them. She'd never loved another man like this. Though putting her trust in him was scary, her heart compelled her to forge ahead.

Reaching out with shaking hands, she cupped Rhett's face and pulled him down until his lips touched hers. "I'll never leave you to face life alone again," he promised. "I'll always be beside you."

As his hands traveled over her body once more, she reveled in his touch. Only Rhett had ever made her feel this incredibly electric, as if her nerve endings were attuned

solely to him. Somehow, like her mother had said, there'd been a man made just for her. And he'd come to make her mind and heart and body sing.

Without any fanfare, Rhett joined their bodies together. It couldn't have felt more right. The solid support of the table beneath her. The firm presence of his body between her thighs. The way he paused, fully inside of her, as if to savor this moment with her.

"I love you, Trinity," he said low as he pressed their bodies as close as possible. "I always will."

Together. Forever.

* * * * *

THE CASE FOR TEMPTATION

ROBYN GRADY

**This story is for Joan,
Teagan Hunter's biggest fan!**

One

As the private elevator continued its climb to the hotel's presidential suite, Jacob Stone couldn't help but admire the woman standing beside him. Forget the *wow* factor of endless waves of silken blond hair. Her beaded off-the-shoulder number must have cost a small fortune, and on that body, it was worth every damn cent.

No one was breaking the law but, if put on the stand, Jacob would have to admit—there was way more than just looking on his mind.

Finally, she glanced across at him. "You know you're staring, right?"

"This'll sound crazy..." Lame even, but he'd put it out there. "This is a first for me."

"If you're saying you've never had anyone back for a drink before tonight," she laughed, "sorry. I'm not buying."

Jacob's teeth skimmed his lower lip as he propped a jacketed shoulder against the mirrored wall of the elevator and crossed his arms. This wasn't about a nightcap after the party. He'd be more specific.

"We've known each other three hours. Four max."

As her gaze eased away from his to the opening doors, one eyebrow hiked up. "Chickening out?"

His turn to laugh.

Not on your life.

Six weeks ago, Jacob had received a wedding invitation from an old friend, a lawyer who'd recently relocated to the West Coast. Marcus Lane had found The One and bought a ring. So Jacob had booked a first-class ticket from New York to LAX and attended today's extravagant garden wed-

ding. After the ceremony, which ended with the traditional release of doves, he followed the trail of pinging crystal flutes to a ballroom more elaborate than any set from a Hollywood blockbuster. Impressive, and he was happy for Marcus and his bride.

But Jacob had been thinking more about the multimillion-dollar lawsuit waiting back home than being in the moment. Then this woman had appeared, seemingly out of nowhere, and his mind-set had done a one-eighty.

When she had stopped at his table, Jacob wasted no time getting to his feet and pulling out her chair. As wine was poured and introductions exchanged, he'd been struck by her eyes—the most sensuous, slumberous green he'd ever seen. He apologized when she'd needed to repeat herself.

Her first name was Teagan. He hadn't caught the last bit.

They'd been so busy talking that he couldn't recall what they'd eaten or who had said what in a run of formal wedding speeches. And that juicy case back in New York? All but forgotten. After the bridal waltz, when the atmosphere dipped into low misty light and *hold me close* music, he'd taken Teagan's hand and led her to the dance floor. Resting his cheek against her sweet-smelling hair—one hand holding hers, the other caressing the warm lower scoop of her back—he'd felt as if they were alone, or sure as hell ought to be.

Jacob never made assumptions, but with his senses homed on her body brushing his and her lips near enough to taste, he'd already decided how this evening would end. When he suggested a nightcap, she'd slid her palm down his lapel and curled two fingers into the fabric. Her exact words had been, "Let's do it."

And yet now, out of the elevator and opening the door to his suite, Jacob saw Teagan hesitate, which, of course, made him hesitate, too.

Earlier conversation had revolved around general interests, politics, business. She was into health and fitness, and

owned a business in Seattle called High Tea Gym. He'd opened up about the law practice he'd inherited, but hadn't elaborated on his reputation, which was cutthroat. Where litigation against the big guns was concerned, Crush or Be Crushed was the only motto to live by.

When they'd discussed friends, he'd shared a couple of tales about Griff and Ajax Rawson, two of his best friends whom he counted as family and vice versa. He had avoided the subject of blood relations and found it interesting that Teagan had done the same. Not a word.

Now listening to the beads of her gown rustling as she moved into the spacious, lavishly appointed room, Jacob had to wonder. Everything about her announced poise and class, but there were plenty of ordinary folk who had learned to master the nuances of the privileged, himself included. So was it possible that Teagan's background was similar to his own? Vastly different from all this glitz and best filed away?

Best forgotten?

As she turned, and then smiled again...hell, what did it matter? Closing the distance separating them with a few easy strides, Jacob set questions and doubts aside. What counted now was finally claiming that first kiss. Everything else—including that defamation case against Hunter Publications—would have to wait.

Jacob Stone was so not her type.

As Teagan turned to see him close the door, she reminded herself again, *I like blue eyes.* Lively and ocean-deep. Tender and kind. The preference went as far back as her first crush freshman year.

Mr. Stone's eyes were the kind of focused amber gold that, combined with the jet-black hair, reminded her of a panther—a mesmerizing, muscled male who hadn't eaten in a week. As Jacob slid the key card onto a marble side table and headed over, that hungry gaze locked onto hers

and Teagan's jaw almost dropped. He even *moved* like a big cat. Completely captivating, and she was a dog person!

As he drew nearer, Teagan puzzled more. In relationships, she wanted openness and honesty. As much as they had talked this evening, she'd gotten the impression that Jacob was more about control and charm—subtle when need be, direct when the time was right. For instance, she could bet he wouldn't stop his approach until he stood squarely in her space, as close as he'd been on the dance floor earlier. Then, of course, he would offer the same confident smile he had used when he'd suggested a drink here in his suite.

At that moment, with his mouth a hair's breadth away from hers, her body had tingled in all the right places. Caution had melted away. Again, not her usual reaction. True substance, real feelings, including the sizzling sexual kind, needed time to grow, didn't they?

Now, as if he'd read her mind, and just to prove her wrong, Jacob stopped more than an arm's length away. No confident smile, either. Instead his eyebrows knitted while that amber-gold gaze penetrated hers. She felt the tingling again and way more than before.

"Teagan? Are you all right?"

She gathered herself, shrugged it off. "Um, last time I looked—sure."

One side of his mouth tugged higher. "You seem…uncertain."

Tearing her gaze away from his, siphoning in much needed air, she glanced around and made an excuse. "I was just taking this place in."

It was Italian marble everywhere, gold-plated everything, along with perfectly lit artwork that might belong in the Louvre. The excess reminded Teagan of her father's home after his new wife had remodeled. Yes, he was a billionaire but, for Teagan's taste, over the top.

None of the "children" were happy about their dad's second marriage. For starters, stepmom Eloise was more about

the almighty dollar than anything else. Nevertheless, they had all supported their father and, of course, their new little brother and baby sister. Family stuck together, no matter their differences—and this clan had a few. But if anyone was in trouble, there was no question, no pause. They closed ranks, now more than ever before.

Jacob was crossing to the suite's phone extension. "I'll order up champagne."

"Actually, I'm good with juice or water."

Without missing a beat, he veered toward the bar's long, gleaming counter. "I'll whip something up."

While eyeing some side shelves, Jacob removed his tie then unfastened the shirt buttons at his throat. Teagan caught a tantalizing glimpse of upper chest. It took her back to their time on the dance floor…to sensations of grazing the hard length of his body and soaking in all that delicious masculine heat.

As he shucked off his jacket, Teagan drifted closer. Beneath the white dress shirt, his chest was strong and chiseled. He folded each sleeve back, revealing two powerful, summer-tanned forearms, then turned to the refrigerator to check out the contents. Teagan told herself not to ogle the lines of his tailored pants then went right ahead and did it anyway.

Long, solid legs.

Even better buns.

Grabbing a stool, Teagan cleared her throat.

"I usually stay clear of alcohol," she said. "The last time I had champagne was at my brother's wedding."

Jacob turned back around and slid a container of chilled berries over the counter toward her. "Nice day?"

"The ceremony was beautiful." It had been a smallish affair held on the estate grounds in a marquee. "Not quite as glam as this one, of course."

His chuckle was a deep rumble. "Of course."

No need to go into how that day had ended—with an ac-

tual bomb going off. That incident had been the latest in a string of attacks targeting their father. While the authorities were on the case, the madman responsible was still at large.

Nothing you can do about it, so deep breath. Focus on the good stuff.

"I caught up with a friend there," she said, selecting a cold berry. "Our families holidayed together one Christmas. Grace Munroe and I became pen pals, but we lost touch over the years. When I found out she was dating my brother, I almost fell off my chair."

"You mean the brother who got married?"

"Another one," she said, and popped the berry in her mouth.

"So, you have *two* brothers?"

"My parents had four children, me and three older boys. When my father remarried, he had two more—another son and a girl."

"Did your mom remarry, too?"

"She passed away."

Jacob stopped laying drink ingredients on the counter. "I'm sorry."

Teagan nodded. *Thanks. So am I.*

"My friend and brother got engaged Christmas Day," she said, getting back to the main thread while Jacob found two chilled martini glasses. "Funny because when we were young, those two hated each other."

Seeing them together now, those two were so obviously in love—so *meant to be*. Teagan knew Grace and Wynn were destined to grow old together, with gray hair and stooped backs, blissfully content, surrounded by a clutch of grandkids. She was happy for them. Envious, in fact. Commitment, marriage, children…everyone seemed to be doing it. But Teagan couldn't see that kind of scenario in her own future. It simply wasn't in the cards.

Jacob found pineapple juice, vanilla syrup, crushed ice and a shiny silver shaker while Teagan drank in the show.

Watching this man move made the nerve endings under her skin quiver and snap alive. And he was just getting started. After tipping in an ounce of syrup, he flipped the shaker into the air and caught it in the same hand—*behind his back*. Not a single drop spilled.

She laughed. "Hey! Good party trick."

"Bartending paid the bills through law school."

Teagan sat straighter. Interesting. He came from money—earlier he had mentioned inheriting a law firm—but he hadn't necessarily relied on it. Maybe Jacob Stone was more her type than she'd thought.

Unlike her older brothers who had accepted jobs with the family company, Teagan had decided to go it alone. The boys had dubbed her The Wild Child, but there was more to her opting out than that. Lately, however, she'd thought about going back. Everyone was on tenterhooks waiting for the next attack. She should be there for her family now.

Jacob was pouring juice into that shaker like a pro.

"Working and studying full-time was a challenge," he said. "But I loved every minute. Passing the New York State Bar was always my dream."

"Do you have a specialty?" Remembering the situation back home in Australia, Teagan leaned closer. "Like criminal law?"

"I deal in reputations. Defamation. Libel."

"Oh, like that case in the news a while back." She recalled the details. "A big-name movie director sued a magazine after they claimed he had indecently assaulted someone."

"The magazine lost." He smacked the juice bottle down like a gavel. "We won."

Get outta here. "That was *your* case?"

"Done and dusted, Your Honor."

Congratulations were in order. But there was a downside. "The amount that director wanted was insane. The magazine worried it would ruin them. That people would lose their jobs."

Jacob studied her before adding a scoop of ice to the shaker. "Not my responsibility."

"Meaning, you'd done your job." *Had brought down the kill.*

"Meaning, if you turn your back on the truth, spread malicious lies, and you come up against me—prepare to pay the price."

Jacob didn't seem agitated. Rather, he looked determined, like Teagan's oldest brother Cole when he was stuck in commander in chief mode. Wynn could be the same way. *Focused*, Grace called it. Even Dex, the chilled middle brother, could switch on that *don't mess with me* trait when need be.

Frankly, the entire family—and their goliath media and news corporation—was known for keeping its eye on the target. Never letting a prize get away. Way too intense for The Wild Child, even if Teagan's father reminded her every chance he got that she shared the same name. That the same blood ran through her veins. He'd said that she couldn't hide from who she was. DNA didn't lie.

While Jacob screwed on the shaker's lid, Teagan joined him behind the bar. "Mind if I try?"

He handed it over. "Be my guest."

She gave the shaker a few slow rotations before going to town. As ice clinked and liquid swished at warp speed, Jacob's eyes widened.

"I'm all about protein shakes, not cocktails." She put a hand on her heart. "I swear."

After she poured the mixture into their glasses, he proposed a fitting toast. "To the truth, the whole truth."

Teagan touched her glass to his. "So help me, God."

She sipped then sighed. Fresh and light and…yeah…

About that toast.

"I need to come clean," she said, setting her glass aside. "I have a confession to make."

"Well, if you need a good lawyer…"

She returned his lopsided grin then admitted, "This is actually a first for me, too…being here with you like this tonight."

His smile changed. The look in his eyes, as well. "As in, two people who just met leaving a party together?"

She nodded. "Needing to be alone for an hour or two."

That amber gaze turned ravenous again. When he stepped closer and a hot palm skimmed beneath the back of her hair—when his head deliberately angled and lowered over hers—it didn't matter that he wasn't what Teagan thought she wanted, needed, maybe even deserved. As his mouth covered hers, there was only one certainty that seemed to shine through. One truth that couldn't be denied.

She was indeed her father's daughter. A Hunter by name. In many respects, a Hunter by nature. And tonight, damn it all, she was hungry, too.

Two

There were times when things felt good. Felt right. There were others when forces conspired or stars aligned and what happened was out of this world.

Like now, Jacob thought, being here with this woman who had come out of nowhere and left zero doubt as to what she was thinking. Where they were heading. Her words alone would have sufficed. The definite yes in her gaze was the icing on the cake.

Let's do it.

As Jacob claimed the first kiss, he felt her dissolve, her two arms coiling around his neck. After blindly setting his glass on the counter, he caressed the curve of her hip while his tongue swept the seam of her lips and they parted. Then she craned up on her toes and pressed her breasts against his ribs. As the kiss deepened and her fingers knotted in his hair, he only grew more certain.

They would need way more than an hour or two.

When Jacob drew away, he kept his gaze on her lips. "Things aren't going too fast?"

A smile played at the corners of her mouth as those gorgeous green eyes drifted open. "Not for me." As she nodded, a waterfall of blond hair cascaded over her shoulder. "How about you? All good?"

So good. Particularly now that she was flicking open every shirt button down to his belt and tracing arcs over his pecs with her nails. Needing to keep up, he found the zipper at her back and eased that baby all the way down. As the gown slipped and rustled into a glittering puddle around her heels, he worked the shirttails from his pants

and cast his shirt to the floor. Then he brought her close and claimed her mouth again.

Only now that wasn't nearly enough.

He bent at the knees and caught her around the waist. Then, inch by inch, he lifted her until her silver heels fanned the air a foot above the ground. And that's how he carried her to his bed. Step by step.

Kiss by kiss.

From the minute Jacob had held her on the dance floor—like they'd been the only ones in the room—she had looked forward to this moment. Getting her out of that dress so fast had been a pleasant surprise. When he'd lifted her up against him, his mouth fused to hers the whole time, Teagan wondered just how good this could get.

She was vaguely aware of leaving the light behind... of moving into the bedroom. He adjusted his hold on her waist to throw back the covers. Then, he laid her down on the cool, crisp sheet.

As his lips left hers, she let her arms fall and curl around her head. Siphoning a giddy breath, she took in the sight of him crouched above her. Light filtered through from the main room. In the soft shadows, the strong angles of his jaw and Roman nose looked more pronounced. Those lidded amber eyes seemed to glow. When he smiled, the thrill of anticipation shot straight to her core.

His voice vibrated through to her bones.

"There's something I need to do."

She plucked at the sheet above her head. "You don't need to ask permission."

He came closer. "Are you sure about that?"

She felt a rush of heat. The need to groan. Arching toward him was pure reflex, one that didn't seem to surprise him at all. When he didn't move, she told him again as she bent her knee and brushed her leg against his.

"Yes, Jacob," she said.

Yes, yes, yes.

He eased back, slipped off one heel, then the other, and dropped both her shoes to the floor. When he flicked on a bedside light, the glow was warm and teasing—perfect for taking in his cut torso. But he was still wearing pants while she was pretty much naked. Not a whole lot to hide, including the scar she'd seen reflected in bathroom mirrors half her life. The jagged line was too long and high for an appendix op, and too prominent to go unnoticed for long, particularly given the way Jacob's lidded gaze was devouring her now.

If he frowned and asked—What the hell happened there?—she would tell him straight up. *Fell off my bicycle when I was a kid. Moving on.* But he didn't seem to notice, even when he knelt over her again and his head gradually went lower.

While the tip of his tongue slid along her panty line, one big hand skimmed up her side until his thumb came to rest under her breast. When his mouth slid even lower and he nuzzled her through the patch of white silk, that thumb brushed higher, grazing and flicking and teasing her nipple.

Teagan gripped the sheet, closed her eyes and arched up again.

Sparks were flying, the majority of them having a party under his lips. Then—*dear God!*—he used his teeth. Every pulse point in her body instantly contracted and hummed.

His next words were matter-of-fact.

"This has to go."

Her underwear?

She was ready to rip her panties off herself when he lifted her behind with one hand and eased down the silk with the other. He kissed that part of her before the tip of his tongue delved deeper, tickling and twirling until she was wound up so tight, she could barely think. When he

raised her hips higher and slid a finger inside, she gripped his hair as a warning.

Don't stop.

She imagined she felt him smile against her before he eased away, taking that final scrap of clothing with him—down her thighs, past her calves, off her feet. After finding his wallet, he set a foil packet on the bedside table then ditched his shoes and pants while she pressed back into the sheet and took in the show.

He braced his long, rock-solid legs so they were slightly apart. His hips were lean and mean, but it was where the lines converged that drew her gaze like a magnet. As he came forward again, setting one knee on the mattress, one hand on the sheet, she pushed up and met him halfway. Their mouths came together as his free hand curved around her back and she held on for all she was worth.

When his mouth finally left hers, he hummed out a breath then looked into her eyes, smiling.

"You said something earlier."

She grazed her toes up the back of his calf. "You mean about not needing to ask?"

"About needing to be alone for an hour or two." He tasted her lips again and stayed close. "Not long enough."

She traced a fingertip around the shell of his ear. "Are you watching the clock?"

He grinned. "I'm watching *you.*" He dropped another lingering kiss at the side of her mouth. "Stay till morning?"

Was he kidding?

Of *course* she would stay.

He rolled on their protection and positioned himself above her. When he pushed inside, she quivered and lost every bit of her breath. In the shadows, he studied her for a long moment before he started moving and slow-kissing her lips.

As he caught her thigh and wrapped her leg around the back of his, she gripped his neck and surrendered it all.

And when his thrusts grew faster—when the friction turned white-hot—she squeezed him tighter, bit her lip harder, and came apart like she'd known she would.

Like she never had before.

Three

The smell of fresh coffee woke her.

Blinking open sleepy eyes, Teagan remembered she wasn't in her own room. The bed looked like a tornado had torn through. Shoes and clothes were strewn all over the place. Jacob Stone was gone from the bed, but his musky scent, and the memories, were everywhere.

Burrowing back into the bedclothes, she circled her head with her arms. What an amazing night! The most intense, and beautiful, of her life. From the instant they'd met, those dark, dreamy looks had grabbed her. Accompanying him from the wedding reception to this suite…

Well, it was always going to end this way—with them twined up together, naked in bed. The decision might have been impulsive, but the reality of making love with Jacob Stone had proved to be more than spur of the moment. It was breathtaking, *liberating*, and she would do it all again in a heartbeat.

Grinning, Teagan caught her lower lip between her teeth. Exactly how long was it before her flight?

Getting to her feet, she picked up on the aroma of pancakes and was suddenly so hungry, needing to refuel. But if Jacob walked through those bedroom doors this minute, she would happily snack on him instead. This was—*he* was—the wake-up call she'd needed.

She'd always prided herself on being strong. Resilient. Then a few months ago she'd suffered a miscarriage, and a relationship she had valued died, too. Now, heading for the attached bath, she felt relief. She could finally look back on that time as a hard lesson learned.

Years after the childhood accident that had left that scar, she'd been told she would likely never conceive. Following her recent loss, however, that prognosis had been modified. Should she become pregnant again, the probability of an early first-trimester spontaneous abortion was high, which had made her feel even *worse*.

But this time spent with Jacob had helped her turn a corner. She would always remember the pain—physical, mental *and* emotional—but she had grieved long enough. She could still live a meaningful and happy life.

Just not the one she would have chosen if she'd had any say.

Jacob heard the shower shut off and waited for Teagan to stroll into the main room. When she did, she was wrapped in an oversize hotel robe, long, damp hair free of salon curls and her beautiful face scrubbed squeaky clean. She took him in, too, in his gray T-shirt and weekend drawstring pants, before studying the room service feast he'd ordered up.

She laughed. "Well, someone's hungry."

His gaze lowered to her mouth. "Always."

They each moved forward until he was close enough to repeat the scene that had gotten things started last night. After sliding a hand around the back of her neck, with great purpose and pleasure, he tasted those sweet lips again.

But this kiss was different. Because it would be one of their last? Or the start of something more? Something new?

He gradually broke the kiss but didn't step away. Being this close again, he felt recharged. Ready for anything, including finding more time to please this woman in every conceivable way.

But first...

"We need coffee." He reached for the silver service pot. "At least I do."

As he poured two cups, she held up a hand. "No sugar for me."

He handed Teagan's cup over then dropped two lumps into his own, as well as an inch of cream. Chugging back a mouthful, he pulled out a seat for her before grabbing a strip of crispy bacon.

Let the feast begin!

After pulling in her chair, Teagan inspected a glass-covered dish. "Is that steak?"

"Filet mignon. Goes great with hollandaise."

There was grilled tomato, smashed avocado, sautéed mushrooms, a pile of golden hash browns and more. It smelled so darn good. But she only reached for the muesli container and shook a modest helping into a bowl. Tacking his smile back on, Jacob helped himself to the smorgasbord. This morning, he could eat enough for two.

Earlier, he'd laid her gown over the back of a couch. She caught sight of it now before eyeing the door to the suite.

"This'll be interesting." She set down the container. "My first walk of shame."

"If anyone can get away with wearing that evening gown this time of day, it's you."

She was busy searching the room-service spread again. *Really* looking this time, like she couldn't find what she wanted. Impossible.

He put his fork down. "Are we missing something?"

"Plant-based milk?"

"Like soy?"

"Or almond."

He got to his feet. "I'll order some up."

Waving him off, she reached for the pancakes. "This is even better."

No trouble, but he wouldn't push. If she was happy, so was he. And after breakfast, before they thought about jetting back to ordinary life, there might be time enough to revisit what they had discovered in each other the night

before. Frankly, he wanted to slip the robe off her shoulders, taste every inch of that incredible body, and then do it all over again.

She was looking at his plate. He looked down, too. *Ha.* He'd forgotten all about the food.

As he pushed a loaded fork into his mouth and Teagan poured syrup over a pancake, she said, "I suppose you need to check out soon and get back."

He chewed and swallowed while pouring them juice. "My flight's not till one."

"Mine's around that time, too."

"You need a lift to the airport?"

"No, no. I just don't want to hold you up."

"I'm in no hurry." Watching how she was downing that juice, he asked, "Are you?"

She set down her empty glass. "It's Sunday."

Right. "The weekend. Time to relax. Forget about work."

Although tomorrow would be a day and a half. He had depositions to sort, background notes, too. There was an afternoon meeting scheduled with that defamation client—former Londoner, Grant Howcroft. Hunter Publications was in for a very public kick in the corporate pants. Making up tales might sell magazines but—moral of the story, boys—dishonesty does not pay.

"It must be full-on being a big-name lawyer," Teagan said as she cut into her syrup-soaked pancake.

Was he looking preoccupied?

"It can get busy," he said, loading his fork again.

"Even on weekends?"

Remembering how her legs had dug into the back of his thighs as she'd bucked up against him, Jacob gave her his word. "Not this weekend."

"Are you sure?"

He wanted to laugh. "Absolutely."

"It's just... I've seen that expression before. The *gotta get back to the grind* look."

Sure. "There's an element of that. You'd know, with a business of your own."

"A *small* business. That's more than enough." She hastened to add, "Of course, people should make their own choices. Ambition isn't necessarily a bad thing."

Ambition was a very *good* thing, particularly when someone had a past like his: a legacy of poverty, despair and *why the hell bother*.

"I had a weird upbringing. Guess that's where I get my drive." He put a little more sugar in his cup and listened to the tinkle of the spoon as he stirred. "How about you?"

"As far as drive goes? I want my business to do well."

"It's important to you?"

"Of course."

He looped back to the heart of the question. "And your upbringing?" Her childhood?

"I wouldn't say it was weird. More filled with challenges, I suppose."

The previous night, they had learned so much about each other, and not all of it purely physical. And yet now, in the morning light, Teagan still seemed largely a mystery.

They both had flights to catch. Nevertheless, he wanted to know more—*feel* more, which was a big step for him. It was the right time, right place.

Certainly right girl.

After she'd finished two pancakes and Jacob had put a decent dent in his generous helping, he dabbed the corners of his mouth with a linen napkin then tapped back into that question.

"So, where did you grow up again?" When they'd met, he'd asked about the accent, which wasn't always noticeable but definitely cute.

"Australia. Sydney." She chose a fat strawberry from the fruit platter. "My family's still there. Well, my father and his wife and their kids. My oldest brother and his wife, too."

"And the rest of the clan?"

"My other brothers are in the States now. Actually, the middle one lives here in LA. He's engaged to someone who grew up in Oklahoma so he spends a lot of downtime there. The other brother's in New York."

"Hey. Small world."

"Wynn's a dyed-in-the-wool workaholic. Although, now that he has Grace in his life, I'm sure that'll change. Or I hope that it does."

In the middle of topping up coffee cups, Jacob hesitated as a chill rippled over his scalp. He shook it off. Found a smile.

"Wynn? That's an unusual name. I'm putting a case together at the moment. The defendant, if it gets that far—" *which it would* "—his name is Wynn."

"Wow. How about that."

He nodded. Smiled again. *Yeah.* "How about that."

Seeming to read his mind, Teagan laughed. "Don't worry. It couldn't be my Wynn. He keeps his cards close to his chest, but a libel suit? He'd have said something about that. Social media would be all over it."

"We haven't submitted yet. No one knows."

Teagan reached for another berry while Jacob finished his second cup of coffee. She hadn't spoken about her family the previous night and hadn't gone into much detail now, not that he'd been particularly forthcoming in that area, either. Admitting that his background was weird was the tip of a Titanic-size iceberg. His childhood had been beyond toxic.

But right now he was more interested in Teagan. And Wynn.

"So what does your brother in New York do? We might know each other."

"How many Wynns have you met again?"

He grinned and conceded. "Only one, and that's on paper."

"So you *couldn't* know my brother."

Ha. Right.

Still…

"What did you say he does for a living?"

Teagan gave him an odd look, like, "maybe drop this." And he would, as soon as this was squared away, because the back of his neck was prickling now. Could be nothing, but he'd learned the hard way to always pay attention to that.

"Wynn works for my father's company," she said. "Or an arm of it. All the boys do."

The prickling grew.

One arm of a family company? "Sounds as if your father runs a big enterprise."

"It's big, all right. Out of college, I decided to do my own thing. I didn't want any part of the drama."

"You're not estranged from your family, though."

Her eyebrows snapped together. "God, no."

"Everyone went to that wedding?"

"Everyone was there."

"So you're all close."

"We've had our differences, between my brothers and father particularly. Too much alike. Although, as they get older, it's not as intense. And, yes. We are close. Protective." She pulled the lapels of her robe together, up around her throat. "That's the way it is with our family. We can say what we want about each other, but anyone throwing shade from the outside needs to brace himself for a smackdown." She set her napkin on the table. "What about you?"

Jacob was still thinking about Wynn and family companies with arms in Sydney, LA and New York.

He tried to focus. "Sorry? What was that?"

"Your family, Jacob. Do you have any siblings? Nieces or nephews?"

"No siblings." As far as blood went, anyway.

"So, it's just your parents and you?"

He rubbed the back of his neck. "It's complicated."

Her laugh was forced. "More complicated than mine?"

Shrugging, he got to his feet. Teagan got to hers, too.

There were questions in her eyes. Doubts about where he'd come from, who he really was. Okay. Let's see.

His A-hole father had jumped ship before Jacob was in school, right before Mom had screwed up monu*freaking*mentally. As a teenager, he'd gone off the rails and literally crashed before lucking out and finding a buoy at just the right moment.

But that was a lifetime ago. So forget about the past and concentrate on this. On now.

Jacob took her hands and stated the glaringly obvious.

"I had a great time last night."

Her expression softened. "Me, too. Really nice."

When he lifted her hand and pressed his lips to her palm, every fiber in his body sat up and took notice.

"You smell so good," he said. Like vanilla.

"It's called soap."

"I skipped the shower. Didn't want to wake you up."

She tilted her head and gave him a teasing look. "I'm awake now."

His gaze roamed her face...the thousand different curves and dips he'd adored and kissed long into the night. Then he considered their backgrounds again, and that *yet to be filed* libel suit. He thought about *his* Wynn, and he thought about *hers*.

It didn't matter. At least, it didn't matter right now.

Leaning in, he circled the tip of her nose with his and murmured, "That robe needs to go."

Her beautiful eyes smiled before she unraveled the bulky tie at her waist. A second later, the robe lay pooled on the floor and they were headed for the bedroom again.

Four

All six shower nozzles were well placed and set to warm and ready. Add two large, soapy hands indulging every part of her body, and Teagan was riding the fast track to *Take Me Now*. Or was that *Take Me Again*? Evidently, Jacob Stone's sole purpose in life was to leave her feeling completely satisfied. Totally adored.

Who was she to complain?

But there were things she wanted for him, too, and precious minutes were flying by. There was no time to lose. So she slid a palm down over that ripped six-pack and curled her fingers around the part of him that so badly wanted to play.

His jaw grazed her temple as he groaned.

"Please say we're not leaving today."

"We have maybe an hour."

When she tightened her hold and slid her hand all the way down his shaft, he groaned again—deeper this time.

"An hour's not enough."

She grinned. "We're not doing that again."

But when he backed her up to the marble wall and slapped his palms against it high on either side of her head, Teagan seriously wanted to reconsider.

As she continued to work his erection, he lowered his head and tasted a line from the slope of one wet shoulder to her neck. By the time he reached her earlobe, he'd begun to move along with her, falling into the rhythm, his pelvis slowly rocking in time with her stroke. When she'd built up the tempo enough, he gripped her hand and buried his face in her hair.

"Tea… Christ…you're killing me."

"Oh. Sorry."

Not.

"You know I'll get you back."

She whispered in his ear, "You'd better."

Being naked with Jacob Stone set her on fire. As long as their bodies were touching, she felt completely consumed. It was helping to elbow out some of those memories from breakfast.

She didn't care that she was a vegetarian and Jacob loved his meat, or that he wanted to save her from walking out this morning wearing an evening gown. What *hadn't* sat well was their conversation about family.

He'd asked questions, which she'd answered. But he wouldn't let up about Wynn. Yes, it was an unusual name, and she was certain Hunter Enterprises' lawyers had dealt with libel suits before. Sometimes reporters needed to dig around in the dirt to uncover the truth.

Of course, the media should be responsible when sharing information, but Wynn was the poster boy for ethics— thorough and principled to the point of driving people nuts. Nothing anyone might say, or try to bring against him in a court of law, could ever change her opinion on that.

But now, as Jacob's mouth began working its magic again in a feverous kiss, Teagan pushed all that other stuff from her mind. This slice of time was about filling the well. About being human and truly feeling again.

When his lips left hers, he took his time searching her eyes while she pledged to memory the chiseled angle of his jaw and how water dripped off the tip of his nose. She wanted to remember the way he was looking at her now, like he would do anything to never let her go.

"We wasted too much time sleeping last night." Droplets fell from his black lashes as his gaze burned into hers. "I need to be inside you."

It was a statement of fact. A heartfelt plea.

Yes, I want that, too.

Just one problem.

As compelling as this moment was, safety came first.

Obviously, Jacob agreed. "Condoms are in the bedroom," he said.

"So we should turn off the faucets."

"Or we could go with something else."

She grinned. "Something new?"

"There is nothing new. There's only *better*."

He edged them both around, swapping places while coaxing her to about-face. With his shoulders propped against the wall and that rock-hard body cradling her back and behind, he began nuzzling her neck, caressing her breasts, while one hot palm slid down her front. But when he reached her scar and stopped, she pressed back against him and stiffened.

He kissed the crown of her head. "That's been there a while. Must have hurt."

"I fell off my bike in middle school."

"We should compare battle scars sometime. I've got a couple of whoppers."

As he talked, his hand slipped lower and a finger curved between the apex of her thighs.

Jacob was back to his old tricks, concentrating solely on her. And as he began to tease and gently rub, she forgot about childhood accidents, the fact that time was running out, or anything else that might interfere. She only wanted to concentrate on the outgoing tide and look forward to being carried away.

All too soon, she was trembling and contracting inside. There was a sense of friction building…of everything else blurring and fading away.

His words were warm at the shell of her ear.

"This was a good idea."

"Don't…" She swallowed, caught her breath. "Don't talk."

Pinpricks of heat were flying together, joining and com-

pressing until finally her hips bucked forward, her head rocked back. And before all that intensity came close to burning out, she climaxed again, higher and brighter and, yes, just that bit better. Still touching her, *loving* her, he wrung out the last spasm until she couldn't stand. Couldn't think. She was officially mindless.

Unreservedly his.

But as he scooped her up and carried her to their bed—curled up in his arms, dripping wet—Teagan knew this wasn't over yet. Jacob Stone wasn't done with her. Not even close.

Nothing was ever perfect, but if Jacob had to come up with something darn close, these hours spent with Teagan would be it. And as much as he had enjoyed the previous night—the talking, the dancing, the mind-blowing sex—this morning's installment in the shower had blown that all clean away.

Now, after making love again, they were lying together, face-to-face, nose to nose. As she looked into his eyes and he looked back, he could only think of the slice of time they had left. Bottom line: he wanted to see her again. But, unless his guess was wrong—and that wasn't likely—this liaison was about to wind up, not for *now*, but for *good*.

The finality of that goodbye hinged on something he needed to say. Something she wouldn't be able to look past. And, frankly, neither would he.

"We need to go," she said, her gaze lingering on his lips. His insides gave a kick that was a whole lot of desire but even more regret.

He exhaled. "How are we going to do that?"

"We get off this bed and say goodbye at the door."

"I don't like that plan."

"Okay. You stay here and I'll pick up my things on the way out."

"That won't work, either."

Her eyes glistened as she smiled. "I think we're out of options."

He came closer and brushed his lips over hers. "Not quite."

Drawing back, she gave him a playful, admonishing look. "We don't have time for another shower."

"No?"

She laughed softly. *"No."*

"Okay. Get ready for Stone's option number two."

He leaned up on an elbow, resting his jaw in his palm as she pushed to her feet and turned to face him.

Waiting, she cocked her head. "I'm listening."

Looking at her awesome nakedness, he was stuck.

"Yeah. I forgot."

Smiling, shaking her head, she headed for the bathroom. "And don't you dare follow me."

He spoke to her through the open doorway. "The walk of shame."

She called back. "What about it?"

"I, for one, would love to see you in that gown again. But we can call one of the boutiques in the lobby and have something in your size sent up. Shoes, too."

Easy. Done.

"That's sweet, but I don't need an Edward Lewis."

Jacob was on his feet, still figuring that out—*Edward who?*—when she returned to the room. She was wearing the T-shirt he'd peeled off before they'd flipped on the shower faucets. It almost came down to her knees.

Striking a *hands on hips* model pose, she asked, "How do I look?"

"Like a goddess."

She blinked and then laughed, but he'd never been more serious in his life. Which made this even harder...what had to be done. They needed to have one more conversation. Better that she found out now, and from him.

While Teagan searched for her shoes, he pulled on his

drawstring pants and then rummaged around in his bag for a shirt, which turned out to be a starched business number. Even when he headed off to chill with the Rawsons for a couple of days, he packed one—along with a dark blue jacket and dress pants. That's what lawyers did. Those who ran a firm on Lexington Avenue, at least.

Teagan had slung her heels over her shoulder. She was ready to go. But before she could say another word—*It's been nice...see you next wedding*—Jacob spoke up.

"I'll walk you to your hotel room."

"You don't have to do that."

"I want to." He looked down at himself, his mismatched clothes, his bare feet. "We can do the walk of shame together."

"I'm a big girl. I don't need anyone to hold my hand."

"Then hold *mine*." When she gave a *maybe not* look, he added, "I won't beg. Unless I have to."

She surrendered a smile. "Okay. But remember, we have flights to catch."

He held up one hand and put the other out, horizontal and palm down. "I swear on the Bible. Best behavior."

Her brows pinched and for a moment he thought she was going to say he was trying too hard. Maybe, but not to make an impression or to cling. He liked Teagan, more than any woman he'd known, but he didn't have a stalkerish bone in his body. When he finally said what *needed* to be said, he wanted Teagan to be in the position of power. In her own space. Closing the door in his face if need be.

Moving out of the bedroom, she collected her gown and evening bag while he found the key card. They took the elevator to her floor and made their way down the hall. After she'd swiped and stepped inside, he did it.

He came clean.

"I need to ask you something," he said. "Confirm... something. Your surname. It's Hunter, isn't it?"

Her smile was tight. "Jacob, I told you that last night when we met."

"I, uh, didn't catch it."

"It's okay. All's forgiven."

Rubbing his temple, he muttered, "I wish."

"What was that?"

"I didn't realize it until we spoke over breakfast. About your family. About your brother. Wynn Hunter." *All your cards on the table now, bro.* "He's the Wynn I'm looking to sue."

Teagan's shoulders slumped. Finally, she exhaled. "What a crap note to finish on."

Crap was right. "I'm sorry."

"Sorry that you want to take down my brother? Or sorry that you didn't share this with me before the shower?"

"The last one."

"That's what I figured."

But she appeared calm, as though he'd admitted to liking baseball more than hockey. Where was the name calling? The face slapping? He wanted to sue the pants off her brother, for Pete's sake.

"I thought you'd be more cut up about it," he said.

"Oh?"

Maybe he hadn't been clear. "I intend to decimate Wynn when I get him on the stand."

"I assume that's what clients pay you for."

He dragged a hand down his face, shifted his weight. "You told me how close your family is. When news of this hits, when your brother receives the verdict…it will affect the entire Hunter conglomerate."

Again. Totally unruffled.

He lowered his voice. "I don't play around in a courtroom, Teagan."

"Thanks," she said. "Got it."

Then it hit. Her reaction.

Well, of course.

"You'd already worked it out," he said.

"When you said the case hadn't been filed yet. Before we shared that shower." Her mouth hitched to one side. "I didn't want to spoil things, either."

"So you're not mad?"

"I told you. I grew up with the constant drama of big business. Everything's about control and making sure you're top dog. Kill or be killed." Leaning against the doorjamb, she sighed. "No, I'm not mad. I'm just over it."

So… *Okay, then.*

This didn't have to be goodbye. Of course, they would want to be completely transparent from now on. No more misunderstandings. No holding things back.

He told her, "We won't be able to see each other while I'm working on that case."

"Conflict of interest."

And then some. "But sometime in the future…" Finally giving in to a smile, he edged forward. "We really need to see each other again."

When he moved in to seal it with a kiss, she stepped back.

"I'm afraid that isn't possible," she told him, "and I think you know why."

Jacob looked like he wanted to laugh, but Teagan wasn't joking. Now that they had reached the crossroads, this was as serious as it got.

"You said you weren't angry," he said. "You said you understood how things work in the corporate world."

"Right. You're trying to bring down my brother. His company. My family's name. I understand perfectly."

"So you *are* mad."

"You have principles. So do I."

Standing in the hall in those smoking sweatpants and an overly starched business shirt, he looked so blindsided— for once, so *not* in control. The moment he'd realized that

the man he wanted to sue was her brother, he should have spoken up. But, to be fair, that wouldn't have changed her decision now. She couldn't continue to see someone who was determined to use a courtroom to destroy a member of her family.

However, given the circumstances, she obviously didn't hate the guy. She wanted to show some understanding. Soften the blow.

"I really enjoyed our time together. It was exactly what I needed." More than Jacob, or anyone else, could ever know. "But this is where it ends."

He cocked a brow. "In a hotel hallway?"

"That was your choice." She would have much preferred to have this conversation in private.

"Would you ever have said anything? That you knew?"

"I thought I would if you asked for my number and called."

He ran a hand through his drying hair and scrunched his toes in the carpet. "There's no way around this?"

"Not unless you drop your client. Drop the case."

His jaw tightened. "You know I can't do that."

Sure. "I understand."

Jacob studied her like he was sizing up an opponent. Then he squared his shoulders and summoned a nondescript smile. "I'm glad we did this face-to-face."

"Me, too."

He nodded and then nodded again. "This isn't going to end with a kiss."

"Afraid not." When he nodded a third time, her chest squeezed and she added, "Put yourself in my place. You'd do the exact same thing. Family is family, Jacob. Blood is blood. You can't turn your back on that."

His eyebrows hitched and his gaze dropped to the floor. "You can if your family sucks."

Teagan blinked. She must have heard wrong.

"Can you say that again?"

"Nothing," he muttered. "Forget it."

"Jacob, did you actually say what I *think* you said?" *That my family sucks?* The idea was too juvenile, too spiteful, to comprehend.

He only exhaled and wrapped it up. "I should go."

Before she could think to pull back, he dropped a quick kiss on her cheek and left, striding back down the hall, disappearing into the elevator. It was all she could do to stop from calling him back to bawl him out.

What a jerk. And to think she'd practically fallen for that guy. Who was one hundred percent *definitely* not her type.

A week later, when Jacob Stone tracked down her business number, Teagan was still fuming. But she'd gotten over her urge to let him know how childish his parting jab at her family had been. She preferred to simply never hear from him again. So she told her receptionist to let Mr. Stone know that she was preparing for an overseas vacation. And a trip was indeed penciled in. So she wasn't lying.

And dealing with the likes of him, so what if she was?

Five

Jacob slammed the phone down, which wasn't like him, or hadn't been in a long while. He'd learned to control his temper, roll with the punches, get his frustrations out in other ways. And, hey, what he'd heard just now wasn't exactly a surprise.

The receptionist at High Tea Gym in Seattle had politely but firmly stated that Teagan was unable to take his call. Ms. Hunter was about to head out of the country and hadn't scheduled a date for her return. She'd be sure to pass any message along.

Translation: *Move on, pal.*

The night he and Teagan had spent together in LA had ended with a massive twist. She was related to the defendant in an upcoming defamation suit. The bigger reveal? They had both been aware of the fact before diving in for an even steamier shower/bedroom finale the next morning.

Jacob swung his high-backed chair toward the window, set his elbows on the armrests and steepled his fingers under his chin as he took in the incredible view of the Chrysler Building. When they'd met, Teagan couldn't have known that a Hunter lawsuit was in his pipeline. She would never have feigned interest purely to gain an advantage…to glean some inside information on her brother's pending case, perhaps. She definitely wouldn't have sex to hold the incident over his head. Nevertheless, a headline had built up in his mind's eye: *Sleazy New York Lawyer Sleeps with Defendant's Sister.*

But, conspiracy theories aside, Teagan refusing to speak with him now was more about *how* they had parted than

why. She had said no one should turn her back on family. He'd responded with a dig about doing just that if the family concerned didn't deserve loyalty. He might have used the word "sucked." But he hadn't meant *her* family. He'd been talking about *his*. He was a master at keeping any residual feelings about his background and not being good enough at bay, but at the worst possible moment that old serpent had reared up to bite him in the balls.

The office intercom buzzed. Jacob ignored it. He needed time to cool down, get a grip.

He'd had relationships with women before and, other than one he refused to think about ever again, he'd always been the party to walk away. Everyone got dumped sometime.

Grow up, Stone. It's water under the bridge.

He heard a tap on the door, then his secretary's voice.

"Mr. Howcroft is here," Waverley McCune said in a subdued tone. "He knows he doesn't have an appointment." Her voice lowered to almost a whisper. "He says he's tired of 'all mouth and no trousers,' whatever that means."

Jacob continued to glare at the view, biting his thumbnail now, which he hadn't done since ninth grade, but whatever.

"Jay? What would you like me to tell him?"

Jacob swung his chair around at the same moment Grant Howcroft strode into the room, hands fisted at his sides.

"This bloody well has to stop! I'll see that bastard on his knees before this is through."

Tamping down the air with his hands, Jacob pushed to his feet. "Take a seat, Grant."

The older man threw himself onto a tufted leather couch while Waverley pressed the bridge of her Mr. Magoo eyeglasses back up her nose and quietly closed the door.

"Have you seen social media this morning?"

Jacob moved to the front of his desk, leaned against the edge and folded his arms. "You mean the small-time blogger opinion piece?" Yeah. He'd seen it. The other pieces concerning Howcroft, too.

"I want them shut down." The older man dabbed at his brow with his jacket cuff. "I want them *shut up!*"

"These things take time."

"While my career goes down the bloody toilet?"

"We'll get compensation."

"Tattered reputations don't mend that easily, Jakey boy."

"When the truth comes out they do."

Howcroft scratched at his wiry ginger-gray hair. "According to this latest piece, I'm a sodding drug lord now!"

"It's a piggyback small-time troll."

Grant wasn't listening. "How do I come back at that? I ask you. *How?*"

"By addressing the heart of the lies. By going after the one with the money." Wynn Hunter and his big-time "untouchable" media arm. "We only need to meet the standard for actual malice and prove the accusations are unfounded, which they are."

Then the wrong would be righted and Hunter Publications could kiss both sides of Howcroft's butt.

His client's brow was beaded with sweat. Jacob poured him a glass of water and brought it over.

Howcroft downed half and then closed his eyes at the same time he grit his teeth and his trembling lips turned white.

"I want to see Wynn Hunter destroyed. The rest of his blood-sucking family, too." An image of Teagan flashed into Jacob's mind while Howcroft took another mouthful then eased out a shuddering sigh. "How far away are we from getting this done?"

Jacob went into the fundamentals of where they were with the case. Today was only Thursday, so there wasn't much to add since Monday when they had spoken last. But when a person's life was falling apart, Jacob understood— minutes could feel like years.

Howcroft pushed back into the couch as his eyes darted

around the room. "Maybe I should do a runner. Hole up somewhere in Mexico until this thing blows over."

Jacob's chin went down. What happened to wanting to see Wynn Hunter destroyed? "We agreed. This is a process. Now we need to hold our course." Then go for the jugular.

"You know I was born a charwoman's son," Howcroft said, like Jacob didn't research the shit out of his clients' backgrounds. "My first job was as a filing clerk. Respectable, but rubbish pay. I got into theater and climbed the industry ladder from assistant stage manager to walk-on parts. Those first few years were brutal, mate. Young people nowadays don't know the half."

Jacob disagreed. There were lots who did.

"There were a few TV appearances," Howcroft went on, "the move to Hollywood, then the role that launched my career. Instant overnight success, the papers said. There were parties, marriages... And, yes, I made mistakes."

Jacob saw how Howcroft's eyes were edged with moisture and worried he might cry. But his client found his feet and tried to square his hunched shoulders instead.

"I don't know if I can..."

Jacob felt a prickling at the back of his neck. "Know if you can *what*?"

Putting up his hands like he'd heard and said enough, Howcroft headed for the door. "I'll be in touch. One way or another. Probably another."

Which was code for what exactly? "Are you saying you want to put the lawsuit on hold?"

"I'm saying I don't know if I want to continue, period." Howcroft swung open the door. "In fact, drop the whole bloody thing. I need time to get away. Clear my head."

"You want to drop the lawsuit?"

But Howcroft was already gone, which left Jacob wanting to slam the door the same way he had slammed down the phone earlier. He wasn't pissed at his client. The guy

had every right to be upset. If he wanted to put a brake on things, it was his time and his dime.

The thing that stuck in Jacob's craw was the situation with Teagan. If it hadn't been for this lawsuit, their time together would have ended on a very different note. She'd have taken his call today...*if* the time they had spent together had meant more to Teagan than simply letting loose. *If* she hadn't planned to somehow set him up.

After thinking that all through again, Jacob made another call. Not to High Tea Gym this time. To people who had never let him down before and weren't about to now.

The moment the image popped up on her laptop screen, Teagan knew why her eldest brother and his bride were video calling. Good news. The *best*. And when they actually said the words, Teagan promised herself to look happy for them both because she was. Genuinely thrilled.

Attending their wedding last year, hearing their vows and seeing the love they so obviously shared, Teagan had no doubt that Taryn and Cole would last until death do them part. Now, her brother looked proud, but also calm. A huge difference from his former *everything depends on me* demeanor—as if the fate of Hunter Enterprises rested solely on his shoulders. But Taryn's appearance struck Teagan even more. With her long hair draped around her shoulders like a thick, glossy mantle, she looked radiant. Blissfully content.

The couple said it together. "We're pregnant!"

"Ohmigod! Congratulations!" Teagan sucked down a breath and bolstered herself. "When did you find out?"

With an arm around his girl, Cole replied, "Four months ago. Taryn wanted to keep it under wraps for a while."

"I figure I'll be showing soon," Taryn added. "So time to let the cat out of the bag."

The newlyweds looked into each other's eyes like life would always be this way. Bright and wonderful. Never a

tear. Although they *had* been grounded enough to delay the announcement.

Teagan could recite the statistics in her sleep: more than eighty percent of miscarriages occurred in the first three months of pregnancy. When fertilized eggs that failed to implant were also factored in, around seventy-five percent of all conceptions didn't go full term.

But this one absolutely would.

Teagan shored up her smile. "So, too early to know if I'm getting a niece or a nephew?"

"We're not sure we want to find out," Cole said.

"We'll be happy no matter what," Taryn added.

"Whichever it turns out to be," Cole said, "we want another one."

Teagan's smile held firm.

More than one. Imagine that.

"How does Dad feel about being a grandfather?" she asked.

Cole's eyebrows pinched. "We haven't told him yet. These past months… It's been tough, particularly recently."

Teagan's heart beat faster. "Has something happened?"

"No more attempts on his life. Unfortunately, no new leads, either." Cole's eyes grew darker. "I don't think he'd care if that madman ever got caught as long as he could stop looking over his shoulder."

"How's Tate?" Teagan missed her youngest brother so much. He was cute and loving, and such a brave little soul.

"We have him over a lot," Taryn said. "The baby, too. It's easier now that Honey's a little older."

Teagan asked, "And Eloise?" His father's young wife.

Cole grunted. "That woman is worse than ever."

Eloise had a problem with the bottle—any bottle she could lay her hands on. She also had a problem with men. She'd come onto their father right after their mother's funeral in her hometown of Atlanta. Eloise had been after a rich man, and Guthrie Hunter was certainly that.

But clearly being the new Mrs. Hunter wasn't enough. Last year, hours before Honey was born, Guthrie learned that Eloise had tried to seduce Cole in the past. He'd been crushed. But, thinking of the children, he'd given her another chance.

After wrapping up the call, Teagan sat back in her office chair, thinking of how happy Taryn must be. But she wouldn't let her thoughts spiral any further down that rabbit hole. She had Tate and Honey, and would be a first-time auntie very soon.

Wasn't that blessing enough?

Pushing out of her chair, Teagan began packing up. She was due an afternoon off. Later she might call some friends. A new restaurant around the corner had rave reviews. Then again, she hadn't had much of an appetite lately…not since those syrup-soaked pancakes the previous Sunday.

A moment later, Teagan said goodbye to the receptionist and left through the gym's main sliding-glass doors. But while she was walking to her car, something caught her eye. A man was climbing out of a cab. Around six-two, killer build, wearing jeans, a casual pale blue button-down and the sexiest pair of shades on the planet.

Teagan's heart hit her throat.

What the hell was Jacob Stone doing there?

He saw her, headed straight over and, in that instant, all the memories came flooding back. Talking, dancing, making love, and suddenly she was tingling all over again, ready to melt.

His clean-shaven jaw tensed as he stopped a short distance from her and removed his sunglasses. "We need to talk."

"So you just dropped in from New York?"

"You wouldn't take my call."

"There's a good reason for that."

"Because of how we said goodbye. I can explain."

Teagan's heart was pounding against her ribs. Her legs felt as weak as cooked noodles.

I can explain.

Seriously?

Continuing on to the parking lot, she gave him the bird then retorted over her shoulder, "And stay away from clichés." *So lame.*

"I grew up with a mother who believed her drug addiction was more important than her only kid," he called after her. "My father was a grifter. He specialized in taking down the elderly and people with special needs."

Teagan pulled up. Slowly turned around. *"What did you say?"*

"He would fix their pipes, mend broken furniture, but he was really casing their homes, making plans to break in and take anything of value. Cash was best, but jewelry, power tools and TVs worked, too. When I was six, he pulled a Houdini. Never heard from him again. His lousy bones could be rotting on Hart Island for all I know."

Teagan could feel her mouth hanging open. Jacob was obviously telling the truth. Who made up stuff like that? And was that a Brooklyn accent she heard coming through?

As he shifted his weight, his amber eyes flashed in the early afternoon sun. "And thinking about it… I *like* clichés. Here's another one." He slipped his hands into his back pockets, cocked his head. "At fourteen, I got into a bad crowd. Smoked, drank. One night, we stole a '69 Chevy Camaro and put the roof down. We skidded out on Pitkin taking a corner. Almost creamed a guy before taking out a pole."

A chill scuttled up Teagan's spine. And her family had thought *she* was wild.

"You were driving?"

"No. Mad Mikey was at the wheel. He turned fifteen the week before and had aspirations of following his brother into

the pimp trade. I was riding shotgun. Cost me six months in juvie."

Teagan simply couldn't see it. This refined, powerful, controlled man was once a delinquent? A danger to society?

"Anyway…yeah. That was my life. My family. Who sucked. What I said…it had nothing to do with you. It was all about *me*. I should have told you that then."

"That's why you flew out here today…"

"I needed to apologize." His chin kicked up as his gaze glinted and narrowed on hers. "And there's something else I need to say. Or want to ask."

Let me guess. "While you're here, you'd like to take me to dinner?" *Followed by a long shower for two, I suppose.*

"I *do* want to ask you to dinner. But home cooked, and not here. In upstate New York. I'd like you to meet my family."

Her jaw dropped again. "Now I'm confused. Your *family*?"

"The people who took me in after the fustercluck that was my childhood. When I needed a real home and someone to care about what I was doing and how I was doing it. The Rawsons saved my life. That's not a cliché or an exaggeration. It's the truth."

She took a moment, let it sink in.

"You want me to fly across the country to have dinner with your adoptive family?"

"Correct."

"You know that sounds *bagful of cats* crazy."

"Yeah. You could say that."

He was forgetting… "Jacob, you're taking my brother to court."

"Not anymore. My client had second thoughts."

"So you're *not* trying to decimate my brother now?"

He grinned and then shrugged. "You'd really like my family."

Maybe she would. They sounded like an amazing bunch.

But *come on*. Dinner all the way in New York state? Just like that?

She shook her head. "Not possible."

"You'd be surprised at what's possible if you try."

He started walking toward her again, cutting the distance between them with that languid gait at the same time she remembered the two pink lines on that home pregnancy test a few months ago. She certainly hadn't believed *that* was possible…the most thrilling, completely positive moment of her life.

And suddenly Jacob was standing in front of her and all she could see were those gorgeous amber eyes, willing her to set aside logistics and do this insane thing.

He asked her, "How long will it take to pack?"

"You mean *now*?"

"It's on Friday. The weekend."

But on top of packing, there was informing his family, organizing a flight. She tried to think ahead.

"How many hours does it take to fly to New York anyway?"

"In a private jet—" he reached for her hand "—no time at all."

Six

Soaring eastward from Seattle to New York, the Rawson family's Cirrus SF50 settled into a cruising altitude of forty-thousand feet. Toward the tail end of the aircraft, Teagan sat beside Jacob, wondering what surprises lay ahead. She had flown around the world—finishing school in Switzerland, vacations in the Mediterranean, business jaunts to the UK. Flying across the country should be a breeze, and yet she'd never felt more keyed up about a trip. Choosing to spend the weekend with Jacob's family was pure impulse on both their parts. Come Sunday, would she regret having given in to the urge or would she be looking forward to next time?

Jacob was opening a photo album on his phone. "I hope you like horses. Over the next couple of days, you'll see a few."

"I had some riding lessons when I was young, before—"

When Teagan cut herself off, swallowing those next words, he smiled. "Before what?"

"Before I got into other stuff."

He knew about the fall from her bike and the scar, but he didn't need to know about the consequences. So, enjoying the view—of the man next to her, not the clouds—she focused on the photo he'd brought up on his phone.

"Who's that?"

Jacob angled the screen more her way. "That's Ajax on the back of a prize stallion, Coming Home."

"Wow. All rippling muscle and sleek lines. The horse is nice, too."

Jacob chuckled. "Oh, you and Ajax will get along great."

Perhaps she was being overly optimistic, but Teagan had

a feeling she would get along with all the Rawsons. She wanted to hear more about Jacob's adoptive family, the father and two sons who had taken in a troubled teen when he'd needed a soft place to land. And if he wanted to share more about those earlier abusive years, she would listen then, too. Although opening up old wounds could be tough.

Since moving to Seattle, she hadn't told a soul about her accident, the moment that changed her life. She would never forget the pain and how she'd had no energy left to cry. The operations had been endless, and so much time seemed wasted waiting to heal.

But through it all, Teagan had had two parents who had loved her dearly and made certain she was cared for by the best. In comparison, Jacob's childhood sounded like a lonely, desperate, living hell. The memories must be haunting. They must be frightening.

Still, with the Rawsons' help, Jacob had turned his life around. Now he was in the clear, not only surviving but in every way *thriving*.

"Tell me more about the Rawson Stud Farm."

Her hand was resting on the console between their chairs. He took hold of it, grazing his thumb over hers as he replied.

"The property sits between Albany and Lake George, a short drive from one of the country's oldest and most respected racecourses. It offers a full thoroughbred boarding facility along with state-of-the-art breeding needs as well as our own stables. Family owned and run since 1888."

She nodded. "Very informative."

"Like a blurb from Wikipedia, right?" His gaze grew reflective. "The first time I saw those hills and pastures, I couldn't believe it was real. I grew up in East New York. In the '90s, there was a murder every other day. So much robbery and truancy, and don't forget the crack." He shook his head as if to clear it. "I mentioned that stolen car incident. As part of my sentence slash rehabilitation, I was sent to the Rawsons' farm for a couple of weeks. The owner had

a program for juvenile offenders. Hux Rawson helped turn more than a few lives around."

"So you went to Rawsons' and never left?"

He gave her a wry grin. "That would've been too easy. After I'd done my time, I got mixed up with a gang that got pinched busting into small businesses—grocers, pawn shops, delis. They took everything they could lay their sticky hands on."

Teagan remembered Jacob's description of his biological father—that he'd been a con man. A thief. "You must've been feeling really messed up at the time."

"I wasn't involved in the robberies. We'd been seen hanging out together, and an eyewitness placed me at the scene of a break-in."

"But if you weren't involved..."

"Over seventy percent of all convictions overturned since DNA evidence was introduced have been based on eyewitness testimony. The human mind doesn't play memories back on cue, like most people think. It reconstructs, trying to put pieces of a puzzle back together. That eyewitness was mistaken, but I went down with the others anyway.

"So I wrote Mr. Rawson, asked if he'd consider having me at the farm again. When I told him I was innocent, he got his brother involved. Uncle Ted, the lawyer, filed some papers, shored up my alibi and my conviction was reversed. But they knew if I went back home, I'd sink into the slime again. A high school freshman with a smack-loving mom and no other support... It's hard to turn things around."

"But you *did* turn it around."

"I will *always* be grateful for my second chance. My second family." Jacob was bringing up another snap on his phone, grinning now. "That's Griff posing with a couple of big-earning mares. He's a kingpin on Wall Street now."

The man was similar in build to Ajax. Both oozed self-confidence and had rugged cowboy good looks. And when Jacob showed her a picture of Hux Rawson, it became ob-

vious where they'd inherited those qualities. In his sixties, Jacob's adoptive father was still bright-eyed and square-shouldered.

Teagan asked, "And Mrs. Rawson?"

"She passed away before I came on the scene."

That made Teagan feel even closer to the Rawsons. She still missed her own mother so much.

Jacob was swiping again. "Hux says Lanie grew into a spitting image of her mom, in looks as well as temperament. Nowadays, Lanie can be particularly stubborn."

Teagan did a double take. "Lanie?"

"Hux's daughter. Our younger sister."

The picture on his phone showed Jacob, around senior year, with a girl in her early teens. Standing in front of an industrial-size red barn, their arms were looped around each other's waists. Lanie wore bright yellow riding breeches and was looking up at Jacob like he was the bee's knees. Like no one had a brother like hers.

"She's a dressage champion," he said. "Too many medals to count."

Teagan smiled at the adoring expression on Lanie's face. "I can't wait to meet her."

She couldn't wait to meet them all.

After landing at a private airstrip, she and Jacob climbed into a cab waiting in the hangar. As they drove, three thoroughbreds on the other side of a timber-rail fence raced alongside their vehicle right up to the homestead, a cream, shingle-style Victorian that was equal parts grace and warmth.

Huxley Rawson was waiting on the porch. With neat steel-gray hair and a prominent widow's peak, Jacob's adoptive father was indeed tall and broad through the shoulders, like his sons. As they mounted the steps, Teagan noticed a golden retriever by his side.

When Jacob introduced her, Hux ignored the hand she

extended. Instead he offered a hug that felt incredibly real. She imagined the troubled youths who, over the years, had found their way here. How at ease and supported they must have felt. How many had wished they could have stayed, too?

"Welcome to our home, Teagan. We're so pleased to have you here." Hux's attention turned to his son and the smile in his burnt-umber eyes shone brighter. "Jay, what a wonderful surprise."

This hug was longer, stronger, with a couple of hearty slaps on the back before pulling away. Without a doubt, Jacob was a good-looking man. But here, in his family home, it was even more pronounced. His eyes were clearer, his voice richer, and the energy behind his smile radiated pure magic, particularly as he turned to study the gentle hills and deepening sunset that had turned the sky into a breathtaking canvas of blue-gray pillows ribboned with rose.

"This place just keeps getting better."

With a hand resting on his son's shoulder, Hux Rawson surveyed the property, too. "If there's a more peaceful place on earth, I'd like to hear about it. Have you been to this part of the country before, Teagan?"

She eased her gaze away from Jacob's profile—that strong Roman nose and proud, jutting jaw. "To New York City," she replied, "but not upstate."

"Jacob mentioned that you live in Seattle."

"For a few years now."

"Is that an English accent?"

"Australian. I get back a couple of times a year. My father and some siblings live in Sydney." She added, "I'll be an aunt soon. My eldest brother was married last year."

Jacob's eyebrows shot up. "That's great news."

She held her smile. Nodded. "Yes it is."

"Children." The corners of Hux's eyes crinkled as he sighed and angled to rub the golden retriever's head. "Nothing brings a family closer. Your dad must be so proud."

Teagan wouldn't go into details, like how her aging father had a six-year-old and new baby all his own. But, yes, Guthrie would be happy to know he was going to be a grandfather. Hopefully soon he would be able to sit back and enjoy those aspects of his life without worrying that someone wanted him dead.

From the homestead's front doorway, another male voice joined in.

"Well now the party can begin!"

Ajax Rawson's build and gait were bronco busting. His grin was lopsided and the wink he sent Teagan was full of mischief. This was the fun-loving brother who, Teagan guessed, had a hard time fighting off the girls.

The brothers clasped each other's shoulders and shook hands. "This is a turnup for the books," Ajax told Jacob before adding an aside to Teagan. "He works a couple of hours' drive away, but decides to fly thousands of miles just to drop in for a Friday night feed."

Teagan laughed. "Last-minute arrangements."

Ajax gave his brother a playful nudge in the ribs. "You ought to take a gamble more often."

Hux was ushering everyone inside when he stopped to peer off into the distance. Teagan caught the sound then, too—galloping hooves beating the ground, growing louder. Closer. A jet-black horse thundered toward them. The rider was folded forward, yellow breeches raised in the saddle. A stream of dark hair flew behind her like a battle flag.

Lanie Rawson, Teagan thought, charging home to greet her brother, too.

While her horse was still skating to a stop, the young woman jumped off her ride and bolted up the steps, two at a time. Then she hurled herself into Jacob's arms with a force that swung them both around.

Lanie was Teagan's age. In her knee-high riding boots, she was the same height, too. That river of dark hair, with its abundance of natural curl, hung in a wind-beaten braid that

ended at the lowest dip of her back. Her energy reminded Teagan of a storm on the cusp, and too bad for anyone who wasn't holding on.

Jacob exclaimed, "What an entrance!" and Hux laughed. Ajax set his hands on either side of his belt buckle as his grin widened. There was so much energy…so much open, honest affection. It made Teagan all the happier for Jacob's situation. She was happy for them all.

But then the picture began to shift.

Lanie peeled herself away from Jacob while Teagan prepared herself for a friendly welcome—perhaps another hug. But the warmth that Lanie had showered upon Jacob seemed to evaporate the instant she laid eyes on her brother's guest. Her wide cornflower-blue gaze hardened. The pointed chin of her heart-shaped face edged higher. Then came her words of welcome, if anyone could call them that.

"So, *you're* what all this fuss is about?"

Teagan had inherited her parents' poise and self-confidence. She didn't normally allow situations to get under her skin. And yet now she felt stuck, wanting to gape. But no one else seemed to notice the goading tone or icy glint in the other woman's gaze. And they didn't comment when Lanie's attention zipped straight back to Jacob and Teagan was left hanging, regrouping…comparing.

This past year, the Hunters had welcomed three women into their family. Teagan had been happy that her brothers had found love, and she was stoked at the idea of having similar-aged "sisters" at long last. On the other hand, Eloise had been her regular hot 'n' cold self, especially when it came to other females. But Teagan had never let her stepmom's selfish personality rattle her. She simply kept memories of her real mother close and tried her best to get along for all their sakes.

Here and now, too, Teagan could have set aside those sinking feelings and concentrated on the pluses. Only one thing stopped her. Something she *couldn't* ignore.

As they went inside to enjoy a cool drink before washing up for dinner, Teagan knew to her bones that Lanie's leveling remark was just the beginning. From the way she held on to Jacob's arm, looking up at him with adoration in her eyes, clearly Lanie not only loved her brother very much, she was protective of him, too. And she viewed Teagan as a threat.

Which was ridiculous. Nonsensical.

Unless there was more to Lanie's feelings for Jacob... emotions that had grown way beyond the scope of an adopted brother and his younger sis.

Seven

Climbing the stairs to their room, which was tucked away in the far end of the stately Victorian's eastern wing, Jacob's thoughts were solely on Teagan. Should he be worried?

When she'd met the family, Teagan had seemed genuinely connected. Happy to be there. But when they'd gone in to talk some more, her tone changed. Teagan wasn't the effusive type. She was composed and in some ways reserved. But there was more to her current mood than that, he was certain.

As Jacob set down their bags, Teagan offered a small smile that he couldn't hope to decipher. If he had to put a caption beneath the expression, it would be: *Landed. Got Here. Next.*

And the way she was looking around the room reminded him of when she'd entered his hotel suite a week ago. Back then, her wariness had quickly thawed. Now? She looked like she wanted to run.

He'd learned his lesson. If something needed airing, sooner was way better than later. *The only approach was total transparency. Nothing but the truth.*

"Tea, is something wrong?"

She'd been studying a filigree-framed mirror hung over a side table. Now her gaze edged across to him.

"Nothing at all."

She wore a casual, flowing, floral dress that fit this rural setting, and her body, to perfection. Although she could never look anything other than poised, her jaw was tight, her pupils tellingly large.

Jacob slid his hands into his front jeans' pockets. "There's definitely something wrong."

"I'm a little tired. Long trip."

"You want to skip dinner?"

"After flying across the country?" She walked over to the other end of the room, which housed two couches, the TV and a bookshelf. "I'm having a second helping, thank you. Possibly even a third."

Looking out the window at the sunset draping the hills, she nodded to herself and then turned to face him.

"Your family is very special, Jacob."

It took a moment to smile. So she *did* like the Rawsons. Well, of course she did. Just for a minute there… But she'd said she was tired. Well, he could promise a relaxing weekend ahead.

"Every time I see Hux, I get that same *now I'm safe* feeling."

Teagan's smile deepened. "I get that feeling, too."

He joined her by the window, close enough for her to lean in if she wanted. But she only clasped her hands and returned her gaze to the rising moon.

"When was the last time you came to visit?" she asked.

"A couple of months back."

"You'd think it'd been years. They're so happy to see you." She caught his gaze. "Particularly Lanie."

He chuckled. "Over the top, right?"

"A little."

"Believe it or not, when she was young, Lanie was a wallflower with braces, skin problems, next to no meat on her bones. Back then she was waiting to grow into her nose and feet."

"She came out of the awkward stage pretty well."

"Oh, she's *beyond* confident now."

"And beautiful. Mesmerizing, in fact."

"Like watching a comet about to strike."

He laughed while Teagan's lips curved with an overly

polite smile. But she must have come across full-on types before. Hell, her own family had a surplus of fireballs. Researching for that lawsuit, he had learned that Wynn Hunter, for example, was an intense character—the kind of person everyone noticed and listened to.

Before flying to Seattle to take that gamble, Jacob had looked into Teagan's family some more. Dex, the middle brother who looked after the movie studio side of Hunter Enterprises in LA, had a playboy reputation, although he was engaged to be married now. The media had painted Cole, the oldest sibling and head of the Australian broadcasting arm, as a domineering hothead, which sounded very much like Guthrie Hunter, the father, back in the day. Recently the Hunter patriarch had retreated from the front lines, handing over the reins to his boys.

There had been some speculation over assassination attempts, too, which had been confirmed when a bomb had exploded at the Hunter family's estate in Sydney during the eldest son's recent wedding.

Jacob had stopped his research there. If Teagan wanted to open up about any of it, that was her choice. Her business. Right now they were discussing his family. Lanie in particular.

Yes indeed, that girl had changed.

"When Lanie was a teen, before I went to college, we would sit together by the main dam and talk about what the future might hold. I wanted to be a kick-ass lawyer, bringing down the bad guys one by one. She only wanted to ride horses and have a family."

Teagan leaned a shoulder against the window frame. "Your sister can certainly ride."

"In a saddle, she's fearless."

"And having a family of her own? Does she have a partner?"

Jacob thought back. Surely there'd been boyfriends, but now he couldn't put his finger on even one.

"I guess she hasn't found the right guy." He grinned as the memories came back. "When she was fifteen, sixteen, she used to joke around and say that one day, if no one else wanted us, we could marry each other."

"Really? And what did you say?"

"I punched her arm and said, 'Gross.' Then she laughed and said it back."

Gross.

"And what about you?"

"What about me?"

"Having a family of your own."

Jacob was caught between wanting to grin and giving her a look that said, *Seriously?* "You mean marriage? Kids?"

Wow. He was coming up with a blank there. Outside of the Rawsons, Jacob's career was his driving force, his focus.

"I've been busy building the firm. I mean, I haven't given it a lot of thought. It's a huge responsibility."

"The biggest."

"I had the worst kinds of role models." He could think of far better things to do than pass those genes on. In fact, he'd rather not have kids. "I don't want to screw anything up."

Like he didn't want to screw up with Teagan again. He had developed feelings for her in a very short span of time. But he wasn't anywhere near ready to think about exchanging vows. And, despite the conversation they were having now, he was sure Teagan wasn't, either.

She had everything going for her, most important, knowing who she was. She might want children of her own one day—he wouldn't be surprised—but she certainly didn't need to chase any guy down an aisle.

Taking her hands in his, he looked into her eyes and smiled. "I'm glad I took the chance and flew to Seattle."

Her gaze softened. "I am, too."

"You look amazing in that dress."

"Who needs an evening gown, right?"

He came near enough for the tips of their noses to touch. Then he slipped one arm around her back and tugged her that bit closer. "I wish there was some music."

"And a dance floor?"

"We could always make our own music."

She cringe-laughed. "Cliché alert!"

"It's not original?" He slowly tasted her lips. "I'm sure I hear violins."

Before his mouth could claim hers, something nudged the back of his knee. He swung around, saw the culprit and pretended to growl.

"Chester? How'd you get in here?"

While the retriever plonked down on his rear end, Jacob checked out the partly opened bedroom door—he must not have closed it properly—while Teagan squatted to the dog's height.

"We didn't get introduced, did we, fella?" When Chester put out his paw for a shake, Teagan turned to marshmallow. "You're not only gorgeous, you're polite."

Jacob hunkered down, too. "He could either be telling us that dinner's on the table or that he wants to camp out here for the night."

"I won't say no."

Teagan was running both hands over Chester's ears and jowls. Chester's expression said, *Love me and I promise to love you back.*

Jacob knew when he was licked.

He pushed to his feet. "While you and Casanova get better acquainted, please excuse me. I'm going to wash up."

He was about to enter the attached bathroom when Teagan called after him.

"Jacob, I really am glad I came."

Good. And when they retired later this evening, he would be locking the door. No interruptions—four-legged or any other type.

* * *

Teagan grew up understanding the power of money. She also knew good taste when she saw it. As she and Jacob entered the Rawsons' large dining room, she was impressed by the nineteenth-century Eastlake chandelier hanging from the vaulted ceiling and the sparkling vintage plates laid out upon a stunning raw-edge maple table.

At the same time Hux and Ajax waved them over to a matching maple wet bar, a set of swing doors on an adjacent wall pushed open and a woman appeared. She wore no makeup or jewelry. Her deep auburn hair was cut so that it swayed like a neat curtain an inch above her shoulders as she walked. Wearing a simple, dark blue linen dress, she exuded a sense of familiarity—or more accurately, a sense of *family*—particularly when she made a beeline for Teagan.

"I'm Susan Copeland." As she smiled, two dimples hijacked her cheeks. "I take care of the house."

"Our Susan does a lot more than that. She takes care of us all," Hux explained.

Susan's smile softened. "And they take care of me."

Teagan didn't miss the look the pair shared, or the way their fingers brushed as they stood side by side. Mrs. Rawson had passed away years ago. Teagan guessed that Susan had come onto the scene sometime after that and had found an ideal haven here, too.

Jacob dropped a kiss on Susan's cheek. "You look beautiful, as always."

Susan smiled at Jacob like a mother should smile at her son, with love and unbridled affection. "For that, you get a second helping of grape pie."

He smacked his lips. "I can smell it baking."

Teagan could, too. The aroma was sweet and delicious. Earlier Jacob had mentioned the district's best-known dessert. She couldn't wait to try it.

"Can I help with anything?" she asked Susan.

"Table's all set." Susan studied the silverware glinting in

the chandelier's light. "And Hux just finished carving the roast. So the dishes are ready to be brought out, if you'd like to lend a hand with that."

The men were already in a discussion about a multiprize-winning mare due to give birth that weekend. As Teagan followed Susan back through the doors to the kitchen, she heard Ajax mention an in-house veterinarian who was examining the expectant mother now.

The kitchen was very large, very clean—all polished, honeyed timber and high-quality stainless steel. And suddenly Teagan felt so hungry. The combined aromas of family dinner at the Rawsons were literally mouthwatering.

"Roast vegetables there," Susan said, crossing to the counter. "Pie's resting, ready to be sliced."

Beyond an expansive window, the rising moon had laced the hills with trails of silver. "What an amazing view," Teagan said, looking out over the land.

"It's a special time of day. So quiet and peaceful, like God himself is getting ready to tuck us all in." Susan joined her by the window. "I'd be happy never to leave this place. What more could a person wish for?"

"I don't think anyone here would *let* you leave."

Susan sighed. "Those boys are like my own. And Huxley is a wonderful father. So patient. Always willing to listen."

"He certainly listened to Jacob when he needed help."

When Susan tucked some hair behind her ear, one of two diamond earrings was revealed—a sizable yet elegant teardrop stud. A gift from Hux? Lucky woman.

"I remember the day we received that letter from young Jacob," Susan said, "asking if he could come back. Huxley knew the boy was telling the truth, that he wasn't involved in that robbery. And he had faith Jacob could turn his life around."

"Jacob still feels lucky to have you all behind him."

"I know exactly how he feels. When I arrived here, my life was in tatters." She hesitated before opening up more.

"I'd been married to a man who treated me like most people wouldn't treat a dog. I stayed because I thought I loved him. Because I thought I could *fix* him. The abuse only got worse. While he was out fishing one day, I packed a single bag and never looked back. When I heard about a job tending house on a quiet estate, I applied and came clean to Huxley about my story. He didn't judge. He never does."

Susan brought herself back from the memory and returned to the expansive center counter. "Have you known Jacob long?"

"We met last weekend."

Rather than look surprised, Susan gave her a bigger smile. "It must have been some weekend."

"It was…" *Incredible. Magical.* "Unexpected."

"Well, although it doesn't need to be said, you are both welcome here anytime, for as long as you'd like to stay. There's nothing better than the sound of family coming together, catching up." As if on cue, laughter seeped through under the doors and Susan sighed. "That has to be the best medicine in the world." She blinked and seemed to catch herself before that easy smile returned. "We'd better get this food out while it's hot."

They each collected a platter. When they rejoined the others, Lanie was there, too. As soon as Teagan laid eyes on Jacob's sister, all the warm feelings from her conversation with Susan iced over. And then she realized… Susan had said the boys were like her own but she hadn't mentioned Hux's daughter.

While Teagan and Susan set down the platters, Lanie didn't once look their way. She was too busy hanging off Jacob's every word, arm looped through his as if she wanted to yank him away. He was simply too wonderful to share.

Hux came straight over to pull out a chair. "Teagan, let's sit you here between Jacob and Lanie."

Lanie broke from her conversation with Jacob to breeze over.

"Dad, I'm sure our guest would like to sit next to you at the head of the table."

Hux looked pleased. "Well, fine by me."

Wearing a white dress with a halter neckline, open back and a billowing ruffled skirt that danced around her ankles—a thousand times different from her breeches and boots earlier—Lanie found her spot on the other side of Jacob while Susan took a chair next to Hux and Ajax.

After Hux said grace and people began serving themselves, Teagan joined in the discussion; they were still talking about the pregnant mare. Ajax was going to check on her as soon as dessert was cleared. Lanie didn't deliver a single word Teagan's way. In fact, she focused her full attention on Jacob.

Then pie was served and Lanie's MO not only changed, it ramped up, like a guillotine blade getting ready to fall.

This visit was back on track.

Jacob had sensed that something wasn't quite right with Teagan after she'd met his family. She'd seemed reserved. Almost irritated. Then Chester, in all his doggy glory, had wriggled onto the scene and Tea had reclaimed her spark. Over dinner, she'd been her usual self-assured self, enjoying the conversations and fitting in like Jacob had known she would.

Although he had felt a little awkward at times, it had nothing to do with his date for the weekend.

Seated on his other side, Lanie was eager to catch up. These days his adoptive sister was full-on, particularly when they hadn't seen each other for a while. Last time he'd visited, she'd been at the World Cup Dressage finals. So now she had plenty to say. And he really wanted to listen. Except he had a special guest to take care of.

He was neglecting Teagan.

The others were discussing two yearlings going up for

sale at Saratoga in August while Lanie was still filling him in on how well her current ride was performing.

"At the start of passage work," she was saying, "you don't want high cadence. You want to confirm the regularity. No uneven steps. Always regularity behind."

"Teagan had riding lessons," he replied, looking at Teagan, wanting to include her.

"Well, we should get you in a saddle while you're here, Teagan," Hux chimed in. "Over the years, Jacob's become quite the master."

"Hux means I haven't fallen off for a while," Jacob clarified.

"I don't have a lot of experience riding," Teagan said, "so maybe nothing too strenuous."

Ajax set down his beer. "Horse riding will give your muscles a good workout. Muscles you never knew you had."

"Teagan owns a gym in Seattle." Jacob added, "She's probably the fittest person here."

Lanie looked around him to study Teagan.

"How long have you owned the gym?" Susan asked, slicing the pie she'd set on the table. "I love Pilates classes."

"A few years now." Teagan leaned in and inhaled. "That smells so good."

"Teagan, you're originally from Australia?" Lanie asked.

Teagan looked around Jacob. "From Sydney. That's right."

"It's supposed to be a pretty little corner of the world." Lanie sighed. "Imagine growing up on an island in the middle of nowhere."

Teagan accepted a dessert plate. "Australia *is* an island. The biggest in the world. Actually, it's almost the size of the States, if you leave out Alaska."

"I didn't know that." Lanie waved away the plate Susan was offering. "I've always wanted to go down and visit."

"There are some amazing beaches and the Great Barrier Reef, of course. The Opera House, the Harbour Bridge—"

"And kangaroos." Lanie fell back in her chair. "They're so funny looking. Like a cross between a cow and a T. rex. They come across as so…"

"Cute?" Susan supplied.

Lanie exhaled. "Docile," she said.

Teagan cocked a brow. "Don't get too close to a big red. You're likely to get your ears boxed in."

"He can try," Lanie replied, slinging a fall of brunette hair over her shoulder. "I don't go down easily."

Jacob's hand tightened around his dessert spoon. His sister had her opinions. She wasn't shy about speaking up—or she wasn't shy *anymore*. But she wasn't normally defensive. So had he imagined that tone in her voice? What did Lanie have to be gripey about? She'd seemed okay a minute ago.

And then…

Well, it got bad.

Teagan and Susan had finished discussing a recipe for a sweet cherry-almond smoothie and Ajax asked for another slab of pie when Lanie leaned forward and set her elbows on the table.

"Your surname," she said while everyone else was scraping their pie plates. "Hunter, isn't it? Dad mentioned it."

"Nice strong name," Hux said, looking at his bowl like he wanted to run a finger around the edge.

"Hunter." Teagan nodded. "That's right."

"Any relation to Guthrie Hunter?"

"He's my father."

Hux paused. "I know that name."

"Of Hunter Enterprises," Lanie supplied. "Broadcasting in Australia, movies in LA. Print media in New York. Very influential. Money coming out of their—"

"Are you sure you don't want some pie, Lanie?" Susan asked.

Lanie smiled. "I'm good. Thanks."

Teagan finished her final mouthful before responding. "I don't have anything to do with that."

Lanie looked taken aback. "You don't have anything to do with your family?"

Jacob spoke up. "Teagan didn't say that "

"I remember catching something on a feed a few months ago," Lanie went on. "A little before Christmas. Is it true?"

Teagan looked calm. Unperturbed. "Is what true?"

"A bomb went off in your father's Sydney mansion."

Hux's head went back and Susan's eyebrows shot up.

Even Ajax's gaze snapped up from his plate. "A bomb?"

Lanie was nodding. "I hope no one was hurt."

Jacob found Teagan's hand under the table and squeezed. He wanted to give Lanie the benefit of the doubt. She was curious. But it wasn't so much the topic as the tone.

If Griff and Ajax were his best friends, Lanie was a confidante. Like he'd told Teagan earlier, this brother and sister had a special relationship. But now Lanie needed to back off.

Teagan was responding. "It was a difficult time. Thanks for asking."

"And there was something else," Lanie added, "about death threats against your father..."

Before Jacob could intervene, Susan pushed to her feet and cut in. "I'm going to put the ice cream back in the freezer before it melts."

Jacob was looking at Lanie. What was the deal? It was like she was sixteen again—awkward, overly sensitive. Was there something she needed to get off her chest? Maybe to do with her horses. Maybe to do with a boy. Or should he say *man*? She wasn't a kid anymore, even with her arms folded tight on the table looking like she wanted to break loose.

Like he must've looked fifteen years ago.

Ajax was answering a text he'd just received. "Sorry, guys. I need to head out."

Hux sat straighter. "The mare's foaling?"

Ajax pushed back his chair. "Her water just broke." About to dash out the door, he stopped to study Teagan.

Beneath the light, his blue eyes twinkled. "Would you like to see a foal being born?"

Teagan blinked several times before an uncertain smile caught her lips. "The mare won't mind?"

"We'll be quiet."

Ajax wasn't joking.

Jacob took Teagan's hand and was following Hux and Ajax out the door—the foaling stalls were within walking distance—when he remembered Lanie. Glancing back, he narrowed his eyes at her in warning. She had some serious explaining to do.

Ignoring his look, Lanie got to her feet to help Susan clear the table. She had seen her fair share of mares giving birth, but if you hadn't witnessed it before, the experience was something to remember.

But, of course, there were times when something went wrong.

Heading down the porch steps, Ajax's smile was a little strained. "Shake a leg, guys. We don't have much time."

Eight

Teagan hadn't bargained for this. Lanie Rawson's barrage of questions and put-downs at the dinner table was pressure enough. Now she was about to see a mother give birth?

As Jacob took her hand and they followed Hux and Ajax to a large foaling barn, Teagan hoped no one could tell that her stomach was tied up in knots. She shouldn't be so nervous about a natural process. How many births were there every day, every year? But as those barn doors drew closer and she squeezed Jacob's hand harder, Teagan was well aware that things didn't always go according to plan.

Whenever she remembered her miscarriage, every minute played out seamlessly in her mind. More than anything, she remembered the aching sense of loss. Entering the barn now, with the vet quietly waving them over, those memories resurfaced with a vengeance.

She took in the scent of fresh hay and spread of gentle light as they approached a middle stall that was free of clutter—just a clean bed of straw. Her coat shining with sweat, a pregnant mare was plodding around the enclosure, constantly swishing her tail. While Teagan and Jacob sat on a bench that gave a clear view into the stall, Hux and Ajax waited near the railing.

Eventually the mare stopped pacing and lay down.

Sitting forward, Teagan concentrated on the mare's movements—rolling around then sitting up to look at her stomach while Tea continued to hold onto hers.

"She must want this over."

"As long as the foal is in position," Jacob said, "front legs forward, nose in between—it should be relatively fast."

Teagan frowned. "*If* the foal's in position?"

"The vet would have checked."

When Teagan blew out a shaky breath, Jacob put his arm around her and pulled her close. As the mare began to breathe more heavily, she lay flat on her side. When the vet crouched down and shifted her tail, Teagan saw the foal—its front legs, at least—wrapped in an opaque bag, the amniotic sac.

Soon the mare's snorting became more like groans, almost human. Rhythmic, laboring, like she needed this done. The vet was holding—maybe pulling—the foal's front legs while repeating, "Good girl, good girl." But nothing more seemed to be happening.

Finally, there was a rush. The foal's head emerged, followed by the body. Teagan and Jacob got to their feet as the foal's front hooves broke through the sac and its two hind legs were delivered. Teagan could see the new baby's heart beating while the mare lay spent. Happy. Relieved.

She wasn't the only one.

Jacob watched her sleep.

Stroking Teagan's hair, listening to her breathe…this "morning after the night before" was even better than the first time. And not because of the sex. After witnessing the birth of that foal, they had returned to this room, shed their clothes and, aside from cuddling, that was it.

In a week he'd gone from being smitten with Teagan to feeling different…feeling so much more, and to the point of now asking himself a serious question.

Could this really go somewhere?

Could this be it?

She stirred, an unconscious lifting of her chin and rounding of a bare shoulder. As he smiled and waited, her eyelids fluttered, then opened. There was the moment of "Where am I?" before she focused and hit him with a croaky question.

"The foal…?"

"Is doing great. I just got back from speaking with Ajax and Hux."

She pushed hair from her brow and looked toward the window. "What time is it?"

"Time for this."

When his mouth lowered over hers, she hummed in her throat, stretched and then arched in against him, curving a languid arm around his neck.

Of course Jacob had been with women before. Only one had come close to stealing his heart. The end of that relationship had left him feeling like he'd been kicked in the teeth. It had put him off wanting that kind of connection again.

Then he'd gone to that wedding in LA.

When he gradually broke the kiss, Teagan gave him a dreamy *I want you, too* smile.

"Can we see them today?"

Jacob recalibrated his thoughts. She meant the mare and her colt. "You bet. The little guy's walking around. The star on his head's really showing up now."

"Has he got a name?"

"Not yet."

"And when does the father get to meet his boy?"

The question took Jacob by surprise. "Not anytime soon, I'm afraid."

"You mean like in a couple of weeks when he's stronger?"

"A stallion is very much an instinctive, territorial creature. Even when a horse is definitely the father of a foal, sometimes, for whatever reason, he isn't sure."

Teagan looked confused. How could he put this delicately?

"Let's just say that studs don't like competition. It's best not to introduce a stallion to any foal, including their own."

Teagan's expression deepened, and then twisted. "You're saying he might try to hurt his own blood?"

"It can happen. And when it does—when a stallion isn't sure—it's purely about looking after the gene pool. It happens among other species, too. Zebras...well, they're closely related to horses, of course. Some monkeys, bears, bats, lions—"

"Panthers?"

"I'm not sure about that."

It hurt to think about, but there were cases of humans doing it, too.

Hell, maybe that was why the old man hadn't lifted a finger to help him grow up. Jacob remembered Stanley calling him a bastard more than once. Maybe the insults had a more primitive motivation. Maybe he was some other man's biological son.

Just fine by him.

Jacob edged the conversation onto a more pleasant and imminent topic. "I'm going to whip us up some pancakes."

She obviously was ready to drop the subject, too. "Pancakes sound great. Lots of syrup."

"Maybe I should bring breakfast back up here." Leaning in, he brushed his lips over hers. "Including the syrup."

"That might be awkward."

"I won't spill a drop." His lips lingered on hers. "And if I do—"

"I mean your family will think we're up to something."

"Like kissing and stuff? Heaven forbid."

She grinned. "You remind me of Dex."

"Your brother?"

"He likes to think he's funny. And he's a bit of a charmer, too."

"I'll take that as a compliment."

"You *should*. You two would get along." She winced and added, "Or maybe not."

He read between the lines. "Because of the lawsuit against Wynn. That's not happening now, remember?"

"You're sure about that?"

"My client said to drop the whole bloody thing, quote, unquote. No one ever needs to know."

"My family is very well connected, Jacob. My father and brothers have people who keep them informed about all kinds of things, including potential legal threats."

He got that. And perhaps news of Howcroft's shelved defamation case against Hunter Enterprises would leak. Hell, the fighter in him almost prayed that it would. Give them something to worry about other than how to spend their billions.

His tone was dry. "Being part of the elite does have its drawbacks, I suppose."

"Like constantly needing to watch your back."

He hesitated.

"You're talking about physical threats now." The assassination attempts on her father's life.

"Not fun," she concluded. "Particularly for the little ones."

Meaning Teagan's two much younger siblings.

"What your family is going through on that front … I wouldn't wish it on anyone. But my beef with your brother was professional, not personal."

"Somehow I don't think Wynn would see it that way."

He shifted up onto an elbow. "And how do you see it, Tea? Do you really think I'm a greedy predator or someone trying to keep the scales of justice aligned? A person simply believing in and doing their job."

"I think I'd like to see you perform in front of a jury. You're very persuasive." Her lips twitched. "But you already know that."

That was a cue if ever he'd heard one.

He was about to kiss her again, and to hell with dead lawsuits or pancakes, when his phone beeped. He'd check the message later. But the sound shifted Teagan out of her playful mood. Next time they were alone, he'd turn the damn phone off.

She pulled away. "We aren't going to get sidetracked."

When she got to her feet, his gaze swept over her naked body and he groaned. "That's not helping."

She grabbed a pillow and hid what she could. "Better?"

"It would be better if you came back here."

When he scrambled to grab her, Teagan trotted off toward the bathroom. The pillow might have covered her front, but her bare behind was in full heart-stopping view. Then the door closed and Jacob let out a breath.

He could really use a distraction about now.

He found his phone. A voice mail was waiting. When he recognized the number, he shut his eyes and growled.

What the hell did Ivy Schluter want? Not that he cared. Especially this weekend. Especially *now*. He ought to delete the message without listening.

Except he was a *cross all the Ts* type of guy. He'd listen, *then* he'd delete.

Only the message wasn't anything he could have expected. It might as well have been that a meteor had crash landed at his feet. Or a brick wall was falling on his head.

"We need to meet," the message said. *"It's about us, Jacob. About our child."*

Nine

Jacob scribbled a note for Teagan and left it on the coffee table.

Back soon.
J. XO.

Then he strode out the door knowing exactly where he was headed and whom he needed to see. Not Hux. Yes, his adoptive father would absolutely sit and listen. He always did. Undoubtedly he would offer advice and Jacob knew it would be sound.

But at this stage he only wanted to vent. Get it out. Quite possibly hit something. Ivy leaving a message that referred to "our child" was beyond insane. It had to be the biggest crock ever.

Had to be.

Jacob found Ajax in the stud farm office going over contracts.

"Hey, bro. Your girl ready to pay that new colt a visit?" Ajax put down the papers and sauntered over, a satisfied grin on his face. "She was pretty blown away by it all. I remember the first time I saw a foal come into the world—" Ajax's brow pinched together. "Man, you look *pissed*. Did you two have a fight?"

"No fight. And I don't know what I'm feeling, but anger would have to be up there."

"You want a coffee?"

"Only if it's too early for Scotch."

Ajax was already pouring two cups, setting them up in

the sitting area near a set of sliding-glass doors that over-looked the biggest arena. A gray was having trouble settling down—shaking his head, rearing up, hitting back.

"I heard from Ivy this morning."

Ajax's eyes rounded. "Did you tell her to have a nice life and leave you the hell alone?"

"It's more complicated than that."

Ajax finished swallowing a big mouthful of coffee. "Look, no one wants bad karma. Couples split up. It's so much better if there're no hard feelings. No…clinging. But you don't need to play games with that woman. Do not reply. That breakup was utterly—"

He ended with a nasty expletive with which Jacob whole-heartedly agreed.

The breakup. Jacob remembered it well.

First, Ivy's Lhasa apso had come down with a fungal complaint, which, she said, would take up every available speck of her time and emotional energy. A couple of weeks after that, she'd sent a CD with the song that had been play-ing when they'd first met at a fancy charity do. The hand-crafted CD cover read "Let's Press Replay."

There were three months of "getting better all the time" and then, right before a planned vacation to Sweden's archi-pelagos, because that was Ivy's favorite place in June, she'd sent a friend over to his office to say she was pulling out. When she wouldn't pick up her phone, he'd gone straight to her apartment. She'd spoken to him via the intercom. The general gist was, "Why are you bothering me? Goodbye for good." He'd punched the panel a couple of times before getting himself together. There had been no further contact until now. Until this.

Jacob put his head in his hands and took a few deep breaths. He felt his brother's hand patting and rubbing his back.

"It's really shaken you up."

"Jax, apparently I'm a father."

His brother frowned and then blinked. When comprehension finally hit, he jolted and slopped coffee all over the place.

"A father? Since when? You guys broke up a freaking year ago."

"The baby would have to be three or four months old. Or more."

"How do you feel about it? Other than being livid knowing that she should have told you way sooner than this."

"I feel… I don't know. Numb? Surreal?" Jacob cupped his hands around his mouth and breathed in and out. He'd never had a panic attack but now seemed the perfect time to start.

"I can't believe it, you know. We always used protection. I understand that nothing is one hundred percent safe…"

"Have you stopped to think that it might not be yours?"

"Of course I have. Then I thought, why the hell would anybody do that? Even Ivy."

Ajax's shoulders squared. "Straight off the bat, you need to have that checked out, not only for your sake but for the child's."

"Absolutely."

And if he *was* this baby's daddy, of course he would step up. If he wasn't… He'd have dodged a mighty big bullet. He pitied anyone who had to coparent with someone like Ivy Schluter.

But right now…

"How do I tell Teagan?"

Ajax's grin was lopsided. "You like her a lot."

"A *lot* a lot."

"Hold back. Ivy could be playing another one of her games." He pulled a face like he'd sucked a rotten grapefruit. "That woman is so superficial. I have no problem with people coming from money, but it grates when they need to let everyone know. I'm pretty sure Ivy's the type to have her own professional picture hanger and kidnap in-

surance." Ajax put his boots up on the end of the table and threaded his fingers behind his head, his favorite thinking posture. "She never asked you to meet her folks, did she? We all met *her*."

"It didn't seem like a big deal at the time."

"If a girl doesn't want you to meet her family, she's not serious." Ajax's lip curled. "Ivy was *never* serious."

"She was serious enough to have my child."

Ajax grunted. *We'll see.* "So, a boy or a girl?"

"She didn't say. Doesn't matter. He or she will need my support."

"Money and the other kind. The most *important* kind."

Acceptance and buckets of love. Given his own history, Jacob was determined to let this child know he was anything but a burden.

If this child is mine.

Ajax circled back to Jacob's question. "So, breaking the news to Teagan…" He wrinkled his hawkish nose. "Seriously, don't say anything yet."

"I can't act like nothing's happened." Jacob told Ajax about the mix-up when he and Teagan had both guessed that the man he had wanted to take to court and her brother were the same.

Jacob nodded. "It's going to be hard." *Maybe even fatal.* "But I won't hold anything back from her. Not again."

Teagan had finished showering and was reading Jacob's note when her phone pinged. It was a message from Grace Munroe. Apparently, Grace *Hunter* as of this week.

Tea, your wonderful brother and I have tied the knot! We both agreed that small was better. No stress and more time for the honeymoon. Which brings me to… We're visiting your family on our way back from Italy. (Doesn't Venice sound like the ideal honeymoon escape?) If you could

make it, Wynn and I would love to see you in Sydney. Will video call as soon as we have more deets. XOXO

The friends hadn't seen each other since Taryn and Cole's wedding last year. The start of that day had been as magical as the end—the explosion—had been horrific. Then stepmom Eloise had gone into labor. Around the same time, Guthrie had learned that his young wife had put the moves on his oldest son.

There was just no way to get your head around that.

In the new year, back in Seattle, Teagan had gone through her own crisis—the miscarriage. Although she was the one to end the relationship, once Damon Barringer had discovered her reason, he hadn't put up a fight.

Now, months later, she was seeing someone new. A man her family would happily shun once the truth about that lawsuit came out. Jacob's ability to argue a point wouldn't make a scrap of difference where Wynn was concerned. Not that she had ever considered introducing them. The thought had never entered her head. Or not seriously.

Until now.

Setting aside Grace's invitation and the phone, Teagan slipped into a pair of three-quarter-length pants, a sleeveless shirt and gym shoes. While she ran a brush through her hair, she wondered more. Her relationship with Jacob certainly hadn't traveled a conventional route. She'd been ready to say goodbye after their night, and morning, together in LA. But that misunderstanding surrounding his "family sucks" comment had been cleared up. And now she couldn't deny she wasn't unhappy that Jacob had pursued her. He'd pulled out all the stops to make this weekend happen, and she had enjoyed meeting his family...minus Lanie, of course. The chemistry she and Jacob shared was something she had never experienced before, even with Damon, a man she had adored.

She hadn't invited Damon to Cole and Taryn's wed-

ding; she hadn't been able to see a future for them together. Damon came from a big family, and one of his biggest priorities was having one of his own. After her home pregnancy test, there'd been a brief window of time when she had begun to believe it was possible. But after the miscarriage, when doctors had confirmed any subsequent (unlikely) pregnancies would fail in the first trimester, she and Damon had talked. They'd touched on the surrogacy option. He wasn't convinced; too many risks and complications. When adoption was brought up, despite the brave face, he had obviously wanted more.

Teagan didn't know how Jacob felt about being a parent. Frankly, this minute, she didn't want to think about it. Wasn't it enough to simply enjoy this time they had together?

Her brothers were all settled with lifelong partners. She would like to have someone special at her side this coming family visit, too. And as dangerous as it might sound, regardless of the risks, she would love for that someone to be Jacob.

When she turned and saw the unmade bed, her insides fluttered with longing. She and Jacob hadn't made love the previous night. After watching the birth of that foal, she'd preferred to simply curl up and soak in his heat before dropping off to sleep. But she was looking forward to being alone with him tonight. Heck, she was looking forward to seeing Jacob walk back through that door.

On cue, the door fanned open and Teagan felt the *zap*. Tall and built, Jacob looked so sexy in jeans and a button-down shirt, especially with that wedge of throat and chest visible at his open collar. With morning light slicing in through the window, his amber eyes were narrowed and even more intense.

He crossed over to her and, without a word, clasped her shoulders and drew her in for a kiss that reduced her to a steamy mess. Apparently he'd missed her, too.

When he broke the kiss, she gripped his shirt and pulled him close again.

"Where'd you go?"

"To see Ajax."

"Oh, yeah. How come?"

Jacob's gaze followed his hand as he pushed hair away from her cheek. "I was probably gone too long."

"You weren't gone too long." She fanned her palms over the hard, hot expanse of his chest. "But I'm happy you're back."

"I'm happy you're happy."

Something different in his eyes made her stop and look deeper. What had he and Ajax discussed? Family stuff, no doubt. His business, not hers. But she did have some news of her own to share.

"A text came in while you were out. Wynn and Grace got married on the quiet. They're visiting Sydney soon to celebrate with family. They asked if I could fly out."

He nodded. Shrugged. "Of course."

Teagan paused. Was it imagination or was he acting low-key weird, like he wasn't certain what to say or where to look? Did the mention of Wynn make him feel awkward? It shouldn't. Earlier he'd said that his conflict with her brother was professional, not personal.

She took a step back. "It'll probably be in a couple of weeks. I'm really looking forward to seeing everyone again."

"Right." His eyes glazed over. "Family is important. Is everything."

A chill raced up Teagan's spine. What the hell had happened since he'd left her earlier? He'd seen Ajax. Had he spoken to Lanie, too?

Teagan crossed her arms. She had wondered about inviting him to Australia. Now she wanted to put it out there just to get his reaction.

"Would you like to join me?"

He blinked and then frowned. "Join you where?"

"In Sydney. You could meet everyone. They could meet you."

When he only looked at her—or rather *through* her—she felt that chill again.

She held his arm. "For God's sake, Jacob, what's wrong?"

He shut his eyes tight, rubbed his brow. "I received a message this morning, too. It was from my ex. Ivy and I broke up a year ago. I almost deleted the message sight unseen. But she had something to share...about family."

"Is someone ill?" He shook his head. "Passed away?"

"There's been a birth."

"So...congratulations."

"That's pretty much how she ended the message."

"I don't understand."

But the strain bracing his jaw, the stormy depth in his gaze...

Suddenly all the blood fell from Teagan's head to the soles of her feet.

Jacob and this woman had broken up a year ago, there'd been a birth, and the ex was passing on her congratulations...

"Your ex had a baby?"

"Apparently so."

"*Your* baby, Jacob?"

"That's what she said."

Teagan waited for the buzzing in her brain to subside. Then, feeling unsteady, she took a seat on the edge of the mattress. *That's what she said.*

Teagan pinned him with a look. "You think she's lying?"

"I didn't say that."

"Have you called her?"

"I'll wait till Monday."

What the...? "You can't wait that long."

He was pacing to the window and back again. "Crazy, but I'd have liked a little more time to prepare."

At the risk of sounding entirely selfish, so did *she*.

Her chest felt so tight. The backs of her eyes were burning. She had taken a chance and accepted an invitation to spend the weekend with a man she barely knew. It turned out she knew far less than she could ever have imagined.

She got to her feet, got a grip. The situation called for civility, but she deserved some answers.

"Why did you break up?"

"I think she got bored. I was cut up about it at the time. But Ivy and I were never going to make it. She comes from big money. A *huge* sense of entitlement."

Teagan bristled. "Wealth doesn't *always* mean a sense of entitlement." Case in point.

Jacob was so preoccupied, her last remark didn't seem to register.

"I spoke to Ajax about it," he said. "We couldn't work out why she hadn't contacted me sooner."

"Maybe she was afraid. Maybe she'd only just worked up the courage to tell you."

"I don't think Ivy's afraid of anything."

Okay. "Maybe she wanted to bring the child up herself."

"Why? I'm not some *creep*. If he's mine, of course I'm gonna look after him."

Teagan paused. There was that Brooklyn accent again.

He was pacing again, talking to himself more than to her. "Obviously, I need to make sure the baby is mine."

"Would this woman lie about something like that?"

"She could've gotten the dates mixed up. In which case, not my baby. Not my problem."

Teagan flinched.

Jacob's world had been flipped on its head. He needed time, and he needed it without distractions. And, from her end, she needed to get out of there—the sooner, the better.

"Jacob, we need to cut this weekend short."

He shot a glance at her like he wanted to disagree. But

then his shoulders drooped and he walked to the window again. Finally, he nodded.

"Bad timing."

As upset as she was, Teagan wanted to comfort him. But her thoughts were suddenly so crowded. She was thinking about little Tate and Honey, and her miscarriage, as well as Ivy's new baby. And she was thinking about that foal's father, too—a powerful, instinctive male who couldn't necessarily be trusted to bond with his own spawn.

Ten

Taking a seat behind her office desk, Teagan patted her postworkout face with a towel as she brought up emails.

Ah. A confirmation from the travel agent. And Grace had sent word that she and Wynn had landed in Australia. Her own flight was due to depart Sea-Tac later that evening. *Home, sweet home, here I come.*

She couldn't wait to raise a glass to the newlyweds. The second toast she had planned would be just as thrilling—to Cole and Taryn on their baby news. She needed to see and hug her dad again. She was desperate for a cuddle from her darling Tate, and her heart ached to hold little Honey. The latest addition to the Hunter clan was six months old now.

Not much older than Jacob Stone's child.

If the baby was indeed his.

After cutting short their weekend at the Rawsons', Jacob had phoned from New York. They'd reminisced over details of their trip, particularly the birth of the foal. Then he'd apologized again for "screwing it up." He'd gone on to say that he'd set up a meeting with the ex to ask some initial questions. In closing, he'd said how much he missed Teagan…that he couldn't wait to see her. He had promised to phone again soon.

Jacob's second call had been brief. The meeting with the ex had been delayed. Prickly Ivy was trying his patience. He'd sounded on edge.

That was three weeks ago.

Closing her eyes, Teagan sat back and drew her palm across the raised scar beneath her sweat-damp top. There were so many questions.

Was Jacob the father of Ivy Schluter's baby? Given the lapse between phone calls, Teagan guessed probably yes. Would Jacob marry Ivy for the baby's sake? Perhaps, if he thought that would give his child the stable home life he had never enjoyed growing up.

If Jacob called again, how would she react? Hopefully with grace, although she had fantasized about hanging up in his ear. He'd left her hanging. Just plain rude.

And then there was the most obscure and haunting question...the one that spoke directly to her miscarriage and she couldn't seem to drown out.

Had Ivy been pregnant before? Had she ever lost a baby?

These last few months Teagan had pored over stories of others who had suffered similar losses to her own. Even after multiple miscarriages, which weren't at all uncommon, many rallied to try and try again. Teagan had nothing but respect for those women and their partners. She could never face that kind of heartache twice, let alone a third, fourth or fifth time.

Hitting Print on the email containing her flight information, she thought of Jacob again. Their short time together had been amazing, but now she hoped he wouldn't try to contact her again. She didn't need apologies and the *thanks for being so understanding* treatment. She only wanted to be left alone to concentrate on her own life and what she *did* have, which included a growing family...just not a family of her own.

The restaurant accepted bookings three weeks in advance, which was why she had needed to postpone their meeting. The new chef was the crème de la crème, Ivy had said. The patrons here of a similar ilk.

Oh, puh-leeze.

Now as the maître d' ushered Jacob to a booth, he made an effort to push all that crap from his mind. But he couldn't block out the name Ivy had chosen for her boy. Benson

Rockwell. Sounded like a character from a vomit-inducing rom-com. And that was the last time he would think that way. This kid needed to know that everything about him was amazing, including his handle. He could totally work with Benson… Ben, Benny.

How about Buddy?

Now *that* was a cool name.

As Jacob neared the table, Ivy saw him and sat up, preening in her white silk blouse. She was as beautiful as he remembered, although the copper-colored hair wasn't quiet as styled and her makeup lacked her former meticulous technique. But being a new mother would mean cutting back on "Ivy time," even with a nanny and laundry service. Jacob imagined her parents would help out, too, which he appreciated.

He guessed he'd finally get to meet the family.

As he drew closer, Jacob dragged his damp palms down the sides of his pants. There was no baby stroller around, and Ivy wasn't holding a baby, either. Perhaps Buddy was lying or sitting on the cushioned seat beside her. Then Jacob got closer.

*Un*freaking*believable.*

Jaw clenched tight, Jacob rubbed the back of his neck. "You didn't bring him, did you?"

Ivy's spider-leg lashes grew heavy. *Bor-ring.* "This isn't your local pizzeria, Jacob."

Jacob felt his lip curl. He should tell her that *he* would choose the venue next time. Walking out would feel even better. But that baby deserved at least one rational parent.

So he took a seat, cleared his throat. With fingers locked together on the tabletop, he proceeded in a calm and mature manner.

"Ivy. We agreed. You said you would bring him."

Looking innocent—or trying to—she swirled her creamy mocktail. That was one thing he could rest easy about. Ivy

had her faults, but she wasn't a lush. And she would never do drugs.

"I thought we could talk more easily without having to soothe him every five minutes."

Jacob frowned. "He needs a lot of soothing?"

She brought the straw to her painted lips. "No more than other babies, I suppose."

"Do you have any photos?"

He had held off asking. It made no sense to drive himself crazy comparing noses and eyes, searching for signs that junior looked like his old man. And he'd had *every* intention of having a paternity test performed by now. Why get emotionally invested, analyze baby pictures, if the point was moot? But days and weeks of no contact had crawled by. Now, damn it, he needed a visual.

Setting the glass aside, Ivy dawdled, finally finding her phone. While Jacob clasped his hands tighter, he watched the inch-long acrylic nail tip swipe, and swipe, and swipe again. Finally, she handed the device over.

The album contained shots of a newborn with mom at the hospital, one in a car capsule, another being held by a woman who looked besotted and a little worn.

"Who's that?"

Ivy glanced at the screen. "Mother. *Granma.*"

Jacob looked harder. Holy crap. She was kidding, right? But there wasn't a hint of humor in Ivy's icy-green gaze.

"Mom knows practically everything about diaper rash and colic."

"He has colic?" Wasn't that when a baby cried and hurled all the time?

"He's over it now." Ivy shuddered. "Never going through *that* again."

And the woman—Granma—that *couldn't* be Ivy's mother. Where was the privileged air and haute-couture outfit? She looked like someone's eccentric great-aunt. But one should never judge a book by its cover. And if Ivy's

mother was…well, *reserved* in her desire to appear privileged, it kind of made sense that her daughter might rebel
and flaunt it every chance she got.

Ivy was tapping that fake fingernail on the table like,
Enough with the small talk already. "We need to discuss
child support."

He handed the phone back. "And visitation."

"Thoughts?"

"I'd like every other weekend."

She looked severely underwhelmed.

"And we need to organize that paternity test," he told
her again, like he had during all their phone conversations.
"They're accurate. Ninety-nine point nine-nine percent on
a positive match. Zero if it's negative."

"Well, he's got your eyes."

Jacob snatched back the phone. "He does?"

"They were blue at first but going brownish now."

Brownish? Teagan said his eyes were amber-gold. She
said she'd never met anyone with eyes like his.

He couldn't count the times he'd debated calling Teagan
these past weeks. He remembered how his body had reacted
whenever they'd made love…how good it had felt to simply
watch her sleep. He wanted to move forward with the relationship, but that couldn't happen until *this* situation was
sorted. When he spoke to Teagan next, he wanted to have
all the answers as well as a plan.

And the first step, damn it, was that *test*.

"I've been in touch with a reputable professional," he
said while Ivy collected her menu and scanned the appe-
tizers. "The sooner we get that out of the way, the better.
Don't you agree?"

"Uh-huh." She turned the page. "The sooner, the better."

His temples began to throb. Steam was rising from
around his collar.

"For God's sake, Ivy, this isn't a game."

"Of course it's not a game." She slapped down the menu.

"That's insulting, Jacob. It's insulting to *Benson*. If you don't want to take care of your own son, just tell me now."

His gut twisted so sharply, he groaned. "I would never try to run away from my responsibility." Never in a million years.

Looking into his eyes, she slanted her head, exhaled and then reached for his hand. When her fingers curled around it and her nails dug in, he wanted to pull away. He didn't need this contact. With or without a baby, that boat had sailed long ago.

He hoped that his expression said it all.

We're a team in this, but not "together."

Then he slid his hand from beneath hers.

Sitting back, Ivy returned her attention to the menu. She tapped on an item. "I need to try the duck liver crème brûlée," she said. "Definitely the hazelnut soufflé for dessert."

Eleven

"Sorry I didn't call sooner."

Teagan wanted to laugh. As if those words were in any way near good enough.

"I guess you've been busy," she replied, gazing, unseeing, from the back seat of a cab on her way from Sydney Airport to her father's house.

"I didn't want to phone until there'd been some movement," he said. "I just got back from giving a sample for a paternity test."

Teagan's stomach muscles twisted. She'd been making headway getting over Jacob Stone, pushing him plum out of her mind. What had begun with a bang had run out of gas and ultimately died. As far as his paternity test was concerned? *Good luck.*

And goodbye.

"Teagan?"

She didn't want to talk. She wanted to hang up then calmly pitch her phone out the window so he couldn't call again.

His voice in her ear was low and rich.

"Tea, I don't blame you for being angry."

"I am not *angry.*"

She wouldn't allow herself to be. She was simply a tad busy herself now. After her flight had touched down ahead of time, she had called Wynn to say to expect her soon. Her brother had said he'd be there in thirty minutes to collect her. But as she had told Jacob, she was a big girl. She could deal on her own, and had hailed a cab.

"Ivy's being Ivy," Jacob was saying.

Sorry. Not interested. But she let him get it all out—the story behind finally meeting with the ex and how she hadn't brought the baby along as agreed. He'd seen photos, though. It was a boy. Benson. Lovely name. Not that Teagan's opinion mattered one bit.

And as the rehash went on, Teagan's grip on the phone tightened. This conversation brought back memories she didn't need now...the excitement of seeing those pink lines form on the stick from the home pregnancy kit...the bliss of anticipating sonogram images, hearing first words, seeing first steps.

Jacob had come full circle. He was back on the paternity test now.

"The results will take anywhere from a few days to three weeks."

The cab was nearing her street. She wanted to be focused—*happy*—when she saw everyone again.

"Teagan? Are you there?"

"Uh-huh. Needing to cut this short, though."

And then the cab pulled into the driveway and, in the distance, the Hunter mansion came into view, a huge, white structure set in an idyllic leafy enclave. The understanding hit her like a medicine ball to the gut.

God, I'm glad to be home.

"I'll call later," Jacob said.

As a security man opened the electronic gates, Teagan swallowed against the ache that had grown to the size of a peach in her throat. "I'm tied up for a week or two. So... good luck with it all."

He hesitated before grunting.

"Wow."

She frowned. "*Wow* what?"

"Nothing."

She pulled the phone away from her ear. Time to hang up. But then she caught his next words.

"Tea, a bomb exploded in my life and I'm still sorting through the pieces."

The cab was rolling down the drive, past the area where last year's wedding marquee had stood…the place where the blast had gone off and precious lives had almost been lost.

"I know I left you hanging," he went on.

She pressed her lips together as tears stung behind her eyes.

"I need to go."

"We can't do this over the phone," he said. "We need to talk face-to-face."

She was gripping the door handle, needing to get out. "Not possible."

"I'll fly over."

He thought she was in Seattle. "You'd need to add another twenty thousand miles to the trip. I'm in Australia." Before he could interrupt, she wrapped it up. "We had a nice time." The absolute best of her life. "But it was two nights followed by two phone calls. We don't owe each other anything."

As the cab approached the front doors, she heard him exhale.

"How long are you out of the country?"

"A week. Maybe longer." She closed her stinging eyes. Why was she even telling him this?

"I'm coming over," he said.

She coughed out a laugh. "No, you are not."

"I should have called sooner."

"You already said that."

"You wanted me to meet your family."

"That was before—"

"Before I was a plus one?"

Did he mean the baby?

She withered, shook her head and murmured, "That's not it."

"Tea, I want to see you. I need to *hold* you. A few hours on a plane…"

She didn't respond. That ache in her throat was so big now, she didn't know whether she could.

He asked her, "Did I read us wrong?"

"You weren't reading anything wrong three weeks ago," she told him as the cab pulled up. "We don't have anything more to say."

Long pause, then…

"Okay."

She breathed out. *Finally*. "Okay."

"You have a great time with everyone."

She would. And she was going to hang up.

Damn it, she wasn't being a bitch.

Still, she had to add, "This isn't going anywhere."

"Okay."

"Anyway… I can't just tell everyone that you're coming over out of the blue. They have no idea I was seeing someone."

"Okay."

"Stop *saying* that," she snapped.

"Okay." When she growled again, he chuckled. Then, "No. Really. I understand."

She held her roiling stomach and closed her eyes. "No, you don't understand." There was so much he *didn't* know. Would *never* know.

"If you're happy, I'm happy for you."

"That's a cliché." But she almost grinned as she said it.

There was another long pause before he admitted, "I wish I could hold you right now."

"Well, you can't."

The driver was taking luggage from the trunk. Soon she would be inside, hugging her family, not listening to Jacob's deep, rumbly, gorgeous voice that made her remember the amazing color of his eyes and the incredible way he made her feel when they touched…when they kissed.

She bit her lip but the tingling only grew.

"Jacob?"

"Yeah?"

Damn it. "I miss you, too."

"I'll be there in twenty-four hours. Okay?"

She eased out a smile and nodded. "Okay."

And then she saw Grace hurrying out through the front doors, waving her arms, pointing to a sparkling diamond solitaire and gold band on her wedding finger. While her friend did a fairy-tale twirl, Wynn appeared and the driver opened Teagan's door. She told Jacob, "I have to go," and as she approached the steps, her brother strode forward with a *just married* grin plastered across his face. Wynn grabbed her up, swung her around and Teagan finally cast Jacob Stone from her mind.

Of course, that didn't last long.

July in Australia was the middle of winter. In Sydney, temperatures were traditionally mild. Early frost and fog were common. In all recorded history, the sands of Bondi Beach had been covered in snow only once. On the morning of June 28, 1836, the colonial outpost had awoken to a drift that coated the streets in a crisp white fall an inch deep.

Today, however, was all endless blue skies and seventy-five degrees—more than comfortable enough for a mug of something warm while lounging outside on the patio area near the pool. As Teagan and Grace strolled out holding hands, with Wynn a step behind, the rest of the family turned in their seats.

Cole sent over a salute before bringing his beautiful wife close. Resting a gentle hand on her belly, he mouthed the words, *Baby on board.*

So much taller—and older—than he'd looked a few months earlier, Tate sprinted over. He didn't stop until he flew into her arms. Swinging him up, she held on tight. Her baby brother felt so warm and...well, *heavy.* He smelled of Aussie sunshine and fresh oranges, his favorite fruit. She'd

come home to congratulate Grace and Wynn, but this single moment of bliss was better than just about anything.

She balanced Tate on her hip and dropped a dozen kisses on both his cheeks. "You've grown."

"I'm in grade two next year."

"Bet you're loving it."

"I have a good teacher. Her name's Ms. Walton. She's older than my kindie one."

"Older like a grandma?"

He thought about it. "Older like you."

Teagan laughed. "Have you made lots of friends?"

His eyes twinkled. "I have a girlfriend, Tea."

"Awesome. What's her name?"

"Bella Blossom Bird. That's alit-ration." He scratched his head then pointed to the others. "Cole told me that."

"You can learn a lot from your brothers." She winked at Wynn. "All three of them."

Her father was sitting in a high-backed lounger. His hair was more salt than pepper now. His eyes were less lively and more wrinkled at the corners. Beneath the royal-blue sweater, his shoulders were stooped, like they were bearing an enormous weight. Guthrie Hunter was a highly intelligent man. He could see his way through any business challenge and come out on top. Teagan's Georgian-born mother had possessed a different kind of smarts—a wily but also demure way of navigating the trickier barriers that life sometimes threw a person's way.

As Teagan set Tate on his feet, then took his hand and headed over, her chest constricted so much, she could barely get a breath down. She wished her mom were here now. If she could have anything, any wish, it would be to wipe out disease from the world.

As Tate scampered off to his father's side, Teagan saw the bundle sloped against her father's chest. Honey was wrapped in a soft pink baby blanket, fast asleep.

What an angel.

Teagan kissed her father's cheek as he said welcome home. Then she focused on the baby. Her eyelashes were so long, they brushed her cheeks. Her mouth was the perfect shape and color. A rosebud. One tiny hand was bunched up, peeping outside of the blanket. Her skin was so fine, it was almost translucent.

Cole and Taryn had moved closer.

"Isn't she adorable?" Taryn said quietly. "Such a delicate little thing."

"Lolly Legs," Cole said. "I reckon our cat weighs more."

Teagan caught the teasing tone in her brother's voice but she didn't miss the element of concern, either. Some kids were chubby, like Dex before his growth spurt. Others were naturally smaller...thinner.

Her father asked, "Would you like to have a hold?"

"Oh, I don't want to wake her up."

"She's due a feed about now," he said.

"We should wake her soon then," Taryn said almost gravely.

Teagan looked around at them all. Wynn's expression said, *We'll talk about Honey later when Dad's not around.*

Tate was tugging on Taryn's skirt. "I'm hungry, too."

"Would you like me to peel you another orange?"

He beamed. "Yes, please."

Taking Tate's hand, Taryn said, "Why don't you come into the kitchen and help?"

As the pair headed off, Teagan was careful scooping Honey up. She felt warm and, yes, small and absolutely perfect. What did her life have in store? Teagan brought her baby sister higher and inhaled that sweet baby scent.

It's all about getting up when you're down, Honey. Finding your own way. Trying always to believe in yourself.

"I'm guessing someone must have told you."

Teagan focused on her father. "Told me what, Dad?"

"That Eloise and I...it's not going to work out."

She slid a quick look Cole's way. His eyebrows jumped

and everyone except Teagan took their seats again. With Honey in her arms, she preferred to stand.

"I'm sorry," she said. "I'd really hoped you could see a way through."

He propped an elbow on the chair arm and rubbed his brow with that hand. "Eloise is a mess. Drinking more and more. She wanted her own place, so I arranged another nanny for the kids, but they're not getting what they need."

Honey's tiny hand flexed as if to say she agreed.

Teagan asked, "Has the baby gone to all her pediatric appointments?"

"She doesn't have any problems," Taryn said, "although she is in the fifth percentile for weight."

Which meant ninety-five percent of babies her age weighed more.

Teagan was usually happy to help but not control things. Only now, looking down into this precious innocent face, something new and fierce roared up inside her.

Eloise is a mess.

"You can't let Honey stay there," she said. "Babies are so fragile." During that brief window when she'd been pregnant, she'd done so much research. "Their brains and bones need every bit of nourishment."

Cole was nodding. "Dad knows that, Tea."

"He's going to file for custody," Wynn added.

Teagan was taken aback. "For Tate, too?"

"For them both," Wynn confirmed.

Eloise was the farthest thing from a model mother, but these kids must love her nonetheless. Of course, her father would bring in more help to try to compensate. But it wasn't the same as having your mom.

Wynn read her mind. "There's no other way. You said it yourself. That baby deserves the best start in life and Eloise isn't capable of giving her that. It's our responsibility to step in. We need to protect them both, end of story."

The atmosphere was so dark and heavy. The topic needed

discussing, but this time was also meant to be about family getting together to celebrate. Teagan tried to lift the mood.

"So, tell me more about this whirlwind wedding," she said to Grace and Wynn. "Was anything planned or did you plunge in on a whim?"

Grace's face brightened. "We started talking one night about all the arrangements a big wedding would involve."

Wynn took his bride's hand. "The following week, we stood before a celebrant and signed the papers."

"And the honeymoon was in Italy?" Teagan asked.

Grace's head rocked back as she sighed. "We are definitely going back."

"Not for a while, though." Wynn winked at his new wife. "I have an office to run."

Cole and Taryn were sitting in a love seat. Now he put an arm around his wife and sent a manufactured frown his younger brother's way. "Surely they can do without you for another month or so."

Wynn laughed. "That's strange coming from you. Before you met Taryn, you practically slept at the office, weekends included."

Guthrie's bushy eyebrows jumped. "It's good to slow down."

"I haven't slowed down." Cole leaned in to steal a kiss from his wife. "I've simply directed certain passions elsewhere."

"We'll all be calling you Daddy soon."

Cole gave Wynn a deadpan look. "You won't be far behind."

Grace and Wynn turned to each other, a sparkle in their eyes.

When Wynn's phone beeped, he growled but opened the text anyway. "I've funneled down the incoming messages to only those that *seriously can't wait*." After reading, he growled again. "Unbelievable."

Guthrie perked up. "Bad news from New York?"

"Nothing we can't handle with a fly swatter." Sitting back again, Wynn crossed one ankle over a knee. "We did a feature on an actor recently, a guy who used in the '60s. He's in his late seventies now, but still a big name. A reliable source said this man was not only at it again, he was small-time dealing. This is after a very public display of obviously being off his tree."

Suddenly the baby felt heavy in Teagan's arms. Her throat was convulsing. Grace seemed to notice. She got to her feet and took Honey.

"You take my seat," Grace said. "I'm going to enjoy this little sweetie for a while."

Teagan folded into a chair while Guthrie offered a prediction. "So, the actor's got some hotshot lawyer to see if he can drag a few million out of your kitty?"

Now Teagan felt ill. Her father didn't like lawyers at the best of times. He thought they were a necessary evil, perhaps like a lot of the world.

"It seems the actor *did* lawyer up," Wynn said, "but later chickened out. Only goes to show."

Teagan was holding her churning stomach. "Goes to show what?"

"That the story was *fact*. Obviously this actor, Grant Howcroft, panicked when he was caught out. He wanted to file but then saw reason when his junkie brain cleared."

Oh, this was bad. But it could be worse. Teagan didn't know if she wanted to ask.

"Did they say who the lawyer was?"

Wynn shook his head. "Doesn't make any difference." Then the phone beeped again. "Ah. Here we go. He's apparently a big deal in his world. Jacob Stone, Esquire."

A dozen exit strategies whipped through Teagan's mind. But she had always welcomed everyone else's companions, partners. This was awkward but, damn it, she wouldn't tell Jacob to cancel their plans, not after the torment she'd gone through to make the decision. In fact, despite all the down

talk about attorneys, she wasn't embarrassed to introduce Jacob as her...friend. And she wasn't going to stew on it for however long before he got here.

"I know Jacob Stone," she said.

Wynn's expression was pinched. "*How?* He's on the other side of the country from you."

"We met at a wedding in LA. He knew the groom. I'm friends with the bride."

Reaching for his coffee, Wynn replied, "Ha. Small world."

Teagan paused. That was exactly what Jacob had said when she'd first mentioned Wynn.

"He's very clued in," she went on. "I think he'd be a good lawyer."

Wynn's expression oozed disinterest. "You don't say."

Grace asked, "How old is this Jacob Stone?"

"Around Wynn's age."

Taryn seemed to have caught on, too. "So you and he talked a lot at the wedding?"

"We talked." Teagan pushed out the rest. "And danced."

Cole's eyebrows swept together as he sat straighter. "Did you see Stone again?"

"As a matter of fact, I met his family on a visit to upstate New York."

Her father's elbow slid off the chair arm while Wynn froze and then blinked once.

"When?" he asked.

"Three weeks ago."

"Have you seen him since?"

"No. No, I haven't."

The hard line of Wynn's mouth eased. "Probably best."

"We have spoken, though. Most recently this morning. I invited him here."

Wynn jerked forward in his chair like a knife had slammed between his shoulder blades. "You didn't."

"I did. Jacob should arrive sometime tomorrow."

Looking around at all the shocked faces, Taryn made her point of view known. "Well, I can't wait to meet him."

"Me, too," Grace said, rocking the baby again at the same time Cole studied Wynn's fuming face and groaned, *"Oh, shit."*

Twelve

Jacob tried to call Teagan—six times now since his flight had landed.

Again. No one picked up.

Sitting in a cab with the engine running, Jacob studied the entrance gates decorated with the sweeping Hunter Enterprises logo. He had three choices. Check into a hotel, fly back home, or buzz that intercom and make a complete dick of himself because if she wasn't answering her phone, there was zero chance of anyone letting him in.

He sat a few seconds longer then threw open the cab door.

Screw it.

"I'll get out here."

The driver's hands stayed on the wheel. "That's one hell of a driveway. You're gonna need a packed lunch."

"I need to stretch my legs." *And clear my head, and drill down on what the hell's going on.*

After receiving that message from Ivy Schluter, he and Teagan had parted on uncertain terms. He'd phoned a couple of times, but Teagan had been hurt when she hadn't heard from him more recently. During yesterday's phone conversation, thankfully they'd gotten back on track. He'd offered to join her during her break Down Under. At the same time, he could meet the family.

Yeah. That was the plan.

The driver had gotten out of the cab and was collecting the luggage while Jacob pulled a bill from his wallet, currency he'd swapped out at the airport exchange.

"Keep the change."

The driver hesitated before accepting the money. "You sure, mate? That's twice the fare."

"I'm sure."

The driver had fallen all over himself to be courteous and chatty to an international visitor who was on his way to meet people who would at best view him as a gate-crasher, and at worst had already made arrangements to have him lynched. Jacob had been about to board his flight at JFK when Teagan phoned to say that her family knew about the defamation lawsuit and the attorney behind it. That was the last time they had spoken.

So had Wynn and the other Hunters convinced her to freeze him out? He'd thought Teagan was stronger than that. Then again, he hadn't forgotten what she'd said about the Hunter clan being protective of its own. Sticking together no matter what.

Jacob was about to try the gate's intercom when a man appeared, strolling along the sidewalk on this side of the ten-foot-high block fence. Big guy, black suit, opaque aviator shades. Not here for the fun. Given what he knew about the attempts on Guthrie Hunter's life, Jacob guessed the man was security.

The guy stopped a good distance away. "Are you looking for someone, sir?"

"Teagan Hunter's expecting me."

The dude turned his head as if to assess the mansion at the same time his iron jaw edged forward. "A friend of hers?"

"That's right. I'm visiting from New York."

"You've been in contact with her recently then."

When Jacob reached for the cell phone inside his jacket, the guy shifted enough for his own jacket to part, revealing a gun holster. *Welcome to the hood.*

Jacob's movements slowed as he extracted his cell and tried to call her again. "I've left messages. She's not picking up."

"Maybe she doesn't want to pick up."

"Maybe there's something wrong with the connection."

"Maybe you'd better move on."

"Maybe you need to *chill*."

A white Lexus zoomed into the driveway. Teagan jumped out and headed straight over. Jacob wanted to wrap his arms around her, tell her he was happy to see her—despite her not answering his calls and Goon Boy here wanting him to disappear. And that's why his greeting was less than it could have been. He gave her a kiss on the cheek, a tight smile, and then stepped back.

It killed to see her smile fade as she gave him a questioning look.

"I thought I'd be back before you got here," she said.

"My flight was early."

"Have you been trying to call?"

"A couple of times."

She winced. "I'm out of charge."

There. Simple explanation. She didn't hate him. Hadn't thrown him under the bus.

He was pretty sure about that.

She spoke to Goon Boy. "Brandon Powell, this is a friend of mine. Jacob Stone."

Goon Boy didn't remove the shades. Nor did he offer a smile, let alone an apology.

"Yeah. Don't worry about the misunderstanding," Jacob said with just enough *shove it* behind the words. "We've all got jobs to do."

The other man's lip curled in a grin that said, *Bet your ass we do.*

Teagan had returned to her vehicle, so Jacob tossed his bag in the back while she thumbed a button on her remote. The gates fanned back and they headed down the pine-lined drive, leaving Mr. Personality Plus behind.

"Serious security," he said, rubbing the back of his neck.

"Brandon's the head of a PI firm. He's also a longtime

friend of the family. One of Cole's mates from his Navy cadet days."

"So, is this a regular thing or because of the trouble?"

After Lanie had brought up the attacks on Guthrie Hunter over dinner, Jacob hadn't found the time to discuss the details with Teagan. He got the feeling she would rather not discuss it now.

"There hasn't been another incident since Cole's wedding," she said. "But no one's been caught yet, either. Until he, or she, is locked away, Dad needs all the help he can get."

"Must be something the super rich have to deal with."

She gave him an unimpressed look. "Thanks for the support."

"No. I didn't mean that the way it sounded." Like, *Boohoo, poor you.* "It's just that those with wealth are more visible, and there are a lot of crackpots out there. People with no scruples and even less conscience."

He'd dealt with them more often than he'd like to admit.

Turning into the elaborate porte cochere, which led to a ramp of granite steps and set of soaring front doors, she shut down the engine.

He wanted to lean across and kiss her like he'd dreamed so often of doing these past weeks. But her posture and expression now said, *Not so fast.* He had hoped that with his coming here they could get back to where they'd been before he'd received Ivy's message that day. But his relationship with Teagan was obviously still on shaky ground, and not only because the paternity question was still up in the air. Her family knew about the lawsuit. They were aware he had planned to cut Wynn Hunter off at the corporate knees.

Yesterday, he'd been pumped when Teagan had given him the go-ahead to jump on a plane. Now he couldn't help but wonder if he'd walked into some kind of trap. If her family were less than friendly—if they came down on him like a ton of bricks—would she come to his defense or sit back and watch the fireworks?

* * *

From the moment she'd spotted Jacob standing at the gates to the Hunter estate, Teagan's scalp had been tingling. He hadn't looked impressed, and not purely because Brandon Powell had been doing his job and checking the situation out. Jacob's greeting had been stiff, and he hadn't warmed after she explained that her phone had run out of charge. She had no idea that he'd arrived early.

Now as they made their way through the house, headed for the great room where her family had arranged to gather this afternoon, Teagan couldn't shake the sinking feeling. When Jacob hadn't bothered to keep in touch, she'd written their relationship off. But hearing his voice again yesterday had brought back into sharp focus how he made her feel. Alive and desirable. Vulnerable and yet strong. Rather than sticking to her guns and saying goodbye for good, she'd been gripped by an overwhelming need to feel that way again.

Now she was rethinking that, big time.

On top of not being able to contact her and receiving a grilling from Brandon, Jacob must be on edge about those pending paternity test results. She understood why he hoped they were negative. But if he did turn out to be that baby's father, would he still feel angry and cornered or, ultimately, proud?

Teagan couldn't help but be envious. She had even fantasized about that baby being their own. Pointless. Even upsetting. But sometimes, lying awake in bed at night, she just couldn't help it.

And then there was that other matter.

Her family knew that Jacob had planned to drag the Hunter name through the courts. How would Jacob and Wynn handle this face-to-face? She doubted her father or Cole would be overly welcoming, either. Frankly, she couldn't blame them.

On top of all that, everyone was dealing with escalat-

ing pressures brought on by another "outsider." It seemed Eloise had really gone off the rails this time. But Teagan felt torn over Guthrie's decision to file for full custody. Of course her little brother and sister needed to be protected, which meant being without their mother most of the time.

That wasn't how it was supposed to be. Teagan still missed her own mom so much. If she were in Eloise's position, she would want to spend every moment with those kids.

So, in hindsight, Jacob being here now was not a good idea. Not a good idea at all. In fact, she wanted to pull up and tell him to just forget the whole damn thing.

But then they were walking into the room and everyone was turning to look their way. Wynn's scowl said it all.

Pressing her damp palms together, Teagan tacked on her smile.

"Everyone, this is Jacob Stone."

She could have kissed Cole for striding over first and putting out his hand. "Good to meet you, Jacob. I'm Cole, the oldest and wisest sibling."

Teagan saw Jacob's expression relax a little when Taryn introduced herself. The woman was all class and heart.

"I'm Taryn. The wise man's wife."

Her dad stood near the fireplace that Eloise had remodeled to overtake the entire wall, all the way up to the vaulted ceiling. Now he came forward.

"I'm Teagan's father. Please call me Guthrie. A funny name, but it's the only one I have."

Jacob shook the older man's hand. "It's a fine name, sir. Good to meet you."

"Tate, my youngest boy, is outside taking advantage of this warm weather and the sandbox. I also have another daughter—" Guthrie winked at Teagan "—a little younger than the first."

"That would be Honey," Jacob said.

Guthrie's gaze sharpened like, *You've done your homework*. "My Honey. That's right."

"I haven't had much experience with babies." Jacob shrugged. "Actually none up to this point. But I look forward to meeting her, too."

Next up was Grace. "I'm the newest addition to the family. Wynn and I took our trip down the aisle just a few weeks ago."

Jacob's smile reached his eyes like he was genuinely pleased for her. "Congratulations. I hope you have many happy years ahead."

And then there was one introduction left. Teagan prayed it wouldn't be a clash of the titans.

"Jacob, this is Wynn," she said. "My brother who works in New York—"

"For Hunter Publications," Wynn said, stepping up, visibly gritting his teeth as he put out his hand. "I believe you work in Manhattan, too."

"Busy place," Jacob said, all too briefly taking Wynn's hand. "It's good to have some time off."

"I'm due back week after next."

Jacob nodded, looked around. "It's a long way from here."

"These days we're all so connected. It's so much easier to keep up to date than, say, fifty years ago."

"Even twenty."

"It's a different world. Nowhere to hide"

Jacob's smile was tight. "Nowhere at all."

Wynn's jaw shifted. "So, Jacob, you're a lawyer. What are you working on at the moment? Any interesting cases?"

Jacob shrugged. "They come up all the time."

"And when there isn't enough evidence to prosecute? I suppose those cases are dropped?"

"There are other reasons a case will be put aside."

"Oh?" Wynn crossed his arms. "Name one."

Jacob's grin was wry. "Are you in need of a lawyer, Wynn?"

"Actually we have an exceptional team. Always prepared to fight. And win."

Teagan groaned. *Enough.* Obviously, Grace thought so, too. Wynn and Jacob weren't talking; they were shaping up. Grace linked an arm through her husband's while Guthrie interjected. He might not approve of the visiting attorney, but thankfully he wasn't making a show of it.

"It really is a full house today," he said. "I'd like you to meet my nephew, Sebastian."

Teagan hadn't realized Sebastian was there. Sitting in a high-backed chair, facing the fire, he got to his feet.

"An attorney, huh?" Sebastian grinned as he ran a hand through his hair. "Wish I'd gotten a law degree."

Jacob arched a brow. "It's not too late. I hear you have fantastic universities in Australia."

Sebastian was the only son of Guthrie's older brother, Talbot, who had left the family business in a huff decades earlier. The families hadn't spoken since that major falling-out, until Sebastian had reached out and reconnected. That side of the family had attended Cole's wedding, and had witnessed the explosion. Now Sebastian was working for Cole, and while he and Jacob talked, Teagan wondered...

If Talbot hadn't opted out of Hunter Enterprises all those years ago, Sebastian would most likely be a CEO now, wielding as much corporate power as his cousins. That was enough reason for a lot of people to be jealous, vengeful. Not that Sebastian ever came across that way. In fact, he was nothing but accommodating.

Someone else Teagan hadn't noticed was pushing to his feet. His hair was thinner and grayer, but she instantly recognized one of her father's oldest friends. Rather than put out his hand, Milo Vennard studied his perpetually unlit pipe as he spoke to Jacob.

"These are interesting times for your country, young man."

Teagan explained, "Professor Vennard is an expert in Marxian economics."

"An ideology growing in popularity," Vennard added,

meeting Jacob's gaze. "Particularly in your quarter. Capitalism was always doomed."

Jacob slid both hands into his pants' pockets. "There's certainly a lot of debate going on at the moment."

"Of course," Vennard continued, "there are many influences that affect government and economic policy, although the plight of the working class is rarely one of them. Lawmakers, and *people who administer the law* like yourself, should give a nation its backbone. Have you ever asked yourself what you can do to help the cause?" The man's bushy eyebrows knitted together. "Son, are you part of the problem or the solution?"

Jacob appeared to be forming his words. Before he could reply, however, the professor went on.

"Those at the top are a disease, spreading a palsy that will ultimately dry up every shred of opportunity for the common man for generations to come."

Someone cleared his throat.

"Well, I know *I'm* pretty dry at the moment." Cole tilted his chin toward the bar. "What's your poison, Jacob?"

As the men headed over—with Sebastian eager to fit in and Wynn clearly itching for a fight—Teagan hung back with the girls.

Her gaze on Jacob, Taryn kept her voice low. "Teagan. Uh, *yum*."

Grace was smiling at the boys congregating and talking around the bar. "Wynn did pretty well, considering."

Teagan exhaled. "Well, no one threw an actual punch." So disaster averted. At least for now.

Sighing, Taryn put a palm on her baby-bump belly. "You look so right together."

"You mean despite how he was going to drag Wynn to court?" Teagan asked.

Grace didn't seem concerned. "What is a good love affair without some hurdles? Wynn and I had a couple of doozies to overcome."

"Cole and me, too," Taryn said. "When we met, I thought he was the most arrogant, controlling man on the planet."

"I couldn't see any future for Wynn and me. I had so many doubts." Grace looked at Teagan. "Who are we if not our deepest hang-ups?"

Teagan was thinking back. When she'd met Jacob, he had triggered her, too, but only in the bedroom, and in a very good way. But as well as they got along in that regard, she couldn't imagine her and Jacob getting married, and not simply because of all the ill feelings swirling around the specter of that shelved lawsuit, or the fact that it was way too soon to even consider such a thing.

What about having a family?

Jacob must be on tenterhooks waiting for those paternity results. But if he was like Damon Barringer and wanted a family of his own one day—and not via adoption or surrogacy—Teagan knew from experience that could be a deal breaker. As far as she could tell, there was just no getting around that one.

End of story, close the book and goodnight.

Thirteen

As they left the interrogation room and Teagan led the way down an outside path, through a series of magnificent gardens to one of the Hunter estate's guesthouses, Jacob could barely contain a shudder.

The Rawsons were wealthy folk. Nice home, beautiful property, but, *Geez, Louise*, nothing like this. The estate was on a massive parcel of land overlooking Sydney Harbour, complete with a mansion in every decadent sense of the word... This had to be one of the most expensive pieces of real estate in Australia—perhaps in the world.

My, my, how the überwealthy lived.

As they entered the guesthouse's vast main room, well away from earshot, Teagan made a comment. "Well, Dad was pleasant enough."

Because the old guy had smiled? *Once.* Jacob wasn't going to whine about it. Guthrie Hunter obviously had other stuff on his mind, like how to dodge the next assassin attempt.

Teagan added, "Wynn was a little defensive."

A little? The fire blazing in Wynn's eyes had said, *I want to rip out your heart and feed it to a lantern fish*—the kind that live at the murky bottom of the ocean and look like a cross between Freddy Krueger and *Dawn of the Dead*.

"The professor friend of your father's is an interesting character," he said, taking in more of the multimillion dollar surroundings before opening a random door that led to a softly lit, marble-clad room that housed a fifty-foot interior lap pool.

Teagan was headed for the other end of the main room. "They've known each other since college."

"They obviously took different approaches to their study of economics." A Marxism economist would probably barf at the accumulation of this kind of monumental personal wealth. "They must have some knockout debates."

"My father and Professor Vennard have different ideas on how the world ought to be run. Dad believes in the dream." She pressed a button on a remote that opened fifteen-foot-high curtains covering four sets of French doors. "Work hard and you'll reap the rewards."

"And the more rules that bend in your favor, the more lucrative those rewards become."

Teagan's eyebrows knitted. "My father—and brothers—are astute businessmen. They contribute. Create jobs. Isn't that something to celebrate?"

"And yet you chose not to join the party." She'd turned her back on the opportunity to be a part of Hunter Enterprises.

"I prefer a simpler life."

Closing the distance between them, he spread his arms, flipped up his palms and looked around. "Teagan, this is *not* simple."

Her grin was wry. "The Rawsons aren't exactly paupers."

"No. But they give back a lot, and from the heart."

"Right. Because my family doesn't have any philanthropic causes."

"Donations to political connections don't count."

Her beautiful green eyes narrowed. "I don't like this conversation."

As she turned away, he winced and caught her arm, held her back.

"Hey, I'm sorry," he said. "I guess this is harder than I'd thought."

"You mean facing my brother?"

"Not that. *More* than that." He and Teagan had commit-

ted to being transparent—honest—so he soldiered on. "I'm used to doing battle with big corporations, not trying to chum up with people who vacation on hundred-foot yachts."

"I seem to recall a flight to New York in a private aircraft."

"C'mon. That plane isn't worth as much as your annual housekeeping bills."

"*My* housekeeping bills?"

"You know what I mean."

"I think I do." She edged away. "Obviously, Wynn is having trouble putting the idea of that lawsuit aside, but let's be honest. You're still champing at the bit to see him pay. Which is funny, because he didn't do anything wrong in the first place."

"You don't know that." He shook his head. "You *can't* know that."

"I know what he told me. He said—"

"Don't tell me." Jacob threw up his hands and turned away. "I don't want to know."

"Exactly."

Jacob was torn down the middle. He wanted to be here, but he didn't need this rock hanging over his head. Ultimately, if Grant Howcroft came back and said he wanted to go through with that lawsuit, Jacob was no longer in a position to help. Wynn Hunter could very well see this visit—at least in part—as a ruse. A way for him to ferret out incriminating information. Or to intimidate him. A judge would see it that way, too.

Which, of course, he had known when he'd suggested that he join Teagan here.

But, boy, it grated having to pass on the opportunity to score a win against an institution that ruined reputations by positing fiction as fact. The other downside of this exercise pained him just as much.

Jacob knew firsthand about coming from nothing and having no one. That reality was the kindling upon which

his passion for the law had been built. He wanted to fight the good fight. Level the playing field. Teagan, on the other hand, couldn't possibly know how that felt. Whether or not she espoused being independent, by virtue of her family's Midas-level assets, she was the one percent…privileged in a way normal folk could never dream of.

That wasn't her doing, her fault. At least she wasn't shoving it down people's throats every chance she got like another woman he knew.

Ivy Schluter.

Teagan was standing by the French doors. The view was a painter's inspiration—a panorama of that bluest of blue harbor with its lazy water traffic and the sweeping shells of Sydney's famed Opera House. Her arms were crossed tightly and her shoulders were squared in that cute polka-dot jumpsuit. Jacob felt like an ass for venting, but he would make up for it now. Not another word about anything other than how happy he was to be spending time with her again. About taking what they had—despite the distractions—to the next level.

He moved across the room and stopped behind her. Then he gazed out over the vista, too.

"I don't think I've seen a more spectacular sight," he said.

She didn't comment, didn't move.

"It must look amazing at night. All the city lights and stars on the water."

He waited again, and finally she spoke.

"My father bought this block of land for my mother. They'd been looking around for a family home—Cole was on the way—and they saw the For Sale sign. The company was going through some hardships at the time. Mom understood they couldn't afford it, but she'd still fallen in love with this view. She'd said it was so close to heaven, you could reach up and swing from the clouds.

"The next week, Dad took her out for a picnic…fried chicken, cheese straws and sweet tea. When he'd stopped

here again and said that he'd managed to buy the land, she didn't believe him. So he took the deed from his pocket." She shifted and took a deep breath. "Whenever he tells that story, Dad says that Mom couldn't stop crying. Tears of happiness, and of thanks. She knew how lucky they were. How privileged. And every single day she gave back, to her family, to the community. She helped others any way she could."

Jacob's heart was in his throat. He let what she'd said sink in before coaxing her to turn around in his arms. Then he waited for her to look up, meet his gaze.

"When I'm here...when I'm home," she said, "I always think about swinging from the clouds. I always think about how happy my mother and father were."

Yesterday on the phone, Jacob had said he couldn't wait to hold her. *Really* hold her. This minute, he wanted that more than anything.

He told her that with his eyes and then with his lips. And he didn't stop telling her until he felt her resistance and doubt ebb away. Until it was just the two of them, standing on a precipice, reaching for the clouds.

Teagan wasn't sure what she was thinking. She only knew how she *felt*. More than anything, that feeling was relief.

Of course this was always going to be tricky. On top of everything else, she'd never brought anyone home to "meet the folks" before. She had never wanted the questions or to face the expectations. She hadn't even brought Damon Barringer over.

After that breakup—and the miscarriage—Teagan had shut off her feelings. Then she'd met Jacob and knew the time was right to put herself out there again. And being with him was *different*. Jacob had a certain edge that made her feel new and exciting, and not only in the bedroom.

And now, as his lips brushed and teased hers, she didn't

dwell on why. She simply put her earlier concerns and this disagreement aside, and gave in to being with him again this way. She couldn't have stopped herself if she tried.

He nipped her lower lip, so lightly she could have imagined it.

"I missed you so much." He nuzzled one side of her mouth, her cheek. "You feel so good, Tea. So good."

When his mouth took hers, she leaned in, clung on. And as the sparks grew stronger, her bones turned to jelly and her heart began to pound. The heat of his tongue playing with hers—the subtle pressure of his fingertips toying behind her ear—left her feeling giddy with need. So impatient for more.

He was already slipping the shoestring straps of her jumpsuit off her shoulders. When the kiss deepened and he tugged at the fabric, she left off kneading his chest to get rid of the jumpsuit herself. No bra. Just a pair of lacy boy-cut panties and Keds, which she blindly heeled off and kicked away.

He hooked an arm around her waist and pulled her toward the circular lounge. As he fell back, all contact broke. No one was going to walk past, peep in. Still, Teagan reached for the remote, pressed a button, and the curtains closed across those doors again.

There was still enough natural light to make out his penetrating gaze as he undid each button on his shirt. She came forward, straddled his lap, and then they were kissing again. She took control this time, dragging her fingers back through his hair, caressing his mouth with hers, pressing and rubbing her breasts under his chin.

When she ran out of breath, her lips left his to graze over his jaw to his ear. She whispered, "Are you happy?"

His palms were gliding up over her lace-covered hips. "Trick question, right?"

She took his hand and steered it higher until he was cupping her breast. When he plucked the very tip, she bit her

lip to contain the moan. He slid lower until his mouth replaced his hand. Then his tongue looped one way and the
other, gently sucking and savoring. All the while, he explored the backs of her thighs, fingers feathering up and
down, around and between.

Teagan buried her face in his hair. This was the fan-
tasy she'd had every night since they'd been apart. It was
all steam and aching pleasure and breathless anticipation.

Please don't make me wait.

She might have said the words aloud because he took
that moment to release the zipper on his pants. She shifted
to get up and lead him to the bedroom, but he reached to
tug her close again.

"You're not going anywhere," he said around a grin.

Straddling him again, she held on to his shoulders,
which were steaming through the shirt. "This could get
awkward."

He was looking at her breasts. "Awkward how?"

"Getting your pants out of the way. Mine too. And…
other stuff."

Protection.

But he was already fishing around for his wallet, finding
and opening a foil wrapper. Then he bucked up and rolled
the condom straight on.

As he kissed her again and her arms wrapped around
his neck, he trailed his fingertips up the inside of her thigh
before burrowing beneath her panties. She felt his smile
tease her lips while he slid the crotch to one side. Then the
pad of his thumb began to strum. The strokes grew more
precise until he found just the right spot and applied just
the right pressure.

As the pulse at her core deepened, she broke the kiss,
gripped his shoulders again and pressed in. When she
started to quiver, began to quake, he brought her hips down
until her inner thighs sat flat against the tops of his and all
the breath was pushed from her lungs.

He was inside her…*filling* her…unbuttoned, unzipped, but still fully clothed, including his shoes.

Through hair fallen over her eyes, she found his lidded gaze. Then she let her head rock back as she slid both her hands up the hot curves on either side of his neck. As he began to pump, he helped her move. Every thrust sent her that much higher…that much closer…until her climax exploded and the world was raining white hot sparks.

Fourteen

Later that evening when Teagan and Jacob strolled into the dining room, she was taken aback by everyone's expressions. Her stomach pitched and the smile slid from her face.

Who died?

Pushing to his feet, Cole waved them over. "We were discussing a few things."

Taking a seat at the table, Teagan looked around. "Where's Dad?"

Wynn eyed Jacob before tapping the blade of his knife on the tablecloth. "Eloise rang. She wanted the kids back."

"We bundled them up, said goodbye," Cole explained as Teagan and Jacob took their seats. "We didn't want to disturb you guys."

"And if they had to go…" A muscle in Wynn's jaw flexed. "Well, we didn't want to drag it out for Tate."

Teagan was stunned. Was she missing something? "Eloise knows this is a family week, doesn't she?"

Wynn grunted. "I don't think Eloise knows what day it is."

Under the table, Jacob took Teagan's hand. She squeezed back and asked, "Why didn't Dad just say no?"

Ice clicked as Cole swirled his tumbler. "At this point, he thought it best not to upset her."

"Doesn't matter that she upset the kids," Wynn pointed out.

Cole voiced what everyone was thinking. "God, I wish those two had never met. No. I take that back. We have Tate and Honey." He took a gulp and smacked the tumbler back down on the table. "This is going to end badly."

Taryn asked, "You mean with divorce?"

Wynn clarified, "And Eloise scooping up a fortune."

"Money's the least of Dad's worries where she's concerned," Cole pointed out. He turned to Teagan. "We've just found out that she has a boyfriend slash live-in lover. A Kyle Scafe. Brandon's running a deeper check on him. Apparently he's an ex-military man."

Wynn qualified, "One of those soldiers for hire."

"Should Honey and Tate be living with any man other than their father?"

Jacob answered Teagan's question. "Statistics show that minors living with a male not related to them are exponentially more at risk."

While Wynn's eyes burned and narrowed, Cole went on. "So far, there are no red flags in this guy's history. In fact, his record is exemplary."

"I just need to say—" Wynn hacked out a laugh. "I'm sorry, but I bet my life he's not the first."

When Cole's jaw jutted and he looked down, Teagan was reminded that Eloise had even hit on him once. Unbelievable.

"When is Dad filing the custody papers?" she asked.

"This evening's stunt will bump that up," Cole said. "He'll still have to deal with her, though. Dad wants her in their lives."

So did Teagan. "But if she puts them in danger..."

"Supervised visits." Jacob's shoulders rolled back. "If she has a history, that could be the way to go."

Wynn shook his head. "I can't see Eloise going for that."

"If you can prove that she's toxic," Jacob replied, "you'll have the judge's ear."

"What do you term *proof*?" Wynn's tone was edged with sarcasm. "A *reliable source*?"

He was having a dig at Jacob about the information his reporter had received on Grant Howcroft's alleged drug use.

Jacob didn't take the bait. "That would help. But if you

could get solid evidence…photos, police reports, psych evaluations…"

"What if she wants a paternity test?" Cole cringed. "I know Tate is the spitting image of Dad when he was that age. Has all his mannerisms, too. Not that any of that is conclusive. But Honey…?"

"It takes anywhere from a few days to a few weeks to get results back," Jacob said.

"As far as our father is concerned," Wynn pointed out, "Honey is his child. DNA swabs won't change that."

Teagan thought of Jacob's situation, which was obviously very different from her father's. If Jacob's paternity test came back negative, he wouldn't hesitate to walk away. He didn't know the child. Had never met him. Being excluded would leave the way clear for the true father to step up to the plate. Still, blood wasn't necessarily thicker than water. She only had to think of Jacob's past and his relationship with the Rawsons to know that.

As far as Teagan was concerned…she would *die* for those two kids, and her feelings for Honey wouldn't change no matter who her father was. The thought of walking away, never seeing Honey again, made her blood run cold.

"I know we're all concerned about Honey," Grace said. "She doesn't have a voice. But I hate to think of how this time is affecting Tate. What does a six-year-old tell himself when he can see that his family is being torn apart? He's been through enough already."

Taryn gave a thoughtful nod. "There hasn't been any action on the stalker front since the wedding."

Teagan shuddered, remembering how close they had come to losing Tate that day.

"Doesn't mean it's over," Wynn grunted. "I'd like to take them both out of harm's way again until *everything's* sorted."

"Tate has stayed with Dex and me," Teagan told Jacob.

"And I had him over Christmas." Wynn expelled a

breath. "Do you know what he told me Christmas Eve? He thought *he* was to blame for his parents' problems."

Cole's eyes suddenly widened and he straightened as he looked past Teagan to the door. *"Dad."*

Teagan turned in her seat. Her father stood on the threshold. He looked beaten. And yet he pasted on a smile as he headed over to the table.

"This isn't much of a celebration for Wynn and Grace, I'm afraid."

Wynn had gotten to his feet to pull out his father's chair while Cole asked, "How are the kids?"

"Eloise decided that she only wanted Honey. Tate came home with me. He's in bed."

Teagan withered inside. Had Tate cried when they'd left his little sister behind? What was wrong with that woman?

She shoved back her chair. "I'll go up and see him."

Her father held up a hand. "He's asleep, sweetheart. Big day."

Wynn returned to his seat. "Was the soldier boyfriend there?"

"He was. Hate to say it, but he was polite. Even concerned."

"And Eloise?" Cole asked.

"She seemed sober. Which almost worries me more. I don't know what to expect next."

None of them did, Teagan thought. Especially poor Tate.

Jacob had been prepared for a challenge. Coming here, he'd wanted to get along with the Hunters, but he hadn't expected to *sympathize* with the family.

They had everything—money, corporate and social power, intelligence. As far as looks went, hell, they could've been the A-list cast from a blockbuster movie. Or perhaps that comparison was in Jacob's head because someone had mentioned that Dex, the middle brother and head

of Hunter Productions in LA, was due to arrive in the next couple of days.

Given the discussion regarding cheating, divorce and custody issues, he'd felt for everyone at that dinner table, including Wynn, who looked so preoccupied and only pushed around the food on his plate. Taryn and Grace tried to lighten the mood with talk about decorating nurseries and honeymoons in Venice. But overall, the dinner was tense, start to finish; plates went away barely touched.

Before heading back to their guest quarters, Teagan told Jacob, "I need to go check on Tate."

"Sure. Of course." He dropped a kiss on her forehead. "I'm totally there if you want me."

She gave him a weary smile and nodded.

They climbed an extravagant sweeping staircase and headed quietly down a long hallway. The bedroom was awash with a soft yellow glow. In one corner, a pack of stuffed animals and plastic dinosaurs stared back at them like a regiment of mini personal guards. The boy lay on his back, one pajama-clad arm dangling over the mattress.

Jacob followed Teagan as she inched closer. When she stopped to gaze down at the sleeping child, her clasped hands tucked under her chin, something in Jacob's chest wrenched so hard, he had to press his lips together to stop the groan. Like the others, he wanted to know this child would be kept safe. But his reaction involved more than that.

At that moment, he got who Teagan Hunter truly was. Loyal, strong and capable of an ocean-deep commitment. Tate and Honey might be going through a hell of a time right now, but their big sister would do *anything* to have them both come out the other side knowing how much they were loved.

When Teagan found his hand, Jacob beat down the urge to clear the emotions crowding his throat. He'd always had a chip on his shoulder about growing up poor and unwanted. Until a few weeks ago, the idea of having a family of his

own had never entered his head. Why would it? He'd been raised in a hellhole where discipline meant endless stinging slaps across the ear and going to bed hungry more often than not. Given he had inherited his biological parents' genes, Jacob had never wanted to take even the slightest risk of repeating the pattern.

Later, when they went to bed, Teagan curled into him and he stroked her hair, loving her warmth and her scent. He was still thinking about Tate and those paternity results when she shifted and looked up into his eyes.

"Thank you," she said.

He smiled softly. "What for, baby?"

"For tonight," she said. "For being on our side."

Fifteen

The newlyweds had booked the grand ballroom of an exclusive inner city hotel that boasted dazzling views of the harbor at night. There would be family and select friends, but guests had been warned to refrain from sharing details of the coming event on social media. The key words were *privacy* and *security*. With Brandon Powell's crew on the beat and all arrangements hush-hush, this was set to be a wonderful and—fingers crossed—*uneventful* night.

With five days on their hands until then, Teagan decided to show Jacob the highlights of her hometown. They'd started with the Christmas in July markets at The Rocks, a historic tourist precinct on Sydney Harbour's southern shore. They enjoyed delicious mulled wine, traditional carols and an array of early Yuletide pop-up stores.

The next day, they checked out Bondi. After a walk along the famous stretch of white sand, they sat at a café overlooking the Pacific Ocean and ordered coffee with slices of wattle seed and quandong cake. Quandong, Teagan informed Jacob, was Australia's sweet and tangy native peach.

The following day, they checked out the harbor and an assortment of stops via commuter ferry. They spent most of the day at Sydney's best known theme park—Luna Park—which had its own "Coney Island" complete with a fun house from the 1930s; there were rotating barrels, moving platforms, large sliders and arcade games galore. They rode the hair-raising Wild Mouse roller coaster *three times*. When they left the park at dusk, the entrance—a giant laughing face—was lit up along with all the rides.

On the ferry back, a woman seated nearby heard Jacob's

accent and took it upon herself to inform him of the Opera House's history as they passed by the iconic shells, which were illuminated with blown-up moving projections of Aboriginal artwork inspired by the Dreamtime. The woman had been born in 1957, the same year the Opera House architect had won the international design competition.

This was why Teagan would always call Sydney home. The amazing climate, scenery, food and the people. Jacob seemed to feel at home, too. With the wind combing through his hair as he studied the iconic arts center and the sparkling harbor waters while listening to the woman's story, he looked more than interested. Jacob looked like he could truly belong.

Every evening, they hung out with Tate and caught up with family over dinner. Tonight, however, they'd gotten in late and opted for a swim in their very private heated pool.

Wearing an aqua bikini, Teagan dove in first. When she came up for air, somehow Jacob was already right there beside her in the pool, beautiful broad chest and shoulders wet and bare.

She wiped water from her eyes. "How'd you get here so fast?"

"Skill."

She gave his lopsided grin a splash before mermaid diving and swimming away.

Before her accident, Teagan had won plenty of blue ribbons at swim meets. But clearly Jacob had a secret weapon. By the time she got to the other end, there he was again, standing in the shallows, dark hair plastered to his head, upper body glistening, and not the least bit out of breath.

She pretended to pout. "I don't want to race anymore."

His muscled arms looped around her waist. "You want to expend some energy a different way?"

"Oh, you mean like by *talking*?"

His muscles flexed as he grinned and tugged her closer. "Sure. Let's talk."

When he began to twirl them both around, she brought her legs up and locked them around his hips. He was so warm and wet and hard…

"So, what do you want to talk about?" she asked.

"Uh…kangaroos. You piqued my interest at the farm that night."

She remembered well. "I told Lanie to stay away from big reds, our *boxing* kangaroos."

"We didn't come across any this week."

"There are plenty of roos in the Outback—more than there are people in the whole of Australia. But you won't see them in the city. Some on the fringes, though."

"Around here?"

"Not so much."

He twirled them the other way, smiling when she leaned back until her hair drifted through the water and her legs needed to brace his hips more.

"Interesting fact," she said, tipping back up again. "When they hop, roos only ever use their hind legs together. But when they swim, they kick each leg independently like riding a bike."

"I did not know that." His gaze was on her lips. "What about the pouch?"

"Well, they're marsupials. Babies are born when they're maybe an inch long. They travel up through their mommy's fur then slip into her pouch where they hang out for a few months, fattening up, growing big."

"Sounds like a snug but extremely bumpy ride." He twirled her around again. "And they swim, you say?"

"Very well."

"How are they under water?"

Before she could think that through, he put his mouth to hers and pulled them both down.

Her first reaction was to break off and find some air, but she soon learned that she liked smooching that way. When

he brought them both up, her arms were looped around his neck and she was out of breath, in more ways than one.

Humming in her throat, angling her head, she circled the tip of her nose around his. "So, what would you like to discuss now?"

He began to pull her under again. "I think we're all done talking."

The following evening, upon arriving at Grace and Wynn's party, Teagan spotted the happy couple sitting in a chair swing decorated with reams of airy tulle and fragrant cream roses. Grace's taffeta gown was ice pink, with exquisite beading around the sweetheart neckline. A slit up one side revealed a shorter *after the formalities* skirt underneath. Wynn looked debonair, and so proud, in his tailored tux. As their photographer snapped a few shots, Wynn leaned in to kiss his beaming bride while the guests sent up a collective *"Aww."*

Cole and Taryn made their way over through the small crowd.

"Isn't the room gorgeous?" Taryn said to Teagan. The decor had a Venetian honeymoon theme. There was a miniature bridge with a glistening mock canal and gondola, a bar adorned with *carnevale* masks and a starlit "sky."

"The wedding cake is tiramisu." Taryn looked to Jacob, obviously wanting to include him. "Have you been to Italy, Jacob?"

"Aside from the Bahamas, I haven't been out of the States until now."

He'd had a disadvantaged childhood, but Teagan had assumed that he had traveled since then. The fact that he hadn't hesitated to jump on a flight to join her here for this celebration made her feel even better about buckling to his request, even if she'd suffered a huge case of nerves when he'd first arrived.

As Jacob linked her arm through his, Teagan cast a look

around. "Where's Dad?" Cole pointed past the heads and shoulders of the partygoers. Their father was speaking with Milo Vennard. "Oh. I didn't realize the professor was invited."

Cole's grin was slanted. "The other night, Vennard pretty much invited himself. Obviously, he's not finished chewing Dad's ear off about the imminent revolution. He's gotten worse over the years. It's like Hunter Enterprises is responsible for all the economic and social woes of the world. According to him, we need to see the light and make amends."

Watching Guthrie and Vennard, Taryn winced. "Should we rescue him?"

"Dad can take care of himself," Cole said. "At least in that regard."

Looking the part of *on the job* but *under the radar*, in a dark blue suit and matching tie, Brandon Powell strolled up. Cole included his friend in the conversation.

"Has Teagan introduced you to Jacob?"

Straight-faced, Brandon acknowledged Jacob. "We've bumped into each other." With Jacob returning a curt nod, it was obvious the tension between the two men hadn't eased.

Cole was surveying the crowd. "So, everything good?"

With a sweeping, heavy-lidded gaze, Brandon assessed the scene. "Tight as a drum."

"Make sure your guys keep an eye on Tate."

Brandon nodded toward a table where a handful of guests' children were trying on *carnevale* masks. The kids were having fun, but Teagan's mother-hen antennae were quivering.

"Is anyone actually *with* Tate?" she asked.

"Tate has a personal bodyguard assigned." Cole winked at his sister. "Don't worry. We won't let anything happen to him."

Brandon went back to work while Taryn and Cole left to greet friends who had just walked in.

Teagan took the opportunity to bring Jacob up to speed on the details of what led to the current security situation.

"The other weekend, Lanie mentioned the explosion at Cole and Taryn's wedding, but I'm not sure you know the whole story. No one was seriously injured, but Tate came close to being trapped." To being killed. "Wynn found him in the marquee. Another few seconds…"

Jacob bowed his head and swore under his breath. "Poor kid. No wonder…"

Teagan prodded. "No wonder what?"

Jacob's jaw tensed as he looked first at Wynn and Grace and then at Cole and Taryn.

"Well, you all seem so protective of him. I thought I understood why, but that puts your concerns on a whole other level. You had mentioned that Tate stayed with each of you in the States. I have to say, I think that's still a good idea. I think Brandon Powell would even agree with me there."

"Dad and Eloise were still together then. Now they live apart and she's making demands like yesterday when she all of a sudden wanted the kids."

Jacob was frowning…rethinking. "If your father flew either child out of the country without her consent, she could cause all kinds of legal problems for him. And given this ongoing investigation and the continued risk to your father *and* the children…she could have grounds to file for full custody."

Her head was still whirling when Sebastian joined them. After commenting on how lovely the bride looked, he spoke to Teagan.

"My parents pass on their regrets. Talbot hasn't been well. Getting older." With a wry grin, he studied his champagne flute. "Can't turn back time, more's the pity."

Perhaps Jacob could see that Teagan was still wrestling with his legal opinion regarding the possible custody battles. He stepped in with a question.

"Sebastian, you're new to Hunter Broadcasting. How are you enjoying it?"

"It might sound weird, but it feels like home. Of course, I have a lot to learn." Sebastian slid a glance Cole's way. "I know the boss is sick of my questions."

"I'm sure he's not," Teagan assured Sebastian. "You're family."

Sebastian's look said, *That means a lot.* Then he caught sight of Guthrie. "I should go say hi. That Vennard dude's full-on. I feel like the Bolsheviks have their sabers drawn and are marching our way."

When her cousin left, Teagan turned to Jacob. Determined to push those other issues from her mind and enjoy the evening, she ran a fingertip down his black satin lapel. "Are you enjoying yourself?"

His slow, sexy grin drew her in. "There's a dance floor, Tea. And I'm pretty sure they're playing our song."

She laughed. Another cliché. But she really liked the sound of this one.

"I'm in the mood if you are."

"Where you're concerned," he said, "I'm always in the mood."

He was leaning in for a kiss when somewhere behind them an almighty roar went up. Jacob spun around, automatically corralling Teagan behind him, protecting her, while her stomach pitched with panic. All she could think was, *Not again!* and, *Tate!*

But there was no explosion. No flames. No disaster. The roar was the room welcoming newly arrived guests—her brother Dex and his gorgeous fiancée, Shelby.

Releasing that breath, Teagan grabbed Jacob's hand and pulled him over.

"Time to meet more Hunters!"

"What a relief."

From the dance floor, Teagan was watching the last of

the guests bid farewell to Grace and Wynn. The lighting was still subdued, the security detail still on duty, but staff were beginning to clear the tables in earnest now. Decorations were coming down.

Jacob pulled her a bit closer as he asked, "What's a relief?"

"That nothing went wrong."

Her hands trailed across his shoulders and then down until they rested on his shirtfront. Jacob could barely contain the *lucky me* groan. He'd had a nice night, but man, he couldn't wait to move on to the next phase of this evening, which involved him and Teagan being completely alone.

"I can say it aloud now. All night, I kept remembering our last Hunter wedding celebration. But, yay." She glanced around again. "No bomb."

"And no Bolshevik revolution."

As her arms curled higher around his neck and she rested her cheek against his shoulder, Jacob recognized something different going on in his brain. It had to do with being this close, the building heat, looking ahead.

Admitting how he felt.

From the get-go, he'd known Teagan was unique—different from any woman he had ever known...even if there were some similarities where Ivy Schluter was concerned. Both Teagan and his ex came from excessive wealth. They were both beauties with trim builds and confident in every way. Come to think of it, they both had green eyes, too.

As his palm rode up and down Teagan's back and he breathed in that signature vanilla scent, Jacob imagined how much calmer he would feel about the *baby* situation with Ivy if he could swap one woman out for the other. That sounded like he was objectifying them. Like he was sexist. That wasn't it at all. It came down to preferring that Teagan be the mother of his child.

That wasn't wrong. That was fact.

Of course, the paternity test could come back negative,

in which case those kinds of comparisons would be meaningless. But if the baby *did* turn out to be his, nurturing the bond between father and son would take priority over everything else. He would be two hundred percent committed to being the best dad he possibly could be. That kind of commitment took not only time, but also a truckload of energy.

How would Teagan feel about that?

Perhaps the bigger question was, how did Teagan feel about having kids?

Jacob stilled and his ears pricked up. Someone was calling his and Teagan's names.

The Hunters and a couple of stragglers had congregated around a round table by the mock canal. Standing to one side, Wynn was holding Tate, who was slung against his chest and shoulder, sound asleep. As he and Teagan joined them, Jacob shored up his smile. When Dex and his fiancée had arrived earlier, he'd enjoyed a brief conversation with the middle Hunter brother. Dex reminded Jacob of Ajax— the cool chick-magnet dude with the dynamite smile. The guy no one could say no to. His *soon to be* wife, Shelby, was a self-assured redhead with an Okie twang and a brand of charm that was sincere and modest. They both made him feel welcome.

As Jacob and Teagan took a seat, Dex looped an arm around the back of Shelby's chair and made an announcement.

"Shelby and I have something to share." Dex looked into his fiancée's smiling eyes. "Time to come clean."

Shelby told the table, "We've set a date for the big day!"

While Guthrie puffed out his chest, Taryn let out a whoop, and Grace got up to fling her arms around the latest Hunter bride-to-be. And Teagan? Was it imagination or did her response sound forced? Jacob thought she looked happy for her brother and Shelby. Her restraint wasn't due to envy. It felt way more personal than that.

As the congratulations kept coming, Teagan slid a look

his way. Jacob thought she might be thinking about their future, too. Could she be wondering whether he and Ivy might "do the right thing" and tie the knot for the baby's sake? *If* the baby was his. He just couldn't see it.

Guthrie spoke up. "I feel more *future granddad* vibes heading my way."

"Yeah, we want kids." Grinning from ear to ear, Dex stole a kiss from his future bride. "Why waste my darling's special talents?"

Shelby explained for those who didn't know. "I worked with children back home in Mountain Ridge, and I was Tate's nanny while he stayed with Dex in LA." She studied Tate, who was still pushing out z's. "I can't wait to be a mom." She sent a wink Taryn's way. "Can't wait to be an auntie, too."

"I have an adorable niece," Grace said. "Tate met her on Christmas Day...the day Wynn proposed."

"Best day of my life," Wynn said.

Grace sighed. "The older you get, the more you realize children are what makes it all worthwhile. They're what's most important." She looked at Jacob. "Do you have any nieces or nephews, Jacob?"

"My brothers are nowhere near settling down. My sister..." He thought back. "I can't remember if she's ever had a boyfriend. I mean, I'm pretty sure she likes boys."

Teagan gave him a dry look. "Lanie definitely likes boys."

After meeting his sister once, how could Teagan be so sure? Not that it mattered. He loved his sister. He loved all his family, like Teagan so clearly loved hers.

The Vennard dude was sitting at the table, too. Waving that unlit pipe around his head, he put in his two intellectual, and disconnected, cents' worth now.

"The children of future generations are in dire straits. Goliath corporations have taken over, debasing the working wage, destroying the environment, wiping out the fu-

ture for those who breathe the fetid air of the decadently privileged." He pointed the pipe Jacob's way. "The gap between the elite and lower classes is fast evaporating. Soon the homeless will multiply to staggering levels in countries that once bragged about high standards of living."

Everyone was looking either down or away. Great that this man had a passion but, sorry, this was not the place to express it. He was completely over-the-top and out-of-bounds. Still, Jacob had a question. He was living on Easy Street now, but he could never forget the lack of food and opportunity growing up. So many kids were in that same boat today.

"If you were in charge, Professor Vennard, what would be your first command? How would *you* begin to turn it all around?"

Jacob didn't miss Guthrie's grunt of disapproval. Hunter Enterprises was one of those evil Goliath corporations Vennard was ranting about. The family had accrued a massive fortune and, Jacob was sure, saw no reason for change. And the other Hunter men? Cole, Wynn and Dex were looking straight at Jacob as if to ask, *Whose side are you on, Stone?*

"The first thing?" Vennard's eyes gleamed. "I would reclaim all the wealth, those bulging bank accounts, the hoarded property."

Jacob was listening. "How would you do that?"

Vennard gripped his pipe tighter. "Let's assume we had a favorable change of government. The transfer could be achieved quite peacefully."

Cole scratched his ear. "If you're talking about a revolution, they're rarely peaceful."

"Let there be violence then!" Vennard's face was suddenly red. His gaze was burning. "Armies are growing in strength as we speak, waiting in the wings, becoming bolder and smarter, beginning at last to fight back. And, by God, we will *win*."

Jacob had a clear view of the entire room, including the

main entrance. Brandon Powell had stood there surveying the area as guests filed out. Now he moved closer, sending eye signals to his men.

As Jacob had told Teagan, he didn't deal in criminal law, but he had friends who did. Most murders were committed not by strangers but by people known to the deceased. Powell's guys had been thorough when searching guests entering this room. Vennard wasn't armed as such. But his walking stick, Jacob knew, could cause some damage if it came down with enough force. Individuals could die from a sharp object—like a pipe—rammed through an eye socket or throat.

"The elite have used violence in all its forms throughout history," Vennard went on. "They will use any means available to subdue what they term 'the mob.'" When Sebastian cleared his throat, uncomfortable, Vennard spoke directly to him. "*You* know there are people who don't play by the rules. Who are determined to seize power and shut others out."

When Sebastian looked to his cousins around the table for help, Cole spoke up again.

"If you're referring to Hunter Enterprises, Professor, we're all about being fair, offering opportunities. You've worked there a few months now, Sebastian. Tell the professor your experience."

Sebastian's mouth tightened as he shrugged. "It's a great place to work."

Vennard placed his cane on the table as he sat forward. "This boy is reluctant to share his true feelings." With a caring note in his voice now, he addressed Sebastian again. "Decades ago, your father was squeezed out of the Hunter company, wasn't he, son? You should have been perched at the top of the tree now. Instead you are begging for crumbs."

Guthrie intervened. "That's enough, Milo."

Quite enough. Jacob had no objections to people holding fast to their beliefs—philosophical, personal, whatever.

He even agreed with some aspects of Vennard's argument. These days the imbalance between haves and have-nots was staggering. But Jacob was only thinking about Guthrie's safety now.

Vennard's grip on his cane tightened even as he cajoled. Looking at Sebastian, he said, "Let the boy answer."

Sebastian cleared his throat again. "From what I know," he began, "you're right. My father was squeezed out in those early years."

Cole coughed out a humorless laugh. "That's not true. They couldn't agree on—"

"Oh, c'mon. It *is* true. My father still feels betrayed." Sebastian's chin wrenched higher. "And, frankly, I don't blame him. I'd be spitting mad, too."

Jacob was concentrating on Brandon now. He was closing the distance, looking to Cole for a sign to intervene. The situation was going downhill fast.

"It must be hard working alongside me then," Cole replied.

Sebastian's smile didn't quite reach his eyes. "I have great faith it will all even out in the end."

Shooting to his feet, Vennard cried out, "Equality! Liberty!" He swung the cane above his head. "Fraternity against tyranny!"

Cole and Jacob leaped up at the same time Brandon swept in, other guards close behind. As they wrestled with the man, Guthrie, dazed and hurt, stared up at his old friend.

Vennard was struggling, cursing at the brothers. "Get your Fascist hands off me! You can't hold us back."

Tate was stirring awake. While Wynn hurried him away from the commotion, a weary Guthrie made it to his feet.

"Milo…my friend…you're not in your right mind."

"What is genuine is proved in the fire." Vennard's eyes filled with frenzied tears. "We have nothing to lose but our chains."

As Milo Vennard was ushered away, Guthrie muttered to himself again. "He's not well...not well."

Cole sliced a hand through the air. "You can't have that man around anymore. That's the end of it."

"Of course," Guthrie grumbled. "I just wonder..."

"Whether he's been behind the threats on your life?" Dex's eyes narrowed. "He was at the wedding. He mentioned an army waiting in the wings. Does he have connections that are capable of pulling off an explosion?"

"That very first incident, when I was run off the road... I had just spoken to Milo." Guthrie shuddered. "God save us all from fanatics."

Jacob made a point. "The victors in history decide who the fanatics are."

Dex laughed. "You *agree* with Vennard's ranting?"

Jacob thought about his abject poverty growing up. "I think it's fair to say that I have more experience with Vennard's ideas about injustice than you ever could."

Jacob was aware of Teagan sitting beside him, stiff. He moved to take her hand under the table. As soon as their fingers touched, she pulled away.

Sebastian nodded to those at the table. "I'm calling it a night." He pasted on a smile for Grace's sake. "Again, congratulations to you both."

When Sebastian was gone, those left shared a look.

Dex kicked the conversation off. "Sebastian's take on our families' history was an eye-opener."

Guthrie's shoulders slumped further. "I had no idea he was so resentful."

Cole was standing behind his father's chair. "Sebastian appeared on the scene after the attacks began, Dad."

"He was there at your wedding, Cole," Dex added. "And he jumped at the chance to work at Hunter Broadcasting. He's inside now."

Cole speculated. "Keeping his enemy closer?"

Teagan repeated Sebastian's comment. "It will all even out in the end."

Someone's phone was beeping. When Guthrie pulled out his cell, Cole groaned. "Whoever that is can wait."

But Guthrie was already studying the screen.

"It's Eloise," he said and connected.

Jacob didn't think Guthrie's face could get any paler. By the time he disconnected, the older man was visibly shaken. He looked at each of his children and ground out the latest news.

"We need to go. That was Eloise's new beau. She's in hospital. Honey's there, too."

Sixteen

When the Hunters arrived at North Sydney General Hospital, Eloise's lover was waiting. The tall, well-built tank of a man stood by the visitor lounge windows, his hands stuffed into his jeans' pockets as he gazed out at the twinkling city skyline.

Earlier, Kyle Scafe had called on Eloise's phone to inform Guthrie that his estranged wife had suffered head injuries. Apparently, someone from child protection services had taken Honey away.

As they'd rushed from Wynn and Grace's party, Cole had wasted no time contacting the hospital. No one could say whether Honey had been injured, too.

While Taryn, Shelby and Grace had taken Tate home, the rest of the family had piled into Cole's vehicle. Now, like everyone else, Teagan had questions for Kyle Scafe. How had Eloise hit her head? Where was Honey when it happened? Where precisely was the baby now?

Kyle heard them enter the lounge. He edged around, took his hands from his pockets and greeted them with a thousand-yard stare. Teagan had assumed he would be agitated. He only looked detached.

"I'm sorry to meet you under these circumstances," he said as though reciting a line from a play.

Cole, Dex and Wynn stood beside their father while Guthrie stepped forward and demanded, "Is my daughter still on the premises?"

Kyle Scafe's broad brow wrinkled like he was trying to think. "I have no idea."

"I'll go find some answers," Dex told his brothers.

He was about to head off when a doctor joined them. "Who do I speak with about Eloise Hunter?" she asked.

Guthrie straightened. "I'm her husband."

The doctor lowered her folder. "When your wife was brought in, she was under the influence of alcohol. Mrs. Hunter suffered a blow to the head. No fractures, but abrasions and bruising. I've ordered an MRI to check for bleeding on the brain."

Guthrie was nodding. "And my daughter? The baby?"

Kyle moved closer. "I was with Eloise when it happened. When we got here, Honey was taken away."

The doctor looked between the two men. "I'm sure CPS have questions for you both. I'll let the representative know you're here." She spoke to Guthrie. "You can see your wife now. She's awake."

Guthrie exhaled. "Thank you."

As they all moved forward, the doctor held up a hand. "Only Mr. Hunter at this time."

As Guthrie followed the doctor down the hall, Teagan felt the atmosphere in the waiting lounge turn from strained to verging on lethal. No one took a seat while a dazed Kyle ran a hand through his dirty-blond hair.

"Eloise obviously has a problem," he said.

Cole folded his arms. "At least one."

"I've seen her drink before, but never around the kids." Kyle's unshaven jaw clenched as his walnut-size Adam's apple bobbed up and down. "I hadn't realized that she'd downed almost the entire bottle of gin. The last time she came back from the bathroom, she was swaying."

Teagan asked, "Where was the baby?"

"With me, asleep in her playpen."

"And the full-time nanny my father pays for?"

"Eloise sacked her earlier today."

Wynn set his fists low on his hips. "What happened next?"

"I got up to help Ellie," Kyle said, "but she pulled back,

fell and—" He smacked his head to demonstrate. "The ambulance only took a few minutes."

The doctor appeared again. "The family can go through. The baby is with her parents now."

The doctor provided a room number. As she walked off, Kyle started after her.

Dex blocked his way. "Sorry. She said family."

Eloise's lover's face turned dark and hard. His hands clenched but he obviously thought better of starting anything, particularly with all three brothers ready to take him on if need be.

Leaving Kyle behind, they all found the room and edged inside. When Teagan saw Eloise, she winced. Eloise's eyes were puffy and bruised. The amount of bandage wound around her head was daunting. But no one asked how she was. Instead they gravitated to their father's side. Guthrie was holding the baby.

Eloise sounded groggy. Whiny. Still sloshed.

"I'm sorry...so sorry..."

Teagan had always let her stepmother's questionable behavior slide. She'd never wanted to cause or add to any ill feelings. This time Eloise had gone too far.

Teagan felt her nostrils flare as she growled, "You disgust me."

Eloise's swollen eyes widened. "Tea, sweetie, don't say that. I can't take that kinda talk."

Keeping her eyes on the baby, Teagan held up a hand. "I'm only thinking about Honey and Tate now."

Eloise tried to sit up. "Well, Honey's not hurt, is she?"

"Next time, she could be," Dex said.

"You're forgettin'—" Eloise's chin rose "—I'm that child's mama."

Feeling ill, Teagan groaned. "You don't deserve to be."

Standing behind her, Jacob held Teagan's shoulders—his touch warm, strong and supportive. But she hadn't forgotten his earlier comments, which made crystal clear his

opinion of her family. His questions had helped drive that earlier conversation off a cliff. *If you were in charge, Professor Vennard, what would be your first command? How would you begin to turn it around?*

And she had more to worry about now.

Eloise's eyes welled up as she sank back onto the pillow. "I just feel so lost. So afraid. I don't know what to do."

"Here's a start," Wynn said. "Give up the bottle."

As a tear ran down her cheek, Eloise begged Guthrie. "I want to change. I want to be a better mother." Her voice cracked. "I *need* to be a better wife."

"You've said that before." Guthrie shook his head. "This can't go on."

"No. No, it can't." Eloise closed her eyes and held her bandaged brow like she was trying to remember. "You wanted me to go to rehab. I'm ready. Ready tonight. Right now."

Honey was wide awake, her big blue eyes darting between each of their faces as if she were trying to keep up with the conversation. Teagan wanted to tell her, *You'll never have to worry again. We'll protect you from now on, I promise.*

"It's not that easy anymore," Guthrie told his wife. "The authorities are involved now."

Eloise began to sob, maybe for real, maybe for show. "One more chance. Oh, Guthrie. I want to go home."

Cole had a question. "What about the man who brought you here? What will Kyle Scafe have to say about that?"

"Well, Kyle will just have to understand." She reached out an arm, fingers splayed wide. "Bring Honey to me. I want to tell her I'm sorry."

Guthrie hesitated before his mouth tightened and he moved over to the bed. Teagan felt for her father. He had to protect his children. To do that, he needed to keep them away from their mother. Come Monday, she knew he would

file for full custody. From then on, any visits with Eloise would be supervised.

As Eloise fawned over Honey and her husband, the others turned to leave them alone.

Someone stood blocking the doorway.

"Is Ellie all right?" Kyle asked, trying to see into the room. "I heard crying."

Cole crowded the man back. "I'm sure Eloise will be fine."

Kyle tried again to see past the wall of Hunter brothers. "I need to see Ellie. Just a minute or two."

Dex held up a hand. "Buddy, you need to leave."

Kyle took a moment before stepping back. When the brothers were out of the way, however, the ex-military man lunged into the room.

"Kyle!" Eloise's mouth trembled with an uncertain smile. "I didn't know you were still here."

Kyle's head went back. "Where the hell *else* would I be?"

As Guthrie handed the baby to Teagan, a nurse, who had obviously heard the commotion, trounced in.

"Okay." She pointed at the doorway. "Everyone needs to leave now."

But Kyle wouldn't budge. He was staring at Eloise, slowly shaking his head as he murmured, "I'm not leaving, Ellie. I'm not."

Wynn tried to make the man see reason. "Let's not make a scene. Think of the baby."

Kyle only wanted to hear from Eloise. His expression was so pained, he looked as if his insides were being ripped out. "You're not going back to him, are you?"

"You need to go." When the nurse put her hand on Kyle's arm, he flung her off and said again, low but also firm, "Ellie, you can't go back."

Eloise waved her hand in the air dismissively. "We'll talk later. Listen to the lady. You need to go now."

Kyle's pale eyes were glistening. "You don't love him.

You've told me that a thousand times." Then he turned his attention to Guthrie. His voice was thick, on the verge of breaking. "You need to be out of her life."

Guthrie backed up. "Calm down, son."

"You just won't *go*!"

"I'm getting security," Cole said.

But as he turned, Kyle exploded and sucker punched Cole from behind. At the same time, Dex caught Cole as he fell forward. Wynn, who was at the door, called out for security, then shot back into the room to help his father. Jacob got there first.

He grabbed Kyle from behind. As the man swung around, Jacob jabbed him low and hard in the ribs. When Kyle doubled over, Jacob delivered a swift uppercut to the jaw. Kyle was stumbling back when two security men shot inside the room.

As the uniformed men each grabbed an arm, Kyle shook his head and, appearing dazed again, looked around. Then he drew in a breath, straightened to his full height and made an announcement.

"I want a lawyer."

Seventeen

"Sorry to bother you guys so early," Wynn said, stepping inside the guesthouse the next morning, "but I figure you'd want to know. Kyle Scafe confessed to the attempts on Dad's life."

All the breath left Teagan's lungs at the same time Jacob put a bracing arm around her. She was shaking.

"Thank God, thank God, it's finally over."

The previous evening, fingers had been pointed at Milo Vennard and then at Sebastian. But after Kyle had asked for a lawyer at the hospital, people began to seriously wonder. Later, gathered back at the Hunter estate, everyone had talked into the early hours. The general consensus was that Eloise's live-in lover was a far more likely suspect, and they'd been right.

"Something else." Wynn arched a brow. "Kyle thinks he's Honey's father."

Teagan held her sick stomach. "So the affair's been going on a while."

"Apparently there was a one-night stand. Eloise didn't want to see him again, but Kyle grew more and more obsessed. He started out wanting to scare Dad. Some macho crap about needing to prove to Eloise what a weak man she'd married. They only got back together when Eloise and Dad separated."

Jacob asked, "How did he organize the explosion at the wedding?"

"He got friendly with the DJ before the event and managed to slip the device in with the equipment. Brandon's looking into how that could have happened on his watch."

Wynn sucked in air between his teeth. "I would like to know, too."

"Let's just be grateful more harm wasn't done," Teagan said.

Whenever she thought of how close Tate had come to being caught in those flames, she got goose bumps.

Wynn stuck his hand into his pocket. "Another thing. Dad's taking a paternity test. Not that it will make any difference. Kyle Scafe will be put away for a very long time and those results will remain private."

"And Honey," Teagan said, "will stay with us."

From the day Honey was born, she had fallen in love with that little girl. Paternity results could never change that. Honey was family and always would be.

Wynn smiled at his sister. "Grace and I are heading off today to see friends who couldn't make the party. We'll be back later in the week," he said, wrapping up the conversation.

"I'm flying out tomorrow," Jacob said.

Wynn studied the other man and put out his hand. "Thanks for helping out last night. I thought Kyle might break your jaw. You ended up almost breaking his. You must've taken self-defense lessons."

Accepting Wynn's hand, Jacob admitted, "Every day for the first fourteen years of my life."

When she and Jacob were alone again, Teagan moved to the window view. Looking out at the harbor, she hugged herself tight.

"Dad will really need support now." More than ever.

Jacob joined her. "More visits home?"

"I've been thinking. I'm going to put the gym on the market. Come back here to live for a while."

Jacob looked at her like she'd said she'd eaten razor blades for lunch. "Back to Australia? Half a world away?"

"It's not half a world away to me. I lived here most of my life."

"You said you didn't *like* your life."

Uh, no. "I said I wanted to do my own thing. Now I want to do that in Sydney rather than Seattle."

Their gazes were still locked when Jacob's phone pinged.

"You should get that," she said.

"We're talking."

She raised a brow. "Read the message."

He hesitated before digging out his phone. As his eyes shut tight and he seemed to curl into himself, Teagan watched the color drain from his face.

"What happened?" She gripped his arm. "Jacob, what's wrong?"

"That was the paternity testing company. The results... they're *positive*. The baby's mine." His shoulders pulled back as he sucked in a sharp breath and peered into her eyes. "I'm a father."

Teagan's mouth dropped open. She'd known this was a possibility, but deep down she'd believed those results would be negative. Clearly, Jacob had felt the same way.

So what did she do now? Congratulate him? Saying sorry didn't fit.

Jacob was staring off...looking ahead.

"It's weird," he said. "I've only ever seen photos, but these past weeks I've thought so much about how my life would change if he actually were mine. I'd be watching him grow into a man, guiding him along the way. Making sure he gets a solid education. Being there at his wedding. But I honestly didn't think it would turn out like that."

Jacob looked so thrown. Who wouldn't be? Still, Teagan couldn't help but wish this revelation belonged to her... that someone had passed on the news that *she* was a parent.

"He's a lucky boy to have you and the Rawsons behind him."

Jacob seemed to wither at the idea of telling his family. Then he took both her hands in his and searched her eyes.

"Have you thought about children, Tea? Having a family?"

Not so long ago, she hadn't thought of anything else. But now she needed to come at the question from a more impersonal point of view.

"I think most people think about that on some level, at some time."

"Seeing how you are with Tate and Honey… I think you'd make a great mom."

His eyes shone in a way she hadn't seen before. Her throat got so choked up, she wondered if she could push out the words.

"I think so, too."

He cupped her cheek. "If you do move back home…" He smiled. "Well, we'll just need to get inventive."

Oh, Jacob. "It'll take more than that."

"*Whatever* it takes, because the way I feel when I'm with you…it's the way I felt when I went to live with the Rawsons. I feel safe, Tea. I feel *home*. Maybe we could build on that together."

Her stomach was tied up in knots. They'd agreed to be transparent, but she had held on to one deep, dark secret. Now she couldn't keep it back.

"You know about my scar. That childhood accident."

He nodded. "You fell off a bike."

"I had so many surgeries, so much time off school. Later I was told I would never conceive."

His eyes widened before he took a breath and nodded. "That had to be a shock."

"It was more of a shock when I *did* conceive."

"Wait. You're saying you have a child?"

"I miscarried. The worst day of my life." She was going to be a mom—then suddenly she wasn't.

He didn't hesitate. He bundled her up in his arms and murmured against her ear, "Tea… I'm so sorry."

She soaked in the warmth and for the first time wasn't flooded by images of blood on the bathroom floor when

she thought of that night. Still, the upshot was the same. "I will never carry a baby to its full term."

She drew away and held his gaze, waiting for a response.

"I want you to know," he began, "that doesn't make any difference to me. Being a father was never on my agenda. My old man was a complete douche. I hate that I have his genes. I never wanted to pass them on. I never wanted to be put in a position where I could make the same mistakes."

Teagan was blown away—*not* in a good way.

"But you *have* passed them on. You have a son now."

"I know. I *know*. I guess what I'm trying to say is… I'm totally on board with stopping at one."

She should have breathed out a sigh of relief. It sounded like a win-win all around. And yet seeing the uncompromising gleam in his eyes only made the knots in Teagan's stomach twist tighter.

Jacob wanted to do better than his own father had done. But if a person had never wanted a child—if he had pretty much decided to renounce every paternal bone in his body…

How on earth would this relationship between father and son end?

A voice in her head kept whispering, *Maybe not so well.*

Eighteen

A week later, back in Seattle, she took a call from New York. The first thing Jacob said was, *"I miss you so much, baby,"* and Teagan melted inside.

It felt so good to hear his voice again. It brought back how passionate and alive he made her feel. It also made her wish there was some way to fix what was missing between them. Some way to make this work.

"I had to let you know," Jacob said, "Grant Howcroft OD'd yesterday."

A chill crept up her spine. Howcroft was the actor who'd wanted to sue Hunter Publications for defamation over reporting on his use of drugs.

"He died?"

"No, but apparently authorities found a huge stash at his home." Jacob paused. "Go ahead. Say, 'I told you so.'"

"I'm just glad he gets another chance." She added, "And, yes, I'm happy for Wynn."

Her brother's reputation remained firmly intact, as it should. As she'd always known it would.

Jacob changed the subject. "So, what are you up to?"

Dragging her teeth over her lower lip, Teagan took in the scene beyond her office window where scores of enthusiastic clients were enjoying the gym's main workout area.

"Actually, I put the gym on the market."

"Oh. So, you're going ahead with it then?"

"It could take a while to sell."

She waited for him to mention her intended move back to Sydney. When he didn't, she let it slide, too.

"How's your dad doing?" he asked. "Have you heard?"

"With Kyle Scafe locked up until the trial, he's feeling relieved that he doesn't have to look over his shoulder anymore."

"And Eloise?"

"She's in treatment, so fingers crossed there."

Given the circumstances surrounding her stay in the hospital, hopefully Eloise would be motivated enough to turn herself around. Miracles sometimes happened; Teagan truly wanted to believe that.

"And the kids?"

"I spoke to Tate last night. He says that he loves the new nanny Dad hired, and Honey does, too, so I shouldn't worry about them."

Jacob chuckled. "He's a good boy."

Yeah. "He's the best."

"So, what are you doing this weekend?" His tone was purposely upbeat. "I can fly out. Or we can meet midway. How about Colorado? There's a bluegrass fest happening. And I know a great place to stay." He groaned like he was caught between pleasure and pain. "A week's too damn long not to have you in my arms."

Teagan closed her eyes. Every part of her ached to have him close again, too. She wanted his mouth covering hers, his hard heat pressing in. But these past few days she'd had more time to think things through. She felt sick to her stomach having to say it, but there was no way to sugarcoat.

She took a deep breath and forced the words out.

"Jacob, I don't think this is going to work."

The silence was deafening. *Agonizing.* It went on for so long, she wasn't certain he was still there.

"Jacob?"

"Is it because of the distance?" His voice was so raw.

"That's a factor." But hardly the deal breaker.

"We can make that work. Some weekends…vacation time…"

"You have a child to consider now."

And wasn't it telling that she was the one who had to mention that? If she was in his place, a new parent, no one would be able to shut her up.

Jacob sounded uncertain now. "Does that make a difference to how you feel about us?"

She shut the window blinds and withered into a chair. "I don't want to get in the way."

"If you need time, Tea, I'll wait."

"Jacob, that wouldn't be fair."

"On who?"

"You need time to focus on that baby." *You need to make sure that works, not us.*

While another silence stretched out between them, the nerves in Teagan's stomach squeezed and squeezed. She'd broken up with Damon because she hadn't been able to give him the family he'd wanted. Jacob had never wanted children—that fit with her physical but not her emotional makeup. She *loved* kids. And she worried that Jacob's ambivalence would taint his relationship with his son, perhaps deeply.

She couldn't fix that, or be a part of it. Inevitably, it would tear her, and them, apart.

"You're right," he said finally. "I've got a full plate at the moment. You do, too."

Tears were stinging the backs of her eyes. She hated that this was happening, but she just couldn't see any other way.

"There's a lot going on," she agreed.

He cleared his throat. She imagined him running a hand through his hair.

"So, best of luck with selling the gym."

Dying inside, she held the phone closer to her ear. "All the best with…everything."

She was thinking of something more to round off the goodbyes. It all seemed so abrupt. So final. But then it was too late.

Jacob was already gone.

Nineteen

"I know this must be a surprise."

Teagan gaped at the woman standing at High Tea Gym's entrance and admitted, "That's the understatement of the year."

"I was in town for an event," Lanie Rawson said, wearing her jodhpurs and knee-high boots like the best socialites wore Givenchy. "We need to talk."

Teagan wanted to roll her eyes. *Stop with the intimidation tactics already.*

"You obviously haven't heard," Teagan replied. "Jacob and I aren't seeing each other anymore."

They'd said goodbye six long weeks ago. It still hurt, and she still wondered, especially lying awake late at night. But her decision to step away was the right one. Jacob had an important job ahead of him. He needed to work all his issues out for himself. It wouldn't help anyone, including that baby, for her to be involved.

As Lanie looked around, that storm of long brunette hair swished across her shoulders. The main workout area was filled with clients cycling, running, pumping weights. The music was pumping, too. "Can we go somewhere more private to talk?"

What could they possibly have to talk about? What was the point? But then Teagan thought back to how Jacob and Wynn's relationship had started off—they'd been like two bee-stung bulls ready to charge. By the end of their Sydney visit, the pair were shaking hands and meaning it. She wouldn't turn Jacob's sister away now without giving her some time.

Then she'd kick her out.

They went into Teagan's office and took seats around the small conference table. Lanie swept back her hair, clasped her hands on the tabletop and pinned Teagan with a no-holds-barred look.

"First," she began, "I want to apologize. When you were at the farm, I was rude."

Teagan almost spluttered. *Well, yeah.*

"I was angry," Lanie went on. "Worried that Jacob would be hurt again."

Because of his relationship with Ivy Schluter?

"Lanie, you don't even know me."

The other woman paused and then came at it from a different angle.

"We were all surprised to learn that Jacob was a father," she said. "I know he was, too. Until recently, it was the furthest thing from his mind. But when the results came in, there was never any doubt that the rest of the family would accept and love Benson." A thoughtful smile softened her gaze. "He's the most adorable little boy. You can't imagine."

Teagan *could* imagine, because she'd felt the same way when Tate had been born. Instantly smitten. One hundred percent committed. That went for Honey, as well.

"But the mother." Lanie visibly shuddered. "When Jacob and Ivy dated, he was in a constant spin. She was either smoldering or colder than a January frost. Ivy comes from big money and happily admits that it's all about her. Jacob was not a priority. I felt like I was watching a replay of how he must have felt growing up. Entirely dispensable." Lanie's head angled. "You know the story?"

Teagan nodded. A drug-addicted mother and criminal deadbeat dad. No love. No *anything*. Lanie was right. As a child, Jacob must have felt thrown away.

"Naturally, Jacob had baggage to burn," Lanie went on. "But he had faith in my father, and he grew to trust us all. Ivy came along at precisely the wrong time when he was

ready to trust on a different level. She reeled him in, spat him out, reeled him in again. Their breakup hit him hard. When Jacob said he was bringing someone new home to meet the family, I was so glad to hear excitement in his voice again. Ivy was finally a sulky blip in his rearview mirror. Then, like any normal person, I searched you on the internet. I learned that Teagan Hunter was the daughter of one of the top three wealthiest men in Australia. Naturally, I thought, *Here we go again.* Another überrich bitch wanting to jerk my brother's heartstrings. And when I met you, frankly, you looked the part."

Teagan's smile was saccharine sweet.

Don't respond.

"I was bursting to tell you that Jacob didn't need that kind of crap again. I wanted you gone. And if you needed a push, no skin off my nose."

"I'm sure Jacob can look after his own affairs." *In every sense of the word.*

As Lanie leaned forward, a dark wave fell over her eyes. "You have siblings, Teagan. If they were vulnerable, wouldn't you try to protect them?"

Tate and Honey's faces flashed into Teagan's mind. With their mother in rehab, their parents' marriage on life support...

Would she try to protect her siblings?

Teagan lifted her chin. "In a heartbeat."

The heat in Lanie's eyes cooled a few degrees and she settled back in her seat. "Do you know that Jacob has the baby every weekend now?"

Teagan blinked. "Jacob asked for that?"

"Ivy suggested it. Almost *demanded* it. Apparently her beauty sleep has suffered terribly, poor dear. Anyway, Jacob's bought a place in Connecticut and works from home if Ivy wants another day or two's reprieve." Lanie's gaze drifted off. "I'm sure Jacob loves that little boy...but he's

so torn. He *wants* to be happy." Her gaze locked with Teagan's again. "He just misses you so much."

Teagan's stomach pitched. "He told you that?"

Lanie nodded then let out a sigh. "For what it's worth, I don't think you're another version of Ivy. You're not just *me me me*. I think your breakup has to do with Jacob becoming a father out of the blue. But no matter how much you try to hide it, I can see in your eyes that you miss him, too. So maybe there's a chance..." Her smile was wan. "Anyway, I had to try."

Lanie had admitted she'd been wrong about her. Teagan had been wrong about Lanie, too. Her behavior at the Rawsons' farm had had nothing to do with being jealous. Lanie wasn't in love with her stepbrother. She was a caring sister who had taken a chance in coming here today for Jacob's sake.

After the women exchanged numbers and said goodbye, Teagan sat at her desk thinking about Jacob and the challenges they had faced as a couple since that amazing first night. First, there'd been Jacob's pending defamation lawsuit against Wynn. No longer an issue. The second challenge was distance, which would only become more of a problem when she moved back to Sydney. *If* she moved back. This morning she had signed an agreement to sell her business. Although she loved the people—staff as well as clients— she wasn't as sad walking away as she'd thought she might be. But the more time that passed since her last visit home, the more Teagan wondered. With her father's life no longer in danger, and Eloise making a real effort for the first time in her marriage, it didn't seem so critical to make that permanent move for the kids' sakes.

The third challenge involved trying to reconcile the legacy of Jacob's childhood with his present-day points of view. Growing up, Jacob had had it rough. Now he was a crusader for those who had been wronged, particularly by corporations—like Hunter Enterprises.

But the tipping point had come when Jacob received word that he was indeed a father. He admitted that he'd never wanted to be a parent; he certainly didn't want any more children, and he was afraid of making the same mistakes his own father had made. Teagan hadn't been able to see herself with someone who was so anti-kids…who was hardly looking forward to accepting and enjoying such a precious gift. The info Lanie had shared today hadn't convinced Teagan otherwise.

I'm sure Jacob loves that little boy…but he's so torn.

Teagan studied her screen saver—a photo of Tate cuddling Honey—and suddenly a thought came to mind.

Was she missing something—actually *two* things—that might make all the difference? She couldn't know for sure, but there was a way to find out. Of course, it would mean Jacob needing to weather another surprise, and she wasn't at all certain he would like it.

But first she had to make a decision.

Was she even brave enough to try?

Twenty

After getting Jacob's address from Lanie, Teagan flew the next morning into Connecticut, then traveled the last few miles by rental car to this house. The double-story Colonial on Huckleberry Lane wasn't scary. But the anticipation of what came next sure as heck was.

Opening the car door, Teagan reminded herself that *she* had been the one to call things off. On top of that, she and Jacob hadn't spoken in weeks. How would he react when, out of nowhere, she came knocking? Perhaps he would welcome her with open arms.

Or would he slam the door in her face?

Teagan wandered up a path that cut through a large, open yard. She had almost reached the front door—was summoning up enough nerve to ring the bell—when she heard a noise somewhere in the near distance. A low conversation.

She crossed to the side of the house and gingerly peered around the corner. Jacob was standing alongside a children's play area that housed a colorful fort, slide, swing and mini seesaw. He was shoveling from a pile of sand into a boarded-off area—filling a sandbox. His T-shirt was damp around the neck and down the back. It clung to his well-defined shoulders and biceps as he pushed the shovel in and pulled it out. He not only looked more relaxed than she remembered, he also looked *sexier*—around a thousand times more than she was prepared for.

His words were too muffled to make out. And no one else was around. So, was he talking to himself? But then he looked off toward a big elm that bookended the other side of the playground. A bouncer chair was set up under the

tree's shade. A baby lay beneath the mobile animals hanging from the bouncer's handle. Every ounce of his focus was fixed upon Jacob.

On his father.

Jacob set the shovel into the sand then rested a crooked arm on the handle and wiped his brow with the sleeve of his T-shirt. He said something more and then chuckled. Oh God, she *loved* that deep rumbling sound. The baby obviously did, too; his little arms and legs started waving all over the place.

The little guy was dressed in a pale blue sleeveless onesie. Perfect for this late summer weather. His thighs were just chubby enough—so different from Honey's "lolly" legs. He had energy, too, like he wanted to leap out of that bouncer, grab a spade of his own and show Dad how it was done.

Teagan wanted to laugh. She also wanted to cry. The scene was so ordinary and yet special. So near but also out of reach.

Jacob must have sensed someone nearby and turned around. When he saw her, he didn't move for so long, she thought he might have turned to stone.

Showtime. Deep breaths now.

Edging forward, Teagan waved in greeting.

"Hi, there."

Jacob sucked in a breath, which only inflated that amazing chest. But his expression wasn't expansive. He looked pissed. Put out.

"What are you doing here?"

Her stomach was churning. "I thought I'd drop in."

"All the way from Seattle?"

She nodded. "All the way from Seattle."

When the baby squealed, Jacob's attention whipped that way again and, in an instant, any uncertainty or aggravation dissolved from his face. With that beautiful big-cat gait, he ambled over to the bouncer, tossing his yard gloves off and

wiping his brow again along the way. Then he crouched before his son and smiled like nothing else in the whole wide world mattered.

"What's up, little man?" he asked, unfastening the safety harness and scooping the baby up. "Did you see we have a guest?"

Teagan hung back. She didn't want to get in anyone's face, particularly an infant who hadn't laid eyes on her before now.

Jacob saw to the introductions. "Benson, meet Teagan."

"Pleased to meet you, Benson," she said.

The baby looked at her like Jacob had earlier—questioning, probing. But—*ohmigod!*—what about the color of his eyes? They were the exact same shade as his dad's—a mesmerizing, deep amber gold.

Teagan edged closer. "Jacob, he has your eyes."

Focused on the baby, too, Jacob gave in to a lopsided, *proud as punch* grin. "They only turned that color the last couple of weeks."

Then his brows eased together and he looked at her again. Differently this time, like he'd just remembered that six weeks ago she had left him. Goodbye forever and good luck.

His question sounded thin—like he was filling time.

"How's your family?"

"Eloise seems to be cutting it in rehab."

"Hope it sticks. You know what they say about addiction. It's a hard habit to break."

She smiled. It was a joke. And it wasn't.

His lidded gaze raked over her again before he nodded toward the house. "Wanna come in for a cold drink? I have ice water."

"Ice water sounds great."

"You thirsty, too?" he asked Benson.

The baby beamed and tapped his dad's chest as if to say, *Lead the way.*

As Jacob headed off, Teagan asked, "Do you want me to carry the bouncer inside?"

He looked back and then down at the baby. "That's okay. We'll come out again later, right, Buddy?"

As they made their way across the yard, up the back stairs and into the house, Teagan couldn't fight off that sinking feeling. Lanie had said that Jacob had missed her. The vibe she was getting now was more, *Do me a favor and disappear*. On a brighter note, he didn't seem to hate being a father, and the baby certainly wasn't unhappy. Jacob had been so committed to his career. Had she caught him on a good day or was he okay with being a full-on parent every weekend?

Despite dark timber cabinetry, the large kitchen was bright—full of windows welcoming in natural light. Jacob went to the refrigerator and retrieved a yellow sippy cup. Benson put out his hands and took a small sip then another.

"He loves it cold, but not too much." When the baby pushed the cup away, Jacob added, "He's on solids now, so the digestive system's working right. Which reminds me." He crossed to a cushioned bench, lay the baby down and, like a pro, checked his diaper. "It's not good to drop off to sleep when you're wet, or worse."

When Jacob was satisfied his son was dry and clean, he scooped the baby up again and moved to a cupboard to grab a couple of glasses. With only one hand free, he got the first glass down, then the next, which he took to the refrigerator water dispenser. Teagan stepped forward. When you were carrying a baby, everyday activities weren't so easy to negotiate.

"Do you want me to take him?" Then she added, "Or I can take care of the water."

"Want to go to the nice lady?" Jacob asked Benson.

Teagan put out her hands and offered her best *this will be so much fun* look. The baby pushed out his bottom lip

before he snuggled back into Jacob's arm and hid his face. Her stomach plummeted. Not a good start.

She was filling the second glass when Jacob asked, "Why are you really here, Tea?"

She hesitated before giving him the glass and the truth.

"I wanted to see if you liked being a father."

He looked...underwhelmed. Like, *I need your approval now?* Nevertheless, he asked. "How am I doing?"

"You're doing great." From what she had seen.

"I thought I'd have to think about it every minute, you know. But now, whenever Buddy and I are together, it's second nature." He winked at Benson—Buddy—who looked so gorgeous and totally at home resting against Daddy's shoulder. "Did you have any doubt?" he asked her. "Where your younger siblings were concerned, I mean."

"No doubt at all. After each one arrived, it felt as if they'd always been there, a part of our lives. I can't imagine my world without them."

"That's how I feel about Buddy. I know I was thrown by the possibility, and even more taken aback when I knew for sure he was mine. No getting around it. The news was a shock. But we're a team now. Done deal." He looked down, his eyebrows jumped, and then he chuckled. "Even if he thinks I'm a bore."

Buddy's eyes were closed, with his gorgeous little mouth slightly open and his free arm hanging. He was fast asleep and so darn cute. Teagan wanted to reach out and touch the satin of his cheek then inhale that heavenly baby scent.

She whispered, "He's really out of it."

Still gazing at his son, Jacob whispered, too. "I'll put him down. He usually naps around this time for an hour or so."

As he walked away, he lobbed a suggestion over his shoulder. "Maybe take a seat on the back porch. There's a breeze coming through."

She nodded. "Sounds good."

Still, she didn't move until Jacob had disappeared up the staircase. That man knew how to rock a tuxedo or custom-made suit. He had blue jeans and boots down pat. But *sexy daddy putting down baby for his nap* was by far his best look. She could soak it in all day long.

She took a seat on the back porch and thought back on the conversation they had after he'd learned he was a father. He'd admitted that he had never wanted children. That he certainly didn't want any more. Some part of Jacob would always be the boy who had grown up without love or support, and he was smart enough to know that deficit could affect the relationship with his son.

The conviction behind his words that day had stopped Teagan in her tracks. His uncompromising attitude had made her think of people who complained when they heard a child cry, or rolled their eyes and shuddered if a kid was having fun rather than being "seen and not heard." She wasn't able to have one of her own, but she would always love the sound of children playing. She would always feel compassion whenever a young person was in distress or needed help. On the flip side, Jacob had thought life would be better if he never had to deal with any of it. On top of that, when she had come to the decision to call it quits for good, Jacob had bowed out without an argument. Like Damon.

But after Lanie's visit, Teagan had begun to wonder.

Despite his misgivings, could Jacob be the kind of father he had needed growing up? And if the answer to that question was yes, there was another one to ask.

How deeply did his feelings for her run? Had things become all too difficult, or were they worth fighting for? Now Teagan was more optimistic about the first question, not so confident about the second.

Jacob walked out through the back screen door. Resting his water glass on a muscular jean-clad thigh, he gazed out

over the yard and playground while she took in his profile, particularly the faint smile tugging his lips.

"Buddy's in his cot." He showed her a baby monitor. "These are amazing. You can hear every peep."

"Peace of mind, huh?"

"That's the goal."

"I like his nickname."

"I got used to Benson, but he looks more like a Buddy to me. The first time I called him that, he was taking a bath. He squealed and splashed till I was soaked through."

As he brought the glass to his lips, a pulse began to beat high in his bristled cheek and then his gaze went to the porch floorboards. The pause was a long one but she waited. Obviously he had something important to say.

"There's been a new development," he finally said. "Ivy's signed over full custody."

Teagan's mouth dropped open. *What the...?*

Despite Eloise's progress, Guthrie had gone ahead and applied for sole custody of Tate and Honey, too. It was not a small thing.

"She doesn't want Buddy to live with her? Doesn't want to be involved in any of the decisions?"

Jacob shrugged one shoulder and grunted. "As of two days ago, he's all mine. She doesn't even want to visit. Says it's better this way. 'A clean cut,' she called it."

Teagan was near speechless. "I can't believe a mother would do that." Even Eloise wouldn't give her children away.

"Oh, *I* can believe it. And if that's how Ivy feels, it's better that I take over completely."

Teagan had thought that Jacob would have a hard time assimilating to part-time fatherhood. In fact, he had taken on the role *full*-time, and seemed not only committed but happy to do it.

"I'm going to have to think about how to tell Buddy one day. I don't want him growing up thinking it was his fault, because he's perfect. Everything about him."

Teagan felt the tears threatening to fall. His words and tone sealed the deal. Jacob might have his biological father's DNA but he had a mind-set and heart similar to Hux's, his dad through adoption.

"And I'm only grateful that Ivy didn't stretch it out," he went on. "At one stage, she was threatening to take me to court over some half-assed reason. What a waste of time and energy."

Teagan remembered the lawsuit Jacob had wanted to file against Wynn. Not so much fun when the shoe was on the other foot.

"So it's all done?" she asked.

"Signed and binding."

"What if Ivy changes her mind?"

His nose crinkled as he shook his head. "You'd have to know her. She had everything, anytime, in every way. Instead of understanding how lucky she was and giving back, people just don't seem to matter to her. Even her own son. Out of sight. Out of mind."

Teagan had to wonder…had Jacob been drawn to Ivy because of his past? Had he subconsciously chosen a partner who was as emotionally unavailable as his parents had been? A psychologist friend had once said that everyone wanted to recreate and control some aspect of their childhood. For example, Teagan wanted to be a wonderful parent like her own mom.

Which reminded her…

"The gym's sold," she said. "Signed the papers yesterday." She was free to return home if she wanted.

"I might have to do the same with my law firm," he said. "I can worry about having a Manhattan office after Buddy graduates. Or maybe I won't. There's lots of interesting stuff I can do from right here."

He talked about moving away from defamation cases and going into family law. He wanted to work with separated or divorced parents to get them to cooperate rather than pit

one against the other. He talked about helping people with mental health and addiction problems who faced legal ramifications and family breakdown. He got particularly wound up when he explained about wanting to save as many kids as he could from juvie hell. He wanted to create a sanctuary like the Rawson Stud Farm and make certain the facility was available to boys and girls who'd been thrown away by their parents as well as society.

The longer he spoke, the more enthusiasm and belief blazed in his beautiful eyes. Teagan could have listened all day…all night.

He'd changed so much in such a short span of time. He still came across as driven but without the need to dominate. It was like he had found what made him truly happy and now he could sit back, take a breath and simply build on that.

And she got the impression he didn't see her as part of that equation. In the past, whenever they'd been together, he could barely keep from kissing her, touching her, telling her how incredible she made him feel. When she'd arrived unannounced, he'd been taken aback. Annoyed. Now it was more like, *No hard feelings.*

That left Teagan feeling like an idiot, hating that she hadn't believed in him more. Hadn't believed in *them.*

Jacob checked his wristwatch. "I should wake Buddy up. If he sleeps too long during the day, he wants to stay up and play with the owls."

"Does he have a cuddle toy?"

"*Cuddle toy?* I would say no."

"I've read that can help for babies over six, seven months old. Around that age, they become aware of separation. Having a familiar face in the cot can be a comfort."

He was nodding. "Sure. I'll pick one up this week." He cast a look out toward that elm and pushed to his feet. "Better put away that shovel and bring the bouncer in. He's probably had enough of the outdoors for one day."

Was that code for wanting her to hang around a bit longer? Or was she overthinking it? Should she tell him how she felt or bow out gracefully now? This all felt so different to what she'd imagined.

He sauntered across the lawn and scooped up the shovel. Then he inspected the sandbox again before disappearing into the big backyard and ducking through some shrubs, which she presumed hid a shed. Watching his every move, Teagan was left feeling a little giddy. In her eyes, he would always be the sexiest man alive, the person who could make her tingle with just a look. And whenever they kissed... whenever they touched...

If they made love now, would it be the same?

Or would it be better?

Suddenly the baby monitor went off. Buddy wasn't just shifting on his cot up there, or even fussing as he woke up. What Teagan heard was a piercing scream that lifted her out of her shoes.

Fumbling, she snatched the monitor up and checked the video feed. Buddy was standing in his cot—*he was old enough to do that?*—holding on to the rail, his gorgeous little face all puckered up. She called toward the shrubs.

"Jacob! *Jacob!*"

Buddy was crying now. *Really* crying. Teagan whimpered, dropped the monitor and bolted inside.

As she ran through the kitchen, an obvious question dawned. Buddy's bedroom was upstairs, but which one was it? As she raced up the stairs, she realized she only needed to follow the wails.

Still standing in the cot, the baby had one arm flung out like he was trying to snatch a rope. Teagan raced over and, without thinking, scooped him out and into her arms.

"It's okay, Buddy. I'm here. Your daddy's coming, too." She threw a glance at the open bedroom door. "Soon. He'll be here really, really soon."

The baby was nestled upright against her chest, his little chin on her shoulder. The motion she used was a cross between rocking and jostling, a fast jigging movement meant to distract as much as soothe.

Hurry up, Jacob. Hurry the heck up!

But of course she could take Buddy downstairs. Right now. No big deal.

Then she realized the baby had stopped crying. *Completely.* Teagan was almost too scared to look; she didn't want to get him started again.

Slowly she lowered him from her shoulder and held him a little away from her. His face was all red. His cheeks were wet. Watching her now, he didn't smile, but at least he didn't scream again.

That's when Jacob swept into the room like there was a fire. He pulled up sharp and ran a hand down his face. Finally, he smiled.

"Well, I see you two have gotten better acquainted."

"Sorry." She shrugged. "We couldn't wait."

And now that Jacob was here, naturally Buddy would want to go to his dad.

But the baby only kept his gaze on Teagan, like she was some strange curiosity. And while he stared, he clung to her blouse, gently tugging the fabric one way, then the other. She caught their reflection in the windowpane. Weird, but not. The image of her and this baby, with Daddy in the background, reminded her of a family photo.

Joining them, Jacob dropped a kiss on his son's crown. Then he looked at Teagan like she might actually be an asset.

"How are you with giving baby baths?"

"I'm…pretty good, actually."

"Are you available? Or are you on a time line?"

"I haven't booked a flight back yet."

"Well, I'm planning steak for dinner. Mashed veggies for Buddy—if you'd like to stay?"

Lifting her chin, she started putting together a proper response in her mind. But poise didn't count now. This wasn't the time to play it cool.

"I'd like that, Jacob," she said. "I'd like that very much."

Twenty-One

Teagan watched while Jacob gave Buddy his bath.

He was spot-on making sure all the creases and fiddly bits like ears were attended to. When he tickled his son's belly with the washcloth, she laughed along with the baby. And after Jacob had dried him and applied baby powder, she was gobsmacked at the expertise with which he managed the diaper. It was that *sexy baby daddy* thing again. *So* attractive.

But it was more than that. The way Jacob cared for his child touched her so very deeply. It made her feel wistful but also hopeful, particularly whenever he wanted her to join in.

"You seem to have all the baby stuff down pat," she said as they headed downstairs to start on dinner.

"I read a couple of books on basics and got hooked on *You're a New Daddy* videos. If you know a few tricks, it's pretty smooth sailing. Helps when you have a good kid."

Heading into the kitchen, he rubbed his forehead against Buddy's. The baby giggled like he'd heard the world's funniest joke. No one learned *that* from a book or video. Despite earlier misgivings, it seemed Jacob was a natural and Buddy loved him all the more for it.

Jacob set Buddy up in a nearby playpen with some toys while they got to work cooking. Again, she was impressed. In between chopping and marinating and mashing, he talked about time-saving techniques, how he stayed clear of preservatives and food coloring where Buddy was concerned, and how he was going to try out a new spaghetti sauce recipe next week.

The way to a man's heart was supposedly through his

stomach. Now she put her own spin on the adage. The way to *her* heart was watching Jacob master this new domain. On the side, she fantasized about seeing him go about things wearing nothing but an apron.

Which, of course, led to thinking about later when Buddy was asleep and they were alone. Not that she wished this time away. She was enjoying every single moment. She wished it would never end.

When dinner was served, Buddy was set up next to his dad in a high chair. Jacob spoon-fed him some mashed veggies, which he devoured. When he'd had enough, Jacob attached a set of toy keys to the tray to keep him amused while the adults ate. Too easy.

After stacking the dinner dishes on the counter—Teagan had said she would load the dishwasher when Jacob took Buddy to bed—they sat together in the living room. Jacob talked on about all the different things Buddy could do.

"His first word was *buba*," Jacob said, holding Buddy on his lap while the baby gnawed a corner of a plastic book about jungle animals. "Then *Dada*. No coaching."

As if to confirm the point, Buddy said, *"Dada. Dada,"* before going back to chewing. Clever. But his eyelids were drooping now. Then came a yawn.

By the time Jacob had dimmed the lights and read him the book, pointing out and describing all the pictures, Buddy was ready to go down for the night. Teagan wiggled her fingers and singsonged, "Night-night, Buddy," before Jacob took him up to bed.

Watching them go, Teagan told herself again how wrong she had been to prejudge. Jacob was patient with Buddy, and good-humored and kind. He literally *shone* as a father. The real joy was how much they both so obviously loved being together.

Was there room enough for her to visit again? After that shaky start today, was there any hope that Jacob might still feel the same way he had about her? Since the baby monitor

incident, he'd included her in things, but there hadn't been the slightest hint of romance. Nothing in his eyes that spoke to a need to take her in his arms. But after Buddy was put down for the night, perhaps they could discuss the second reason she had come.

Did Jacob care about her still? Or had she literally thrown *them* away?

By the time Jacob got upstairs, Buddy was already asleep. As he laid a light cover over his son, he deliberated more on Teagan's surprise visit today. No phone call, no warning, no, *Sorry I didn't believe in you and dropped your sorry ass cold*. Was he being too harsh or did she have a nerve?

Making his way back downstairs, he wondered how best to convey his feelings on the subject now that there was little chance of them being interrupted. Perhaps, *Thanks for taking the time, now excuse me while Buddy and I get on with our lives*. Like Teagan was getting on with hers. With the gym sold, she would soon be jetting off to rejoin her billionaire clan on the other side of the world. Cool. She had her family and, you'd better believe, he had his.

He'd even met someone who had let him know he was doing a good job. Someone who thought Buddy was the absolute best. A woman they both could trust.

Jacob found Teagan where he'd left her. Sitting on the couch, she was thumbing through Buddy's book, looking hauntingly beautiful beneath the lights' soft glow. These past weeks, he'd thought about her way too much…her hair, her scent, most of all her touch. But when people let you down, you dusted yourself off and moved on. You survived…even when something fierce and deep inside clawed at you to hold on.

When she looked across and smiled, Jacob bit down against the almighty tug in his gut. They had a history in the bedroom like nothing he had experienced before. But

the tender moments they had shared were even more memorable. Watching her sleep, hearing her laugh, holding her extra close just because.

"Buddy's down?" she asked as he walked over. "That didn't take long."

"He should sleep through the night."

She sighed. "He's just so sweet."

Yep. "I know."

Her eyebrows knitted as she put the book aside. "I can't understand his mother…"

"You mean about her not giving a crap?" He sat down. "I understand her perfectly."

Teagan's eyes filled with pity. "Because of your own mother?"

"That woman was so out of it, she didn't care whether I lived or died." Thinking of Buddy again, he growled and shook his head. "Sometimes I feel like I handed down some twisted family curse."

"It's not your fault Ivy Schluter has no heart."

"But I did make the choice to be with her." To *sleep* with her.

"And now you have a beautiful son." Her gaze grew distant as she murmured, "I always wanted kids of my own."

"I never wanted to be a parent, period."

She blinked and then straightened. "That's why I thought we wouldn't work out, Jacob. Why I decided it was best we didn't see each other again."

"And, frankly, I think you were right."

She froze before visibly composing herself. "I didn't know how you would cope with being a father."

"Sure." He shrugged. "Easier to opt out."

Her jaw dropped. "That's not fair."

"Life's not fair."

He didn't like saying it. He liked less the look on her face. But, *Sorry not sorry.* That was God's honest truth.

She was getting to her feet. "I shouldn't have come here."

"So, why did you?"

"Because…" She paused then squared her shoulders. "Because I couldn't forget you."

"I see." Churning inside, he stood, too. "You needed another fix."

Her nostrils flared as the corners of her beautiful mouth turned down. "Now you're being cruel."

He was being cruel? Wow. She really had no idea.

"We were always somehow out of sync," she added.

Jacob's chest was so tight now, it ached. But he kept his voice even. His emotions under control.

"It doesn't matter anymore."

"No," she agreed. "I guess not."

So—*over*. Done. No need to shake hands, remain friends, drag this drama out any further.

But she was looking at him with such intensity, like *her* conclusion was something else entirely. Like maybe they'd just had a lover's spat and she was waiting for the making up part to begin. And in that moment, with his heart blocking his throat and all that pent up stuff off his chest, a pragmatic part of him felt almost willing to listen, and even to goad.

It wasn't as if anyone's life would be irreparably shattered come morning.

He took a step closer. When she drew a breath then did the same, the energy crackling between them flashed and caught fire.

Focusing on her lips, he lowered his voice.

"You didn't answer my question."

"About needing a fix?" Her eyes glistened as she shrugged. "Maybe it's that simple, Jacob. Maybe I'm addicted."

He almost winced, but the language fit. This minute he needed her that much, too. More than he was prepared to ever let her know.

Threading his fingers up through the back of her hair, he enjoyed watching her limpid eyes darken and those lips

quiver then part. And when his mouth claimed hers and she melted against him—when she clung on to his shirt and whimpered in her throat—Jacob embraced the sense of power mixed with relief. He hadn't planned for this to happen, but this coming together would be different from anything they had shared before. This was purely physical. Entirely sexual.

One more fix.

One last time.

Twenty-Two

Teagan woke up with a start.

When she realized where she was—when she remembered in a flash what had happened—she grinned from ear to ear and stretched like a cat. But how long had she been lying here alone?

Last night, after Buddy had gone to bed, the adults had a hard-hitting conversation where painful truths were hashed out. Jacob had been exceptionally blunt and she'd gotten justifiably upset. But underpinning it all had been a reality neither one could deny. No matter how much they disagreed, the attraction they felt for each other only seemed to grow stronger, deeper.

Hotter.

When he had finally kissed her, she practically dissolved. In no time, they were in this guest bedroom, sans clothes and regrets. Afterward, curling up against all that amazing masculine heat, she had clocked out and fallen fast asleep.

Big day.

Now, still feeling as though she were in a dream, she slipped out of bed and into the attached bathroom. She had an overnight bag stowed away in the rental car, but for now she was happy to hurry back into yesterday's clothes. She couldn't wait to find Jacob and talk more because now she was certain. This time there was no turning back.

She was in love with Jacob Stone. More than that, after their day spent together with Buddy and then last night, she was looking forward to spending the future with them both. She'd never felt so sure about anything in her life. In her heart, she knew he felt the same way.

She found him in the kitchen, standing at a counter, laptop open. After rushing both hands through her unbrushed hair, she strode over.

"Guess I overslept," she said with a big smile.

Shifting his focus from the laptop, Jacob looked across. She expected his gorgeous eyes to gleam with approval. She thought a bold grin would instantly light up his face.

Instead, he studied her with a laid-back kind of curiosity. Almost like he'd forgotten about last night. Like he'd forgotten she was even there.

"I just put Buddy down for his morning nap." He made a move toward the percolator. "Want a coffee?"

Teagan shook herself and held up a hand. "Uh… I can get it."

After he nodded and went back to his laptop, Teagan tried to gather her thoughts while she found a cup and poured. Had she woken up in an alternate universe? Because last night had definitely happened. Her body still tingled. Her lips still burned. But what they had shared was way more than mind-blowing sex. It was about an understanding. An irreversible coming together.

Cradling her cup, she joined him by the counter. He smelled so good—fresh out of the shower with hints of his natural scent. His hair was still damp and a pulse was beating in his unshaven jaw. She wanted to lean in and graze her lips over the spot. She wanted to tell him how happy she felt now that everything was good.

But his attention remained fixed to the screen.

She tried to make a joke. "Looking into colleges for Buddy?"

"I'm searching out community organizations around here. Thinking more about moving on from Lexington Avenue." His eyes narrowed, like he was thinking back. "When did you say you were heading back to Sydney?"

Teagan hesitated and then smiled. That must be the reason he was acting so strange. He didn't know.

"Actually," she said, "that was something I wanted to talk to you about."

His brows nudged together as his chin came down. "Has something happened? Are the kids okay?"

"Considering everything that's gone on, they're actually doing really well. Honey's put on weight, and I Skype with Tate all the time."

"So, what's the problem?"

She tried to explain. "These past few months, Dad wasn't the only one in danger. We older kids passed the baton, doing our best to keep Tate, and later Honey, out of harm's way. We all felt we needed to be there when we could. But that danger's definitely over now. Dad and Eloise still have issues to work through, but that's really their business, not mine."

He seemed to soak that in before changing the subject, like what she'd just said didn't naturally lead into another conversation—about *them*.

"Are you hungry?" he asked, moving to a cupboard. "I could whip up some pancakes."

Teagan's stomach knotted. "I don't want pancakes, Jacob. I want to talk."

His mouth pulled to one side as he sized her up. "Talk about what?"

She coughed out a humorless laugh. "Are you serious? You're acting like nothing happened last night."

He scratched his temple. "How do you want me to act?"

That really took her aback. Was he gaslighting or had she truly gone mad?

"Jacob, are you saying that being together again didn't mean anything to you?"

"I'm saying you made the decision for us weeks ago."

"I explained—"

"You made a choice," he cut in. "I made a choice, too." His gaze narrowed. "I have my son to think about now."

A knock on the front door interrupted them. Jacob

blinked before his attention shot that way. Then he checked the time on his wristwatch.

"I'm expecting someone," he said.

Teagan tried to gather her whirling thoughts. What he'd said, how he'd acted…it had taken her completely off guard. Cut her to the quick. But his reasons for putting up this wall made perfect sense. Yes, she had made a choice, which meant when he had really needed her support, she'd stepped away. Shutting her out now probably wasn't so much about *him* being hurt as it was about protecting Buddy.

The same way, not so long ago, she had needed to protect Tate.

Getting a second wind, Teagan followed him. She needed Jacob to know that after he'd taken care of whoever was at the door, they should talk again. These past weeks had been a roller coaster ride, but they were smoothing out all the humps now. This was a long way from over.

Jacob had opened the door. A woman stood on the other side of the threshold—around Teagan's age, with ice-blond hair, wearing modest shorts matched with a midriff shirt. She was naturally pretty in a fresh-faced, *girl next door* kind of way.

And Jacob was expecting her…why?

"Hope you don't mind that I'm early." All smiles, the woman stepped inside. Then her gaze met Teagan's and her expression changed while Teagan's heart missed a few beats.

Jacob looked between the two women before he rolled back his shoulders and stepped back. "Monica, this is Teagan."

Monica's eyes widened before she sent a frown Jacob's way. Teagan imagined the other woman's expression said, *What the hell is she doing here?*

At that moment, baby noises trickled down from upstairs. Monica didn't hesitate. She stepped around Jacob, already on her way.

"Can I go get him?"

Teagan thought of how she had raced to Buddy yesterday when she had heard him cry out on the baby monitor. But Monica obviously didn't need to think about which room. She wasn't worried about Buddy being wary of a new face.

Jacob sent Monica a smile. "Sure. Go up."

While Monica flew up the stairs, Jacob stuck his hands in his jeans' back pockets and met Teagan's gaze. He was waiting for questions, but his silence was all the response she needed. *I made a choice, too.*

Feeling her cheeks burn and her heart drop, she asked, "Who is she?"

His gaze held hers. "I thought that would be obvious."

The backs of her eyes were suddenly prickling with tears. They had slept together when he was seeing another woman? And to think she was ready to trust this guy.

Teagan had left her handbag by the couch. Now Jacob watched as she moved to collect the bag and walk out the door without another look or a word. Rather than see her stride down the path to her car parked on the street, he forced himself to shut the door and turn away.

Monica had started down the stairs with Buddy in her arms. Before Jacob could open his mouth, she got in first.

"You don't have to explain," she said.

He had mentioned Teagan to Monica once in a weak moment. He could admit that he hadn't painted her in a very good light.

"She showed up yesterday out of the blue," he said.

"None of my business," Mon replied. "I'm just the nanny."

Not *just a nanny*. Mon did a fantastic job. He and Buddy had been damn lucky to find her.

Jacob cupped his son's flushed cheek. And when Buddy put out his arms, despite feeling like shit, Daddy found a bigger smile and took him in a heartbeat.

"He'll want a bottle," Monica said. "I can put his laun-

dry on while it heats up." She paused. "Or, if you don't need me today after all, that's fine. We're still working this out."

After learning that he would have Buddy full-time, Jacob had pulled out all the stops to find a nanny whom he and Buddy could trust. The agency had put Monica's application forward. She was back in the area, staying with her folks after a stint working in orphanages overseas. Her credentials were impeccable and her easy way with Buddy had won both father and son over in no time. She was staying for perhaps six months in the district before moving on again. He didn't want to lose her while he searched for someone more permanent.

He hadn't mentioned her to Teagan because—why? He had assumed that she would be gone, well on her way, before Monica showed up today—earlier than expected, as it turned out. No one could accuse Mon of being tardy. She had their best interests at heart.

Taking a seat on the couch, he set Buddy on his lap and let the nanny know, "Everything's sorted out. We're all set."

Still, Monica slid a questioning look toward the door before walking away.

While the baby played with the hairs on his arm and blew bubbles, Jacob talked to him. He did it a lot. Maybe too much. But Buddy never seemed to mind, and, after that horror of a scene, his dad could sure use a sympathetic ear.

"Teagan mustn't think too much of me. Hey, I'm far from *my* favorite person right now. I know she hurt me, probably more than I've ever been hurt before, and that's saying a lot. But I shouldn't have done what I did. I swore I'd always be honest, no matter what, and I *lied* to her. I let her believe we could go back to how it was. But you can never go back, Buddy. The only way is forward, and in our case that means you and me. A tandem team cooking with gas. We don't need anyone else because going that route…" He winced. "It's just too darn hard. Feeling for someone, laying your heart on the line, worrying about when the next

bombshell will land. Not that all surprises turn out to be bad. Not when you get used to the idea."

Jacob tickled his son's belly, which drew a giggle. God, he loved this kid. Would die for him in a heartbeat.

"Some of life's biggest challenges," Jacob went on, "can turn out to be blessings in disguise when you can drill down on what's most important. On what you really want and need and cherish, even when you know there will always be more challenges ahead, because anything worthwhile requires work and trust and—"

Jacob bit down as his chest tightened and his gut wrenched.

"God, I really let her go, didn't I? I seriously just let Teagan believe the absolute worst and walk away."

"She's still out front by her car."

Jacob's head snapped up. Monica was back from the laundry and headed over.

"I don't think she can find her keys," she said, taking Buddy when the baby put out his arms to her. "I was going out to check if she was okay." Mon gave a knowing smile. "But I thought you might want to do that."

The damn key had to be here somewhere. But the more Teagan burrowed around in her purse, the more her face burned and she wanted to fall apart. Soon enough that car key would appear. Then she could jump inside that vehicle and keep driving until this nightmare of a morning was nothing more than a sickening memory.

Jacob Stone. She never wanted to hear his name again. She needed to wipe away every thought she'd ever formed around him, particularly the ones seared into her brain from last night when she'd fallen like a sap into his arms again.

As a tear escaped and rolled down her cheek, Teagan set her jaw and cursed under her breath.

Why had she ever thought that coming here was a good idea? Wynn had it right from the start. Jacob was a first-

class manipulator who couldn't be trusted. He had taken her to bed when he was already seeing someone else—a woman who obviously had no problems with slotting in with this *eligible single dad* lifestyle.

Well, good luck to her, Teagan thought, dumping the contents of her bag on the hood and wincing at the screechy-clatter of lipstick, cell phone and every other damn thing hitting the metal. Good luck, and good riddance, to them all.

Suddenly the key was there, staring back at her. She snatched at the tag, but it somehow slipped under her hand and fell between the tire and the curb. Cursing again, she got down and fished the key out. When she straightened, he was there, looking even more infuriatingly sexy than he had five minutes ago.

"You had trouble finding your key," Jacob said, like she didn't know that already.

Her face was damp with tears, but she wouldn't give him the satisfaction of seeing her wipe them away. And she didn't feel the need to respond, either, other than to turn her back on him. She didn't need his help. She didn't need him, period.

She pressed the remote and the doors beeped open. But then she remembered the handbag stash still strewn all over the hood. As she scooped everything back into her bag, Jacob opened the driver's side door.

Geez, what a gentleman.

"That woman," he said. "Monica—"

"I don't want to know," she replied, pushing around him to get inside.

"I know what you're thinking," he went on, "but you're wrong. Mon is Buddy's nanny."

Teagan stopped dead. Then she scowled and shook her head. That woman did not look like a nanny.

Then again, Dex's fiancée, Shelby, didn't look like Mary Poppins, either.

"This morning I didn't want you to think that I cared

anymore," he said. "But I was trying to convince *myself* more than anyone else." His eyes flashed in the sunshine as he edged closer. "But I *do* care, Tea. I care a lot. In fact, I really need to tell you just how much."

Teagan put up a hand and shut her eyes tight. "I don't need to listen to any of this."

But being the overbearing man that he was, he told her anyway.

"The truth is, I'm in love with you. I've never said that to anyone before. But saying it now, knowing that it's real…" His mouth kicked up at one side. "I can't believe how good it feels."

When the shock subsided, Teagan pushed him hard in the ribs. Then she pushed him again.

"Don't you dare do that," she said. "Don't for a minute think you can play with me that way."

As if what he'd already done wasn't enough.

"I've never been more serious in my life." He held her arms and stepped into the space separating them. "When I saw you yesterday, I didn't want to let myself feel that way again. I didn't want to set myself up for another fall. But when we finally got to be alone and things started to happen, of course I wanted to be with you." His grip on her arms tightened. "Like I want to be with you now."

Teagan suddenly felt so weak. So confused. "That's not what you said a few minutes ago."

"I didn't want to risk being hurt again. But it's way scarier to think about my life without you. Without your smile and your strength and your love."

Her breath caught in her throat and grew into a lump.

"I never said that I loved you."

Cocking his head, he grinned. "Not yet."

She pulled back. "I'm sorry I hurt you, but, Jacob, you hurt me, too."

"So why don't we be grown-ups and just forgive each other?"

She thought about it. "And then what?"

"Then we start again. Start afresh."

Her stomach was a hot knotted mess. But he looked so certain. So...ready.

She bit her lip and almost smiled. "You really think we can?"

"I *know* we can. And one reason is the cute kid inside that house who is dying to have a mom he can depend on."

Her heart was bursting.

"Me?" she squeaked.

His answer was to bring her close at the same time his mouth captured hers with a kiss that turned her blood into molten lava and her heart into mush. And as the kiss deepened and she felt his strength wrap around her, any lingering doubts she might have had evaporated beneath the steam.

When he gradually broke the kiss, he brushed his smile over her lips.

"I love you, Tea. And that will never change. Never die."

Teagan thought about her life ahead with a man she loved so much, too, and with an adorable child who would actually, truly be hers. When her eyes filled again, this time she didn't want to wipe the tears away. Sometimes people cried because they were happy, and she had never been happier in her life.

When he rested his brow against hers, waiting for her answer, she let out a grateful sigh. "This is real—isn't it?"

Before he kissed her again, Jacob promised her with all his heart. "This is the way it's going to be. Us together. A family forever. That's the truth, Tea, so help me God."

* * * * *

MILLS & BOON

THE HEART OF ROMANCE

A ROMANCE FOR EVERY KIND OF READER

MODERN

Prepare to be swept off your feet by sophisticated, sexy and seductive heroes, in some of the world's most glamourous and romantic locations, where power and passion collide.
8 stories per month.

HISTORICAL

Escape with historical heroes from time gone by. Whether your passion is for wicked Regency Rakes, muscled Vikings or rugged Highlanders, awaken the romance of the past.
6 stories per month.

MEDICAL

Set your pulse racing with dedicated, delectable doctors in the high-pressure world of medicine, where emotions run high and passion, comfort and love are the best medicine.
6 stories per month.

True Love

Celebrate true love with tender stories of heartfelt romance, from the rush of falling in love to the joy a new baby can bring, and a focus on the emotional heart of a relationship.
8 stories per month.

Desire

Indulge in secrets and scandal, intense drama and plenty of sizzling hot action with powerful and passionate heroes who have it all: wealth, status, good looks…everything but the right woman.
6 stories per month.

HEROES

Experience all the excitement of a gripping thriller, with an intense romance at its heart. Resourceful, true-to-life women and strong, fearless men face danger and desire - a killer combination!
8 stories per month.

DARE

Sensual love stories featuring smart, sassy heroines you'd want as a best friend, and compelling intense heroes who are worthy of them.
4 stories per month.

To see which titles are coming soon, please visit

millsandboon.co.uk/nextmonth

MILLS & BOON
MEDICAL
Pulse-Racing Passion

Set your pulse racing with dedicated, delectable doctors in the high-pressure world of medicine, where emotions run high and passion, comfort and love are the best medicine.

MILLS & BOON
True Love
Romance from the Heart

Celebrate true love with tender stories of heartfelt romance, from the rush of falling in love to the joy a new baby can bring, and a focus on the emotional heart of a relationship.